**Award-winning screenwriter Malla Nunn
brings back Detective Emmanuel Cooper
in a stunning novel about murder, power and
a dangerous South African underworld.**

Emmanuel Cooper's life has an "ex" through it:
ex-soldier, ex–detective sergeant and ex–white
man. He now works undercover surveillance on the
seedy Durban docks to make a living. All that changes
when the brutal murder of a young boy forces Cooper
out of the shadows. He must elude the police to
conduct his own unofficial investigation. After two
more similar murders, Cooper becomes the police
department's prime suspect. He dives into the Durban underworld for answers and finds that the kill-
ings are part of an international tussle for the political
soul of South Africa. Under the pressure of new racial segregation laws, Cooper must find the killer
before the Durban police pin the crimes on him.

LET THE
DEAD
LIE

A NOVEL

Malla Nunn

WASHINGTON
SQUARE PRESS

NEW YORK LONDON TORONTO SYDNEY

Washington Square Press
A Division of Simon & Schuster, Inc.
1230 Avenue of the Americas
New York, NY 10020

First Washington Square Press paperback edition April 2010

WASHINGTON SQUARE PRESS and colophon are trademarks of Simon & Schuster, Inc.

For information about special discounts for bulk purchases, please contact Simon & Schuster Special Sales at 1-866-506-1949 or business@simonandschuster.com.

The Simon & Schuster Speakers Bureau can bring authors to your live event. For more information or to book an event, contact the Simon & Schuster Speakers Bureau at 1-866-248-3049 or visit our website at www.simonspeakers.com.

Manufactured in the United States of America

10 9 8 7 6 5 4 3 2 1

Library of Congress Cataloging-in-Publication Data is available.

ISBN 978-1-4165-8622-7
ISBN 978-1-4165-8670-8 (ebook)

Literary agents Sophie Hamley of the Cameron Creswell Agency and Catherine Drayton of InkWell Management, who do an amazing job of getting my work out into the world.

For historical and cultural help, special thanks to Terence King, author, police and military researcher and historian. Any errors or omissions are entirely my own.

Deepest thanks to Judith Curr and the stellar team at Atria. Thanks to Emily Bestler, who always asks the right questions and helps get the best version of the story onto the page. It's a pleasure working with such a talented team.

Thank you all.

ACKNOWLEDGMENTS

W RITING IS solitary work made possible with the help of others. I thank the following:

Imkulunkulu, the great, great one. The ancestors. My siblings, Penny, Byron and Jan, and their partners, Brian, Monique and Keith, for opening their homes to my family every summer. To Dr. Gerald Lazarus and Dr. Audrey Jakubowski-Lazarus, Lynne and Andrew Shear, Laura and Saul Goldstein and Elyse De Jong, who allowed us to crash their summer holidays. A generous family is a blessing beyond words.

My husband, Mark, a true partner in everything that I do. You make the impossible possible. My children, Elijah and Sisana, two bright and beautiful sparks who light up the world and start fires with equal ease.

Darryl Robinson for the beautiful author photographs.

Kerrie McGovan and Burcak Muraben for dressing me in goose down and leather for my winter trip to America.

Hannah and David Shear for making a home for me in New York, complete with snowfall and a cat curled at my feet.

Rose and Eric Campbell for use of their lovely beach cottage for writing retreats. Steve Worland and Georgie Parker for friendship and arranging the keys.

To my parents,
Courtney and Patricia Nunn

PROLOGUE

A FLASHING NEON HOTEL sign lit the narrow cobble-stone lane. The night had a spring chill from the showers that had fallen that afternoon across the Tuileries and the Boulevard Saint-Germain, but heat emanated from the GI bars. The smell of sweating bodies, spilled liquor, cigarette smoke and perfume soaked the air. Emmanuel was glad to be free of the crush inside. A group of Negro soldiers entered a subterranean club on the corner of Rue Véron, and a jazz trumpet blared into the night. He strolled the slick lane with three giggling stenographers and Hugh Langton, a BBC war correspondent with impeccable black-market connections.

"That's it up ahead," Langton said. "Two double rooms on the fourth floor. You don't mind a few stairs, do you, girls?"

Five days of R & R, then back to bully beef in a tin and the parade of demolished towns. Emmanuel had five days to forget. Five days to build new memories over the visions of broken churches and people. The brunette in the trio nuzzled closer and pressed a hot kiss to the nape of his neck. He picked up the pace, greedy for the sensation of skin on skin. The hotel sign flashed light into a doorway a few feet ahead. Bare legs, pale and dimpled with rain, jutted into the street. The torn edges of a skirt and an open change purse were visible in the dim recess.

"*Mon Dieu . . .*" The brunette pressed slim fingers to her mouth. "*Regardez! Regardez!*"

Emmanuel unhooked his arm from around her shoulder and moved closer. Another flash of neon illuminated the thickset body of a woman slumped against a door. A bloodied hole was torn into the lapel of the grubby jacket, evidence of a small-caliber entry wound. The blank eyes and slack jaw suggested a passenger who'd missed the last train and would now have to spend the night in the open. Emmanuel checked for a pulse, more a formality than a necessity.

"She's dead."

"Then we're too late to be of help." Langton herded the stenographers toward the Hotel Oasis. This little hiccup could seriously extinguish the mood. "I'll get the concierge to call the police."

"Go ahead," Emmanuel said. "I'll find a gendarme and catch up."

Langton took Emmanuel aside. "Let me point out the obvious in case you missed it, Cooper. Dead woman. Live *women* . . . plural. Let's get the hell out of here."

Emmanuel stayed put. A kit bag stuffed with spare ration packs and a warm hotel room with soap and fresh towels meant the stenographers would wait. Such was the cold pragmatism of war.

"Okay, okay." The Englishman ushered the women toward the flickering neon. "Don't stay out here all night. There'll be plenty of dead back in the field."

That was true, but it was an insult to abandon a body in a city where law and order had been restored. Emmanuel found a stocky policeman enjoying a cigarette under a cherry blossom tree, and an hour later a balding detective with an impressive eagle-beak nose and sad brown eyes arrived on the scene. He peered into the doorway.

"Simone Betancourt." The identification, in heavily accented English, was for the benefit of the foreign soldier. Most cases involving the Allied forces were shifted to the handful of bilingual police. "Fifty-two years old. Listed occupation, washerwoman."

"You recognize her?" Emmanuel said.

"She took in the police station washing and that of many small pensions. I knew her." A hand was thrust in Emmanuel's direction. "Inspecteur Principal Luc Moreau. You discovered the body?"

"Yes."

"Your name, please."

"Major Emmanuel Cooper."

"And you were on your way to . . ."

"The hotel up there," Emmanuel said, certain the French detective had already figured that out.

"The last rain was . . ." Moreau checked a gold wristwatch. "About two hours ago. So, Simone has been here longer than that. Others, no doubt, saw the body. And did nothing. Why did you alert the police and wait here for so long at the crime scene, Major?"

Emmanuel shrugged. "I'm not sure."

The dead were another part of the war's landscape. Soldiers and civilians, the young and the old, were left unattended and without ceremony in the fields and the rubble. But this washerwoman had resurrected memories of another defenseless female abandoned a long time ago. "It felt wrong to leave her, that's all."

Moreau smiled and unwrapped a stick of chewing gum, a habit acquired from the American Military Police. "Even in war, a murder is offensive, is it not, Major?"

"Maybe so." Emmanuel glanced toward the hotel. Stopping to mark the death of Simone Betancourt would not rebalance the scales of justice, nor dull the memory of fallen friends. And yet he'd stayed on. The night had grown colder. Jesus. He could be in bed with a stenographer right now.

"Do me this favor." Moreau scribbled on a page and tore it loose. "Go to your woman. Drink. Eat. Make love. Sleep. If tomorrow Simone Betancourt is still on your mind, please call me."

"What for?" Emmanuel pocketed the crumpled paper.

"When you call, I will give an explanation."

—

Distant church bells chimed eleven a.m. Emmanuel awoke dry-mouthed and loose-limbed amid a tangle of sheets. The brunette stenographer, Justine from Cergy, stood naked by the window, devouring a block of ration-pack chocolate. Her body was perfect in the spring sunshine that dazzled through the glass. A pot of black-market coffee and a dish of butter pastries were set on the table. Justine climbed back into the bed and Emmanuel forgot about war and injustice and fear.

When he awoke a second time, Justine was asleep. He

looked at her peaceful face, like a child's. Every element of happiness was right here in this room. And yet he felt sadness creep in. He slipped from under the sheets and went to the window. Directly below the hotel's precarious wrought-iron balcony was the cobbled lane where Simone Betancourt had died in the rain.

That a life could be so easily taken without justice or recognition was a lesson he'd learned in childhood. Leading a company of soldiers through war confirmed that nothing was sacred or precious. It was strange how, after four years of training and fighting, the memory of his mother's death still lurked in the shadows, ready to ambush the present.

Emmanuel retrieved the detective's telephone number and smoothed the paper flat. He was going to phone Inspector Luc Moreau, but he had the unsettling sensation that the reverse was happening: he was the one being called.

1

THE ENTRANCE TO the freight yards was a dark mouth crowded with rows of dirty boxcars and threads of silver track. A few white prostitutes orbited a weak streetlight. Indian and coloured working girls were tucked into the shadows, away from the passing trade and the police.

Emmanuel Cooper crossed Point Road and moved toward the yards. The prostitutes stared at him, and the boldest of them, a fat redhead with a molting fox fur slung around her shoulders, lifted a skirt to expose a thigh encased in black fishnet.

"Sweetheart," she bellowed. "Are you buying or just window-shopping?"

Emmanuel slipped into the industrial maze. Did he look that desperate? Brine and coal dust blew off Durban Harbor and the lights of a docked cruise ship shone across the water. Stationary gantry cranes loomed over the avenue of boxcars and a bright half-moon lit the rocky ground. He moved to the center of the yards, tracing a now familiar path. He was tired, and not from the late hour. Trawling the docks after midnight was worse than being a foot policeman. They at least had a clearly defined mission: to enforce the law. His job was to witness a mind-numbing parade of petty violence, prostitution and thievery and do nothing.

He scrambled over a heavy coupling and settled into a space between two wagons. Soon, an ant trail of trucks would roll out of the yard, packed to the limit with whiskey and cut tobacco and boxes of eau de cologne. English, Afrikaner, foot police, detectives and railway police: the smuggling operation was a perfect example of how different branches of the force were able to cooperate and coordinate if they shared a common goal.

He flicked the surveillance notebook open. Four columns filled the faintly ruled paper: names, times, license plate numbers and descriptions of stolen goods. Until these cold nights in the freight yard he'd thought the wait for the Normandy landing was the pinnacle of boredom. The restlessness and the fear of the massed army, the bland food and the stink of the latrines: he'd weathered it all without complaint. The discomforts weren't so different from what he'd experienced in the tin and concrete slum shacks his family had lived in on the outskirts of Jo'burg.

This surveillance of corrupt policemen lacked the moral certainty of D-day. What Major van Niekerk, his old boss from the Marshall Square Detective Branch, planned to do with the information in the notebook was unclear.

"Jesus. Oh, Jesus . . ." A groaned exhalation floated across the freight yards, faint on the breeze. Some of the cheaper sugar girls made use of the deserted boxcars come nightfall.

"Oh . . . no . . ." This time the male voice was loud and panicked.

The skin on Emmanuel's neck prickled. The urge to investigate reared up, but he resisted. His job was to watch and record the activities of the smuggling ring, not rescue a drunken whaler lost in the freight yard. Do *not* get involved. Major van Niekerk had been very specific about that.

The hum of traffic along Point Road mingled with a wordless sobbing. Instinct pulled Emmanuel to the sound. He hesitated and then shoved the notepad into a pants pocket. Ten minutes to take a look and then he'd be back to record the truck license plate numbers. Twenty minutes at the outside. He pulled a silver torch from a pocket, switched it on and ran toward the warehouses built along the northeast boundary of the freight terminus.

The sobs faded and then became muffled. Possibly the result of a hand held over a mouth. Emmanuel stopped and tried to isolate the sound. The yards were huge, with miles of track running the length of the working harbor. Loose gravel moved underfoot and a cry came from ahead. Emmanuel turned the torch to high beam and picked up the pace. The world appeared in flashes. Ghostly rows of stationary freight cars, chains, redbrick walls covered in grime and a back lane littered with empty hessian sacks. Then a dark river of blood that formed a question mark in the dirt.

"No . . ."

Emmanuel swung the torch beam in the direction of the voice and caught two Indian men in the full glare of the light.

Both were young, with dark, slicked-back hair that touched their shoulders. They wore white silk shirts and nearly identical suits made from silvery sharkskin material. One, a slim teenager with a tear-streaked face, was slumped against the back wall of the warehouse. The other, somewhere in his early twenties, sported an Errol Flynn mustache and a heavy brow contracted with menace. He hunched over the boy, with his hand over his mouth to keep him quiet.

"Do not move." Emmanuel used his detective sergeant's voice. He reached for his .38 standard Webley revolver and touched an empty space—like a war veteran fumbling for a phantom limb. The most dangerous weapon he had was a pen. No matter. The gun was backup.

"Run!" the older one screamed. "Go!"

The men ran in different directions and Emmanuel targeted the smaller of the two, who stumbled and pitched toward the ground. Emmanuel caught a sleeve and steadied the teenager against the wall.

"Run again and I'll break your arm," he said. A coupling clanked. The older one was still out there somewhere. Emmanuel rested shoulder to shoulder with the boy and waited.

"Parthiv." The boy sniffled. "Don't leave me."

"Amal," a voice called back. "Where are you?"

"Here. He got me."

"What?"

"I've got Amal," Emmanuel said. "You'd better come out and keep him company."

The man emerged from the dark with a gangster swagger. A gold necklace complemented his silvery suit, and a filigree ring topped with a chunk of purple topaz weighed down his index finger.

"And just who the hell are you?" the skollie demanded.

Emmanuel relaxed. He'd put down thugs like this one on a daily basis back in Jo'burg. Back before the trouble in Jacob's Rest.

"I'm Detective Sergeant Emmanuel Cooper," he said.

With the National Party now in control, the police had become the most powerful gang in South Africa. The air went out of the Indian's hard-man act.

"Names," Emmanuel said when the men were against the wall. He'd deal with the fact that he had no authority and no jurisdiction later.

"Dr. Jekyll and Mr. Hyde," the Indian Errol Flynn said. He looked tough and he talked tough but something about the flashy suit and the jewelry made him look a little . . . soft.

"Names," Emmanuel repeated.

"Amal," the youngster said quickly. "My name is Amal Dutta and that's my brother, Parthiv Dutta."

"Stay put," Emmanuel instructed, and dipped the torch-light toward the ground. A bottle of lemonade lay on its side near the pool of blood. Then, in the shadows, Emmanuel made out the curled fingers of a child's hand. They seemed almost to motion him closer. A white boy lay in the dirt, arms out-stretched, skinny legs tangled together. His throat was sliced open from ear to ear like a second mouth.

Emmanuel recognized the victim: an English slum kid, around eleven years old, who picked a living among the box-cars and the whores. Jolly Marks. Who knew if that was his real name?

Starting at the tattered canvas shoes, Emmanuel searched upward over the body. Army-issue fatigues were rolled up at the cuffs and threadbare at the knees. A line of string was tied to the belt loop of the khaki pants and a smear of blood stained the waistband. Streaks of dirt fanned out across the boy's gray shirt and gathered in the creases around his mouth. The search revealed the lack of something in every detail. The lack of money evident in Jolly's shabby clothes. The lack of hygiene in the tangled hair and filthy nails. The lack of a parent who might stop a youngster from going out onto the Durban docks after dark.

Emmanuel focused the light on the stained waistband again. Jolly Marks always had a small notebook attached to the belt loop of the khaki pants, where he wrote orders for smokes and food. The string that held the book was still there, but the book itself was missing. That fact might be significant.

"Did either of you pick up a spiral notebook with a string attached?" he said.

"No," the brothers answered simultaneously.

Emmanuel crouched next to the body. An inch from Jolly's right hand was a rusty penknife with the small blade extended. Emmanuel had owned a similar knife at almost exactly the same age. Jolly had understood that bad things happened out here at night.

Emmanuel knew this boy, knew the details of his life without having to ask a single question. He'd grown up with boys like Jolly Marks. No, that was a lie. This was whom he'd grown up *as*. A dirty white boy. This could have been his fate: first on the streets of a Jo'burg slum and then on the battlefields in Europe. He had escaped and survived. Jolly would never have that chance. Emmanuel returned to the Indian men.

"Either one of you touch this boy?"

"Never." Amal's body shook with the denial. "Never, never ever."

"You?" Emmanuel asked Parthiv.

"No. No ways. We were minding our own business and there he was."

Nobody in the back lanes of the Durban port after midnight was minding his own business unless that business was illegal. There was, however, a big difference between stealing and murder, and the brothers' sharkskin suits were pressed and clean. Emmanuel checked their hands, also clean. Jolly lay in a bloodbath, his neck cut with a single stroke: the work of an experienced butcher.

"Have either of you seen the boy before, maybe talked to him?"

"No," Parthiv said, too quickly. "Don't know him."

"I wish I'd never seen him." Amal's voice broke on the words. "I wish I'd stayed at home."

Emmanuel tilted the torch beam away from the teenager's face. Violent death was shocking, but the violent death of a child was different; the effects sank deeper and lingered longer. Amal was only a few years older than Jolly and probably still a schoolboy.

"Sit down and rest against the wall," Emmanuel said.

Amal sank to the ground and sucked breath in through an open mouth. A panic attack was in the cards. "Are you going to . . . to . . . arrest us, Detective?"

Emmanuel pulled a small flask from a jacket pocket and unscrewed the lid. He handed it to Amal, who pulled back.

"I don't drink. My mother says it makes you stupid."

"Make an exception for tonight," Emmanuel said. "It's mostly coffee anyway."

The teenager took a slurp and coughed till fat tears spilled from his eyes. Parthiv gave a derisive snort, embarrassed by his younger brother's inability to hold liquor. Emmanuel pocketed the flask and checked the narrow alley between the warehouse wall and the goods train.

He had a body in the open, no murder weapon and two witnesses who, in all probability, had stumbled onto the crime scene. This was a detective's nightmare—but also a detective's dream. The scene was all his. There were no foot police to trample evidence into the mud and no senior detectives jockeying for control of the investigation. Clumps of vegetation embedded in the gravel shuddered in a sudden breeze. Beyond Jolly's body, the butt of a hand-rolled cigarette blew on the ground. Emmanuel picked it up and smelled it—vanilla and chocolate. It was a special blend of flavored tobacco.

"You smoke, Parthiv?" Emmanuel asked over his shoulder.

"Of course."

"What brand?"

"Old Gold. They're American."

"I know them," Emmanuel said. Half the Yank army had puffed their way across Europe on Old Gold and Camel. For a few years it seemed that the smell of freedom was American tobacco and corned beef. Old Gold was a mass-market cigarette imported into South Africa. The vanilla and chocolate tobacco was probably made to order.

"What about you, Amal . . . do you smoke?"

"No."

"Not even a puff after school?"

"Only once. I didn't like it. It hurt my lungs."

Parthiv snorted again.

Emmanuel shone the beam on Jolly's hands and face. Amal looked away. There were no defense wounds on the boy's hands despite the open penknife. The killer had worked fast and with maximum efficiency. Maybe it was the night chill that made the murder read cold and dispassionate. The word *professional* came to Emmanuel's mind.

This was hardly a description that fit either one of the Dutta boys. He played the torchlight over the rough ground again, looking for hard evidence. Jolly's order book was nowhere near the body.

A coupling creaked in the darkness. Parthiv and Amal focused on an object in the gloom of the freight yard behind him. Emmanuel swiveled and a black hole opened up and swallowed him.

2

SOMETHING POWERFUL FORCED a sack over Emmanuel's head and pulled it down hard over his shoulders. Rough hessian scraped against his face. He smelled rotting potatoes. Air hissed from his lungs, and muscular arms tightened around his chest like pythons. He was lifted into the air and his feet dangled beneath him like those of a child on a swing.

He could feel a face pressed between his shoulder blades. The man holding him was small, with the strength of a troll. Emmanuel twisted to try to break the hold. The arms tightened a fraction, enough for him to feel the slow crush of his own bones. He stopped struggling and listened to the angry chatter of voices talking in overlapping Hindi. He had no idea what was being said, and couldn't judge from the tone if it was good or bad news for him.

"Shut up, Amal," Parthiv snapped in English. "Find our torch and make sure we haven't dropped anything. I'll get the car."

"He's a policeman," Amal protested. "We have to let him go."

"No chance. Not after you spilled our real names."

"What about the boy?" Amal said.

"Someone will find him in the morning. Now move."

Parthiv fired off a series of commands in Hindi, his voice distant by the final order. Emmanuel's feet scraped over loose stones and the steel spine of the railway tracks. The darkness inside the sack was suffocating. He fought the urge to try to break free. A crushed rib was the only thing he could gain from the exercise. He heard Amal hyperventilating as if he were confined to a hessian sack of his own. A car pulled up, engine idling.

"*Geldi, geldi!*" Parthiv ordered. "Quick."

A door opened and Emmanuel was thrown into the backseat. His captor followed and rested an elbow in the small of his back, a light point of contact with plenty of threat behind it. Emmanuel lay still and breathed slow. Did they plan to dump him in the mangrove swamp that lapped the harbor or bury his body in the bush scrub around Umhlanga Rocks? He should have listened to van Niekerk. Getting involved was a big mistake.

"If Maataa finds out . . ." Amal spoke between shallow breaths.

"We'll go in the side way." Parthiv's tone suggested they were discussing nothing more important than breaking a family curfew.

"Then?"

Silence followed Amal's inquiry. Emmanuel imagined Parthiv's heavy brow furrowed with concentration. Criminals with limited intelligence always resorted to the most obvious solution. Get rid of the problem quickly and hope for the best.

The car took a corner and the suspension bounced. The elbow dug into Emmanuel's back to stop him from rolling onto the floor. So far, the strongman hadn't said a word.

"*Madar-chod,*" Parthiv swore in Hindi, but continued in English. "Keep calm, brother. They're just driving by. They got no reason to stop us."

"Two cars," Amal panted. "Two cars."

"Keep calm. Keep calm," Parthiv said. "They are going somewhere else."

Blue lights flickered across the interior of the car and penetrated the weave of the hessian sack. It was two police vans. Perhaps someone else had called in Jolly's murder. The lights faded. It was just as well. The police would greet the information in van Niekerk's notebook with swinging batons and rhino-hide straps. He was probably safer with the Indians.

"See?" Parthiv was giddy with relief. "Piece of cake. Smooth going, no problems."

The car picked up speed till the engine shifted into fourth gear. Emmanuel didn't try to count the turns or listen for the faint cry of a bird found only in one park in the city. Outside of the movies, all forced rides had the same sound track: the rhythm of the tires meeting the road and the abductee's own heartbeat.

The weight of his body slid back against the leather seat when the car climbed up over a steep ridge, then they continued on a flat for at least fifteen more minutes. The car eased to a stop on a gentle incline and the engine cut.

"You go in the front, quiet, quiet," Parthiv said. "If Maataa or the aunties or the cousins wake up, make nice talk. 'How are you doing today? The house, it looks lovely.' I'll take this one up the side to Giriraj's *kyaha*."

"Okay." Amal sounded skeptical. The holes in the plan were obvious even to a teenager in the middle of a panic attack.

"Be a man," Parthiv said. "We will deal with this problem on our own. No women."

Emmanuel was bundled out of the passenger door and pushed along a pathway. The scent of flowers, sweet with a hint of decay, cut through the fetid potato smell in the hessian bag. The thump of his heartbeat slowed. He was in a garden, being led back toward a servant's room, or *kyaha*. A metal door scraped open.

"Feet up."

Emmanuel stepped into the room and the iron man's hands grabbed him by the shoulders and pushed him into a chair. A match was struck against a box and there was the brief double hiss of cotton wicks being lit. The strong smell of paraffin lamps burning filled the space. He waited a minute, till he was halfway sure that he would sound calm.

"Parthiv . . ." he said. "How about you let me go before your mother comes here and finds out the mess you're in?"

"Tie him up," Parthiv said.

Emmanuel's hands were pinned behind the chair and secured with a length of rough material. The sack was whipped off and he sucked in a lungful of clean air. He was in a small one-room house. The bedroom was a single cot pushed into a corner, the kitchen a small gas burner balanced on a wooden crate stenciled with the words SARIS AND ALL along the side. Two sharpened butcher's knives hung from hooks hammered into the side of the crate. A third hook was empty. Two chairs stood in the middle of the space. A newspaper clipping of an Indian dancer with beguiling eyes stared down from the bedroom wall.

Parthiv pulled up a chair and gave a dramatic sigh. The strongman stayed behind Emmanuel and out of view.

"We got a problem," Parthiv stated. "You know what the problem is?"

"I'm guessing it's me," Emmanuel said.

"Correct."

"You good at solving problems, Parthiv?"

The yellow light from the paraffin lanterns threw dark shadows across the Indian gangster's face so it took on the menacing quality of a skull. It was an illusion. Emmanuel knew bad men, evil men who killed for pleasure and without hesitation. Parthiv was not in that league.

"I'm the best." The Indian man leaned in and cracked his knuckles. "You took a turn into nightmare alley, white man. This room is where danger lives."

"What does that mean?" Emmanuel asked.

"I'm the public enemy: born to kill. I walk alone and brute force is my best friend."

Emmanuel almost smiled. Where else did an Indian youth in subtropical South Africa learn how to be a gangster but at the bioscope?

Emmanuel said, "That's quite a bunch of movies you've seen. James Cagney in *The Public Enemy*, Burt Lancaster in *I Walk Alone* and I can't remember who's in *Brute Force*. The big question is: Who are you in real life, Parthiv? Robert Mitchum or Veronica Lake?"

Parthiv leaned in again and delivered a hard smack to the

side of Emmanuel's head. "You in big trouble," he said. "My man can snap you like a chicken bone."

"If you let me go now, Parthiv, you might get out of this without going to prison and belly dancing for your cell mate."

"Giriraj."

The strongman stepped forward and positioned himself in front of Emmanuel. He was barely five feet five, but wide across the shoulders. His bald head was oiled and a waxed mustache twirled out to sharp points over full lips.

Parthiv waved a hand and the man stripped off his cotton shirt and then hung it neatly on a hook at the foot of the bed. He returned to the center of the room and stood in front of Emmanuel. Green cobras waged war across his chest in a tattooed scene that seemed to have been inked into his dark skin by a rusty nail: the work of a prison artist with limited tools, unlimited time and a subject with the capacity to absorb a lot of pain. Emmanuel noted recent scratch marks on the right forearm. Possibly from fingernails? The strongman stepped closer and stretched his biceps.

Parthiv was all talk but Giriraj was all muscle. Now was the time to confess all.

Emmanuel said, "Okay, there is something I have to tell you . . ."

"Good, because—"

The door scraped open before another overblown threat could be delivered. Parthiv jumped up as if his chair had caught fire. A torrent of Hindi gushed from him. He pointed to Emmanuel, then Giriraj, then back to himself in an effort to explain the situation. A flash of hot-pink sari crossed Emmanuel's eye line and a dozen glass bracelets chimed. An Indian

woman in her fifties with sinewy greyhound limbs grabbed
Parthiv's ear and twisted till his knees buckled. She muttered
insults under her breath and didn't let go even while Parthiv
was writhing on the ground. More bodies squashed into the
room. Emmanuel lost count at twelve. The Duttas weren't just
a family; they were a tribe in which females outnumbered
males three to one. The number and volume of the women's
voices shook the corrugated iron walls of the *kyaha*.

Amal was shoehorned between a walnut-skinned woman
and an old man with no teeth. He made eye contact with
Parthiv and then looked down at the floor, ashamed at his failure to be a man.

Giriraj retreated to the wall, and a young woman in a
floor-length dressing gown followed him and yelled straight
into his face.

"You grabbed a policeman? Is there even half a brain in
that fat head of yours?"

The sinewy woman in the pink sari let go of Parthiv's ear
and collapsed into a chair. "We will lose everything," she said.
"My sons. My shop. We will end up in a shack on the Umgeni
River."

"No, Auntie," the young woman in the long gown said.
"It will be all right. The boy was already dead when Amal and
Parthiv found him. They are innocent."

"They are Indian," a voice called from the doorway. "The
police will make sure they are guilty."

"That is true," the woman in the pink sari said. "They will
hang."

The noise was sucked from the room. A life for a life was
the law in South Africa. Two Indian men found at the scene of
a white boy's homicide would have a hard time convincing an

all-white jury of their innocence. Under the National Party's new racial segregation laws, Indians were classified "non-white." They were ranked above the black population but still below the "Europeans."

The walnut-skinned woman held Amal's hand to her cheek and muttered quietly. Emmanuel spoke no Hindi but he understood every word. The sound of prayer was universal: he'd heard it in the battles and ruined towns of Europe. An appeal to a mute and deaf God. The woman in the pink sari dropped her face into her hands. A girl, dark-haired and tiny and still too young to understand what was happening, began to cry. The Dutta family had started to unravel.

"I'm not a policeman," Emmanuel said.

The woman in the dressing gown turned. She was in her early twenties, with a thick rope of black hair that fell to her waist. Light glinted off the silver petals of her nose ring.

"What was that?" she said.

"I'm not a police detective," Emmanuel said. "I used to be, but I'm not anymore."

"No," Parthiv said. "He's a lawman. A detective sergeant. I heard it in his voice."

"Quiet." The gowned woman waved four female elders closer. They leaned in, head to head, and whispered. The circle broke, but the female council remained tightly bunched. They turned their attention to Emmanuel. The young woman in the dressing gown stepped forward.

"I'm Lakshmi," she said politely. "And you are?"

"Emmanuel Cooper."

"You're a policeman?"

"Not anymore."

"What is it you do now?"

"I work at the Victory Shipyards on the Maydon Wharf."
It was the truth, in part. He couldn't tell them he was also on
a surveillance mission for Major van Niekerk, doing an unofficial investigation of police corruption at the Point freight
yards. That fact was not for public discussion. "I'm a ship-
breaker."

The Victory Shipyards employed only veterans of the
armed forces. All skin colors were folded into the shipyard
ranks and together they constituted the full array of the British Empire's fighting forces. Mixed-race soldiers from the Malay and Cape corps. Hindu and Muslim soldiers from the
Indian Army, European soldiers from the Royal Marines
and the Welsh infantry, all now surplus to the needs of a world
at peace and cut loose from the purse strings of a shrinking
empire.

"Ahh . . ." One of the aunties called Lakshmi over and the
women chattered in quiet voices that were accompanied by
wild hand gestures and the vigorous shaking of heads.

"You're an old soldier," Lakshmi said when the council
had reached a conclusion. "My auntie knows this Victory
Shipyards. Her brother was in the Fourth Indian Division."

An interjection was shouted from the gallery and Lakshmi
gave a small sigh before relaying the message. "My uncle was
at the Battle of Monte Cassino. Have you heard of it?"

"Of course," Emmanuel said. "The Indians fought like li-
ons to get the Germans off that hill."

The aunties nodded their approval of his answer and signaled for Lakshmi to continue.

"What were you doing at the docks?" she said.

"I was lonely. I was looking for a woman to keep me company." Emmanuel used his ready-made excuse. It was the only

believable explanation for being out in the freight yards after dark.

"Oh . . ." Lakshmi was taken aback at the answer and looked to the female elders for help.

The woman in the pink sari lifted her face from her hands. "Out, out, out," she said. "Lakshmi, you stay."

Aunties, uncles and cousins left the room in single file. Parthiv tried to go with them but was stopped dead by a pointed finger. He retreated to the edge of the cot. Giriraj sank down by his side, both men miserable.

"You said you were a detective." Lakshmi frowned. "Why did you lie to Amal and Parthiv?"

"Habit," Emmanuel said.

And a longing to be a detective again. Six months ago his job was to speak for the dead. Other occupations seemed inconsequential. He was, in his bones, still a detective.

"Did you get the sack from the police?" Lakshmi asked.

"I was discharged."

"Why?"

"I didn't have a choice," Emmanuel said. He'd gone up against the powerful police Security Branch on his last official case and lived to tell the story. That should have been enough. He should have been grateful to have his life back, almost intact.

Lakshmi nodded and waited for him to say more. Emmanuel shifted against the wooden backrest. He didn't want to remember how careless he had been. Major van Niekerk was right when he'd said, "Fucking with the Security Branch out in the boondocks is one thing, Cooper. Fucking with them here in Jo'burg where everyone can see . . . that's slapping them in the face."

And that was what Emmanuel had done. He had maligned the most powerful law enforcement body in South Africa by delivering a letter to the mother of a black man wrongly accused of murdering an Afrikaner police captain. The young man, a member of the banned Communist Party, hanged himself in his jail cell on the eve of the trial. Or so the papers said.

"And what was the content of this letter?" Major van Niekerk had asked Emmanuel after calling him into his office at Marshall Square CIB in Jo'burg six months ago. One of the cunning Dutch major's spies had alerted him to a Security Branch investigation in which a Detective Sergeant Emmanuel Cooper was named.

Emmanuel told the truth. Lying to the major was a waste of breath and time. "I wrote that I was sorry for her loss, that her son was innocent of the charges against him and that he was beaten into a confession by the Security Branch."

Van Niekerk absorbed the information and calculated the extent of the damage. "That letter is enough to have you declared unfit to serve in the police force, Cooper."

"I understand, Major."

"Do you also understand that as long as the Security Branch has that letter in their hands, they can do anything they want to you? And I can't help you."

"Yes," Emmanuel said.

He had been careless and ungrateful. After he had returned from Jacob's Rest with broken ribs and no one in custody for the murder of Captain Pretorius, the major had shielded him from criticism and questions. Emmanuel had come back to the city and thrown that shelter away under the delusion that an unsigned letter, even one that told the truth, could wash away the brutal aftermath of the investigation in Jacob's Rest.

"One other thing," the major said. "There was also mention of a murder file being sent over from the Sophiatown police."

Sophiatown, a chaotic jumble of brick and corrugated iron houses and shacks just west of Johannesburg, was home to a mix of blacks, mixed-race "coloureds," Indians, Chinese and poor whites. Overcrowded, poverty-stricken and violent, close-knit and bursting with life and music, Sophiatown was an ugly and beautiful sprawl. And until he was twelve, it was Emmanuel's home.

White noise roared in his ears. The sound he imagined drowning victims heard before going under for the last time. "Security Branch must have asked for the police file on my mother's murder," he said. He was sure of it. "They're going to use the disciplinary hearing to make the information in the file public."

The police file raised awkward questions. Was Emmanuel's father the Afrikaner man he grew up calling "Vader," or was his father the Cape Malay owner of All Hours Traders, where his mother worked six days a week?

The major studied a landscape painting of low green hills hanging on the beige wall, then said, "Security Branch are going to get you dismissed and then they're going to get you reclassified from European to mixed-race. And they're going to do it publicly to inflict maximum damage."

Emmanuel knew the damage would not be limited to him. The attention drawn to the case would taint everyone. His sister was bound to lose her teaching job at Dewfield College, a "European" girls' school run by "European" staff. Major van Niekerk's name would be dropped from promotion lists for allowing a man of uncertain racial origins to rise above the rank of detective constable. Even the Marshall Square Detective Branch was open to attack. They might all be dragged through the mud. Public humiliation and punishment was, Emmanuel suspected, exactly what Lieutenant Piet Lapping of the Security Branch wanted.

Emmanuel knew that there was no one to blame for this situation but himself. He had personally and with great deliberation planned a mission that even the most naïve GI could see was a clusterfuck waiting to unfold.

"I'll take the punishment before they can hand it out," he said. "I'll buy my own discharge and request racial classification before they do."

Van Niekerk mentally turned the suggestion over for a long while, then looked at him. "Fall on your own sword. It might work," he said. "Plus, your record will show a voluntary discharge, not a dismissal. That might leave the door open for you to come back when things cool down."

Van Niekerk's optimism was dizzying. Neither of them would live long enough to see the Security Branch learn to forgive and forget. The major took a piece of paper from a drawer and slid it across the leather-topped desk to Emmanuel. He pulled a pen from his pocket and placed it next to the piece of paper. Emmanuel wrote out a request for discharge and backdated it to Friday, two days before his letter to the black man's mother was delivered.

Van Niekerk scrawled a looped signature on the bottom of the request and said, "I was going to call you in anyway, Cooper, to tell you some news. I'm being transferred to Durban next month. You should consider relocating out of Jo'burg for a while."

And now here he was. In Durban . . . tied to a chair in a servant's room somewhere on the outskirts of the city. Major van Niekerk had given him another chance and he'd failed to follow the simple order "Do not get involved."

"I'm a shipbreaker," Emmanuel said again to Lakshmi. "I went to the yards to find a prostitute. End of story."

"He's lying, Maataa," Parthiv said to the older woman. "He is a policeman. I swear it."

"Check me," Emmanuel said. "I don't have a gun or a police ID."

Lakshmi knotted her fingers together. Physical contact with a sweat-stained male who trawled the docks for prostitutes was akin to plunging her hand into a sewer.

"Let me see." The woman in the pink sari stood and Lakshmi retreated into the "kitchen" area. Emmanuel was pretty sure that Maataa meant "Mother" in Hindi, but this woman had the tenderness of rhino hide. Her dark eyes were rimmed with kohl and devoid of sentiment. He shifted in the chair, conscious of his own sweat and the stink of rotting potatoes that clung to his suit, which even when clean looked old. The suit was the most respectable piece of clothing he owned; all the buttons matched. Maataa opened the jacket to expose a pale blue shirt and dark trousers.

"Look," she said to her son. "No gun. No ID. No nothing."

"But . . ." Parthiv began, and thought better of it. His mother was in charge now. Maataa rifled the other pockets and found the small coffee flask, a pencil and nothing else. The van Niekerk notebook was safe in the back pants pocket. The ID card listing his age and race classification and his driver's license were in a drawer back at his flat. He never took them out anymore. Let the tram conductors figure out where he belonged for themselves. He was done trying.

"The dead boy at the train yard," Maataa said to Emmanuel. "He was white?"

"Under the dirt, yes, he was white."

"You know this boy?"

"He's not a relation," Emmanuel said. "I've seen him around the dock area. That's all."

"Big trouble." The Indian woman narrowed her eyes. "You will go to the police?"

"I won't go to the police," he said. "It was a mistake to get involved."

Maataa's angular face drew closer. She smelled of cloves and a temple fragrance Emmanuel couldn't name.

"You are scared," she said.

"Yes, I am." It was better to stay completely off the Security Branch radar.

"This is very good."

Maataa crooked a finger toward Giriraj. He untied the rope binding Emmanuel's hands, then returned to the bedroom space and awaited the next command.

"I can go?" Emmanuel asked. He didn't want any misunderstanding.

"You will keep your word. This I can see."

She searched Emmanuel's features and frowned. "What is it that you are . . . European? Mixed-race? Or maybe you were born in India?"

Emmanuel said, "You choose."

Maataa laughed at the idea that she would ever have that power. "Ahhh, you are a naughty man. Go with Parthiv but do not go back to the harbor. There are plenty, plenty clean women in Durban."

"I'll go straight home," Emmanuel said. Parthiv escorted him from the small room. The night garden was fragrant and cream flowers the size of babies' hands twirled in the breeze. He was free to finish the last one or two hours of the van Niekerk job and forget that he'd ever attempted to relive the role of detective sergeant. The memory of Jolly's curled fingers was stark.

"What were you doing in the freight yard?" he asked Parthiv when they stepped onto a narrow driveway at the front of the house. The city of Durban glittered below. Out on the dark mass of the Indian Ocean shone the lights of anchored freighters awaiting the call into the harbor. Emmanuel guessed he was in Reservoir Hills, a suburb created especially for the Indian population. Farther out on the urban edges was Cato Manor, the tin and mud catchment area set up for the burgeoning black population.

"I, too, was looking for a woman," Parthiv confessed, and unlocked the kidnap car, a midnight-blue Cadillac low to the ground and gleaming with chrome. "My mother wants Amal only to study, study and study. This is not good. He is clever but he is not a man."

Emmanuel got into the front passenger seat and waited for Parthiv to fire the engine. Giriraj stepped out of the side pathway and climbed into the back. He moved surprisingly quietly for a big man. They reversed out of the sloping drive and drove an unlit road edged with jacaranda trees.

"Why the docks?" Emmanuel asked. The lowest class of prostitute worked the dockyards and the vacant boxcars. Parthiv was behind the wheel of a shiny new Caddy.

"There was no choice," Parthiv said. "If I took Amal to a house where there are paid Indian women, my mother would find out. She wants him only to make the good marks and be a lawyer."

"So," Emmanuel clarified, "you took your little brother to the docks to find a woman. Maybe even a white woman. As a treat."

"Exactly." Parthiv smiled, happy his unselfish motives were understood and appreciated.

Emmanuel wanted to swing back to the house, find Amal and tell him, *Never listen to Parthiv. Unless you want to spend a few years in a tiny cell with a bucket to crap in, keep studying. You can cure virginity quick. Jail goes on forever.*

"He's still a child," Emmanuel said. "He'll find his own way in a few years."

"What happened to that boy in the alley," Parthiv said, "that could also happen to Amal. Gone, just like that. Better to die a man."

"Better not to die at all," Emmanuel said, and tried to block the image of Jolly Marks lying in the dirt. Collecting evidence was what the police did, and Emmanuel wasn't one of them anymore. He was a civilian working for Major van Niekerk. Still, the crime scene bothered him.

"Where was the boy when you first saw him?" he asked.

Once a few facts about the murder were in place, he'd stop and let the Durban police do their job. A dead white child was on the top of the murders-that-matter list. The Detective Branch would throw men and expensive overtime into solving the case.

"The boy was lying there," Parthiv said. "Blood everywhere."

"This is while you were looking for a prostitute?"

"*Ja,* same like you. We found one, red hair with a shiny purple dress and small titties, but she wouldn't do it with a Charra, an Indian." Parthiv was offended again at the memory. "I said, 'Only one of us. Good money. No police to see us.' This whore said no. We kept going and he was there in the lane way, dead as anything."

"Anyone come out of the lane way?"

"No."

"You hear anything? Voices? An argument?"

"Nothing. We were quiet because the police, they see Indians more quickly than they see white people."

"Did you notice any other men in the area?" Was Jolly's murder connected to a bad deal? Did he see something he shouldn't have?

"No one," Parthiv said, and fiddled with the dial of the radio despite all the stations being off the air till daylight.

"But you knew the boy," Emmanuel pushed ahead. "Tonight wasn't the first time you'd seen him. That's right, isn't it?"

"You a cop," Parthiv said. "For sure."

"I'm not." Emmanuel knew he'd pushed too far. "I was just curious."

Parthiv's voice swelled with panic. "You're working undercover, isn't it?"

"I'm not an undercover policeman," Emmanuel said. Or any other kind of police, he reminded himself. "Once you've dropped me at the freight yards, you and I will never see each other again."

"For real?" Parthiv said.

"For real."

The Cadillac sped through the empty streets and zipped past municipal parks with deserted swings and scrappy cricket pitches. They soon arrived at the Point freight yards. A drunk zigzagged along the footpath and a stray dog pawed at the contents of a toppled garbage can. There were no police wagons, no crime scene barricades and no guard positioned at the entrance to the alley where Jolly Marks still lay undiscovered and alone.

"Thanks for the lift," Emmanuel said. Parthiv responded with a humorless snort and swung a U-turn back toward the city center. Red taillights dimmed and then disappeared. Emmanuel scooped loose coins from his pocket. The closest public telephone box was within visual distance of the Point Police Station. A risky position for what he had in mind.

He flipped his jacket collar up, like a second-rate hood in one of Parthiv's gangster films, and ducked into the red and cream circular booth. A tattered telephone directory dangled from a metal chain. He thumbed the pages to the list of police stations and fed coins into the slot.

"Sergeant Whitlam." The voice on the other end was gruff. The morning shift and a soft bed were still hours away. "Point police."

"There's a body in the alley behind the Trident Shipping office."

"What's that?"

"Listen carefully, Sergeant Whitlam. This is not a hoax or a joke. Send someone out to the alley behind Trident Shipping. A boy has been murdered."

"Who is this, please?"

Emmanuel hung up. It had come to this: anonymous phone calls in the dead of night to speed the wheels of justice.

He retreated into the shadows and crouched across from the entrance to the alley, like a thief. Five minutes ticked by, and then ten. Every second magnified just how ludicrous the situation was. He was a grown man hiding in the dark, with no option but to watch and wait. The sensible thing was to get up and walk away.

A gangly foot policeman with sleep-tousled hair turned up to conduct the search a quarter of an hour later. Twenty years old at most, Emmanuel figured, not cynical yet but certain that the charge-office sergeant had sent him out to chase a waste-of-time tip-off. The constable entered the narrow pathway with his torch on high beam and reemerged quickly, gasping for air. The subtropical night was still and the policeman's rasped breath could be heard across the width of the road. Nausea, shock and disbelief . . . Emmanuel waited for the young man to move through the emotions that came with the discovery of a murder victim. The constable wiped his nose with a sleeve and pulled the police whistle free. A long and mournful note sounded across the Point.

3

IT WAS SIX FORTY-FIVE A.M. and the morning light was soft on the shopfront awnings and the tidy redbrick houses sitting behind tidy redbrick walls and trimmed hedges. Emmanuel buttoned up his grubby jacket, plastered down errant strands of hair and approached Dover, the Edwardian-style apartment box that housed his "fully furnished short-term accommodations." The cross-town tram rumbled off toward West Street in the heart of the city, the lion's share of the seats reserved for white office workers, clerks and perfumed shopgirls. Nonwhites were squashed into the last six rows of the carriage in a press of saris, khaki suits and prepacked lunch pails.

He approached the entrance to the Dover flats slowly, the better to judge the chances of slipping in the side gate. He'd waited to see a guard posted at the murder scene before turning for home. That was a mistake. Mrs. Edith Patterson, the landlady, was out on the front footpath pulling up weeds from cracks in the pavement. Her purple hair was wound tight over rollers. The brass ring that held the keys to her building clanked together against the green material of her housecoat as she worked to tame nature.

The black maid, a slight Zulu girl in a patchwork dress, collected the debris and made neat piles ready to be swept up. Rows of paper Union Jacks were strung along the fence to celebrate Princess Elizabeth Windsor's imminent coronation. A dirty Scots terrier panted down the stairs, trotted to Mrs. Patterson and attempted to mate with her arm.

"No, Lancelot." The landlady shook off the dog. "Bad boy!"

Emmanuel did a half turn toward the tram stop. He'd try his luck later.

"Mr. Cooper."

Mrs. Patterson was now standing up, a much better vantage point from which to look down her nose at him. He walked over to her and smiled. Buttoning the jacket was a mistake, he realized. It only made him more pitiful: as if he really believed a simple gesture could wipe the smell from his clothes or rearrange the muddy creases in his suit. He unbuttoned his jacket in a show of defiance. Five months at the Dover, and he'd never been late making the monthly rent. He was still paid up one week in advance. That counted for something.

"Mr. Cooper." The landlady's brown eyes narrowed. "Are you going to make me regret my decision to take you on?"

She pointed to the hand-painted sign nailed under the building's name, which read EUROPEANS AND WELL-BEHAVED MAURITIANS ALLOWED. NO EXCEPTIONS. "Well-behaved Mauritians" being a code for any light-skinned mixed-race person willing to pay the inflated rent and refrain from bringing bar girls into the room for a night of mattress-thumping.

"My car broke down and I missed the last tram," Emman-

uel explained while the mangy Scots terrier began an unsuccessful liaison with the mailbox pole.

Mrs. Patterson pursed her lips. She waited for Emmanuel to make an apology or show regret for confirming
her worst suspicions about mixed-race men. He relaxed his
shoulders, kept eye contact and said nothing. He'd explained
himself enough for one day. The maid's hand hovered above
an unplucked weed, held there by the sudden tension in
the air.

Mrs. Patterson broke eye contact first.

"I run a good house. A clean house." She brushed dirt-
flecked hands against her housecoat, and the keys at her waist
chimed. "I thought you understood that, Mr. Cooper."

Emmanuel sidestepped the landlady and walked to the
front door. He knew that the moment this week was up, Mrs.
Patterson was going to slip an eviction notice under his door.
He'd committed the cardinal South African sin. He was regis-
tered nonwhite. He had failed to express gratitude for being
bullied by a white woman.

"Lancelot. No. Bad boy." The landlady's tone set Emmanuel's teeth on edge. She talked to the dog the same way she
talked to him.

A flicker of material at the downstairs window alerted
him to the fact that Mr. Woodsmith, the retired postman who
rented the ground-floor flat, had witnessed the confrontation.
He nodded in the direction of the curtain and the material
dropped. One week and not a second more.

Inside the building, the oak banister of the staircase shone
with a fresh application of wax. Mrs. Patterson did run a clean
house. Why the Scots terrier had never seen a bath or a bar of
soap was one of life's little mysteries.

The walls of the flat were painted bright yellow. A cheery color scheme that depressed Emmanuel every time he entered it. The room possessed a single bed no wider than a field cot, a two-ring gas burner and a mothball-laced wardrobe that easily contained two suits, six shirts and three pairs of work pants. The private bath and shower squeezed into an alcove and separated from the rest of the room by a wraparound curtain cost him an extra pound each month.

A tenants' phone in the hallway made it easy to call his sister in Jo'burg on the first Sunday of every month. The conversations were brief. He repeated the familiar lies that he'd told her while their parents fought in the kitchen. Life was good and everything was fine. Lies kept them together.

He reached into a jacket pocket and removed a postcard with a tinted photograph of misty hills and deep, silent valleys. On the back, in chicken-scratch writing, was an invitation to visit Zweigman's Medical Clinic in the Valley of a Thousand Hills. Dr. Daniel Zweigman, the old Jew who'd saved Emmanuel's life after a vicious beating by the Security Branch, was a two-hour drive away. He laid the card gently on the bedspread. Maybe one day when he was less worn around the edges . . .

He stripped off the dirty suit and threw it into a small sisal basket in the corner. The young maid took in tenants' laundry along with her other work. Emmanuel washed. He'd already planned to have the day off from the shipyard to rest and regroup after the night of surveillance. But he would not sleep this morning. He would not sleep at all today.

He dressed in a clean suit and checked his reflection in the mirror. Five months at the shipyards had erased any trace of physical softness from his person. Impersonating a church minister or a gentle family man was now out of reach. Yet he loved the hard labor of the yards, doing what most Europeans considered "kaffir work." Hauling, lifting and hammering sapped his energy and left his mind empty. Sleep came like a force of nature, black and unstoppable. Dawn brought only a vague memory of having dreamed. Being too exhausted to think was the closest he'd come to happiness since leaving his old life and the Detective Branch back in Jo'burg.

Emmanuel slipped Zweigman's postcard into the jacket pocket of the clean suit and scooped up his driver's license. The race classification ID card was left behind in the drawer. He still retained the body language of a white detective and no one had so far dared question his right of entry to any venue, be it a "Europeans only" restaurant or a "nonwhite" queue at the bank.

He collected the laundry basket. He was about to break a promise that he'd made to himself when he left the force: never hang around an official police investigation. He was going to go down to the freight yard and make sure the Detective Branch was at the crime scene. Then he was going to try to find out if the search had turned up the notebook. It was a quick ten-minute stop.

Where was the harm in that?

———

Striped police barricades fenced off the crime scene. A black Dodge mortuary van was parked on the street corner. Detectives in porkpie hats and loose cotton suits scribbled in notepads and searched for evidence. Photograph flashes burst out of the alley and lit the crowd of shipping clerks and railway workers pushed against the barricades, hungry for a glimpse of the terrors that lurked behind Durban's sedate façade. Farther along Point Road a group of Onyati, black dockside laborers known as Buffaloes, stood close together. A white supervisor kept them in check by smacking a baton against his thigh while he paced back and forth.

Emmanuel unfolded the *Natal Mercury* newspaper and skimmed the columns in an attempt to distract himself. News of the coming royal coronation took up slabs of space. There were details of the cream satin gown and descriptions of the jewels embedded in the Sovereign's Orb. Emmanuel found the whole thing impossibly dull. News of Jolly's murder was not in print yet, and when the story hit the stands tomorrow, it would probably take second place to the city's coronation celebrations.

Emmanuel looked over the crime scene. The Detective Branch was out in force. He could walk away with a clear conscience. But the energy radiating from the investigation team roped him in and pulled him closer. He missed this: the intense focus on the task and the bending of individual will to the demands of the case. He moved through the crowd of onlookers until he stood next to an Englishman with busy eyebrows and a thin mouth.

"White boy," the man said. "Cut to ribbons in the back alley."

A beanpole redhead slouched next to an older detective with salt-and-pepper hair. Her purple sateen dress shone like discarded tinsel on a barbed-wire fence and the plunging neckline highlighted breasts the size of bee stings. Parthiv's fussy prostitute. The one who didn't sleep with Indians.

"Charras!" The prostitute's shrill voice rose in frustration; yet another of the English migrants who'd come to South Africa in search of a better life and had still found gas and electricity bills and impatient landlords. "All the Charras look the same. Dark, with greasy hair, flash suits. Two of them."

"That figures," said a bearded Afrikaner with hands that could crack walnuts. Emmanuel recognized the aggrieved tone. The fact that Indians, or Charras, as they were called in Durban, owned shops and restaurants and ran their own schools and even built temples with spires and elephant-headed gods right in the middle of town was a source of open resentment.

"Two of them," the Englishman added. "A criminal gang of some sort."

A turbaned Indian clerk slipped into the entrance of the Trident Shipping Company and closed the door behind him. Two coloured men followed, nervous at being mistaken for Indians. Farther down the street, a black street sweeper swung a U-turn and worked away from the crowd. A young detective emerged from the alleyway with an object laid out on a cloth, and the crowd stretched as one to take a look. The front rank of onlookers eased back, disappointed by what they saw.

"Flashlight," the Afrikaner informed the crowd behind him. "Probably belongs to the Charras."

No, Emmanuel thought, the torch does not belong to the Charras. It belongs to me. It had fallen to the ground when Giriraj bagged him. The salt-and-pepper-haired detective dismissed the prostitute and joined the huddle of men around the torch. Emmanuel pushed forward to the first row of onlookers.

"Good work, Bartel," the older detective said. "Where was it?"

"Behind the wheel of one of the freight cars, sir."

"Must have rolled there," the senior detective speculated. "Anything else?"

"Besides the soft-drink bottle, nothing, sir."

The hand-rolled cigarette might have burned away but Jolly's penknife was made of wood and steel. It should still be in the alley. The notebook normally attached to Jolly's pants had not been found, either. That made two pieces of evidence not retrieved by the police. There was one logical place they might be.

Emmanuel stepped back and slowly made his way to the front doors of the Trident Shipping Company. He wanted to run but that would be a mistake. Innocent bystanders drifted away when the routine police work began. No bodies to see, no instant arrests . . . just a big silver torch with a broken light and a bottle of lemonade.

The entrance to the shipping office was decorated with a painting of Poseidon. He walked in under the curve of the sea god's navel. Six open cubicles manned by a mix of Indian and coloured men took up most of the space. In a glass-fronted office in the back, a busty redhead in a green suit took dictation from the baas, a white man lounging behind a teak desk.

The turbaned Indian man who'd slipped away from the crowd was seated at the second cubicle. Emmanuel walked straight up. He had to get in and out of the office quickly. An underfed coloured man with a pencil tucked behind an ear jumped up.

"Can I help you, sir?"

"No," Emmanuel answered, and drew level with the Indian clerk. "Sir" meant the clerks thought he was classified white and wouldn't challenge him.

The turbaned man sprang to attention, another demobbed soldier of the empire ready to present arms. "I have nothing to do with the dead boy, sir. Nothing."

"Saris and All," Emmanuel said. "You know of a shop by that name?"

That was the brand stamped along the side of the wooden crate in Giriraj's room, and Maataa had mentioned owning a shop. Two pieces of information that might lead back to the Dutta family.

"Saris and All?" The clerk repeated the name, surprised and relieved by the unexpected direction of the conversation.

"Yes. Do you know where I can find it?"

The baas glared out of the glass window. He'd be out in a moment, Emmanuel figured, annoyed that someone other than him was bossing his workers around.

The Indian man said, "On Grey Street, I think, sir. Close to the Melody Lounge."

"Thanks."

The baas emerged from the glass fortress to investigate and Emmanuel exited the front door. The crime scene crowd was still five deep.

"To the side," a rotund sergeant instructed the onlookers through a megaphone. "Make way for the van."

The crowd split and the black Dodge van drove through a breach in the barricade. A balding man in a white double-breasted uniform opened the van doors, and two attendants carried a canvas stretcher out of the alley. Jolly Marks's body was a small lump under the sheet.

A dark-skinned Onyati with a broad face pulled off his woolen cap and the rest of the dockworkers did the same. They stood in silence until the van departed and the leader of the Onyati began to sing. His men joined in and the melody swept across the freight yards and Point Road.

"*Senzenina, senzenina . . .*" The black dockworkers' voices rose in a powerful harmony. "*Senzenina, senzenina. Siyo hlangane ezulwini. Siyo hlangane ezulwini . . .*"

"Kaffirs got no respect. This is no time for singing," the bearded Afrikaner man said.

"It's a funeral song," Emmanuel told him. "It says we will meet again in heaven. They are singing the boy away, so his soul won't remain trapped in the alleyway."

Emmanuel had Constable Shabalala, the Zulu policeman on his last case, to thank for that piece of knowledge. Shabalala had taught Emmanuel something else too: at some point today, out of the view of the white supervisor, one of the Onyati would pick up Jolly's soul with the help of a small spirit twig and transport it to a better place. The life of an Onyati was hard enough without the angry ghost of a dead white boy to contend with.

The Afrikaner stared at the ground and listened to the second verse. The Onyati song finished and the street became quiet. After a moment, the black men made their way across Point Road and into the freight yards. Emmanuel moved through the thinning crowd.

"Like blades of grass, we are cut down." A southern American voice cracked the silence left by the Onyati's seamless switch from singing to working. "Was the poor boy found here, on this very yard, prepared to meet his maker, O Lord?"

Emmanuel eyed the wiry preacher, who stood on a wooden

box and held a Bible in the air. What ten-year-old boy was prepared to meet death? What idiot questioned the victim's readiness to die instead of questioning God's unwillingness to protect the innocent? And why, since winning the war, did Americans believe that rescuing the world was their next mission? Emmanuel felt his body tighten.

The preacher lowered the Bible and pointed a bony finger in his direction. He sniffed an unrepentant sinner in the crowd.

"What troubles you, brother? Is there sin in your life? An error against God that you have not confessed to?"

"A punch in the right direction would solve a few of my problems. Brother." Emmanuel emphasized the last word, tipped his hat and then turned toward the Seafarers Club, where the Buick Straight 8, on loan from van Niekerk, was parked.

Uniformed police milled on the sidewalk and picked through garbage cans for evidence. Unmarked Chevrolets and blue Dodge police vans lined Point Road.

"Keep up the good work, men." A tall colonel with muttonchop whiskers marched through the ranks boosting morale. A sign that this murder was being taken seriously.

4

G REY STREET, WIDE and overhung by electric tram wires, was in the very heart of Durban's Indian area. Brightly painted vegetarian restaurants jostled for space with spice emporiums and LADIES' FROCK AND GENTLEMEN'S SUIT retailers. A gaggle of black women ambled down the sidewalk with bags of rice balanced on their heads. Shirtless Indian laborers hauled bamboo poles through the windows of the Melody Lounge, which was temporarily closed for renovations. The air smelled of roasted cardamom seeds and chilies.

Saris and All was a narrow shop that sold English Rose skin-lightening creams, loose tobacco, shoelaces and bulk dried goods under a waterfall of silk and cotton saris that hung from wooden bars bolted to the ceiling. A tall Indian man in a white cotton suit and open-necked shirt approached Emmanuel.

"What may I get you on this fine day, sir?" The shop steward indicated the laden shelves and burlap sacks of dried lentils and rice.

"Parthiv or Amal," Emmanuel said. "Are they in?"

"Mr. Dutta and Mr. Dutta junior. That is who you would like to see?"

"Yes."

"Please." The tall man fiddled with the top button of his shirt. "I cannot help you. It is lunchtime and past that door I cannot go."

"What door?"

"Behind the purple sari. This is very private. For the Dutta family, no one else."

Emmanuel swung the shimmering curtain aside and pushed the hidden door open. He stepped onto an outdoor porch sheltered by a woody bougainvillea vine with sparse pink blooms. A row of reused corn-oil tins were planted with seedlings tied to slender bamboo poles.

Amal sat at a table with a book in one hand and a samosa in the other. Silver bowls of curry, pickles and rice were spread out on a table in front of him. He was so absorbed in his book he didn't look up until Emmanuel pulled up a chair and sat down opposite.

"Detective." A well-thumbed science text dropped to the floor. Pieces of paper with scribbled formulae scattered. "Detective Sergeant."

"It's just Emmanuel."

"But . . . how . . . ."

"Relax, Amal. I want to ask you something."

"Am I in trouble?"

"No." Emmanuel motioned to the bowls of food. "Finish your meal."

Amal collected the book and papers and placed them on the table. He fiddled with the tablecloth, too nervous to eat. Emmanuel nodded at a fried curry puff.

"Mind if I have one?"

"No. Please."

Emmanuel took the spicy pastry and bit into it. Then he selected a samosa and a scoop of chutney, which he placed on a white plate. He ate that, then served himself some chicken biryani with sliced cucumber and a warm disk of roti. The confrontation with the dragon landlady, Mrs. Edith Patterson, had put him off breakfast. He'd eaten nothing since the night before.

"You like Indian food?"

Emmanuel glanced at Amal, who observed him in the same way a child might observe a sword swallower working in a circus tent. "I do," he said. "You should have some before I finish it all."

Amal scooped food onto his plate, still wary but beginning to relax. Emmanuel waited until the boy was halfway through a plate of rice and chicken curry.

"When we left the alley last night"—Emmanuel made it sound like a mutual decision that Giriraj had carted him away in a sack—"what did you pick up as you left?"

Amal threw a nervous glance toward the courtyard door, then pushed a grain of rice around the rim of his plate with a spoon. Silence dragged out.

Emmanuel leaned forward. "This conversation is between you and me," he said. "I won't tell Parthiv or Maataa or anyone else what we've talked about."

"True?" Amal looked up.

"True," Emmanuel repeated, and said, "That is a promise."

"I picked up my torch."

"What else?"

"A small notebook."

Jolly's notebook.

"There are two strings tied to the spiral. One string has a pencil attached to the end," Amal said.

"Have you got it?" Emmanuel asked.

"Not here. It's at home in my bedroom."

"Anything else?"

"No." Amal shifted uncomfortably and went back to toying with the rice grain. "I didn't see anything."

Emmanuel knew his torch had rolled under a rail carriage, which explained how Amal had missed it. What had happened to the penknife was anyone's guess. A police search of the freight yards should have found it. A vital piece of evidence had either disappeared or Amal had lifted it and was now too scared to admit it.

Emmanuel pulled a piece of work paper from the science textbook. "Can I borrow a pen?"

Amal extracted a ballpoint from his pocket and watched Emmanuel draw a rough sketch of the crime scene, with the shunting yards and Point Road labeled. Sometimes the long way around was the quickest way to get information.

"This is the alley where the body was found." He indicated the map. "The X marks the location of the body. You and Parthiv were standing about here against the wall."

"I see."

"Show me where the notebook was."

Amal frowned, then tapped a finger to a spot. "It was about here."

"Are you sure?"

"*Ja*, I picked it up when we were going to the car. I thought it might have something to do with Parthiv's business."

That was a surprise. The notebook was located between the body and the section of alley that led back to the main road. Jolly must have cut and dumped it on his way toward the freight yard where he was killed. Why get rid of the book? Had he done it on purpose?

"Look at the map again," Emmanuel said. "Did you see anything else in the alley that night? Think."

"There was something."

"Go on."

Amal swallowed hard, then whispered, "A small knife was near the boy's hand. I . . . I was too scared to pick it up."

"It's the job of the police to collect evidence," Emmanuel said. "You did the right thing by leaving it."

"And the notebook, is it yours, Detective?"

"Yes. It is," Emmanuel lied. "Can we go and get it?"

"If you drop me off at the school library after," Amal said. "I can do that."

The door leading to the courtyard swung inward and Parthiv appeared. His brows shot up to his hairline at the sight of Emmanuel and his little brother side by side.

"You talk to him?" Parthiv went straight for Amal.

"No." Amal scooted back in his chair. "I said nothing."

"Hold on." Emmanuel addressed the older Dutta male calmly. "I dropped a notebook in the freight yard last night and Amal has it. That's all."

"You dead meat." Parthiv moved in with a raised hand. "What did you tell him?"

"Nothing." The boy ducked away. "I didn't tell."

Parthiv swooped and Emmanuel laid a firm hand on the padded shoulders of Parthiv's blue silk suit. "Step back and leave him alone," he said. Like all policemen who'd worked the regular foot section of the force, he hated domestics. "Amal didn't say anything."

"You think I'm stupid? If you're not a policeman, then you're a spy, isn't it? For Mr. Khan."

"Don't know who Mr. Khan is."

The veins on Parthiv's neck stood out. "You're Mr. Khan's man, isn't it?"

"Calm down and listen," Emmanuel said. The Indian man's reaction was out of proportion to the apparent threat. Something else was going on. "I don't work for Mr. Khan, have never even heard his name before now."

"You're a liar. First you say you are a police, then, sorry, not a police. Then you say I will never see you again but now you are here in my family place squeezing Amal for information to tell Mr. Khan."

"That's not why I'm here," Emmanuel said. "I came to find my notebook."

"You think you can walk in and out of this place like it is yours? I must just take that disrespect?" Parthiv fumbled in a jacket pocket and extracted a bone-handled switchblade that flicked open with a click.

"Put the knife down," Emmanuel said. "Or I will make you put it down."

Parthiv lunged forward with the silver edge exposed. Emmanuel sidestepped the blade and slapped Parthiv's forearm. The knife hit the concrete floor, clattered as it spun across the courtyard and came to rest against the side of an empty corn-oil tin.

Emmanuel grabbed Parthiv's arm. "Amal didn't tell me

anything but I think you might have something to tell me. What do you say?"

"No dice."

Emmanuel pinned Parthiv's arm behind his back and pushed up until he was sure the pain had reached the shoulder socket.

"Wait . . ." Amal cried out. "I'll tell."

Emmanuel took a quick look at the boy and tried to ignore the shocked expression on his face. Over lunch they had been almost friends. Now Emmanuel was a violent stranger hurting his brother.

"No," Emmanuel said. "Your big brother will tell me what happened on the docks last night."

"We were looking for a woman." Parthiv tried to tug free. "I already told you."

"What else?"

"We . . ."

"The quicker you tell me, the quicker your arm will start to heal."

Without his detective's ID, this altercation was a common assault. There was no way to dress up what was happening as a citizen's arrest. A judge would determine that his prior knowledge of the law only made his actions more reprehensible. Emmanuel could see the headline in the *Natal Mercury*: "Ex-Detective Beats Indian in Sari Shop."

"We collected a package," Parthiv confessed. "From a steward on one of the passenger ships."

"What was in it?"

Parthiv stopped talking. Emmanuel shoved his elbow higher.

"Hashish!" The Indian man's shoulders sagged. "You smoke it."

"I know what hashish is," Emmanuel said, and let go. He stepped away from the puddle of silk that was Parthiv, collected the knife, pressed the switch to unlock it and folded the blade back into the ivory handle. Grinning skulls were carved into the sides. It was the kind of weapon an unpopular twelve-year-old might buy to impress classmates.

"You like knives, Parthiv?"

"*Ja*, sure. If they nice like that one." The Indian man rubbed his arm to get the circulation flowing and concentrated on the cracks in the concrete floor. His gangster pride was dented.

"Do you have any other blades?" Emmanuel asked. He remembered the sharpened butcher's knives in Giriraj's *kyaha*, the empty third hook.

"You only need one to do the job," Parthiv said.

"Really? And what's the job of a knife?"

"To frighten people."

"Did you have this knife on you last night?"

Parthiv blinked rapidly, his humiliation pushed aside by fear. The connection between a switchblade and a sliced-open child was obvious.

"No," he said. "I didn't touch that boy."

Emmanuel pressed the raised switch on the handle and the blade snapped out again. His own distorted reflection played across the silver metal surface. The skulls grinned. The knife looked almost unused; there wasn't a scratch on the steel or a speck of dried blood in the grooves of the handle. Emmanuel closed it.

"Was Jolly Marks a customer of yours?" he said. Maybe

Jolly distributed more than food and drinks to the night women and their customers.

"Jolly who?" Parthiv said.

"The boy in the alley. Was he meeting you to buy hashish?"

"No ways." The Indian man shook his head. "I ain't stupid."

"Why did you lie about knowing him last night?"

Parthiv's Adam's apple bobbed when he swallowed, and he blinked rapidly. Emmanuel was all too familiar with this facial dance, had seen it performed a hundred times before. It was the desperate search for a new lie to cover an old one. This was one part of being a detective sergeant that he did not miss. Everyone lied. Some were better at it than others. Parthiv was an amateur.

"Just tell me," Emmanuel said. "Then we can all go home."

"I don't know him. I have seen him. Around the docks and the like: running around to make deliveries. That's the truth. It doesn't pay for an Indian to get friendly with a white boy, so I never asked him to fetch me anything."

That was the plain truth. If Parthiv was on the docks to pick up hashish, he'd never risk a conversation with a European boy. It would have just elicited more attention. Emmanuel moved on.

"What did you do after you picked up the package?"

"Took it back to the car and hid it in the glove box."

"Then what?"

"It's like I said. I took Amal to find a woman."

"Where was Giriraj?"

"At the car."

"No, he wasn't," Emmanuel pointed out. "He was in the alley with the two of you."

Parthiv pulled on an earlobe. "I said to stay and keep guard. Plenty crooks on the docks."

"Did you tell him to keep a lookout for you?"

"No. I told him to keep eyes out for the police. The police take your stuff, you can't steal it back; it's gone and gone."

Emmanuel slipped the knife into his jacket pocket. Giriraj's strength and speed were impressive. Emmanuel hadn't heard him lurking in the alley, wouldn't have looked behind him if the brothers hadn't tipped him off by gazing over his shoulder.

Why was Giriraj in the alley instead of at the car and how did he get the scratches Emmanuel had seen on his arm last night?

Best to concentrate on one thing at a time and take small steps along a path that he would abandon come sunrise tomorrow.

"The notebook," he said to Amal, who was pressed against the wall. "Let's get it."

The boy peeled himself away and they turned to the exit. Maataa stood in the doorway, an unlit clove cigarette in one hand and a box of matches in the other. Emmanuel nodded to her. She'd witnessed the whole scene with Parthiv, he was sure. Seen it and done nothing.

He let her make the first move. He was sure that if Maataa came at him with a knife, she'd find a major artery and the courtyard would be spray-painted a nice shade of "blood from a reclassified white man."

Maataa lit her cigarette and threw the matches onto the floor. She walked over to a corn-oil tin that contained a fruiting aubergine and pulled a bamboo stick loose from the soil. Another puff of her cigarette, and she swished the stick through the air to test its soundness.

"Giriraj!" she called. "Giriraj!"

Amal pressed to the wall again and slid down to a crouching position, smaller targets being harder to hit. Parthiv searched in vain for a magical way to break through the walls and escape.

With a rustle of sari silk from the partition, Giriraj appeared in the courtyard. A tap on the floor with the bamboo stick told him where to stand.

"Down," Maataa said.

Parthiv and Giriraj knelt side by side with blank faces. Maataa laid the bamboo stick lightly on Parthiv's shoulder and then on Giriraj's shoulder, as if knighting them into a secret society.

The bamboo gained height and whistled through the air before smacking against Parthiv's and Giriraj's shoulders and legs. And then all over. Emmanuel inched forward, then thought better of it. Not his fight. Both men absorbed the blows, their bodies like stiff toy soldiers arranged on the battle line.

Emmanuel crouched next to Amal and whispered, "What's going on?"

"They are being punished."

"I can see that. What for?"

"The package. They were not supposed to pick it up."

"Did the package belong to someone else?"

"No, but Mr. Khan, he controls the amount of packages coming into Durban. He does not like others to bring in more packages than him."

"Who's Mr. Khan?" Emmanuel asked. The whack of the bamboo cane hitting flesh was distracting. Parthiv had accused him of being a spy for Khan moments before.

"A Muslim," Amal whispered. "He is in business."

"What business?" Emmanuel asked, but he already knew. It would be a legitimate enterprise, a dress shop or garage, backed up by prostitution, hashish smuggling and anything else that made money.

"Taxis and restaurants and, ah . . . many other things."

"Is your mother in the same business?"

"No. Sometimes she lends money, and when the people don't pay, then Parthiv and Giriraj collect it. That is all. Mr. Khan is big. My mother is small."

Clearly Parthiv wanted more of Durban's criminal action and his mother was not happy about that. Maataa stopped and flicked ash from her clove cigarette. She pointed the bamboo stick toward Emmanuel and Amal. They stood up.

"You will tell Mr. Khan they have been disciplined, yes?"

"I'll tell him," Emmanuel said. Another lie, but there seemed to be no other answer.

"Go," Maataa ordered.

Emmanuel and Amal were out of the courtyard in less than five seconds. Emmanuel had the keys in the ignition of the Buick in under a minute.

—

The waves of the Indian Ocean curled blue against the long sweep of South Beach. Landlocked Dutch farmers and holidaying Rhodesians splashed in the water or sheltered under a canopy of striped umbrellas.

A recently erected sign was cemented into the sand: UNDER

SECTION 37 OF THE DURBAN BYLAWS THIS BATHING AREA IS RE-
SERVED FOR THE SOLE USE OF MEMBERS OF THE WHITE RACE
GROUP. The message was repeated in Afrikaans and in Zulu so
there was no misunderstanding.

A black vendor in a high-collared uniform moved among
the sun worshippers with a tray of ice creams slung from his
neck by a wide leather strap. The law did not apply to those
whose job it was to service the Europeans.

Emmanuel drew level with a bench. A sign painted on the
wood read WHITES ONLY. Like hell. He sat down and sipped
his lemonade. There was between a zero and naught percent
chance that he was going to walk miles to the nonwhites' section of the beach just to take a rest.

Guilt stirred at the sight of the black ice-cream vendor
trudging across the sand. There was no place for him to take a
load off or dip his feet into the ocean when the heat got too
much.

A child, all pigtails and chubby thighs, chased a ball past
the bench. Emmanuel retrieved Jolly's notebook, which he'd
picked up from Amal's house in Reservoir Hills. It fit in the
palm of his hand. Two strings were attached. One had a pencil
at the end, while the other was cut clean, not frayed or snapped.
That explained the penknife. It had been used to sever the
notebook from the khaki pants, not in self-defense.

Emmanuel flipped the pages one by one. Lists of orders
for pies, cool drinks, boerewors rolls—hollowed-out loaves of
bread filled with curry called "bunny chow"—and beer.
Where did an eleven-year-old child get beer? The next page
wasn't a list but a portrait sketched in pencil. A girl with wisps
of hair stared up from the paper with ancient eyes. He flicked
another page to get free of the girl's dark gaze.

The contents of the notebook fell into a rough pattern. Eight or so pages of orders for a variety of take-away foods, followed by a chilling portrait of a child. The children, boys and girls, blacks and whites, might have been ghosts for all the warmth they had in them. They stilled his heart, made him wonder what Jolly had experienced in his short life to be able to draw such desolate children.

"Ice cream. Ice cream," the vendor called out. It was late afternoon and this would be the last run of the day. The baas wanted only empty boxes at sundown. "Vanilla. Chocolate ice cream."

Emmanuel flipped and found an uneven edge where another page had been. He ran a finger over it, then across the surface of the next blank page. Ridges teased his fingertips. He lightly feathered the tip of the attached pencil across the blank page. An image of a bare-breasted mermaid with a fishtail curled beneath her appeared. One eye was closed, the other wide open. A winking mermaid. The image was innocent yet somehow salacious.

"This taken?" a white girl, about fifteen, in a pink dress asked. She had a pretty Dutch boy in tow.

"Not if you qualify," Emmanuel said.

The girl frowned, uncertain.

Emmanuel pointed to the sign on the bench. The girl laughed, a pretty sound in keeping with everything else about her. She sat down, pulled the boy close and rested her head on his shoulder.

"Isn't it perfect?" the girl said with a sigh.

"The best," the boy agreed, and traced circles on the girl's naked shoulder with gentle fingertips.

Light shimmered on the water. The black ice-cream vendor struggled up the stairs from the beach with his wooden box. His polished shoes were covered with fine grains of sand.

"Here." The girl waved her arm in the air. "Here, boy."

The vendor approached, a half smile on his mouth, his gaze a little to the left of the couple. Mindful always to not make eye contact with the little baas and the little madam.

"What is it?" The girl pointed to the lone tub in the box.

"Vanilla, missus. One bob. Very good."

The boy dug into the pockets of his shorts and handed over some coins. The vendor handed back the ice cream and the change.

"Check it," the girl demanded. "Pa says the ones who live in the city cheat you blind."

The boy counted the coins while the vendor concentrated on the row of brightly painted buildings in the background.

"It's all here."

"Go." The girl waved the ice-cream seller away with a flick of her hand. Her fingernails were painted a frosted pink, the color of the sky in fairy-tale books. She replanted her head on the boy's shoulder. He pulled open the top of the tub, then began to spoon tiny paddles of vanilla into her mouth.

An ocean breeze ruffled Jolly's notebook and wrapped the pages around Emmanuel's fingers. He scribbled the pencil along the bottom edge of the page and two words emerged from the gray.

Please help.

Emmanuel felt a chill come over him in the sunshine.

5

THE SUN WAS down but a trace of heat lingered. A breeze tousled the trees, lifted hems and stirred up the exhaust fumes from cars cruising the slow lane of West Street. Lines of smartly dressed couples snaked down the pavement and waited for the Empire Cinema's late-Friday-night movie session to open. Suits, ties, ironed dresses and gloves; the occasional corsage pinned to a tulle ruffle. The nine o'clock double feature was dress formal. *Where the North Begins* followed by *Tarzan's Desert Mystery*.

In the afternoon, Emmanuel had a haircut and shave followed by a shoeshine at the corner stand. He bought coffee, milk and bread for the week. None of these routine domestic tasks had taken his mind off the notebook.

He drove past the central post office. The trunk of a Natal mahogany, known as "dead man's tree," was plastered with white funeral notices edged in black. Jolly Marks would have an announcement posted soon.

At the Point he parked the Buick a block down from the

tram stop. The place he was looking for didn't advertise. The lights from a moored passenger liner called *Pacific Pearl* twinkled like a miniature city at the harbor mouth.

He came to within sight of the crime scene. Scraps of orange and white paper streamers lifted into the air and curled against lamp poles. Jolly had probably worked a ten- to fifteen-minute radius from the freight line. Emmanuel would do the same and look out for takeaway cafés with pies and boerewors rolls on the menu.

A police car crawled up from the harbor terminal and stopped so the officer could shine a flashlight between two storage sheds. The plan, to walk the Point openly, wasn't so much a plan as an invitation to trouble. If the officers in the police cruiser spotted him twice, they'd stop and ask where he was headed. Basic procedure. Jolly's notebook was in his pocket.

That he was an ex-detective pursuing a lead in his own personal homicide investigation would not get him out of trouble with the uniforms if they nabbed him. The thought of explaining to the police that investigating the murder was more than an intellectual challenge, it was a desire to restore order and help the dead on their way, almost made him smile. Surely they'd understand?

And all of this was coupled with an arrogance that he himself acknowledged. Since this particular murder of this particular boy had found *him*, he was certain that he could put it right.

Emmanuel walked quickly toward Browns Road. One circuit and he'd be gone. It was too hazardous otherwise. He turned left and glimpsed a familiar figure, also moving fast.

Dim light from the streetlamps bounced off the high sheen of Giriraj's bald head. Interesting, Giriraj back at the Point so soon after the beating this morning.

The strongman followed a rat run through the back lanes of the harbor. Emmanuel trailed behind in the shadows. This lead was too good to ignore. The Indian curved into a blunt lane and disappeared behind a shoulder-high wooden gate. A solitary streetlamp shone a pool of light onto the uneven ground and lifted the darkness.

Emmanuel took up post outside the gate and waited. The night was heavy with the industrial scent of spilled fuel and engine oil blowing in from the harbor.

"You got it? Let me see." A woman's voice, sharp enough to shred paper, drifted over the fence. A match struck against the side of a box.

"I want more," the woman demanded. "A big chunk more, or I'll tell the police you and your Charra friends was the ones who cut the boy. You hear?"

Giriraj growled. Emmanuel rested a hand against the gate, ready to push into the black nook if the trouble escalated.

"Don't growl at me, Charra."

Emmanuel held back. The rough voice grated against his eardrums. He'd heard it before; it belonged to the prostitute in the purple dress who had talked to the senior detective at the crime scene. The one who didn't do it with Charras. There was the sound of a hard, open-handed slap.

"You like a Doberman my pa used to have," the woman said. "It was an ugly thing. Everyone was scared of him except me. He used to lick my hands and face. That's what you are, Charra. A puppy dog."

The mix of contempt and excitement in the prostitute's voice told Emmanuel exactly how the altercation would end.

"How dare you . . ." The female voice pitched higher, the breath now small, hard gasps. "You should have your hands cut off for even touching me . . ."

Where was there for a European street crawler to go in her fantasy? If she lay down with a white man, she was a whore. The law put a premium on her skin. In Giriraj's dark hands she was a precious white object defiled, a luminous pearl cast before swine.

The groans got louder and Emmanuel walked away. His heart thundered and the breath burned in his chest. Eight months had passed with nothing but the memory of smooth brown legs wrapped around his body and his name whispered in the night.

Davida. Her touch was grafted to his skin in equal parts pleasure and fear. The shy brown mouse with eyes the color of rain clouds. Last he'd seen of her, she was flying across the veldt in a white nightdress; running to find shelter from evil men. Was she building a new life for herself in some distant corner of South Africa, safe from the violence of her past? Some nights, in the stilled hush of the darkness, he dared to imagine her in the doorway of a stone and thatch house, looking up at distant hills, thinking of him.

On the count of twenty, Emmanuel headed back. Some of the heat had dissipated, enough so he could walk straight. He arrived back at the gate for the finale.

"Good boy . . ." The woman was either giving a stellar performance or was actually having an orgasm. Emmanuel guessed the latter. The sound of their breathing died down and he could hear the rustle of clothes being rearranged.

"You come next week with more." The prostitute was all business now that her buttons had been pushed. "Double. Or I'll go to the police, you hear?"

Emmanuel stood back and waited. The woman was the first to emerge, now dressed in a red satin dress with red pumps and holding a large red handbag. She caught sight of him and made a dash for the main street. The cork wedged pumps attached to her feet by thin "vamp" straps were not designed for running. He caught her easily and swung her around.

False eyelashes the size of Japanese fans fluttered in her powdered face.

"He pulled me in. The Charra grabbed me and dragged me behind the gate."

"What's in the bag?" Emmanuel asked.

"What?"

"I'd like to see what's in your bag."

She clutched the handles. "That Charra raped me. Call the police."

Giriraj stepped out into the alley. If the Indian ran, Emmanuel knew he'd catch him. Keeping him down was going to be the problem. He waited for the bald man to make a move. Giriraj stood like an impala caught in the headlights.

"Arrest him. He took advantage of me."

Emmanuel said, "Open the bag."

The prostitute flipped the giant gold clip. Emmanuel moved his hand along the bottom and felt the usual female beauty tools—a disk of rouge, a brush, a lipstick tube—and then a doughy lump. He extracted a round shape held in a small muslin cloth.

"What's this?"

"Don't know. The Charra must have slipped it into my bag."

"Open it."

She shrugged a shoulder before she unfolded the cloth and let the edges drop. A dark matchbox-sized lump lay in the center of the white material. Hashish.

He looked to the woman for an explanation.

"It's chocolate," she said.

"Really?"

"*Ja.*"

"Eat it."

"No." The woman shook her head. "I got a delicate stomach. That much chocolate will make me sick."

"I bet it will," said Emmanuel. "You get all your chocolate from this man?"

She fiddled with the gold clasp of the handbag, trying to take a stand against revealing more damaging information. Emmanuel waited in silence.

"Used to get it from another Charra, but now I got an arrangement with that one over there," she said quickly.

"What kind of arrangement?"

"I don't let him have more than fifteen minutes." She tossed her hair back, full of righteous indignation. She was a whore but a whore with standards.

"Did you get some from him last night?"

"*Ja.*"

"You paid for it?" he asked the woman.

"I told you. We have an arrangement."

"Ahh . . ." Emmanuel understood.

He motioned Giriraj over and got him to stand next to the streetwalker. The Indian man's head was bowed, like that of a recalcitrant child. Emmanuel tapped him on the shoulder and forced him to make eye contact.

"Does Parthiv know you're stealing from him?"

Giriraj shook his head.

"Where were you when Parthiv and Amal went to find a woman? You weren't by the car."

Giriraj pointed to the prostitute.

"The two Indian men you told the detective about . . ." Emmanuel said to the red-haired woman. "When did they speak to you?"

"Don't know. I don't wear a watch. Too risky."

"Did you talk to them before or after you got your delivery?"

"A bit before. This one came with the stuff right after I sent them packing."

In just under half an hour Giriraj had managed to steal a chunk of hash, service a prostitute and initiate a kidnapping. Impressive work.

"The boy that was found in the alley," Emmanuel said to Giriraj. "Did you see him alive?"

The broad-shouldered Indian shook his head again.

"I seen him," the woman said. "He was coming from the Night Owl."

"Where's the Night Owl?"

False eyelashes fluttered downward and threw shadows over her rouged cheeks. She pursed her lips. "What have you got to exchange?"

"Freedom," said Emmanuel. "That's the opposite of jail, where prostitutes with hashish end up. "

She took a breath. "It's two blocks back on Camperdown

Street. Open late even when it's supposed to be shut. The boy had a brown paper bag and a bottle. I seen him walk by fast."

"Alone?"

"Couple of minutes later a white man in a black suit also came by fast."

"Following Jolly?"

"They was going in the same direction."

"You tell the police this?"

She fiddled with the neckline of her satin dress and rearranged the folds. Her long fingernails had flakes of old fire-engine-red varnish. "No. The more I tell them, the more they want to know, and I've got troubles of my own."

"That was the last time you saw Jolly?"

"I had to meet a Norwegian whaler, Sven or Lars, can't remember which." She rubbed her skinny arms. "I worked the dock till morning. He was lying there all the time and I didn't know."

"Tell me about the man that followed Jolly," Emmanuel said when the prostitute had recovered from the specter of a dead boy just a few yards from her nightly beat.

"I told you. White man in a black suit."

"Tall or short? Skinny or fat?"

"Skinny and light on his feet. Quick-like."

"Same height as me?"

She squinted. "Little smaller, maybe. Can't really say."

That would make the suspect just under six feet. Slightly above average height but not enough to stand out in a crowd.

"Anything else?"

She shook her head, her attention on the slide. Emmanuel suspected she dreaded the men who "just wanted to talk."

They took up more time than a shuffle and a grunt between boxcars. Still, the odd pairing of nighttime creatures transcended the ordinary. That a hashish-hungry prostitute and an Indian strongman had found each other was a thing to marvel at, especially in the National Party's color-coded South Africa.

"You can go." Emmanuel waved the woman away but stopped Giriraj when he tried to make a break for the street. "If Parthiv finds out you're stealing from him," he said, "his mother will kill you."

Giriraj shuffled a foot in the dirt, impatient for the awkward moment to end. Emmanuel motioned the muscleman forward and examined the fresh scratches on his neck. They were identical to the ones he'd seen on his arm last night. Now he knew who had made them.

———

The proprietor of the Night Owl was a big-bellied man with short forearms and a dark beard streaked with gray. His place was two rungs down from a café and a half step up from a missionary soup kitchen. A string of naked bulbs lit the chipboard tables and chairs scattered under the awning in front of the business. Two tired Greek flags curled at either side of a browning potted plant placed on the middle table.

The big man took the orders and worked the grill; his dwarflike forearms strained to reach the onions and fried eggs on the back hot plate. The name NESTOR was embroidered onto the pocket of his sweat-stained shirt. A small sign, hastily painted in jungle green and nailed under the orders window, read WHITES ONLY.

"That's for the sailors," Nestor explained gruffly. "Otherwise they get into trouble and then we get into trouble."

Emmanuel pressed straight in. "The kid Jolly Marks, did he get his food from here last night?"

Nestor sized Emmanuel up with a look. Decided he was a policeman, or near enough to one to be given a quick exit.

"Ask around the back. In the 'nonwhite' section. That's where we take his orders," he said, and slid rubbery eggs into a pool of grease.

Emmanuel went to the back and found a rough square of cracked cement that faced a small orders window. No awning, no tables or chairs. One naked bulb dangled from a frayed wire suspended across the cement pad. Two black men in overalls sat on upturned fruit crates and played checkers on a hand-drawn piece of cardboard. Durban was a visibly English town and few natives were granted employment passes to live within the urban area.

"Number twenty-seven," the short-order cook called out. "Bunny chow 'n' chips. Coca-Cola."

A crinkly-headed youth in repatched pants and a loose brown shirt picked up the meal and leaned against the wall to eat. Emmanuel approached the orders hatch. The man behind the window had features borrowed from every nationality to have dropped anchor in Natal Bay. He had Asian eyes flecked green and brown, soft Zulu lips, a long thin nose dusted with freckles and woolly brown hair. Mixed-race, no doubt about it.

"*Ja?*" The narrow eyes were hard.

"Jolly Marks get his orders from here last night?" Emmanuel said.

"Who you? A policeman?"

"No. Just curious."

"Well, you and your curiosity can fuck off."

The short-order cook called out two boerewors rolls with onion and tomato sauce. Emmanuel pressed Jolly's notebook against the glass.

"Recognize this?"

"Nope."

"Take a good look," Emmanuel said. "It belonged to Jolly Marks. He was here last night. What time?"

"I told you," the man said. "I've never seen that book before."

He was defiant. Even with a detective's ID slammed against the window, Emmanuel knew the colored Asian man would not talk. Silence was the only weapon he had against authority.

Emmanuel returned to the front of the Night Owl, intent on questioning Nestor about the time of Jolly's last order. A police car was pulled up to the curb, engine idling, while the uniforms ate sausage and onion rolls. Maybe another time. He peeled to the left and bumped into a wiry man setting up a wooden crate on the sidewalk. A stack of religious tracts illustrated with a lurid drawing of a scantily dressed woman engulfed in towers of flame fluttered to the pavement.

"Do I know you, brother?" the evangelist from the dock asked. "Have we met before on the Lord's highway?"

"Don't think so," Emmanuel said, and kept moving. The roll of car wheels sounded. He glanced over his shoulder to confirm what he already knew. The patrol car was driving toward him. A flashlight aimed out of the passenger window sprayed bright light into doorways and down side streets.

The entrance to the Harpoon Bar, a watering hole for dockworkers and merchant seamen, was right on the corner. Emmanuel fought the urge to sprint for the doorway. Jolly's notebook was still in his pocket. He'd have a hard time explaining that to the police.

The bar entrance was just a few feet away. The front fender of the police car drew almost level with him. Emmanuel dropped slowly to his knee and retied his shoelace. The beam of the torch moved across the pavement and flickered into a doorway two yards ahead. The patrol car was on a door-to-door street search for something or someone. Emmanuel heard the accelerator push the cruiser farther down the street and away into the night. Relief sucked the moisture from his mouth. He needed a drink. Maybe three or four.

The dim interior of the Harpoon Bar reeked of smoke and beer. Three dark-skinned merchant seamen murmured to one another at a corner table. The Separate Amenities Act, which designated places like this into either European or non-European facilities, was being ignored. Some places were beyond classification.

Emmanuel sat down at the bar and his heart rate slowed. A spotlight search twice in one night meant the uniforms were on the lookout for someone in particular. He wouldn't want to be an Indian man out in this part of town tonight.

The younger of the two barmaids approached and leaned an elbow on the counter. She was dark-haired, with pale skin and dark almond-shaped eyes. A scooped neckline revealed the top swell of her breasts. Emmanuel remembered her from the last time he had been to the Harpoon with another ship-breaker, an ex-corporal of the Third Commando Brigade.

"Thirsty?" she said.

Emmanuel cleared his throat. "Double whiskey, thanks."

He slid a pound note onto the wooden surface. The scene with Giriraj and the prostitute had him stirred up. The scare with the police cruiser had set the adrenaline pumping and his body was awake. Memories of Davida's mouth on his had re-ignited a desire to touch and to feel, to lose himself in the tangle of a lover. A tumbler of whiskey appeared close to his hand.

"Anything else?"

He risked an upward glance, and a moment of eye contact sent a jolt to every nerve ending. Heat burned his neck. With a penny from every man who wanted her, she could own the bar and a big slice of the waterfront.

"I'm fine." He heard the lie in his voice and thought she did, too.

"If you say so."

Two slack-jawed sailors seated at the bar watched her collect used glasses and stack them onto a tray. The men looked as if they'd turned up at the dock to find their ship headed out to sea without them.

Emmanuel focused on a black-and-white photograph of a whaler nailed to the wall above a row of gin bottles. It was a long way yet before he turned into a barside pervert. But the languid movements of the barmaid's body and the dark fall of her hair were hard to ignore.

He swallowed his drink. Whiskey flooded through his arms and legs as if through the branches in the tree of life, and his mind focused. The decision to follow leads in Jolly's murder was foolish, and this attempt to re-create his past life was more than that, it was dangerous. Walking near the crime scene with Jolly's notebook in his pocket was bloody-minded stupidity and an invitation to dance the hangman's jig.

The words *Please help* were not a personal plea from the dead boy. He had to let the kid go.

"Major," said the barmaid.

Emmanuel sat up at the use of his old army title and recognized his mistake instantly. The major was a silver-haired man with broken blood vessels in his cheeks. It was a classic drinker's face, with every bottle accounted for.

"The usual," the major said.

The dark-haired barmaid flashed a look at Emmanuel and caught his eye. Electric currents sent his heart into near-arrest. He checked the level of alcohol in the tumbler. Half full. The eye contact held a moment too long was not a fantasy.

He finished the whiskey in one hit and considered the alternative. A beautiful woman, the center of every man's attention, had expressed an unspoken desire for physical connection.

"More?"

"Same again," Emmanuel said. Another hit, and he would go back to the single cot with its neat hospital corners and folded-down blanket. The bed of a soldier or a priest.

The full whiskey tumbler slid back into view.

"It's on the house," the pretty barmaid said, and moved down the counter, filling a line of shot glasses along the way.

"What's the occasion?" Emmanuel asked the older barmaid, who wore cat's-eye glasses and a sour expression. She was pushing fifty and it appeared that every one of those years had been hard-fought and hard-won.

"It's Lana's last night. She's moving up. Got a job at a posh ladies' boutique on West Street working as a house model." The barmaid's smile was nasty. "Let's hope they don't give her the combination to the safe."

She moved away and left Emmanuel to tussle with the enigmatic comment. Stealing was a common criminal activity and if he had to pick the dark-haired barmaid's area of operation, he'd pick fraud. A smile opened a lot of doors and even more wallets. Not that the older woman's word was a solid foundation on which to base anything. She'd made no effort to hide her malice. Emmanuel drained the whiskey and pushed back the barstool. Lana collected the empty tumbler.

"Do you have a car?" she said.

"Yes."

"I need a lift. Can you take me?"

She's never been turned down, Emmanuel imagined. Never had a man say no. Who was he to change the course of history?

"My car's around the corner," he said.

6

A WHISPER RUSTLED ACROSS Emmanuel's conscious-ness like a skirt trailed against the floor. He sat up and blinked hard into the unfamiliar environment. A garden of floral prints crowded the tiny room. A lavender-bush motif on the curtains crashed into daisies embroidered on scatter cushions thrown on a couch. On a small table pushed up against the window stood a ceramic vase with a dozen white roses in bloom.

Last night's lift home had turned into much more.

The black shadow of Jolly Marks's murder had made him reckless. The need to chase life in order to outrun death was a soldier's response to fear and one that he recognized from wartime Europe. Trouble was, he'd awakened in South Africa and not Paris.

"Relax, Major," a woman's voice teased. "The war's been over for eight years. You won, remember?"

Emmanuel examined the barmaid in the clear light of the morning after. Lana Rose. A name so perfect it had to be made up. She stretched her body out against the cream sheets, comfortable in her own skin.

"My slip at the bar," he said. "You noticed."

"I picked you long before that. I just didn't know if you were army or police. I'm betting it was both."

"All that brainpower stuck behind the Harpoon bar. Shouldn't you be running the country?"

"I'm finished with the Harpoon. Today is the start of a new life. I just needed to get some things out of my system first." Lana unknotted a stocking from the headboard and draped the flimsy length of silk over Emmanuel's left shoulder where an old bullet wound marked his flesh. "I ticked off quite a few boxes with you last night, Mr. Cooper."

Ah, yes. The stocking. Emmanuel rubbed his face to cover his embarrassment. It was a common enough game. What bothered him was the enthusiasm he'd brought to it . . . the ragged authenticity of a policeman enjoying the full exercise of power after a long absence.

Emmanuel got out of the bed and searched for items of discarded clothing. The memory from another time of door hinges flying inward and the breath of the law on his neck quickened his movements. Technically, the snug little flat was a crime scene. Sexual contact across the color line was a punishable offense in the new South Africa. He located a hat and belt. No sign of his trousers or shirt.

"Relax," Lana said. "There won't be any trouble."

"Really?"

"Yes, really."

Emmanuel found his trousers, improbably wedged between the sofa cushions and the seat springs. Jolly's notebook was still in the back pocket. Everything in the flat, including a chunky Bakelite radio, looked as if the price tag had just been removed: high-quality items for a woman who'd worked a low-end bar until last night. Had these things been given to Lana or had she stolen them?

He found his shirt at the foot of the bed entangled with a lace brassiere. Lana motioned toward the bathroom.

"Have a shower," she suggested. "You might be shy this morning but you weren't shy last night."

Her relaxed posture and the dozen white roses on the table eased the tension from his body. The law would not come. This flat was an illicit haven, set up for whoever had paid for the flowers and the transistor radio in the kitchen. It was the South African demilitarized zone. The normal rules separating race groups did not apply. Lana had waved off Emmanuel's racial identification last night because she was protected and she knew it.

He headed for the blue-and-yellow-tiled nook that contained a shower suspended over the bathtub. He closed the door and turned the water on. The spray was warm and soothing but a little fear remained. He was safe. He was satisfied. He was lucky. He ticked off the list, but the onset of a headache pressed against his skull. Images collided and tangled together. The curve of Lana's naked back, the slender stems of the roses, pale legs jutting into a cobbled Parisian lane and Jolly's hand against the dirt of the freight yard. His mind jumped from one thought to another like a radio receiver scanning for a clear signal. A quick needle of pain stabbed behind his eye and the force of it threw his head back.

"*Did you really think that a night in the sack was going to make it all okay, soldier?*" a ragged Scots voice said. "*It didn't work in Paris after Simone Betancourt's murder and it's not going to work now. That little fucker needs you, Cooper."*

Emmanuel switched off the shower and gripped the wet taps. The last he'd heard from the Scotsman was eight months ago, laid out on the veldt between Zweigman the old Jew and Shabalala the Zulu Shangaan constable. Like a vulture, the voice of his sergeant major from army basic training eight years previous appeared only when there was a fresh carcass to feed on. If the Scotsman was here in Durban, that could mean only one thing.

"That's right. Your arse is in big trouble," the sergeant major said. *"That's the only reason I'm here. I don't like the ocean and I hate the bloody heat."*

"I don't need looking after . . ." Emmanuel dried himself and dressed quickly. This appearance by the sergeant major broke all the rules. His was the voice of war, not of a soft winter morning in peacetime Durban.

"Okay, I know I'm only supposed to front up when the blood sprays the walls," the sergeant said. *"But we've got to talk about the dead boy."*

"There's nothing I can do about him." Emmanuel opened the medicine cabinet above the sink. "It was a mistake to get involved. Investigating murder is a police matter."

"What's that got to do with it? I've got a bad feeling, soldier."

Four or five painkillers were all Emmanuel needed, just enough to quiet the voice and get out of Lana's flat without incident. He searched rows of face creams, plastic rollers and metal hair clips on the narrow shelves.

"Look, you've spent the last ten hours listening to your dick," the Scotsman said. *"Give me five minutes."*

A glass container of Bayer aspirin was on the second shelf. Emmanuel checked the bathroom door and took the painkillers down.

"*Come on, lad.*" The sergeant major adopted a friendlier tone. "*We have to talk.*"

"There is no 'we.'" This time Emmanuel answered without talking out loud. It was a small step back from crazy but nowhere in the vicinity of normal. He shook out six pills and swallowed them with tap water.

"*They're not going to do anything. Morphine, maybe, but six wee pills? It's insulting. A piddling dose like that underestimates my power to fuck with you, soldier.*"

Emmanuel ignored him. The medication would take hold soon. Then he would be free to escape the bathroom and leave the flat. He replaced the bottle of pills and spotted a piece of paper the size of a playing card glued to the back of the cabinet.

The Scotsman said, "*I'd never have guessed it of her. She doesn't seem the type.*"

"No, she doesn't," Emmanuel said softly, and examined the image printed on the front of the cardboard square. A doe-eyed Virgin Mary wrapped in a royal blue cloak held an adoring baby Jesus on her lap. The holy child, painted as a miniature adult, was kissing his mother's cheek. Silver whorls and Eastern crosses surrounded the Madonna and child.

"*Papist rubbish,*" the Scotsman said.

Not papist, Emmanuel knew. The image was a Russian Orthodox icon. He'd seen plenty tucked into kit bags and hidden in the folds of the uniforms worn by the apparently godless Red army. He replaced the bottle of pills and closed the cabinet door. The Virgin Mary icon was private, in the same way that Zweigman's postcard was to Emmanuel: both were symbols of faith and an unspoken belief in safe haven.

"Okay," the sergeant major said. *"I'll admit she's prettier than I am and you've got no time for me right now. But listen well, Cooper. The fight has just begun."*

"What fight?"

"Heavy artillery. Expect casualties."

"What does that mean?"

There was no reply. The Scotsman had vanished. Emmanuel splashed cold water onto his face. This was Durban. The war was won. There was no fight. He rested another minute and then went out to face the awkward social shuffle of two strangers who had nothing in common but a carnal knowledge of each other.

Lana had a pot of coffee on the stove and the transistor tuned to Lourenço Marques Radio, which played a mix of American country music, English torch songs and the daring new sound of Negro rhythm and blues.

"Coffee?" She turned the radio volume down low and leaned against a kitchen counter when Emmanuel approached. Her silk slip was pale green and faded at the hem.

"Milk with two sugars, thanks," Emmanuel said. "But I'll leave right away if you want me to."

She handed him a mug. "There's no rush. I have to be somewhere in three hours."

Lunch with the benefactor and then back here to pay for the new furniture. If Lana saw Emmanuel on the street this afternoon, she'd look right through him. Her boxes were ticked off. The moment he stepped out of the flat, he'd revert to a shipyard worker from the wrong side of the color bar and a white girl's secret.

"Thanks," Emmanuel said, and accepted the mug. He was going to enjoy the coffee and the view while they were on offer. Lana poured herself a cup and leaned her hip against the kitchen sink.

"Don't look at me like that," she said.

"How's that?"

"Like I'm a question you have no idea how to answer."

"Sorry." Emmanuel drained the coffee mug and placed it on the counter. Any questions about the dark-haired ex-barmaid would remain unanswered. In his daylight world she, too, would remain a secret.

"Oh, I almost forgot." Lana slipped into the lounge room. "It was under the table."

She handed over his leather wallet, and the sour barmaid's comment from last night came back. He tucked the wallet into his jacket without checking the contents. He didn't have anything worth stealing and there was no way to place a value on last night. The old Emmanuel Cooper had returned for a few happy hours.

"Another?" Lana gestured to the empty mug.

"Please," he said. He was reluctant to leave. Here, right now, in this room, he was a man and she was a woman. The complications of race, the law, the past and the future didn't exist. It was good to stand with her in the quiet kitchen.

Lana handed him a fresh coffee and pulled the curtain open. The hum of traffic drifted into the room.

"I love the beginning of winter," she said. "Everything looks so clean, even the tarred roads and the cars."

Emmanuel joined her and peered through the glass. City traffic held no interest but being close to her for a few more minutes did. Through the sharp morning light, an aged bus disgorged a flow of black maids dressed in green and blue cotton housecoats. Sunday was the domestics' day off, so this was the last ten-hour shift of the working week. A white man in a dark suit leaned against the wall of a hardware store and read the weekend newspaper. His hat was angled to block the sun and it was impossible to make out his features.

Emmanuel waited for the turn of a page or any movement of the head left to right to indicate the paper was being read. The edge of the newspaper dipped and the man in the suit did a three-point check that took in the parked Buick, Lana's front door and the windows of the flat. Emmanuel stepped back into the kitchen.

"Something wrong?" Lana asked.

"Nothing." Adrenaline, the old flame from the battle and the crime scene, warmed his blood.

"Are you sure?"

"Yes, I'm fine."

Imaginary voices giving commands and enemies lying in ambush were classic signs of the old soldier's disease. None of it was real. The man across the street was a Saturday-morning pedestrian catching up on the news before jumping on a bus. Emmanuel stepped back to the window and looked out. The newspaper reader was gone, replaced by a tall black man sweeping the sidewalk with a grass broom.

He was not being followed. He was not in danger.

Lana pressed her palm to the wild beat of his heart.

"Are you crazy, Emmanuel?"

"A little," he said.

The emerald lawn was punctured by a blue-tiled swimming pool, and the view of Durban was exquisite. Red-hulled freighters and a few graceful sailboats dotted the harbor.

Two buxom women in polka-dot bikinis splashed in the pool while a group of men fed wood into the belly of a portable barbecue made from half a steel drum. A clutch of couples danced closely to a sentimental country-and-western ballad that played on the record player. The black servants had been sent home for the day. The sight of half-naked white women was reserved for the baas and his friends.

A photograph of Princess Elizabeth Windsor was propped on a wooden easel, the corners decorated with red, white and blue streamers. Lipstick kisses dotted the Princess's cheek.

"Are they all professional girls?" Emmanuel asked. He watched the party from the study of van Niekerk's Victorian mansion perched on the Berea Ridge.

"A mix of professionals and other girls who just want to be here," the major said. "Some of these men like to think they got lucky."

"What's the occasion?"

"The royal coronation. A party is the easiest way to get to know my men and to thank them for their hard work."

It was also the easiest way for the major to establish a power base within Durban's predominantly English police. He was new in town and a Dutchman—a potentially fatal combination. Decades of war for control of land and diamonds kept the two white communities wary of each other. The Afrikaners believed they were the white tribe of Africa, born, nursed and raised on the veldt. To them, the British were newly arrived interlopers interested only in profit and power.

The British believed that the Boers had neither the intelligence nor the drive to rule South Africa.

Van Niekerk was the son of a rich Dutch father and an English mother with more blue blood in her veins than the entire Durban force. That fact made no difference. His Afrikaner name branded him inferior. Free booze, food and women would help erode any anti-Afrikaner prejudice.

Emmanuel sat down in a chair facing a mahogany desk that bounced light off its waxed surface and onto the ceiling. "This should give you a clear idea of your men." He placed the surveillance notebook on the desk. Half the police on the lawn were listed in it.

The major ignored the book and pushed an unmarked envelope across the smooth surface. "Thank you, Cooper," he said.

Emmanuel took the packet and stuffed it into a breast pocket. The weight of it pressed against his heart. This was the closest he'd get to the job of detective sergeant, and no amount of money could make up for the loss.

"Back to swinging a hammer at the shipyard?" van Niekerk asked.

"Yes," Emmanuel said.

The major leaned back in his chair with his long legs stretched out. His dark hair was cropped short as if to emphasize the close ties between the South African police and the military.

"Why did you take the surveillance job, Cooper?"

"For the money," he said.

"It had nothing to do with missing the Detective Branch?"

Emmanuel shrugged, hoping to convey a casual disinterest in the subject. He'd spent the last day and a half conducting an unofficial murder investigation. That was proof enough of how quickly he could be drawn back in.

"I miss the job," he said. "I miss the camaraderie and the European pay."

Blank spaces ran through his life where people and places had once been. His sister and memories of Davida Ellis were hidden in one. His past in the Detective Branch was hidden in another. He missed being a policeman and, most shaming of all, he missed the ease and power that came with being a white man. None of these things seemed to matter in the closed world of the Victory Shipyards. It was an unusual place for South Africa. All that mattered was whether or not you could do the backbreaking work.

"Work for me again," van Niekerk said. "I can use you. The wages will be set to European standards."

"More undercover surveillance?" Emmanuel said.

"Something like that."

Emmanuel considered the proposal. Being this close to police work without being a policeman was like picking at a wound. If he stayed, the wound would never heal. The major didn't have the power to reinstate him in the Detective Branch and nothing less would do.

"No, thanks," he said. "The hours are murder."

Van Niekerk smiled. "I thought you'd say that."

Music from the record player in the garden blended with laughter and the splash of swimmers in the pool. Van Niekerk filled two tumblers with generous slugs of whiskey from a drinks tray on the table and slid one across to Emmanuel.

"Don't rush off," he said. "Everything is on the house. No one will check your ID papers."

"Thanks." Emmanuel drank a mouthful. He had no intention of staying. A night with Lana Rose had eased the ache in him. For a little while.

"Take some time to think about my offer," van Niekerk said. "The Victory is a waste of your time and your talents."

Emmanuel wasn't entirely sure about that. He stood up and collected his hat from beside the chair. He smoothed the rim with his fingers. It was time to decide if he lived in the past or in the present.

"Thanks for the job offer and the drink," he said, and left the room. It was time to start living in Durban and in the here and now.

—

Emmanuel pulled his hat low onto his brow and took the stairs leading to the wide gravel driveway two at a time. Ornate steel gates guarded the major's mini-estate. There were no devils or gargoyles placed at the entrance to ward off the evil eye, however. The devils, Emmanuel knew, were in the garden and splashing in the pool. There was plenty of evidence in the surveillance book to back up that statement.

On the last stair he connected with a shoulder. A woman grabbed his arm to break her fall and Emmanuel looked up. The shock of recognition held him still for longer than was natural. It was Lana Rose, dressed in a scrap of white silk. A dozen questions pressed onto Emmanuel in the silence that fell between them. Was Lana one more girl for the pool or a paid professional brought in to reward van Niekerk's men?

She recovered first. "What are you doing here?" she said. Her dark eyes were fearful.

"Business with the major."

"Did you say anything about last night?"

Van Niekerk's garden was jammed with men whose job it was to enforce the strict racial segregation laws. Combine that with the belief, common among many of the police, that a white woman engaged in unlawful sexual adventures across the color bar was on par with a child molester. Emmanuel understood her fear. He felt it, too.

"My business wasn't about you," he said.

"Oh . . ." She cast a wary glance toward the white gabled house. "Will you tell him?"

"Of course not." Van Niekerk's ego was covered by a very thin skin. "I won't ever do that. And you won't, either, if you're smart."

"Don't worry." Her smile was filled with knowledge of things not learned in school. "I'm good at keeping secrets."

Emmanuel pushed his hands deep into his pockets to stop himself: he wanted to kiss her in full view of everyone, then take her hand and lead her away.

"Lana." The name was grunted from the top of the stairs. "Come now."

A ginger-haired man with a thick neck stood on the veranda with one hand resting casually against the leather holster of his Webley service revolver. A flattened nose and an eyebrow bisected by a silver scar testified to a round or two in the boxing ring. In the heavyweight division.

"Are you deaf, girl? I said come quick. The major is waiting."

"Thanks, Emmanuel," she whispered, and he moved away from the subtle floral scent of her perfume. The henchman cleared the stairs two at a time, obviously furious that a civilian and a female ignored his direct order. He reached for Lana's arm.

"Touch me," she said, "and the major will hear about it."

The man backed away. He glared at Emmanuel, the only witness to his demotion from tough guy to flunky. "You going to stand there all fucking day?" he demanded.

Emmanuel maintained eye contact but didn't move. Life on the tough streets of Sophiatown had educated him in the ways of the bully. It was better to be knocked down than to back down. The heavyweight's hand dropped from the gun holster and Emmanuel moved toward the gates.

He had to get Jolly's notebook out of the flour tin where he'd hidden it after getting home from Lana's flat and post it to the Point Police Station. And then he was going to forget he'd ever chased murderers for a living. The memory of Lana Rose leaning against the kitchen cabinet with sleep-tousled hair and a coffee nestled between her palms drew his attention back to the major's house. Emmanuel didn't know for sure, but he suspected they were both flies caught in van Niekerk's web and that last night had been a brief flutter against the constraint.

7

THE BACKYARD OF the Dover flats was empty. The dragon landlady was nowhere to be seen. Emmanuel made a dash for the stairs. Another encounter with the tight-lipped Englishwoman and his temper was going to flare.

An upturned enamel bowl and spilled carrots were scattered across the back stoep. A knife with a shred of carrot skin clinging to the blade lay on the trimmed skirt of lawn. The Zulu maid had left a job half done. Odd.

The fly screen that led to Mrs. Patterson's lair banged against the back wall. Lancelot, the filthy Scots terrier, shivered in the doorway. A radio played a World War II song heavy on the good cheer and the violin.

The dog whimpered in fear.

Emmanuel crossed the lawn and scooped up the peeling knife. The blade was blunt and the tip was broken off, a useful weapon if one's opponent was a slab of butter. He slipped it into his jacket pocket, held the screen door open and did a visual sweep. Mrs. Patterson would kick him out of his flat immediately if he entered her home without permission. The dog retreated into a pile of dirty laundry. The interior of the flat was unlit. Something was wrong. Apprehension prickled the skin on the back of his neck but he kept moving forward. Raising Mrs. Patterson's ire was a risk he had to take.

"Mrs. Patterson?" he called out, in case she was in the lounge room listening to World War II torch songs with her maid in the middle of the day with the curtains closed and the lights turned off.

"It's Emmanuel Cooper from upstairs. I'm coming in."

The dog snuffled its nose into the neck of a frilled nightgown on the floor and whined. The song on the radio assured the boys at the front that they'd be home soon.

Emmanuel eased the laundry door open and stepped into the kitchen. It was hard to see. The drip of a tap punctuated the music floating in from the sitting room. He stepped toward the covered window and his feet slid from under him with a wet sound. The inky outline of the sink and the silver handles of the cupboards flashed by and he flipped backward and landed hard on the floor. The breath was knocked from his lungs and pain shot up his spine. A heavy hessian bag marked EXPORT toppled over and raw sugar spilled across the tiles.

Emmanuel turned to the right. The young Zulu maid stared straight at him with a startled expression. *How,* her open mouth seemed to ask, *did I end up on the kitchen floor in a pool of blood?* Emmanuel scrambled upright and steadied himself against the lip of the sink. He jerked the curtains open. Bloody handprints, his own, were stamped onto the sink's white porcelain surface.

Seams of black and pink liquid stained the material of his suit. Blood dripped from a sleeve and splashed onto the floor.

His stomach churned but van Niekerk's whiskey stayed down. He wiped his hands against the legs of his pants and felt them shaking.

Steady, steady on. Hold the line, soldier.

The words stilled him; he took a deep breath and knelt by the maid, a crumpled rag doll in a hand-me-down housecoat. Mbali. That was her name. It meant "flower" in Zulu. Had she ever owned a dress of her own? Loops of blue cotton thread were sewn through her earlobes in place of earrings. Two dead children in two days. Only savages kill their own young. The maid had a single cut across her neck, just like Jolly. What connected a white boy who worked the docks and a black servant girl who lived miles from the harbor?

The darkened doorway of the next room exerted a magnetic pull on Emmanuel. He stood up and walked toward it. He stepped into the dusky room. The air smelled of wax polish, mothballs and the metal scent of blood. Pieces of broken figurines were scattered across a Persian rug. An upholstered chair lay on its side. Emmanuel fumbled the maid's knife free from his pocket and moved deeper into the lounge. Marlene Dietrich crooned the anthem of the desert warrior, "Lili Marlene," in her distinctive, mannish voice. Violins swelled and an accordion kicked in.

"D-don't move," a male voice stuttered. "Y-you're under arr-arres-arres-tt."

Adrenaline cut Emmanuel's reaction time to zero. He swung hard at the voice. A dark shape crumpled onto the flowered carpet in a blur of olive drab. Animal impulse propelled Emmanuel to swoop and land two more solid hits to the torso. The wood handle of the knife bit into the flesh of his palm with every punch, but he hung on to it.

Cool steel touched his neck.

"Drop the knife and get away from McDonald or I will shoot you," a cocky male voice said. "It'll save the judge the trouble of sending you to the hangman."

The butt of the gun hit Emmanuel's shoulder blade and he was slammed to the carpet. A boot pressed onto his throat. Olive drab uniform pants crossed his line of sight, and beyond that Mrs. Patterson's feather duster snapped in two.

—

Emmanuel's neck muscles ached. The smack from the Webley revolver would take days to heal. Handcuffs bit into his wrists.

The door to the stark interview room opened and a slim man in gray flannel pants and a pressed shirt ambled in. It was the salt-and-pepper-haired detective from the crime scene at the freight yards. He nodded in greeting and placed a leather satchel gently on the floor. He'll be the nice one, Emmanuel thought. The good detective.

A second man swaggered through the door, ginger hair damp with perspiration, a heavy hand resting casually on a leather holster. It was the redheaded policeman flicked away like a fly by Lana Rose. Emmanuel shook his head. The Negro soldiers had an expression, "If it wasn't for bad luck, I'd have no luck at all." Now Emmanuel knew how funny that was.

Recognition flickered across the detective's beaten features before he pulled up a chair opposite the interview table and sat down with his legs spread apart.

"I'm Detective Head Constable Robinson," the good detective introduced himself. "And this is my partner, Detective Constable Fletcher."

"Two counts of murder, assault of a policeman, resisting arrest," Fletcher said. "You've had a very busy afternoon, haven't you?"

Emmanuel cleared his throat and the muscles constricted in protest. Robinson offered a glass of water and a smile. Emmanuel downed the water in one gulp.

"I didn't kill anyone," he said. The smudge of blood his fingertips left on the glass mocked that statement.

"It was a coincidence," Fletcher said, and scooted forward. "You being in the flat when the policemen arrived to investigate a disturbance?"

"Yes," Emmanuel said.

"Ever been in the landlady's flat before?"

"No. I went in because I thought something was wrong."

"Is that why you were armed?" Fletcher said.

"What?" Blood pounded in Emmanuel's ears and the pressure in his head had returned with a vengeance. A dark force seemed intent on breaking through the bones of his skull.

Robinson reached down, opened the leather satchel and withdrew the kitchen knife. He tilted it so the electric light hit the metal and made it shine.

"You had this weapon in your hand when the uniforms broke in," Robinson said. "Do you always carry a knife?"

Emmanuel rested his forehead in the palm of his hand. The chain securing the handcuffs swung against his nose. He needed to make sense of things.

"You're aware that the landlady and the maid had their throats cut?" Robinson continued.

"The maid, yes. I didn't see Mrs. Patterson."

"Can you imagine how it looks? You with a knife and the

victims' throats sliced from ear to ear. What's a judge going to make of that?"

"It's a blunt knife without a tip," Emmanuel said. "It couldn't cut a sponge cake."

"You have a good knowledge of knives, then?"

"Enough to know when one is blunt."

Fletcher picked up Emmanuel's driver's license from the table and read over the details. It listed an outdated Johannesburg address. The license hit the wood with a slap. The detective's eyes reflected the utter contempt reserved for lowlifes.

"Want to know what upsets me, Mr. Cooper? The fact that a degenerate from Jo'burg thinks he can come to my town and commit all manner of filthy acts."

"I didn't kill anyone," Emmanuel repeated. The smooth surface of the concrete floor was inviting. It was the perfect place to rest an aching head. Then, an ice pack for the boot print branded onto his neck.

Robinson said gently, "Your neighbor Mr. Woodsmith claims you had a fight with the landlady yesterday morning. Do you recall that incident?"

Mr. Woodsmith, the harmless window peeper, had supplied the police with a time-honored motive for foul play, bad blood between the landlady and the lodger, a story line lifted from *Detective Tales*. Emmanuel closed his eyes and focused beyond the pain that split his temple. Should he tell the truth or take evasive action?

"There was no fight," he said.

"Really?"

"We talked about dogs. Small versus big."

"Mr. Woodsmith claims the landlady was scared of you. Couldn't wait for you to vacate the premises," Robinson said.

"I don't know anything about that." Disks of light flickered across the room in a bright meteor shower. It was getting hard to hold up the weight of his head.

The detectives' attention was drawn away when the interview door swung inward. A young constable in an olive drab uniform entered and placed a shoebox on the table with boyish awkwardness. White puffs of bloody cotton wool protruded from his nostrils. Fletcher patted the constable's shoulder, a gesture that said, *We are both men bloodied in the fight against crime.*

Stuttering constable to station hero: this afternoon would be a career highlight for the young policeman who'd taken blows from a vicious killer. His incompetence might even get him a medal from the police commissioner. The injured constable whispered something to Fletcher that made him smile.

"What's in here?" Robinson, the good detective, reached into the shoebox once the constable had cleared the room. He extracted a bone-handled knife. It was Parthiv's gangster switchblade. Emmanuel had forgotten it in his pocket when he rushed from Saris and All, then shoved it into a drawer. Out of sight, out of mind.

His head lifted a fraction. The uniforms had searched his room. Robinson dipped into the box again and produced Jolly's notebook. He dusted off the cover and rubbed the white powder between his fingers, curious.

"Where did the constable find this?" he asked.

"Wrapped in newspaper and hidden in a flour tin," Fletcher said with satisfaction. "In Mr. Cooper's kitchen."

"Strange place to keep something." Robinson flicked through the pages and then glanced at Emmanuel, waiting for edification on the notebook's placement.

Emmanuel didn't even try to explain how an imaginary Scottish sergeant major's warning had made him cautious to the point of paranoia.

"The boy on the docks . . ." Robinson handed the notebook to his partner. "What was it his ma said about him?"

"Ran errands at the port. Collected food and booze for various people. Kept everything written in a book."

"You know a boy by the name of Jolly Marks, Mr. Cooper?" Robinson asked.

The empty glass rattled against the metal chain of Emmanuel's cuffs. The shakes were coming on strong. White clusters of light erased outlines of objects and people. The detectives were soft Vaseline smears.

"I can't think," Emmanuel said. "I need painkillers . . . something for my head and my neck."

"Medicine's not going to fix what's wrong with you. The hangman will set you straight," Fletcher said.

Emmanuel forced his chin up and tried to focus. The white snow haze of his migraine blinded him.

"Your eye is fucked, soldier." The rough Scottish voice filled his head. *"I'll tell you what they have. The Indian's knife and the dead boy's notebook. Now you know. Your eye's not the only thing that's fucked."*

Emmanuel rocked backward. The glass flew into the air and smashed against the concrete floor. Darkness swamped him. Fletcher grabbed him by the lapels and pulled him to his feet.

"Faking illness?" he said. "Don't even think about going soft now."

"Wait." Robinson examined Emmanuel's pale face and the

sweat on his bruised neck. "The arresting constable clobbered him too hard. Probably knocked some bones loose."

"He's pretending."

"Put him down, Fletcher." The order was given quietly. "Get Dr. Brownlow in here to give him a once-over."

"No disrespect, sir, but—"

"We have him on three counts of murder. All the evidence is right here on the table. I want him in top shape when he appears in court."

Emmanuel's body slid to the floor.

"*A small drop compared to the gallows,*" the Scots voice rasped.

———

Emmanuel rested his head on his forearm. The absence of pain was pure joy. He felt better than fine. The fistful of codeine painkillers the doctor had pushed down his throat were working. The demented sergeant major's voice was crushed into silence and happiness was five minutes' sleep away.

The door to the interview room opened. Emmanuel sat up.

"Major." He greeted van Niekerk with a nod.

The major was in full uniform, the pleats of the trousers and jacket ironed to a razor's edge. A subtle floral scent mixed with whiskey lingered on his person. No surprise as to how the perfume had been transferred to van Niekerk's skin.

"Sit down, Cooper." The major held the door open for a second man, who entered the room carrying a dented blue toolbox. The newcomer, pale-haired and pale-skinned, mid-thirties, sat in the corner. Emmanuel waited for an introduction. None came. Van Niekerk closed the door. What was the major doing in the interview room with a man who wore a suit and carried a toolbox?

"They've got you on three counts, Cooper," the major said. "There's enough evidence to make the charges stick. Plus the fact that you were caught, literally, red-handed."

"I know."

"Are you going to answer my questions truthfully, Cooper?" The ghostly man in the corner spoke for the first time. Emmanuel glanced at him. He hadn't moved an inch.

"I'll answer," Emmanuel said.

"You knew Jolly Marks?"

"Not well. He worked the freight yards and the passenger terminal. Ran errands. I knew him by sight."

"You were at the yards the night before last?" The pale man's voice was emotionless and, like his skin, leached of color.

"I was in the yards," Emmanuel said.

"Doing what?"

Emmanuel hesitated. The major didn't mean for him to answer that question truthfully, did he? There was nothing illegal about observing corrupt police conducting their business. Hiring an ex-detective to record proof was in another league, however.

"I get bad headaches. I went to the docks to buy hashish. It helps me sleep."

A flicker of emotion crossed the major's face. Relief? Emmanuel couldn't tell. The man in the corner shifted position but stayed put.

"How did you get Jolly's notebook?" the major said.

"From the freight yards." He wanted to keep the Dutta family out of it. Amal especially. The young man's only sin was having a stupid older brother. "It was in the alleyway near the body."

The major nodded. "Did you kill the boy, Cooper?"

"No. He was dead when I found him."

"Like the landlady and the maid?"

"Yes."

"Hard to believe."

"The truth often is."

The man in the corner walked toward the table, leaving the toolbox behind, and Emmanuel's skin tingled with relief. The toolbox shut and out of reach seemed like a good thing. The man's clean fingernails and unwrinkled black suit confirmed that he was not a tradesman in the traditional sense. Emmanuel suspected he knew how to break and fix things— none of them domestic.

"You lied about what you were doing at the docks." The accent was South African with an undertone of English public school. A colonial boy sent back to the motherland for an education in bad food and bullying. His eyes were an indeterminate color, like pieces of quartz lit by an unknown source. "Major van Niekerk has already confirmed that you were doing private work for him. Surveillance."

Emmanuel shifted under the intense scrutiny. Why would van Niekerk confirm anything unless he'd been forced to? The thought was disturbing. It was nearly impossible to get the jump on an old fox like the major.

"I've worked for the major before," Emmanuel said. And like so many who'd served under van Niekerk, Emmanuel thought him arrogant, even ruthless. But it wasn't his job to bring the major down. His conscience was already burdened by three murders and the fact that he somehow connected them. Best let van Niekerk go to hell without help. "Night before last was private business. The major knew nothing about it."

"Are you calling the major a liar?"

"No. I'm saying I lied to the major."

The tradesman smiled at van Niekerk. "He'll do nicely," he said.

"I never doubted it," van Niekerk said.

Van Niekerk and the pale man were visibly relaxed, pleased, even. He'd passed a test they'd set for him with a mix of lies and discretion.

"Will getting out be a problem?" the tradesman said.

"It won't be comfortable." Van Niekerk glanced at the interview room door. "My men will keep it under control, but we have to move quickly."

"Where are we going?" Emmanuel said.

"Out of the station," van Niekerk said. "There's a car waiting for us at the front."

"I'm free?"

"No." The tradesman collected the toolbox and placed it on the table. His alabaster hands rested lightly on the dented surface. "You're being transferred from police custody into my custody."

"And you are?"

"The only one who can keep you off death row."

"Why would you want to do that?"

Emmanuel needed to know the price of his freedom. Walking away from three counts of murder did not come cheap.

"Because you didn't kill the landlady or the maid, at least not with the knives they have in evidence."

"And Jolly?"

"Jolly was killed by the same person who killed the two women. You didn't kill the women, therefore you didn't kill the boy."

The station detectives and the arresting policemen would not agree with the tradesman's conclusion. They'd be furious when they learned their suspect had been released.

"Exactly what am I going to do once I'm in your custody?" Emmanuel asked.

"Investigate Jolly Marks's murder," came the tradesman's deadpan reply.

"And Mrs. Patterson and her maid. What about them?"

"Clear Jolly's murder from the board first," the tradesman said. "Concentrate your resources on one investigation at a time."

"I'm the prime suspect in all three murders. How's that going to work?"

"Your investigation will run parallel with that of the regular force," the major explained smoothly. "You'll report directly to me."

"Or stay here and wait for the fingerprint results on the torch that was found in the alley to come back from Pretoria." The tradesman picked up the metal box and moved to the door. "They can do that now, you know. Lift prints from objects with a powder. It's a world first, developed right here in South Africa."

The bloodstains on Emmanuel's fingertips made the whorls and ridges stand out like contours on a map. He'd left clear prints on the torch and on the lip of the landlady's porcelain sink. The results might take months to come back, but when they did, he was going to swing.

"What will it be, Cooper?" the major said.

Emmanuel stood up and moved to the door. The murders of Jolly Marks and Mbali the maid were identical in style and execution. He wouldn't find the connection between the two victims from a jail cell.

"We'll leave those on until we've exited the station." Van Niekerk indicated the handcuffs. "Keep your head down, do not make eye contact and keep walking. I'll deal with the flak."

Olive drab police uniform pants, polished black boots and plain cotton trousers crowded the edges of Emmanuel's vision. He kept his head down. A low murmur accompanied their speedy exit from the station house.

"Pig . . ." "Murderer . . ." "Special favors . . ." "Bastard . . ." "Fucking disgrace . . ."

A filthy, blood-covered criminal walks to freedom. Emmanuel knew how it looked. Knew how it felt, too, when a guilty party slipped the net and cheated the law. It made good policemen want to do bad things.

They emerged onto the street. A gob of spit hit the pavement in front of him. Emmanuel looked up. The stuttering constable with the injured nose sneered. Fletcher balled his hands into fists.

"If we meet again," the detective constable warned, "I'll make sure it's your own blood you're covered in."

They kept moving. Emmanuel glanced over his shoulder. Twelve or so policemen now stood on the station steps and watched the killer go. Anger and frustration bound them together. If this special investigation was running parallel with the regular force's, as van Niekerk said, the men on the stairs knew nothing about it.

"Popular move," Emmanuel said when they stopped at a gold-leaf Chevrolet Deluxe with its motor chugging.

"You'll be working alone," the major said.

8

THE DRIVER OF the Chevrolet was a skinny white woman who'd given up being a blond. A trench of dark brown hair ran down the center of her head like a deserted landing strip. The major unlocked the handcuffs and Emmanuel caught a glimpse of the driver's green eyes examining him in the rearview mirror. A freckled hand flicked ash from the end of a cigarette onto the chrome-plated ashtray built into the dash. The woman's fingernails were chewed down to the quick.

"Drive on, Hélène," the major said, and the woman eased the car into a steady stream of Fords, Packards and Rovers. Up ahead the traffic robot turned green and she piloted the Chevrolet through the intersection. The police station receded behind them, but Emmanuel knew that as far as the Durban police force was concerned, it was open season on his hide.

"Pull over," the tradesman instructed after a two-minute ride during which he sat silent and unmoving, like a crow on a gravestone. The Chevrolet slid to a stop in front of a tailor's shop advertising A WHALE OF A SALE. He got out, shut the car door and disappeared into the Saturday market crowd of Indian traders, European shoppers and Zulu rickshaw pullers without a backward glance. A skinny white male of above-average height, dressed in a dark suit and moving "quick-like."

"Who was that man?" Emmanuel asked van Niekerk.

"Constable John Smith. Commissioner's office." The major's voice was heavy with sarcasm. "Recent transfer from Cape Town."

"You don't believe it," Emmanuel said. And neither did he. The tradesman was not a garden-variety police recruit. His quiet intensity suggested he belonged to a group beginning with the letter *s*; Security Branch or Special Services.

"I got a call about two hours ago from a brigadier who got a call from a major general. It must have been just after your arrest. Cooperate. That was the message. It seemed like a good idea," van Niekerk said. "The . . . uh, albino was waiting at the police station for me. He asked questions. I answered."

"All this cloak-and-dagger for a boy with no family connections? Doesn't make any sense, not even when you include the murders this afternoon."

"That's your job, Cooper. To make sense of things."

Emmanuel wound the window down to get some air. The pills had stopped the throb against his skull but dulled his thoughts. On the pavement, a double-chinned dame festooned with gaudy seashell necklaces reeled at the sight of him. She clutched her suede handbag with both chubby fists. None of the pretty Durban postcards showed a bloodied man being chauffeured around town in a Chevrolet Deluxe.

"Head back to the house, Hélène," the major said to the driver, then made a detailed study of the side panels of a sluggish bus, which advertised J. GUSTAVE COIFFEUR BELGE on West Street.

Emmanuel closed the car window. His release from custody was wrong on every level. Catching a triple murderer at the scene covered in blood was the equivalent of winning the July handicap horse race at five hundred to one. The police would never walk away from this case. The department's hand had been forced from somewhere high up.

"Who signed my release forms?" he said.

"I did." Van Niekerk loosened the top three buttons of his uniform jacket and tugged at the starched collar. His lean face was impassive and his hooded eyes were unreadable.

"Why?"

"To the victor belong the spoils. If you pull this off, the major general will remember your name and mine. You'll get your detective's ID back and I'll have friends in high places."

"And if I don't?" Emmanuel said.

"That's not an option. For either of us. I vouched for you, Cooper. Gave a personal guarantee. If you don't deliver, they'll come after you, then they'll come after me."

Emmanuel rubbed the bruised muscles of his neck. It was possible that signing off on the backdated letter of discharge in Jo'burg six months ago had gotten van Niekerk blackbanned from the promotions list. That would explain why the major was taking a huge gamble on the results of a one-man investigation. Maybe he needed friends in high places.

"What now?" Emmanuel said.

"Investigate the Marks boy's murder and report to me. That's the sum of it." The major pulled Jolly's notebook from his jacket pocket and threw it onto Emmanuel's lap. "The victim's address is penciled in the back. Some hovel out on the Point."

"How did you get this?"

A piece of evidence liberated from the hands of legitimate law enforcement without a fight? That was another action that made no sense.

"I took it," the major said, then handed over a mimeographed piece of paper printed with a black-and-white mug shot of a European male with a Frankenstein head. Dark eyes glared from the police portrait. "Until you turned up with bloody hands and a knife in your pocket, this man was the number one suspect. A low-level heavy called Joe Flowers."

The escaped prisoner, Joe Wesley Flowers, was proof that the disproved science of phrenology wasn't completely off the mark. His very large square head, shifty eyes and slack mouth all said criminal. Petty theft, housebreaking and malicious wounding showcased his versatile talents.

"What makes him right for the murders?" Emmanuel said.

"He was in for stabbing two men in a bar fight, and he worked as a flenser at the whaling station for a year and a half. He knows knives."

A single cut to the throat had killed Jolly and Mbali the maid. Whoever killed them knew knives, too.

"Was Mrs. Patterson killed the same way as the maid?" he asked.

"No. The killer made a mess of that one. She was cut across the shoulder, made a run for it and knocked over a table of porcelain figurines. The crash alerted the neighbor, who called in the police. A single cut across the neck finally killed her."

"Does Flowers have the legs for this kind of crime?" Emmanuel said. "It's a big jump up from cutting whale carcasses to murdering two children and an old lady."

"Maybe he's trying his hand at something new." Van Niekerk's tone was dry. "Moving up the criminal ladder."

"Any leads?"

"Patrol cars haven't caught sight of him. His mother has vanished as well."

"No other family?"

"A dirt-farming uncle who lives out past Pietermaritzburg. The police called in yesterday and found nothing." The major shrugged. "Rootless whites. You know what they're like, Cooper. No fixed address, no forwarding address and no better than the kaffirs."

Yes, he knew all about that life.

Out the window, redbrick shop fronts and flats gave way to peacock-green lawns and mature shade trees with limbs that overhung the road like the beams of a cathedral. The rest of the country was dressed in brown for winter, but Durban still had orange, purple and sunny bursts of yellow.

"Leafy" was one of his ex-wife Angela's favorite words and also one of her biggest criticisms of South Africa. The country was not "leafy" enough. Not quaint enough. Not English enough. Perhaps if they'd lived in Durban they might still be together. He did not long for the past or for her cool embrace, though. She was one of the unsuccessful ways that he had tried to escape the past.

"Where are we headed?" he asked.

"Glenwood. You're staying with some friends of mine."

The Chevrolet turned into a driveway set between whitewashed brick columns. A brass plate on the right-hand column read CHÂTEAU LA MER. The car stopped in front of a vine-covered trellis flecked with purple blooms. The woman driver slipped out from behind the wheel and held van Niekerk's door open.

"*Merci*, Hélène," the major said, pulling the lines of his uniform jacket straight.

"*De rien*, Major," Hélène replied, and kept the door ajar for Emmanuel, like a hotel valet. He crunched onto the gravel drive and checked the neat suburban surroundings.

Château la Mer was a handsome brick house with leadlight roses decorating the windows and a wide veranda that ran along three sides. High on the roof, an iron weathercock swayed east in the breeze. A white marble statue of a nude female balanced in the middle of a tinkling fountain set up on the front lawn. The driver shut the door and moved to van Niekerk's side.

"Cooper." The major waved him over. "This is Hélène Gerard. You'll be staying with her for a few days."

"Very kind." Emmanuel substituted a nod for a handshake. His hands still had dried blood on them.

Hélène's smile was tight but the skin on her cheeks and neck sagged, as if she'd recently lost a great deal of weight. What kind of a friend agrees to accommodate a man fresh out of police custody?

"Hélène, this is Detective Sergeant Emmanuel Cooper," the major said. "He scrubs up fine, so pay no attention to his appearance."

"A pleasure to meet you, Detective Cooper."

Hélène was grace itself; she might be welcoming a guest to a civic reception and not talking to a disheveled man with a boot print on his neck. Van Niekerk must have something big on Hélène to get her to take a murder suspect into her home.

"I'll arrange for a bath and fresh clothes. Please come in when you're ready." Hélène dropped a half curtsy in van Niekerk's direction, then slipped away into the red and green blaze of the garden.

"Well . . ." The major checked his watch. "I'll leave you to settle in, Cooper. Hélène will take good care of you."

Does she have a choice? Emmanuel wondered.

The major frowned, a piece of trivial information popping into his mind.

"You don't have a lot of time, Cooper."

"Meaning?"

"In forty-eight hours members of the Durban police will issue a warrant for your arrest on three counts of murder, one count of assault of a police officer and one count of resisting arrest. Those are the terms of the deal for your release."

"What can I achieve in that time?" He was being set up to fail before the investigation had even started.

"You've been given a second chance at life, Cooper. Stick to the Marks boy's murder the way you've been told. There's not enough time to chase three separate inquiries." The major extended his hand. "Call me with any updates. Or better, call around to my house if it's after hours."

They shook hands and van Niekerk got into a car that was parked off to the side of the drive. The engine started up and Major van Niekerk pulled away without looking back.

A company of Cape canaries bickered on a swaying telephone wire. Emmanuel sat down on the front steps of La Mer. The blood on his palm was bright with moisture. The ice-cool major was sweating heavily on a mild winter's day. Now, that was a miracle.

A single question kept Emmanuel immobile. Why was he

sitting in a pool of sunshine instead of a jail cell? There was no answer to that question yet. The Cape canaries took to the wing and arched across the blue sky.

Forty-eight hours. He checked his watch. It was four forty-five. Time to get moving.

—

The two-story brick house had lost chunks of its Victorian façade to wind and weather and was now a classic slum mansion. A warren of cold-water flats occupied spaces originally set out for a prosperous family with need of a library and a music room. The long blast of a harbor tug horn sounded across the water.

A shrunken man in an antiquated wheelchair was parked out on the pavement. Emmanuel rechecked the address and approached the invalid, who stared out at the railway lines and the distant ships in dock. A sign on the sagging fence read SLEGS BLANKES. Whites Only.

"Does the Marks family live here?" he asked.

The man was thin as a string, with unwashed hair that grew past his shoulders. No response. Not even a flicker of an eyelash.

Emmanuel proceeded to the once-grand entranceway, selected the first flat and knocked. The door opened and a barefoot girl stared up at him. He recognized her from a sketch in Jolly's notebook. It was the child with the desperate eyes.

"This the Markses' place?"

The girl nodded, turned and ran into the interior of the flat. Emmanuel followed her down a long shotgun corridor. Detritus and dirt crunched underfoot. Small alcoves that might originally have been hall closets ran off the sides and were now sleeping quarters. A baby in a cloth nappy played with a wooden spoon in the bare kitchen. Emmanuel kept going. The filth and the poverty did not disturb him. The sense of familiarity he encountered in hovels such as this one did. Slums in Durban and slums in Johannesburg were the same.

He entered a sitting room, where the runaway girl was bent over the side of a toy pram. A woman slept on a tatty couch, her body curled up like a drunk's on a park bench. Her snores competed with the squabbling of children who played hopscotch in the dirt and concrete yard outside the window.

Emmanuel touched the woman on the shoulder. Her eyes flew open and she sat up with a jerk. An unclipped nylon stocking fell around her ankle.

"Who're you?"

"He's come about Jolly," the little girl said, and pushed the pram back and forth with motherly concern.

"My name's Emmanuel Cooper." He couldn't use his old title. Without his official police ID to back him, it was all make-believe. "I work for the police."

"Oh . . . you don't look like a policeman."

The cream silk suit, cream shirt and pale-mint-colored tie that Hélène Gerard had laid out on the bed before he emerged from the bath at the château were more suited to the high-roller marquee at the racetrack than to a police station. If Jolly's mother had picked him as a dapper armed robber or a pimp, Emmanuel would not be surprised.

"Besides, I already told the other two everything." Close-set brown eyes narrowed in concentration. "Jolly went out like usual and he didn't come back. Miss Morgensen from the Zion Gospel Hall . . . she's the one who went down to make sure it was him that the police found. I didn't have the heart."

Or the energy. Emmanuel had counted six children so far. Two indoors and four in the yard. The husband was most likely at sea, in jail or holding down a bar with his elbows. Emmanuel knew the score: a family diet of plain bread with lard for dinner and meat once a fortnight. Vegetables were exotic novelties. No matter how long Jolly's mother slept, she would always be too tired to face life.

"The Zion Gospel Hall?" Emmanuel asked. It sounded like a Holy Roller, speaking-in-tongues kind of place.

"It's just here in Southampton Street. The young ones get a blessing whenever we go."

Whenever we go . . . Emmanuel doubted the Marks family were regular churchgoers, but come Sunday morning he knew he'd be there. Churches were places where people confessed.

"I'd like you to look at something." He perched on the edge of a wooden chair and pulled Jolly's notebook out of his pocket. "Do you recognize this?"

" 'Course. It's Jolly's. He was always scribbling things. Got that from his dad. Artistic. Head in the clouds."

Jolly had cut the notebook free and dumped it. Maybe the children sketched in it were the reason. Emmanuel found the first portrait and held it up. "Who's this?"

"It's Sophie, the harbormaster's daughter."

"She was a friend of Jolly's?"

"I wouldn't say that. They played together sometimes."

"And she's still around . . . not in any trouble that you know of?"

"No. I saw her yesterday morning at the corner shop."

The barefoot girl tiptoed away from the pram and craned over Emmanuel's shoulder while he worked through the portraits and collected names and addresses. All the children were local to the Point area and not particularly close to Jolly. None appeared to be in any trouble.

"That's me," the girl said when they came to the last sketch. "That's me."

"Jolly was a good artist. It looks just like you," Emmanuel said, and flicked through to the end of the notebook. Forty-eight hours was not a long enough time frame to interview every child individually. If Jolly's murder was connected to the mass exploitation of children, he might as well give up now. The bare-breasted mermaid winked from the page and Emmanuel covered the picture with his hand, conscious of the girl's young age.

"And that's the Flying Dutchman's mermaid," Jolly's little sister said. "She lives on the land, not in the water."

Emmanuel turned to her. "What's your name?"

"Susannah. It has two *s*'s and two *n*'s."

"Who is the Flying Dutchman, Susannah?"

"A man in a nice car."

The girl recrossed the room and peered into the toy pram. She gave a loud exhalation, then rearranged a scrap of material in the carriage and pushed the pram back and forth. Emmanuel waited till she got her rhythm up.

"Have you seen the mermaid before?" he asked. The girl had an unhinged quality that was disturbing.

"*Ja*. In the back window of the Flying Dutchman's car when he came to pick up Jolly."

"Is the mermaid a picture or is she real like you and me?"

"A picture, like Jolly drew. She was stuck up against the glass, looking out," the girl said, and hummed snatches of "London Bridge Is Falling Down" to the doll in the pram.

The mermaid was a sign, an advertisement of some kind, for a business run by a man in a nice car. Not an ordinary tax-paying venture but one that probably took customers to places not listed in tourist guides.

"Where did Jolly go with the Flying Dutchman?" Emmanuel said.

"I don't know, but he brought back sweeties for us and American cigarettes for Ma."

Jolly's mother mustered enough energy to pull her unclipped stocking up over her knee. A soccer ball hit the window and rolled back to a button-nosed boy in long shorts playing in the yard.

"There's six of them." She brushed tears away with the back of her hand. "The building is full of children coming and going . . . I can't keep an eye on every one."

Not from the couch. And the complimentary cigarettes came in handy. Except that nothing in the world, especially the dockside world, was free. Jolly had paid for the candy and the smokes somehow.

"Who is the Flying Dutchman?" he asked the mother.

"Don't know . . ." Her back stiffened. "We don't mix with the coons or the riffraff."

"Except when they have cigarettes," he pointed out.

The pitiable mix of pride and poverty wore on his patience. Black or white, riffraff or missionary, what did it matter? A cigarette was a cigarette. Jolly had known that.

"Well, I've never seen this Dutchman," she said. "Don't know anything about him or his mermaid."

It was a lie and it wasn't. The Dutchman was a sinister Father Christmas who had passed through her life unseen and left chocolate and cigarettes to prove his existence.

A filthy hand tugged at Emmanuel's sleeve. The girl had abandoned her pram. Her feathery blond hair was clumped with knots, her dark brown eyes were as Jolly had drawn them: older than the sun but with no warmth in them.

"Come look," Susannah said. "My baby's sick."

Emmanuel followed her to the pram. This scenario was one his sister had enacted a dozen times in an afternoon. It seemed she had loved her dolls most when they were sick and she could fix them. The world could be put right with a little medicine and a pat on the back.

Susannah motioned him closer. He squatted down next to the pram and peered in. A porcelain doll with creamy skin and startling blue eyes lay in a nest of rags.

"What's wrong with her?" Emmanuel asked.

"Someone cut her throat."

—

The sky was streaked pink when Emmanuel emerged from the dilapidated mansion. A long-necked ibis pecked at a mango pip discarded on the sidewalk. The wheelchair-bound man was still there, a silent witness to the fall of night across the harbor.

Emmanuel peeled off in the direction of the Buick. He'd picked the car up from opposite his apartment where he'd parked it a lifetime ago. Hélène had driven him from the château to the Dover, smiling every mile of the way. The ibis took flight and circled overhead. Two men in a hurry walked toward the stairs that led to Jolly's home. It was Detective Constable Fletcher and Detective Head Constable Robinson. Emmanuel turned away and showed them his back. The Buick was a quarter block away. He'd make a run for it if he had to.

Footsteps sounded on the stairs and then faded. Emmanuel sprinted for the Buick. Robinson and Fletcher would be back on the street the moment Jolly's mother mentioned a visit from a lone police officer.

He was just here, she'd say. *Now, now.*

Emmanuel unlocked the driver's door and slid in. He turned the engine on, reversed back a foot and made an illegal U-turn.

The side mirror reflected the image of the two detectives flying down the stairs of the decrepit mansion. They split and began a search of the street. Emmanuel shifted up to third and saw Fletcher sprint to close the distance between himself and the departing Buick.

Jesse Owens in his prime couldn't have run down an American eight-cylinder engine. The detective diminished to a black bump on the horizon. This will be the pattern, Emmanuel figured. Wherever I go, the police will follow. Five minutes with Jolly's mother and they'd know about the mermaid illustration and to whom it belonged.

He had to find the Flying Dutchman. The mystery man with the sharp car might have been the last person to see Jolly Marks alive.

9

NESTOR WAS DROWNING a mix of chopped onions and potatoes in a whirlpool of vegetable oil. He glanced up at Emmanuel's approach but kept working. The early-Saturday-evening crowd of sailors, sugar girls and dockworkers crowded in under the awning and fueled up for the long party ahead. Legitimate Durban may shut down at eleven-thirty p.m., but Nestor's Night Owl clients belonged to the world between midnight to dawn when illegal pool halls, all-hours liquor joints and "adult only" cinema lounges operated under the paternal eyes of the police.

"The Flying Dutchman," Emmanuel asked the Greek cook, "is he around?"

Nestor shoveled a glistening mountain of fried potatoes onto a chipped plate and handed it to a tarty brunette with purple bruises on her arms.

"Haven't seen him," Nestor said. "Maybe he's not working today."

"He takes Saturdays off?" That had to be a lie. It was 7:25 p.m. on the busiest night of the week.

Nestor scratched an unshaven cheek. "Normally he is here looking for clients. Not tonight."

"Know where I can find him?"

"No."

The Greek loaded up a second plate and pushed it over the counter to a tall woman in a lace dress brightened with pink crochet flowers. Emmanuel pushed the order back across the counter before the customer could touch it, and smiled.

"Really?" Emmanuel kept his fingers lightly against the side of the plate and made sure Nestor got the message: *I can do this all night.*

"Check the passenger quay," Nestor said. "That's where he normally parks when there's a liner in port."

"What am I looking for?"

If Nestor was wasting his time, then he'd be back within an hour and they'd celebrate in true Greek fashion with the smashing of plates.

"Tall man in a blue suit. He drives a white DeSoto convertible with silver chrome along the side and white wheel hubs. You can't miss it."

Emmanuel picked the plate off the counter and handed it to the woman in the lace dress, who, at close quarters, had the muscled bulk of a longshoreman. Dark stubble bristled through her white powder and rouge. To Emmanuel, the beauty mark positioned over her top lip was a step too far.

"Miss . . ." He handed the food over and was rewarded with a wink and a smile.

"Kind thanks, sailor . . ." The strapping she-male dropped a curtsy and strutted over to a side table where a small white man in dirty work overalls waited.

Port towns, Emmanuel thought. You can find anything if
you just know where to look.

———

Emmanuel parked the Buick in a tight space on Quayside
Road and headed to the passenger terminal on foot. The
docked liner *Pacific Pearl* had pulled a mix of Indian families,
Christian youth groups and courting couples to the quay.
White cars dotted the curb of the redbrick streetscape. Find-
ing the Dutchman was going to be a challenge.

A Rolls-Royce Silver Wraith limousine cruised along the
wharf. Emmanuel checked both sides of the street for a white
convertible with silver trim and for the police. The Durban
boys couldn't arrest him but they could break a couple of ribs.
The Rolls pulled over to the sidewalk and stopped a few feet
ahead. The engine still hummed.

Emmanuel turned to see two dark-skinned men a few
yards behind him. They seemed to have sprung out of the
ground. In front of him, the back passenger door of the Rolls
swung open and blocked the footpath. He glimpsed polished
wood panels and cream leather inside.

A rich honey and tobacco scent drifted out of the car's interior. A British bulldog of a man in a checkered suit emerged
from the front passenger seat and motioned for Emmanuel to
lift his arms. Emmanuel complied. The man patted him down
for weapons and then nodded to the Rolls. *Please accept my
gracious invitation,* his manner indicated, *or my friends will
break your legs.*

"Get in," the bulldog said.

Emmanuel slid into the limousine. The passenger door
sealed with a click and the Silver Wraith rolled into traffic. Soft

leather and plush carpet hushed the engine and the world outside. The red tip of a lit cigar cast the only light in the dim interior.

The passenger-compartment light switched on and Emmanuel blinked in the sudden glow. An Indian with dark skin, black hair and black eyes sat to his right. The man wore a gray linen suit. The material stretched tight across the powerful width of his shoulders and chest.

"You're supposed to work for me," the Indian said. "But I don't know who the fuck you are."

"I'm Emmanuel Cooper." Emmanuel held his hand out politely. Parthiv was a pretend gangster; this man was the real thing. "You're Mr. Khan."

The man said nothing and ignored the offer of a handshake. He continued to examine Emmanuel. "You have a message for me, from the Duttas. What is it?"

"Mrs. Dutta wants you to know that Parthiv and Giriraj have been disciplined." Emmanuel decided this was no time to explain that he wasn't involved with the Duttas or their business. Somehow, Khan seemed to already know what had happened in the backyard of Saris and All.

"What does that mean?"

"A beating. With a stick," Emmanuel said.

Khan smiled but the black center of his pupils remained dead. "I like that. The old ways are the best. Did Mrs. Dutta know about her son's hash dealing?"

"She wasn't happy. That's all I know."

"Good. I don't want to start trouble with the Dutta family, but if I have to, then . . ." Khan left the rest of the sentence hanging.

The Rolls turned onto Marine Parade and cruised past art

deco hotels and beachfront bars where colorful crowds spilled onto the pavement. A Zulu rickshaw boy in animal skins and a feathered headdress posed for pictures with two Englishwomen in tweed. The street bustled with people. That was a good sign. If he could be seen, he was safe.

The Rolls took a sharp turn onto a dark service lane and parked at the rear entrance of a closed warehouse. A sign on the steel-reinforced door read COLD MEAT STORAGE. No lights and no passing traffic. Emmanuel tensed. Being light-skinned didn't count for much in the back of a Rolls with an Indian gangster where no one could see you. Khan was on the second-rate "nonwhite" rung of the South African ladder, but he had a thug, a Rolls and a complete lack of fear. The scent of blood and meat crept in from the alley.

Khan leaned to within an inch of Emmanuel's face and breathed out smoke. "Working for Parthiv Dutta and that mute is a mistake." His voice was ice. "It could get you killed."

"I don't work for Parthiv or the Dutta family," Emmanuel said. He wanted to make that clear. "I work at the Victory Shipyards."

It was better to throw out correct information right away. It might stop Khan from digging deeper later.

"Ah . . . the Victory," Khan said. "The famous refuge for the old men of war. What theater were you in? North Africa or the Mediterranean?"

"Europe. The Western Front. France and then Germany."

"Tell me, do you miss the fighting?"

"No," Emmanuel said. Not even the temptation to sit around a bar and rehash memories of the war had appealed to him.

"That is my big regret." Khan crushed his cigar into the ashtray. "Not being able to join the Indian Army. I was ruled morally unfit. In a war!" Khan laughed. "I would have loved war, I think."

"Some men do."

Khan retrieved a wooden box from the floor and placed it on his knee. He clicked open the brass latch of the box and Emmanuel noticed that the index finger on his right hand was severed at the middle joint.

"I have a message for Parthiv. Pass it along for me, Mr. Cooper."

Emmanuel did not want to be caught in the middle of a feud over hashish. Life was complicated enough and the clock was ticking down to his rearrest.

"I'll pass the message on," Emmanuel said anyway. If Jolly Marks's killer was found in the next forty-five hours, then maybe he'd swing by Saris and All. If not, he'd be in jail and Khan's disappointment would be the least of his worries.

"Tell Parthiv he is no longer in the hashish business. If I hear he is selling it anywhere, it will not go well for him. You understand?"

"I'll let him know," Emmanuel said.

Khan rapped on the glass privacy screen that separated the front from the backseats. The Rolls reversed out of the alley and swung back to the Point. Khan unclipped the lid of the wooden box and pushed it open. The scent of tobacco and cannabis bud spiced the air. He selected a lumpy hand-rolled cigarette as thick as a baby's wrist and offered it up.

"What is it?" Emmanuel said. The vanilla and chocolate butt at Jolly's murder scene had probably come from a box

like the one on Khan's knee. He considered a connection between the Indian man and Jolly Marks but nothing seemed
to fit.

"This is a gift," the Indian man said. "Kentucky burley
mixed with Swazi Gold and a sprinkle of Durban Poison."

"Thank you, but I'll pass."

Swazi Gold and Durban Poison were two of the most potent daggas on the market. Together they might be lethal. A
few puffs and the night would be spent searching wardrobe
corners for invisible enemies. Real life provided all the paranoia he could handle.

"You don't smoke?"

"Not since I was a kid."

All part and parcel of a slum childhood and adolescence
spent in a country boarding school long on discipline and
short on fun. He had been wild until the army tamed him. The
police force and the Detective Branch had harnessed his mental and physical energy. Even the Victory Shipyards kept him
straight up. If he stepped off the path now, he might end up
exactly where his teachers had predicted: in jail.

"Maybe next time," Khan said, and Emmanuel's jaw
clenched involuntarily. The Indian gangster was not going to
let him walk away from their acquaintance. Khan would know
him from now till the end of time.

"Maybe," Emmanuel said.

The Rolls came full circle and stopped at the intersection
of Quayside Road and Old Station Street. The bullish white
man who'd conducted the weapons search opened the passenger door and leaned in.

"Walk Mr. Cooper to his car and make sure he knows
where he is going," Khan said.

"Will do, sir."

The message for Parthiv was supposed to be delivered to-night. Well, he needed something from this encounter.

"Where can I find the Flying Dutchman if he's not at the passenger quay?" Emmanuel said. Knowing a criminal boss had to have advantages.

Khan smiled but, again, no emotion showed in the black eyes. "I can get you a woman," he said. "Any color, any size. For the right price. Just say the word."

The free marijuana and now a woman had both been of-fered with a smile, but Khan sat back watching Emmanuel like a spider, waiting for a weakness to show.

Emmanuel said, "Not tonight."

"You should reconsider," Khan said. "The Dutchman left town Friday morning and won't be back till tomorrow."

"Where can I find him tomorrow?"

The Indian man lit up the giant spliff and settled back into the leather seat. Smoke drifted from his mouth in a thick plume. "Try back at the quay in the middle of the afternoon. Sundays are slow and he'll be trawling for tourists off the boat."

"Time's up," the bodyguard said, and laid a hand on Em-manuel's shoulder.

Emmanuel shrugged off the heavy sausage fingers and climbed out of the car. The two men who'd earlier blocked him between the Rolls door and the pavement materialized from the shadows of a closed tea shop.

Khan's voice reached out from the gloom of the passenger compartment. "I will see you again, Mr. Cooper. Soon, I think."

10

ONE FORTY-FIVE A.M. Electric streetlights lit the sleeping city. The tram lines were empty and the police cells full of drunks, barroom brawlers and natives caught without the official passbook that allowed them to overnight in white urban areas.

Emmanuel let himself into Château la Mer with the key that Hélène had *too* kindly given him in the afternoon and went straight for the guest bathroom. His shoulder blades and neck had begun to throb and the presence of the mad Scottish sergeant major hovered at the edge of the pain.

"Please be here . . ." Emmanuel pulled the medicine cabinet open. His luck had to change. The last few hours had been a waste.

He'd ignored Khan's errand and pushed ahead with the murder investigation. The Zion Gospel Hall was locked, and the Cat and Fiddle Pub where Joe Flowers had knifed two men in a fight had gone out of business. Flashing Joe's mug shot to lowlifes in every drinking hole on the Point turned up nothing. No white DeSoto with white hubcaps and a mermaid

picture in the window, either. He knew no more about the
Flying Dutchman than what Jolly's sister had told him. In fact,
all he'd managed to do was appear on Khan's radar.

"Christ above . . ." Emmanuel shook his head. He was on
a losing streak. The cabinet shelves were empty and wiped
clean. He moved to the bedroom to continue the hunt.

A brown paper envelope lay on the quilted duvet. He up-
ended the contents onto the bed and a pair of silver police-
issue handcuffs and keys weighed down the luxurious cover.
An official police ID card with his name, photo and detective
sergeant's rank came out to rest next to a freshly printed race
identification card. Just like that. Two small pieces of laminated paper and he was white again, a detective again.

The race identification card wove a dark magic. People lied
and cheated to get the word *European* on this square of green
paper. Others turned their backs on South Africa for lack of
it. How could such a small thing—a plastic-covered piece of
paper—control an individual's whole world?

One flimsy document and he could walk through the front
entrance of Dewfield College where his sister, Olivia, taught
maths and science. He could sit in the manicured grounds, a
stone's throw from a dozen white schoolgirls, and not be considered a moral hazard.

He threw the cards down and pressed his thumbs to his
temples. The presence of the Scottish sergeant major continued to search for a breach. Emmanuel headed for the kitchen.
He'd chew on cloves and garlic if he had to. Anything to hold
back the Scotsman and the splintering pain gathering force behind his eye socket.

He switched on the kitchen light and found the pantry.
Glass tubs of goose fat, tall cans of peaches suspended in juice,

cake flour and jars of raw sugar: Hélène Gerard was thin now, but this was a fat person's larder. He moved aside bottles of olive oil and checked behind them.

"Mr. Cooper?" The French-accented voice was slurred. "Is that you?"

"It's me." Emmanuel stepped out of the pantry. "Sorry to wake you, Mrs. Gerard."

"No matter." Hélène leaned her weight against the long oak table that ran across the middle of the room. "No matter."

The gracious woman he'd met this afternoon had disappeared. In her place was a sloppy housewife with unpinned hair and dull eyes. She straightened herself up in the overly dignified pose adopted by drunks trying to appear sober.

"Please." She formed her words laboriously. "How can I help? I told the major I would help you."

"I'm fine. You should go to bed."

"No," she insisted. "Whatever you want, I can find it for you. Then you can tell Major van Niekerk that I did everything that I promised."

Emmanuel glimpsed the panic in her eyes. "Painkillers," he said. "I have a headache. That's all. Nothing the major has to know about."

"Aahhaa . . ." Hélène sailed toward a ceramic tea canister like a rudderless ship and lifted the lid. She rifled inside and produced a bottle of pills. "Not ordinary painkillers, Detective Sergeant Cooper. The best. It's morphine," she whispered. "For you."

Morphine was a controlled drug. Was Hélène Gerard an opium eater as well as a drunk? Emmanuel checked her face, her eyes, and found none of the dreamy washout that morphine left behind. He knew the look from the war. He had seen wounded soldiers and even some of the doctors wrapped in those dreams.

"Please." Hélène pushed the bottle into his hands. "Take them. There are only a few left. They are yours."

Emmanuel turned the glass bottle over and the pills rattled. He didn't trust himself. Four white beauties and he'd sail out of a window and stretch out on a cloud till midday. And that was the problem with good drugs. They worked so long as you kept taking them. And if they were good, that's all you wanted to do: keep taking them. He opened the bottle and shook out four pills, thought better of it and returned one to the container. Two for now and one against the possibility that he didn't crack the case: that's when he'd need calm. He screwed the aluminium top back in place and read the label stuck onto the front of the medication. The pills were prescribed for a Vincent Maurice Gerard. Two months ago.

"Your husband?" he asked.

"That's right."

"Doesn't he need the morphine anymore?"

Emmanuel was curious. There was no evidence of Vincent Gerard in the house. In fact, there were no family photographs of any kind on display.

"He copes without the pills." Hélène took the bottle and replaced it in the tea canister, then filled a glass with water and gave it to Emmanuel. "You'll tell the major I helped?"

"Of course."

"Don't forget."

Hélène tottered out of the kitchen on unsteady pins. A chair toppled over in the hallway and Emmanuel heard a soft curse. Why was the French Mauritian so desperate to please van Niekerk?

He swallowed two pills and slipped the spare into the breast pocket of his jacket. Not his jacket. It was Vincent Maurice Gerard's property and on loan to him, along with the police ID, for a shrinking period of time.

———

Emmanuel climbed into the wide expanse of the provincial-style bed, safe in his morphine lifeboat. He drifted over rusted corrugated iron roofs and chimneys breathing woodsmoke into the air. A dirt lane ran behind a row of ragged shops. His mother sat on the back steps of the All Hours General Store and shared a cigarette with a dark-skinned Sotho woman. Emmanuel rushed toward her. A hand gripped his shoulder and dug into the flesh.

"Do you see . . . ?" His father's voice was angry. "How careless she is?"

The scrape of a chair leg against the bedroom floor cut across the liquid play of memory and Emmanuel pulled himself upright. The solid shape of a man was perched on the edge of the bench in front of the mirrored vanity.

"Who are you?" Emmanuel said.

The outline wavered. There was someone in the room, within arm's length of him. He pushed himself up onto his elbows, muddled by the morphine and disoriented by the unfamiliar surroundings.

"You're the man who was outside Lana's flat," he said. "You've been following me."

The male figure stood up and floated to the door. Emmanuel struggled from under the quilt and the boom of his heart drowned out the warm hush of the morphine.

"Wait . . ." His feet hit the floor and he stumbled after the retreating figure. A tree branch scraped against the window and night shadows flickered across the walls. The bedroom door opened and the man disappeared into the hallway.

Emmanuel lunged forward and bumped the sharp edge of the dressing bureau with his hip. The police-issue handcuffs skated across the wood surface and the ID cards and clothes thumped to the floor.

"Shit . . ." He steadied himself against the furniture and checked the door. It was closed. The fog in his head shifted and ebbed. Morphine took the edge off the fear, but not enough. He switched on the bedside lamp and checked the room. The windows were locked and the corners were empty. He was alone. He collected the cards and clothes strewn across the floor and restacked them.

Zweigman's battered postcard had fallen out of the inner pocket of the stained crime scene jacket, which Hélène had neatly folded on the bureau. Emmanuel picked it up and turned it over. A dried spot of the dead maid's blood colored the handwriting scratched onto the back of the card and made the script appear ancient.

In the small hours of the morning the bloodstain was an omen that foretold violence and death. Emmanuel flipped the card and studied the pristine beauty of the misty hills and kloofs. Where the Zweigmans in danger?

Don't worry, the morphine whispered. *The drop of blood doesn't mean anything. Go to the deep valley. Listen to the waterfalls.* Emmanuel laid his head down in the nest of pillows and rested the postcard on his chest. The morphine opened a door to the past and he stepped through it into a landscape of mud ditches and burned trees. The steel ribs of a bridge twisted at an impossible angle and plunged into a swollen river. Emmanuel crouched in the dirt and rested. The air smelled of spent aviation fuel and shredded lemon trees, the scent of spring in wartime. Tracer fire lit the night sky with bright lines of green, blue and white and he marveled at how beautiful death looked.

A Lancaster bomber swooped over the river. A group of boys sat in the limbs of a bare, burned tree and their hands reached out to try to touch the plane as it flew just above them. One of the boys turned to Emmanuel. He had Jolly Marks's face. He pointed upward.

"Look," he said.

—

The bicker of mynah birds awoke Emmanuel and he rolled out of bed. The morphine tablets had taken him to the briny deep but daylight brought real problems and serious consequences for failing to solve them.

Zweigman's bloodied postcard was placed neatly on the bedside table. Last night it had been on his chest. He checked the room quickly. A pale lemon two-piece suit hung from the back of the chair where yesterday's cream silk jacket had been.

Emmanuel crossed the room. The police ID, van Niekerk's money, the morphine tablet, the Buick's keys and the new race ID card were arranged in a neat row along the top of the oak dressing bureau.

Hélène Gerard had been into the room. The idea of being observed while asleep made Emmanuel uncomfortable. Angry, also. The dawn intruder could easily have been detectives Fletcher and Robinson. Or maybe someone else? He still couldn't be sure if the man sitting by the dresser last night was real or a drug phantom.

No more morphine, then.

The IDs were laid out in the same manner as the contents of an evidence folder awaiting a signature to verify that all was present and accounted for. Hélène Gerard had not stolen or tampered with a thing, but Emmanuel was sure that she'd looked over the cards.

11

ZION GOSPEL HALL was a gray demountable building squeezed between a scrapyard and an abandoned shop with chicken wire over the windows. The first verse of the hymn "Arise, My Soul, Arise" drifted out of the open church door. Emmanuel looked in. Many of the congregation had thrown their arms in the air and swayed from side to side as if caught in a strong crosscurrent. Black and white limbs, skinny and malformed by poverty, reached like saplings to the ceiling.

Three more verses to go, Emmanuel thought. He knew the song by heart. Five years of mandatory prayer meetings and weekly church services at boarding school had left an imprint.

He backtracked along the length of the chain-link fence separating the scrapyard from the gospel hall and absently pulled up a chunk of kaffirweed along the way. The bitter scent lingered on his hands and brought back memories of endless Saturdays spent weeding the gardens alongside the Ndebele laborers, standard punishment for being unruly and wild at Ligfontein Kosskool—the Fountain of Light Boarding School. His offer to weed the gardens on Sundays as well was refused. He reached the street and turned back to the gospel hall. The dying notes of the hymn drifted out, followed by a loud chorus of "Amen." The congregation filed out of the demountable and gathered around the front entrance: black, brown and white all mixed together. They looked at Emmanuel, curious about the stranger loitering in their yard. A gray-haired white woman approached with squared shoulders. She wore no jewelry, no makeup, no stockings and no adornments in her plaited hair. Emmanuel couldn't imagine a way to improve her.

"Can I help you?" Wary blue eyes matched her Scandinavian accent.

"I'm Detective Sergeant Emmanuel Cooper," Emmanuel said. "I've got a few questions about Jolly Marks, if you don't mind."

"You weren't with the other detectives at the morgue. I've never seen you before."

"Transfer from Johannesburg. It's my first week."

"All the same, I'll be seeing some identification first," she said. "Then we'll take the next step."

"Of course." Emmanuel withdrew the brand-new ID from his pocket and handed it over. The plastic cover was pristine and the ink fresh. He wondered if the woman would notice.

"Never met a policeman that looked the way you do." She gave the ID back after reading it and made a point of studying the dark silk tie and the pale-citrus-colored suit with the delicate mother-of-pearl buttons hand-sewn down the front of the jacket.

"Never met a woman preacher before," Emmanuel said. "So that makes us even."

"Miss Bergis Morgensen." She introduced herself with a nod. "I've got to get back to my family and give them a parting blessing. Wait here. I'll answer your questions when everyone has gone. Jolly's passing has shaken people's faith, so we'll keep this quiet, if that's all right."

Emmanuel was happy to step back. He wanted to stay on the right side of Miss Morgensen, but more than that, he wanted to keep a safe distance from the broken members of the missionary woman's congregation.

They passed him on their way out of the churchyard in a parade of human frailty. A stumpy leg, a mouth with more gaps than teeth, a dark hollow where once an eye had been. Most disturbing of all was the combination of black skin and a physical impediment, which amounted to double punishment under the National Party laws that squeezed natives out of skilled labor and secondary schools.

Emmanuel waited for Miss Morgensen to bless the last member of her flock, a malnourished Afrikaner girl with cropped brown hair and a snub nose. The preacher held her hands, palms down, over the girl's bowed head.

"You are a holy temple. May the Lord provide you shelter from the storm."

"Amen." The girl received the prayer and hurried to the street with her bony arms swinging by her sides. The girl appeared to be running from church into the arms of the devil, which was the pattern Emmanuel had followed during his years of religious instruction.

"This way." Miss Morgensen unlocked the door to a small shed nailed onto the back wall of the church. The storeroom shelves held a paltry collection of commodities that Old Mother Hubbard would have turned her nose up at. "I pack and distribute charity boxes on Sunday afternoon. We can talk while I work."

Miss Morgensen took a small wooden crate from a shelf and started to fill it from an assortment of dented cans and bulky paper bags stacked on a round table. Her movements were brisk and strong for a woman who must be in her seventies.

Emmanuel shrugged off Gerard's jacket and hung it over the back of a chair. Silk seemed a vanity in the spartan room. He lifted a box from the shelf and placed it on the table. Bergis Morgensen did not like talking to the police, and perversely, he liked her more for it.

"One of each item?" he said.

The missionary hesitated, then thrust her chin in the direction of the meager stockpile. "Three of sardines, two of Spam, a bag of flour and sugar, then hand the box over to me."

Emmanuel sorted through the cans and found the sardines and the canned meat, all with the labels peeling away from the metal. The flour and sugar bags were light, perhaps five cups inside.

"Now." Miss Morgensen received the first completed box and topped it up with half a bar of soap and a washcloth that had been cut down from a towel and resewn. "What do you want to know about Jolly Marks?"

"You identified the body?"

"His mother asked me to, so I went to the morgue and signed the papers. The police have me in a few times a year, normally when they need to put a name to an unidentified body that's been found around the Point." She shut the box and tied it off with string, then wrote the name *Ephraim Nakasa* along the side with a pencil attached to the table by a string. "Jolly was the first child I've had to identify, and I pray the Lord never gives me that errand again."

Emmanuel took down another box and arranged the cans and bags so they at least covered the bottom. "You knew Jolly and his family pretty well, then?"

"His attendance at Zion wasn't regular but he came often enough to be called one of my flock."

"Do you know anyone who could have hurt him?"

"Hard to say. The children in and around the docks live in a floating world. One day the tide brings in gold, the next day poison. Normal does not exist. Prostitution and violence are a part of everyday life."

"What about his father?"

"In and out of jail. In and out of bars. Never in church. He's got seven more months to serve in Durban Central Prison for holding up the local milkman for a couple of bob. That tells you all you need to know about Jolly's father."

"Is there someone else in his everyday life that made you suspicious? An odd relative or a man who makes a nuisance of himself around children in this area?"

"I've prayed on it. But God is stubborn and hasn't answered me yet." Miss Morgensen tilted her head and frowned. "How did a stranger get close enough to harm Jolly? That's the question on my mind."

"You think Jolly knew his killer?"

"I believe he did," Miss Morgensen said.

"What makes you think so?"

The crime scene was cold and impersonal. The knife wound clean and precise. Murders where the people knew each other were normally messy and driven by emotion.

"Jolly worked on the docks but he was careful," she said.

"All his customers were regulars. He knew the railyards and the quays better than the harbormaster. It would have been hard for a stranger to surprise him."

Emmanuel considered Miss Morgensen's theory but wasn't convinced. Out on the docks, a stranger with money was an instant friend. It was wishful thinking to believe that Jolly Marks worked exclusively for a select band of prostitutes and thieves. He couldn't throw away any leads at this point, however.

"Nobody comes to mind?" he said, and pushed a box of supplies across the table. If the Flying Dutchman wasn't at the passenger quay, he'd need a new lead to pursue. Fast.

"Nothing so far, but God and I are working on it, Detective Sergeant." The missionary scribbled the name *Brian Hardy* on the second charity box and *Bettie Dlamini* on the third. "He hears every prayer and He notices every death. 'Are not two sparrows sold for a penny? And yet not one of them will fall to the ground apart from our father.' Matthew 10:29."

If a hundred years were as nothing to God, then both he and Miss Morgensen might die awaiting a divine answer to the question of who killed Jolly Marks. Man's forty-eight-hour clock was winding down and the suspect's description was still "a white man in a black suit," except that Emmanuel could now add "and possibly known to Jolly."

"You don't believe," Miss Morgensen said without rancor, and began to pack the charity boxes into a wheelbarrow with a punctured tire.

"I've seen forests of sparrows fall into trenches filled with bodies," Emmanuel said. "I'm a little thin on belief."

"The war, eh? Infuriating, isn't it?" The missionary chuckled. "How stubborn God is? I often wonder what He's up to with the famines and the wars and now with this poor country."

She tied the last box with string and wrote the name *Delia Flowers* along the side, then placed it in the wheelbarrow. She retrieved an oak walking stick with a curved handle from the corner and laid it across the top of the charity supplies.

Flowers. Not a rare surname but not common, either. The warren of decrepit cottages and cold-water flats served by Miss Morgensen's charity was the natural nesting ground for the people the major had called "rootless whites." Emmanuel was fresh out of leads and it was hours yet before he could search for the Flying Dutchman at the passenger quay. He stopped the missionary when she began to wheel her load to the door.

"I have a car," he said. "I'll take you on your deliveries, if you like."

"Are you sure, Detective Sergeant?"

"My good deed for the day," he said.

—

A chain-link fence with barbed wire along the top encircled the back entrance of a redbrick industrial building. Rusted paint cans leaked color onto the drive that led from the street to the factory. Miss Morgensen lobbed a stone across the yard and hit the back door, which opened a fraction.

"Come," Miss Morgensen called, and a lopsided black man sprinted across the concrete with his night watchman's coat flapping behind him. The man lifted a loose section of the fence and the missionary pushed the care package into the yard. Points of sharp wire punctured the man's hands but he appeared not to notice.

"*Ngiyabonga*." He mumbled his thanks and ran back to the shelter of the factory with the box. The whole exchange took less than a minute. Silhouettes flittered in the doorway and then disappeared when the man reached the door.

"He's not alone," Emmanuel said.

"You are mistaken." Miss Morgensen turned to the car, chin out and shoulders back. "He is a single man."

She walked away quickly and Emmanuel had to extend his stride to keep up. The wariness from in the churchyard was back and he knew why.

"I'm investigating a murder. Natives who are in town without a proper passbook are not my concern."

And thank God for that, he thought. The National Party's passbook laws came into effect after he made the jump from the foot police to the Detective Branch. Yes, he'd used the passbook laws to extract information from vulnerable suspects, but the endless trawl for natives who had trespassed too long on white streets was never one of his duties.

"And neither are their families," he added. Two or more people could have cast the flickering silhouettes in the factory doorway.

Miss Morgensen reached the Buick and rested against the hood. She studied Emmanuel's face closely. He let her. A minute passed and, satisfied by whatever she saw, the missionary said, "The factory owner lets Ephraim stay in the storeroom with his wife and two children. She doesn't have the passbook that allows her to work and live in the city, so they have to be careful. The package helps keep the family together."

"So things haven't improved in the black locations," he said.

"Not enough. Men still have to leave their kin and find work in the white man's world. And what are we without family, Detective Sergeant? We are dust in the wind."

"You have family in South Africa?" Emmanuel asked. The missionary was as solid and individual as a rock.

"My blood relations are in Norway," she said. "But my real family is here at the Zion Church. And you?"

"My parents are dead and I don't see my sister much anymore."

It was a lie. His father was still alive. The last time he'd seen him was twenty years earlier: standing on the front steps of the Johannesburg central courthouse, awkward in a pressed suit on loan to him for the duration of the murder trial.

"Wave," his sister, Olivia, had whispered, desperate even at that young age to appear normal. "Wave good-bye."

Emmanuel had waved and his father had turned his back. It was a final parting, with no words. Twenty years. His father might as well be dead. His sister lived hundreds of miles away in Jo'burg.

"It's not good for man to be alone," Miss Morgensen said. "That goes double for you, Detective Sergeant."

"Double?" She didn't know one thing about him.

She corrected herself. "No. Triple. You are no more suited to being a speck of dust than I am. We were born to take up space in this world, Detective Sergeant. There's no running from that."

Miss Morgensen had her broken family to fuss over and protect. He had three murders to solve in a dwindling amount of time. Maybe after that, when life was less complicated,

maybe then he'd think about family and just where his speck
of dust would land.

———

"Next stop, Mrs. Flowers," Miss Morgensen said when they'd
delivered all but the last of the charity boxes. Emmanuel
parked at the edge of a wide field pockmarked with the rem-
nants of night fires and switched off the engine.

"We'll have to go cross-country to deliver this one." She
indicated a path that cut into the derelict land.

Emmanuel carried the box in the crook of his arm and followed the missionary down the narrow path. They headed for
an abandoned two-story structure set amid waist-high grass
and guava trees sown by bird droppings. Most of the windows
on the decaying building were boarded up and the remainder
appeared as black spaces punched into the bricks. The faint
outline of the word SOUP ghosted across a sooty wall. Maydon
Wharf, the industrial heart of the port, loomed in the background. A family of vervet monkeys trooped along the buckled roofline and clambered into the branches of an overhanging
fig tree.

"Has she been here long?" Emmanuel asked. He felt for
the handcuffs in his back pocket to make sure they were acces-
sible. The field was open on all sides, allowing escape routes in
every direction. Too much ground for a single man to cover. If
he flushed out Joe Flowers, he'd have to grab him and pin him
down quickly.

"She's been here a few weeks." Miss Morgensen led him
along the pathway with the walking stick clutched like a
weapon. "A rent increase forced her out of her last boarding-
house and she's too ill to work, so she landed here. I'm hoping

this situation is temporary. This isn't the safest building. Too close to the port."

"Has she got family?"

"A son, but he's in all-male lodgings," came the tactful reply.

The vegetation on either side of the path was thick and the wind made a thin whistling when it blew across the wild field.

Emmanuel slowed before they entered the building, and checked the area. All clear. Miss Morgensen tramped toward a buckled concrete and steel staircase that led to the upper level.

"The ground floor is for the more transient types," the missionary said while they climbed higher. "The first floor has a few rooms with doors and locks. Mrs. Flowers is in one of those, thank the Lord."

There wasn't much to thank a higher power for in the gutted soup factory. Shoots of green vines curled through the gaps in the boarded-up windows; cracks in the ceiling admitted weak shafts of sunlight. Emmanuel's eyes adjusted to the darkness.

The upper floor contained a series of rooms squared around the staircase. They moved to a door at the far end of a corridor where the shadows were at their deepest. Force of habit dipped Emmanuel's hand down to his hip to unclip his revolver and he touched the empty loop of his belt instead.

He followed Miss Morgensen into a rectangular room with four mattresses laid out on the blistered linoleum tiles and stood just inside the doorway. A charred hot-water urn was bolted to the side wall where the staff's morning tea table must once have been. Three of the beds were unoccupied; the fourth was home to a faded woman with thinning brown hair.

He placed the box on one of the empty beds and moved back against the wall.

The woman struggled to a sitting position and wrapped a fringed shawl around her shoulders. Her cheeks were sunk so deeply into her face that she resembled a mine collapse.

"Mrs. Flowers . . ." The missionary hesitated at the foot of the mattress, her way barred by a wooden box packed with apples wrapped in purple crepe paper. A bulging sack stamped EXPORT leaked a pool of raw sugar onto the floor. The silver trim of a new Primus gas burner sparkled like a diamond in the dim room.

"I forgot you were coming," the woman said, and plucked nervously at the tassels of her shawl. "I was just resting."

The box of apples and the sugar sack had come straight off the docks on the Maydon Wharf. They were common enough items to be listed missing or stolen in shipping company ledgers and then forgotten. Mrs. Flowers's new woolen shawl and the pyramid-shaped bottle of perfume placed on the crate next to her bedding were the kind of gifts a thoughtful son might shoplift for his ailing mother.

"You look well." Miss Morgensen squeezed herself onto the end of the mattress and glanced at the new things surrounding Mrs. Flowers. The Zion charity box was paltry compared with the gas burner and the boxes of candles and matches stacked along the wall.

"I feel well," Mrs. Flowers said. "I've got some of my strength back."

"That's good news. You need to rest, and when the hospital gets its shipment of medicines, I'll bring your pills straight over."

A whistled tune accompanied the slap of shoes on the central staircase. Mrs. Flowers tried to lift her weight off the bed, but her strength failed her. The whistling grew louder and Emmanuel kept out of sight.

"Don't fret, sister." Miss Morgensen patted the woman's hand. "We'll leave you in peace."

The Norwegian missionary picked up her walking stick and straightened her skirt. Emmanuel stayed put and listened.

A tall female figure wrapped in an ankle-length mauve coat appeared in the doorway. A box of fresh tomatoes was cradled in the woman's arms, and the chiffon veil of her jaunty straw hat shielded her face from the world. She stepped forward and flashed a broad shin. Dark hair sprouted through the nylon stocking.

Mrs. Flowers whispered, "My boy . . ."

The box of tomatoes smashed to the floor and red fruit bounced across the tiles. Emmanuel grabbed for Joe, but he was quick and slid through the doorway like an eel. Emmanuel caught a handful of material and tugged. The coat came away in his hands and Joe ran the length of the corridor.

Emmanuel sprinted and closed the gap to a body length at the top of the stairs. Joe cleared two at a time, his muscular arms flapping away from his body in an effort to gain speed. Emmanuel lunged and Joe went airborne, sailing over the last four stairs in a mighty leap that sent a cloud of ash exploding off the floor when he landed. He sprinted out of the front entrance and disappeared into the grass.

Emmanuel ran the perimeter of the crumbling building. Joe Flowers was fast despite the weight of his huge head. A woman's leather shoe in a ridiculously large size lay at the edge of the field.

A breath came from deep in the faded greenery.

Emmanuel approached carefully and broke through the vegetation. A small man stood in a trampled circle of grass with his trousers around his ankles. An impossibly fat girl with lank brown hair was busy removing her bloomers. They swung around, panicked at being discovered. The girl was more experienced than her customer. She slipped into the brush with her underwear bunched in her hand.

The man struggled with his trousers, breath coming hard with fear now, not anticipation. A wedding ring flashed dull gold when his hands fumbled with the buttons of his fly.

"Please, mister," the man mumbled. "I've never done nothing like this before. Promise."

"Button up your pants," Emmanuel said. "And go home."

———

Miss Morgensen stood outside the abandoned soup factory with her walking stick clutched in her hands, like General Patton about to address the Third Army.

"You knew," she said.

"I suspected." Emmanuel kept an eye on the oak stick that had not once been used for walking.

"You knew," she repeated with narrowed eyes, and marched onto the path that led back to the car. The wide swing of her walking stick cleared the overgrown vegetation. Shredded grass seeds and greenery flew into the air. "You pretended charity, Detective Sergeant, but your heart was full of deceit. Mrs. Flowers now thinks I led you to her son and she will never trust me again. The bond is broken."

Emmanuel let Miss Morgensen continue her violent land-clearing. He had used her, that was true, but even the infirm

Mrs. Flowers must know that Joe was only a moment ahead of the law. The street came into view and the missionary stopped to get her breath back.

"I thought you were investigating Jolly's murder," she said, and turned to him. Her cheeks were pink but her eyes had the calm of a sea after a storm.

"I am. Joe's escape and Jolly's murder may be connected," Emmanuel said. "Was Joe Flowers a member of your congregation?"

"We can't talk here. Too many of my family live in the area, and after that trick you pulled with Mrs. Flowers, it's better if I'm not seen with you."

"Whither thou goest, I goest," Emmanuel said, and had the unexpected pleasure of Miss Morgensen's laugh.

12

THE SWELL TIMES Café on South Beach sold scoops of ice cream in waxed-paper cups. Miss Morgensen chose chocolate and strawberry sprinkled with chopped nuts. Emmanuel stuck with vanilla. They strolled the beachfront on the lookout for a place to sit and talk. A vacant bench faced the ocean. Miss Morgensen pointed to the WHITES ONLY sign.

"If members of my family can't sit down here, then I don't sit here, either."

"Well, that rules out the beach and the cafés," Emmanuel said. "This whole strip is for Europeans only."

"Then we'll walk."

"Happy to," Emmanuel said, and kept alongside the missionary. The ocean curled onto the sand, and tanned families splashed in the waves. A tanker glided along the horizon line. He was comfortable in the silence. Sometimes the people he spoke to felt the need to fill it. Miss Morgensen was not one of them. She licked her ice-cream spoon and admired the ocean.

"You're a servant of God," he said after three minutes of quiet. "But you're worldly enough to know that the murder of a child isn't going to go away. Silence won't give you, or any of your family, protection from the police. Talk to *me* now—or talk to somebody else later."

Miss Morgensen paused and began walking again, more slowly. "Joe was a member of the Zion family for a short while," she said. "But it didn't take."

"This was before he went to prison?"

"He left a few months before he stabbed those two poor men in a bar fight. He's a poor, lost man himself."

"What happened?"

"Joe's spirit was willing but his flesh was weak. Very weak. He got involved with one of the young sisters in the congregation, and when money was tight, he was happy for her to work the docks."

"He was a pimp?"

Miss Morgensen's look said yes, but she couldn't bring herself to say it. "We talked about these bad habits and we prayed for power to resist the devil, but nothing changed. Then I discovered Joe had brought other young sisters into his arrangement and that's when he was told to find another family."

Emmanuel had met a few murdering pimps back in Jo'burg. The victims were usually "disobedient" girls who'd run away or customers who bruised the merchandise.

"Were Jolly and Joe members of Zion at the same time?"

"They were."

"Jolly knew him?"

Miss Morgensen hesitated. "Yes, he did."

The missionary had earlier said that Jolly might have known his killer and now the connection between Joe and the murdered boy was established. Was there also a connection between the escaped prisoner and Mrs. Patterson and her maid? Emmanuel remembered the sack of sugar toppled over in his landlady's kitchen. Maybe goods stolen off the docks linked the murders.

"Are any of Joe's girls still around?"

"A few are in the area, yes."

"Names and addresses?"

"Let's see." Miss Morgensen ate a scoop of chocolate. "Stella is married to a policeman now. Newborn baby. Joe won't go anywhere near her. He tried it once and got a beating. Patty is around, but I haven't seen her the last month or two. Anne is still a member of the Zion. She lives in the same building as the Marks family."

It was worth a try. Joe wouldn't risk a return to the soup factory now that he'd been spotted there. He'd be hunting for a new hiding place. "What number?"

"You really think there's a connection between Jolly's murder and the Flowers boy?"

"There's a connection," Emmanuel said. "But I don't know what it is yet."

Miss Morgensen contemplated the crash of the waves and said, "I'd better take you. Anne will go out the back window the moment you knock on her door, and it's better for the family if we can clear up questions about Jolly's death without delay."

"Better for all of us," Emmanuel said.

———

The crippled man in the Victorian-era wheelchair was parked at the front of the crumbling flats, same as yesterday. A straw hat was jammed onto his head to keep off the midday sun.

Two mangy kittens burrowed into the blanket tossed over his paralyzed legs.

"Anne's father," Miss Morgensen said when they reached the front door. "Used to be a railway shunter. Hit by a train. That's all that's left. Anne's mother took off with another man about six months after the accident."

They climbed to the second floor and Miss Morgensen rapped her knuckles on the door. There was a shuffle of feet inside the flat but no answer. Emmanuel maneuvered closer to the wall and out of sight.

"Sister Anne?" Miss Morgensen said. "I won't take more than a minute of your time."

The door creaked open and a young white woman's angular face appeared in the gap. Her stubby nose was dusted with freckles and her thick brown hair was cropped close to her skull; in the wrong light she could easily be mistaken for a boy. Red cold sores cracked the corners of her mouth. Miss Morgensen's "holy temple" blessing this morning had not erased the reality of life in the shadow of the port.

A tawny kitten slipped into the corridor and rubbed itself against the missionary's leg. The woman unclipped the chain lock and scooped the kitten up in her thin arms. It was hard to tell who needed milk most: Anne or the starving cat.

"Have you got Pa's medicine?" The kitten dug its claws into Anne's shoulder. "A few more days and he'll be out."

"The clinic is waiting on supplies," Miss Morgensen said. "I'll bring the medicine the moment it's ready."

"*Ja*, sure." The young woman's voice wavered when she caught sight of Emmanuel leaning against the wall. She reached for the door handle.

"He won't hurt you, Sister Anne. I'll be with you the whole time."

"What's he want?"

"You're not in trouble," Emmanuel said. "I just want to talk with you."

Anne retreated into the flat and Emmanuel trailed close enough to grab her if she made a run for it. Winter light seeped in from the front window. Fingers of rising damp curled strips of green wallpaper from the walls and gave the flat a musty smell. A litter of kittens frolicked in a broken chest drawer and the overflowing contents of the litter box added an animal odor to the small space. The peeling wallpaper and the grim poverty of this flat at the center of a dilapidated mansion were one of the reasons for the National Party's rise to power. In and around Durban, there were blacks who lived better than this. To the National Party and their constituents, this was untenable. Anne scooped up a second kitten and held it to her chest. Her eyes flickered to the opened window, judging the distance to the street.

"Have a seat, Anne," Emmanuel said, and leaned back against the edge of the windowsill, legs outstretched. Casual body language to signal the fact that he wasn't worried she would make a break for it, because if she did, he would catch her. Anne slumped onto a tartan couch that had been mended with scraps from a box of random patches. She scratched a kitten behind the ears till its body vibrated.

"Are you a friend of Joe Flowers?"

"Used to be," she said.

"Have you seen Joe lately?"

"Joe?" Bony fingers curled into the kitten's mangy coat. "No."

"You sure about that?"

"*Ja,* of course." The kitten leaped to the floor but she pulled it back by the tail and held it down by force. Cat claws dug through her cotton dress and into her skinny thighs.

"You haven't seen him at all? Like across the street or maybe near the Zion Church?"

The captive kitten squirmed free and streaked across the room to the safety of the drawer. Anne turned her attentions to the tawny kitten burrowing into the crook of her neck. She massaged it with rough hands and avoided eye contact.

"Last time I seen Joe was before he went to Durban Central, a long time back. I don't know where he is now."

"What's through there?" Emmanuel indicated a hole in the wall that had once been a doorway.

"That's the bedroom."

"Can you show me?"

She dragged herself over to the entrance like a deep-sea diver working against the current. "My pa sleeps in the big bed and I sleep in the corner," she said.

A double bed and a narrow cot were neatly made up. A tallboy, half-wardrobe-sized, held Anne's and her father's Sunday clothes. A porcelain ballerina with a missing foot pirouetted on a small side table. Emmanuel moved to the window at the back of the room. It was shut, but the latch was open. Rusted iron stairs spiraled down to the common yard. An older Zulu woman hung wet clothes on a wire line while a small white child drew pictures in the dirt with a stick. Even destitute Europeans could not live without help. A wooden gate, painted an optimistic yellow, opened from the yard to a night-soil lane.

"You ever use these stairs?" he asked.

"No. Never."

A tin plate and a mug of the kind normally reserved for servants were laid out on the iron ledge just outside the window. Ants pulled bread crumbs over the lip.

"Never?" he said.

"Never."

"Okay, I believe you."

Anne's head dipped against the kitten's fur to hide a smile. A lie swallowed whole by the police; if Joe came around, she'd tell him the flat was safe and that the police detective was a fool. Fine by Emmanuel.

Still, there was something familiar about the room. Not from childhood but from the last few days. Emmanuel stepped closer to Anne and the sensation increased, so he stopped and examined her. He'd seen her receive a blessing outside the Zion Church but that wasn't it. There was something that made him feel that he knew her well enough to touch her. He leaned in. The scent of flowers was faint on her neck, a trace of something exotic in the broken-down room. The perfume smelled expensive. Like Lana Rose had worn at van Niekerk's coronation party. Joe had been shopping for his "sister."

"Detective Sergeant," Miss Morgensen said. "Sister Anne has answered your questions fully and I believe it is time for us to move on."

"Of course." Emmanuel returned to the windowsill. He wrote Château la Mer's phone number onto a page in his notebook, then tore it loose and handed it to Anne. "If you see Joe, call me or tell Miss Morgensen and she'll contact me. Will you do that?"

"*Ja.* Of course."

Emmanuel almost laughed at the easy promise. The only

working phones in a two-block radius likely belonged to the bookmakers and the public barkeepers.

"We're done here, sister. Peace be with you," Miss Morgensen said.

"And with you," Anne said, and rushed to the door. She cracked it open to let them out. The purring kitten sank its claws through the fabric of her dress again and burrowed its face against her nape. Red scratch marks appeared on the freckled skin of Anne's neck and shoulder.

She enjoys it, Emmanuel realized: the simple combination of love and pain and need.

—

"It's not what you think," Emmanuel said. "Back in the flat."

"What was it I witnessed, Detective Sergeant? Fatherly concern?"

"Did you smell the perfume? Expensive." He held the front door open for the missionary, who stepped out into the bright sunlight.

"I . . . well, yes . . ."

"I don't think she bought it herself."

"You come from these people, I think." Miss Morgensen stopped by the antique wheelchair and adjusted the straw hat, which had slid down over the crippled man's eyes. The kittens played with a piece of newspaper stuck between the wheel spokes.

"I grew up surrounded by Annes," Emmanuel said. "The fact that I noticed her is what's strange."

Anne should have smelled of caustic soap and hard times. Not a subtle mix of lilac and spice.

"Speaking of strange." The missionary gestured toward a

skinny man in a dark suit spreading pamphlets in a semicircle around a wooden box. It was the preacher from the crime scene and the Night Owl Café.

"Bumped into him twice," Emmanuel said. "He works the harbor, doesn't he?"

"Three, sometimes four times a week he hands out those leaflets and threatens everyone with damnation. What he does with the rest of his working hours, I can't tell."

"That makes him strange?"

The preacher was Miss Morgensen's competition. Both gathered souls that were notoriously hard to hold on to.

"I pray for charity," she said. "But there's something about Brother Jonah that makes me want to . . ."

"Punch him?"

"Yes." Her rumbling laugh startled the kittens and they scampered under the seat of the wheelchair.

"I know the feeling," Emmanuel said. Any man who tried to drum up business at the scene of a child's murder was no Christian.

"Sister Bergis." The preacher lifted a cream felt hat and revealed shoulder-length black hair. He smiled and his lively brown eyes twinkled.

"Brother Jonah." Miss Morgensen returned the greeting but did not break stride. Her fingers gripped the handle of her walking stick. Brother Jonah stepped across their path and shoved his hand at Emmanuel.

"You're new to these parts, aren't you, brother? What's your name, so I might remember you in prayer?"

"I don't have a brother," Emmanuel said, and shepherded Miss Morgensen around the fruit-box pulpit. She didn't need protection but there was something in Brother Jonah's smile, a hint of pity and condescension, that irked him. Or maybe it was his Jesus-like hair, which was brushed back from his forehead to reveal the sharp V of a widow's peak.

Emmanuel and the missionary walked on at a brisk pace till they reached the street corner.

"What I said earlier about not knowing anyone suspicious around this area," Miss Morgensen said, "I've changed my mind." She jerked a thumb in Brother Jonah's direction. "The last few weeks he's been around the Point and the passenger terminal every hour of the day and the night, talking especially to the children."

"Jolly?"

"I saw him with Jolly on Wednesday. They were walking past the terraces on Wellington Street. Brother Jonah had his arm around Jolly's shoulder."

"That was the day before Jolly died?"

"Well, yes."

"What time?" Emmanuel asked. Brother Jonah was a white man in a black suit, which made him a match for the prostitute's description . . . along with a thousand other males in Durban.

"Around six-fifteen. It was getting dark but I recognized them."

"You didn't think it was strange at the time?"

"We both work in this area and we know the same people. It didn't seem odd."

Emmanuel maneuvered Miss Morgensen around the corner and out of Brother Jonah's sight. Protecting witnesses from potential retaliation was second nature to anyone who'd worked in the Detective Branch.

"What else?"

A moment, then, "You'll think I'm a silly old woman."

"Try me and we'll see."

"Brother Jonah is not who he says he is. He disappears for days at a time and he keeps strange company in strange places."

"So do you."

Most white people would run screaming from the abandoned soup factory and turn away from the native night watchman hiding his wife and children in the city.

"Female intuition?" Emmanuel suggested.

"No. I followed him."

"Ahh . . ."

"Brother Jonah arrived without the backing of a church or an evangelical mission." The Norwegian missionary set off quickly and the end of her stick hit the pavement hard. "Yet he hands out money. Not much. A few bob to buy food or a school textbook. He doesn't collect donations or ask for charity from the local shopkeepers. So where does the money come from?"

They turned onto Point Road, where a line of customers waited in front of a kiosk. Among the cigarettes and newspapers were colorful handmade paper badges featuring Princess Elizabeth, the royal-Queen-in-waiting. The city would be lit up tonight, on the last day of May, in honor of her upcoming coronation. The *Natal Mercury* newspaper expected record crowds to witness Durban's attempt to be "one of the most colorful coronation cities in the Commonwealth." Brass bands and flag-waving. Emmanuel made a mental note to stay away.

Miss Morgensen pushed her walking stick between two men and forced a space. The kiosk line parted like the Red Sea and they sailed through without breaking stride.

"My motives were dishonorable, Detective Sergeant. I don't like Brother Jonah. I wanted to catch him in sin. Envy led me down the path of temptation."

"Find anything?"

She paused outside a ship's chandlery to catch her breath. A white and blue mural of a right whale and her calf breaking the ocean's surface was tiled into the footpath. "He went to Larsen's Scrap Metal Yard near the black stevedores' barracks. There's an office at the back of the yard, away from the street. He was in there with another man."

"Doing?"

"Talking," she said. "The blinds were drawn in the office, so I hid by the side of the stairs and listened. They used English words but I didn't understand what they said."

"For example?" Emmanuel kept the ball rolling. She was ashamed of her unchristian behavior and he was her confessor. Ask, listen and nod. A surprising amount of police work hinged on these three simple actions.

"Brother Jonah said, 'They are not going to send a dogface on a mission to extract this Ivan . . .' "

A pause stretched out and Emmanuel lifted an eyebrow.

"The language was not good," Miss Morgensen said.

"I'll give you a bob for every word I've never heard before." Emmanuel extracted his wallet and flipped it open. "Let's see if you can make some money for the collection box, sister."

Miss Morgensen hesitated, then wrote the word *mother-*

fucker onto the dusty surface of the chandlery window with the tip of her finger.

"Well?" Her eyes twinkled. "Do you owe me a bob, Detective Sergeant?"

"Afraid not," Emmanuel said. "It was a favorite of the Yank GIs. First time I've ever seen it written down so neatly, though."

"That must be worth a bob," she said. "For penmanship."

Emmanuel paid up and switched the wallet for a notebook. He wrote down the unfinished sentence and read it back to the missionary, who was slipping the coins into a breast pocket with a tiny smile.

They are not going to send a dogface on a mission to extract this Ivan . . . ? He tapped the word *motherfucker* instead of saying it out loud in front of Miss Morgensen. *Ivan* was a slang term for the Russian soldiers that had flooded across Europe in the wake of the Allied victory. *Dogface* was the nickname given to the men of the U.S. infantry. Together they made no sense. Was the American evangelist a soldier turned preacher?

"Anything else?" he said. Brother Jonah seemed to be in the middle of a military mission.

"No. The night watchman came out of his shed and I ran out to the street. A moment later a big silver car drove by very slow and there was a burning feeling here in my chest." She pointed to her heart. "Brother Jonah was in the car and he knew that I had followed him."

"You saw him?"

"No. I felt him. Judging me."

The sign of a well-trained Christian was the deep and certain belief that God saw all and judged all, almost always in the negative. Miss Morgensen knew her actions were wrong and, as promised in the Book, God—in the form of Brother Jonah—had caught her red-handed.

"Tell me about the car," he said.

"It was Mr. Khan's Rolls-Royce."

He cocked his head in surprise. "You know Mr. Khan?"

"He's one of the local merchants who supports the Zion family with donations." A red tinge worked its way across her cheeks. "He supplies medicine for the sick."

Dirty money washed clean through charity.

Emmanuel said, "Maybe Brother Jonah gets his money from Mr. Khan. Same as you."

"I do not take money from Afzal Khan." She tapped her cane against the footpath to emphasize the words. "Mr. Khan supports Christian and Muslim organizations. Twice a year Zion gets a box of medicine. Bandages, headache tablets, cough syrup and disinfectants. Mr. Khan's very particular about the donations being given out to the poor. Brother Jonah gives out nothing but pamphlets."

"Was Mr. Khan the man that Jonah was talking to at the scrapyard?"

She shook her head. "I can't say for sure. Brother Jonah was the one who did the talking."

"What do you think Brother Jonah was doing in Mr. Khan's car?"

If he'd been in the Rolls at all—a fact yet to be established beyond the feeling that burned inside Miss Morgensen's chest.

"A man of God in Mr. Khan's limousine just before midnight? My thoughts on that subject are uncharitable, so I will keep them to myself." She erased the swear word from the dusty window with a sweep of her palm. "After that, I put temptation behind me. But the feeling of being observed by Brother Jonah . . . that has not gone away. It's stronger."

The line in front of the kiosk had thinned and Emmanuel got a clear view to the end of the block. A man in a dark suit and dark hat stood on the corner with the *Natal Mercury* newspaper held open in front of him. Pale alabaster hands clutched the pages. Blood thundered in Emmanuel's ears. Was the tradesman from the police interrogation room tailing him? Emmanuel stepped forward and the man on the corner turned and walked away.

"Something wrong, Detective Sergeant?"

Fear spread once it was whispered out loud. The magic charm against it, in battle and in peacetime, was silence. Knowing when to shut the fuck up.

"Coronation fever," he said, and pointed to a girl in a short cotton shift tying red, white and blue balloons to the points of a wrought-iron fence with the help of a maid only a few years older than herself.

"Will you be celebrating?" Miss Morgensen asked. "The newspaper says the buildings in town will be lit up like a fairyland."

"I'll be working." Emmanuel closed the notebook at the mermaid sketch and shoved it into his pocket. His hands were steady but his heart raced. The night with Lana Rose happened before the murders at the Dover. Why would anyone have been following him then?

"Looking for Joe?" Miss Morgensen asked.

"Among other things." Like checking over his shoulder every five minutes to confirm that he was being tailed. His watch read 3:45 p.m. Time to head back to the passenger ship quay and try to find the Flying Dutchman.

"Is Joe your only suspect?" The prospect clearly worried the Norwegian missionary. How would she explain that someone who'd once been called "brother" had committed the murder of a family member? The delicate bonds of trust that held the congregation together would break and the Zion Church would fracture.

Emmanuel mentally scratched together a suspect list. Flowers was a white man in a dark suit who moved fast and was known to Jolly. Joe also knew the docks, having pimped a variety of girls there. And now there was Brother Jonah, the possible ex-soldier who worked the docks and talked to children. He wore a dark suit and had gotten close enough to the skittish Jolly to put an arm around his shoulder.

"No," Emmanuel said. "Joe isn't the only suspect."

13

A WHITE DeSoto FOUR-DOOR with silver trim and white hubcaps was parked in the shadow of the ocean liner moored at the Southampton Street pier. A muscular black man in fresh blue overalls buttoned to the collar worked a cloth over the car's wheel arch while a crew of Zulu stevedores loaded the ship's cargo hold and chanted a work song. Sun-kissed passengers leaned over the railing and enjoyed the sound of black Africa at work.

The man acknowledged Emmanuel's approach with the wide smile offered by servants to Europeans. Emmanuel did not disabuse him.

"Greetings," the man said, and continued buffing the vehicle with long, even strokes the way a stable hand might groom a horse.

"Nice car." Emmanuel pretended to study the silver chrome that ran along the vehicle's side. Instead he studied the cleaner. His hands were smooth and his clean fingernails were clipped short.

"Does the baas have a car also?" the black man asked without looking up from his work. The weather, automobiles and the coronation of the English queen were all safe things to talk about with white men.

"No car," Emmanuel said, and caught sight of the two-tone leather shoes peeking from the bottom of the overalls. The soles were unworn and the laces new. They were not an employer's throwaways. If this man turned out to be just a humble domestic, then Emmanuel would eat the shoes for dinner.

"I'd like to talk to the Flying Dutchman," he said.

That got the car cleaner's attention. He glanced up. The wide smile contracted a fraction but the man managed to hold it in place by force of will. *"Hiya ..."* He made a sound of regret. "I'm sorry, ma' baas, but I do not know about this man. Sorry, ma baas. Sorry."

Emmanuel said, "You can cut the 'baas, sorry ma' baas' routine. Take a good look at me. I'm not a policeman. I just want to find the Flying Dutchman."

The man twisted the cloth around his finger, then slowly examined Vincent Gerard's borrowed suit. The silk tie, the imported quality fabric, the hand-sewn buttons ...

"What is it you want with the Dutchman?" he said, still cautious.

"I'll tell him myself," Emmanuel said. "It's private business."

"Private?" The black man whistled. "That's an expensive word in South Africa, ma' baas. A man must pay and pay for these private things."

"I've got money," Emmanuel said. Van Niekerk's bankroll was now stay-out-of-jail money. Twenty-five hours and both he and the stack of notes might be signed into police evidence.

"Who told the baas about the Dutchman? I must give a name or he will not come."

Mentioning Jolly Marks this early in the negotiations might scare the Dutchman away. Dead children had that effect. Not giving a name would definitely send the Dutchman packing. He pulled out Jolly's notebook and showed the mermaid sketch. "Will this do?"

The man's dark brown eyes studied the picture, weighing up the potential risks and rewards of taking on a new client.

"Wait here and I will see."

The black man shoved the cleaning cloth into a pocket and disappeared behind a row of sheds at the side of the two-story passenger terminal. Emmanuel rested against the DeSoto. The sun was still well above the horizon line.

"Union Jack flags. Union Jack buttons . . ." An Indian street vendor carted a bucket of coronation decorations along the pier. The sunshine was warm on Emmanuel's skin but he could not enjoy it. Seeing the pale man hidden behind the newspaper had brought back the big question: why had he been released from police custody? He had a feeling that the real reason for the forty-eight-hour deal was more complex than van Niekerk had said.

A black man in a dark green suit, white shirt and green tie stepped out from behind the storage sheds and walked quickly along the planks of the wharf. Blue overalls were folded neatly over his arm. Emmanuel squinted into the bright afternoon light. The black man opened the boot of the DeSoto, threw in the overalls and retrieved a dark gray fedora with a green satin trim. Three minutes behind the sheds and the servant in overalls had become a "town Jack"—someone streetwise and sharp, who had never hoed a field or herded cows back to the kraal at dusk.

"You?" Emmanuel said. The wild-haired mermaid winked from an illustrated cardboard square neatly stowed in the clean boot. Faint clip marks bit into the top edge of the sign.

The black man angled the brim of the fedora so his expression was unreadable. "Don't I look Dutch, ma' baas?"

"Like windmills and tulips," Emmanuel said.

And maybe that was the point of the name. Here was a black man whose ambition ignored the color barrier.

"Do you want to go to the same place as your friend?" the man asked after he'd locked the boot and wiped his own fingerprints off the chrome with a handkerchief.

Emmanuel drew a blank. What friend?

"The one who came to me with the boy's picture. Do you want to go to the same place that I took him?"

"The boy's picture . . ." Jolly had given the sketch to someone else to use as an introduction to the cagey Dutchman. "*Ja*. The same place," Emmanuel said. "How much to take me?"

"Two pounds for transport there and back. Cash up front."

That was nearly a month's rent. A jail cell, on the other hand, was free. He crossed the man's palm with a couple of portraits of the king and wondered where the ride would take him.

"What's your proper name?" he said. "I can't have someone called the Flying Dutchman knowing my secrets."

"It is Exodus." The man rustled the pound notes between his thumb and forefinger before tucking them carefully into a breast pocket. He pulled the car door open and waved Emmanuel inside. "That is my church-given name. We Basotho had to leave our land and come to the city just like the people in the Bible."

Maybe that was true, but Emmanuel doubted it. Multiple names gave multiple covers to hide behind. It might take the police weeks to unravel the connection between Exodus and the Flying Dutchman.

The polished leather interior of the DeSoto smelled of fresh beeswax and the plush carpets were springy underfoot. Two metal clips were glued above the passenger window. That's how Jolly's sister, Susannah, had seen the mermaid. Her picture was hung against the glass: a coded invitation to Durban's underworld.

Exodus reversed out of the parking space and drove along Quayside Road toward town. Rows of wide-fronted ware-houses gave way to art deco apartment buildings and balco-nied hotels with dress circle rooms facing the Esplanade and Natal Bay. Golden veins of sand threaded the water. A solitary gray heron fished the shallows, while men with buckets, spades and turned-up trousers mined the tidal shoreline for worms. The Bluff headland, covered in wild green, protected the harbor from the open sea.

"So . . ." The Basotho man tilted the rearview mirror to get a better view of the passenger seat. "Is the baas married? Got a girlfriend, maybe?"

Emmanuel wasn't bothered by the scrutiny. Vincent Gerard's high-class suit was better than a clown disguise. The reflection in the mirror was a million miles from the reality of his life.

"A girlfriend," he said. Memories of Lana Rose were still fresh, while the wedding-ring indentation on his finger was now faint. Three years had not been a long enough time for the weight of the gold band to leave a permanent mark.

Dark fingers drummed against the steering wheel. "And she is a good woman?"

"Sure." Two lies in a row, and the ride was five minutes old. A man in this kind of job couldn't expect the truth from his customers.

"Tell me," Emmanuel said. "Will the right amount of money get me anything I want?"

A fine suit and a fine car were two things normally out of reach of a black man. Money made it all possible. And Jolly Marks was somehow hooked into this operation. The cigarettes and sweets were not charity; they'd been earned.

Exodus shook his head. "There are those who work the docks who will help scratch any itch. I am not one of those men. I do not do the young boys and the girls. Also, the man who likes to draw blood from a woman with his fists, I cannot help. These are my rules."

That criminals and thugs loved rules and chivalrous codes had always amused Emmanuel. Firebomb a restaurant, murder a police informer, terrorize a whole community—that was all right as long as no children or dogs or old ladies were harmed. The rules were, in Emmanuel's experience, the laziest way a man had to convince himself of his own worth. In any case, the rules were fiction. They all came with a dozen out clauses.

"Story around the docks is that you did business with that kid Jolly Marks," he said, and waited for the car brakes to slam. A conversation about a dead European child was dangerous territory for a man in Exodus's position.

"That boy is good with the numbers, like a machine," Exodus said with a smile. The easy two-pound payment had put him in a good mood. It was more than most nonwhites made in a month. "For him to keep track of five different hands in a poker game; that is nothing."

Exodus had used the present tense and Emmanuel realized why. He'd left town on Friday morning and had only just returned. The Basotho man didn't know the Marks kid was dead.

"You use him as a card counter?"

"For card games at 'Europeans only' parties. Better money than working the docks. Safer, also."

Durban, the most English of all South African cities, appeared easygoing, but influx control gates at every major entry road kept most black people corralled in the sprawling township of Cato Manor. It was not possible for a native man to stumble upon the mathematical talents of a white child by accident.

"How did you know Jolly was good with numbers?" Emmanuel asked.

"My mother's sister. She is a cleaner at one of the houses on Point Road, the one run by the fat Irishwoman who wears the men's clothing. You know it?"

"No."

"The boy's father brought him into the house to do card tricks for the cat women and their customers. This is how my auntie knew about the numbers."

It was always behind closed doors that race groups mixed. The DeSoto slowed to a crawl along a deserted stretch of Edwin Swales Drive. A drunk slept off a hard night in the doorway of a ship repair yard. Out here, it was a dead-quiet Sunday afternoon.

"I took this boy Jolly to three parties only." The black man glanced over his shoulder, suspicious. "How is it that the baas knows these things unless he is a policeman?"

The "baas, ma' baas" would come thick and fast while Exodus planned an escape strategy.

"I'm not a policeman," Emmanuel said.

"How do you know this boy worked for me?"

"Give me two pounds and I'll tell you," Emmanuel said. If he didn't stem the panic, Exodus might swing a U-turn back to town.

"And why must I do that?"

"Because my sources are private, and *private* is an expensive word in South Africa. A man must pay and pay for these private things. Right?"

Exodus laughed and said, "I think that maybe you are not a policeman."

"No, but I am in a hurry. My girl wants me back in time for the coronation lights." A few more hours on this job, and lying would come easier than breathing.

The industrial buildings thinned out and a mangrove swamp grew up, thick and tangled along the water's edge. A gang of juvenile boys with jutting elbows and scraped knees sprinted across the road with homemade fishing rods over their shoulders. The bridge spanning the Umhlatuzana Channel was a slender umbilical cord connecting the Bluff to the more cosmopolitan confines of Durban town.

"Are we crossing over the bridge, or heading back to the passenger terminal?" Emmanuel said. "That's the two-pound question."

The DeSoto rumbled across the bridge. He had his answer.

The road sloped upward toward the spine of the headland. Small houses occupied the cusp of land overlooking swamp-lands and the harbor wharfs. European women gossiped over low fences while men in overalls tinkered with car skeletons or burned off the weekly rubbish in tin drums perforated with oxygen holes. The windblown petals of a kaffirboom tree painted the dirt verge red.

Two Union Jack flags flew from a makeshift line strung across the front garden of a brick house. Across the road, a white banner with the word REPUBLIC fluttered from the front fence of an equally small dwelling.

"English versus Afrikaner," Exodus said. "One side is for the queen and her country and the other side is for Prime Minister Malan and a republic."

"Are you taking bets on the winner?" Emmanuel asked.

The odds had swung behind Malan, the ex–Dutch Reformed Church minister with pants hitched high over his prosperous gut. He was in London for the coronation but was talking up plans for an independent South Africa, while the bones of British soldiers interred in the fields of Zululand and the Transvaal turned in their graves.

"I must give more money now that Malan and his people are the chiefs. Many laws to break means many bribes to pay the police. But to say the truth . . . both the Dutch and the British, they can go and dance off a cliff. No hard feelings, baas."

Emmanuel shrugged to indicate that no offense was taken. Reclassification from white to mixed-race had forced him outside the confines of the white world. From the perimeter he had experienced the singular truth that governed the lives of a majority of nonwhite South Africans: the weight of the boot on your back, Boer or British, was equally heavy.

"Look at this clown." Exodus drew focus away from his bold remark and indicated a fair-haired youth who tore circles into a field of dirt with a motorbike. Smoke and dust blew from the tires. Two girls looked on from the edge of the field, vaguely impressed by the roar of the engine and the smell of burned fuel.

"Rough and tough from the Bluff. That's what we say in town. Have you been out to this place before?"

"First time," Emmanuel said. Almost six months in Durban with nothing to show but rough hands and corded muscle. The loop between the Dover flats and the Victory Shipyard was almost the entire orbit of his universe.

The DeSoto climbed steadily upward, then swung left onto a road that followed the spine of the headland. A thick blanket of vegetation covered the slopes and spread downward to the edge of the bright ocean water. A breeze blew in a stench of soured pork and fish.

"That is the whaling station," Exodus said. "They are cutting and boiling the fat in big vats. Will you still be able to enjoy your visit?"

"I'll give it my best shot. And my name is Emmanuel."

This afternoon would be special if it led to one of the last people to see Jolly Marks alive. Possibly. Maybe. Hopefully. Words for a prayer, not a police investigation. Facts, hard evidence, witnesses. That's what he needed to stay out of jail.

They peeled off the main road onto a dirt track that cut into a mass of thornbush and creeping triffid weed. A white mailbox marked the presence of a dwelling somewhere in the thicket. Red dirt, blue sky and fifteen different shades of green surrounded the car. The sound of an automobile driving on the main road receded into the quiet.

The DeSoto bumped downward and the silver teeth of the front grille leveled the underbrush to lawn. The chrome hood ornament, a bust of Spanish explorer Hernando de Soto, cast a steely gaze into the bush.

"We are here." Exodus pulled into an untidy lot overshadowed by ancient Natal mahogany trees. A tumbledown house occupied a square of land that had been cleared of all vegetation. A flock of glossy starlings perched along the broken fence line, their feathers iridescent in the sunlight.

"You sure this is it?" Emmanuel said.

A deserted dwelling off the main road and far from prying eyes was the perfect setting for a shakedown. Men who used Exodus's services were easy targets. Rob them, and they rarely reported the theft to police. Rough them up, and they sometimes hit back, but mostly they crawled into a corner and licked their wounds, their shameful secret safe.

"This is the place," Exodus said. "I left them here. It was pitch-black, but we found the mailbox and then the house."

Them. More than one person had been dropped off in the dead of night. Emmanuel opened the car door and the caustic stench of the whaling factory brought the smell of death. It was too late to back out now. If he mentioned the word *police,* Exodus would drive away without a good-bye. The two pounds were already in his pocket.

14

THE ENTIRE FRONT yard of the dilapidated house was a solid block of cement over which a collection of plaster-cast animals stalked. Three snarling wolves encircled a spotted deer with huge brown eyes, and a knee-high brown bear grappled with an elk. They were all Northern Hemisphere animals of prey arranged on a barren slab that resembled the unforgiving snowfields of winter. The owner of the house was a European, Emmanuel figured. A man with fond memories of the hunt and kill.

The windows were shut and a faint glow of light was discernible from under the curtain's edge, maybe a lantern low on oil. The absence of power lines confirmed the lack of electricity. If things went wrong, there'd be nowhere to make an emergency phone call and nowhere to hide except the green expanse encircling the house. The parked DeSoto with Exodus still at the wheel was the only point of escape.

Emmanuel knocked on the front door and it swung inward. A sharp metallic sound broke the silence, then stopped. Someone or something was moving around inside.

"Police," he said. "I'm coming in."

An open window at the back of the room let in enough daylight to illuminate rows of shelves buckling under the weight of rusting harpoons, fishing hooks and spools of anchor chain. A yellowing shark fetus floated in a specimen jar and next to it, a pyramid of bleached bones. The hollow eye sockets of a human skull stared out from the graveyard pile. A prickle of warning raised the hairs on the back of Emmanuel's neck.

"Police," he said a little louder.

No answer.

A polished leather suitcase leaned against a wall and the flame of the oil lamp suspended from the ceiling beam flickered weakly. A bowl of pickled eggs and brown onions was set up on a small table, with a fork still stuck into the food. A crate of empty vodka bottles was jammed against the back door.

Emmanuel crouched down to examine the unfinished meal. The onion on the end of the fork was bitten in half. Someone had left the house in a hurry or had retreated to another room.

The flame of the oil lamp flared bright and then expired on a curl of gray smoke. A length of silver chain swung across Emmanuel's view and tightened against his throat.

He leaned backward and jammed his right hand between the hard line of the choke chain and his neck, which still bore the boot marks left by yesterday's encounter with the police. The world seemed intent on cutting off his air supply.

A quick jerk on the silver chain and it loosened. The person on the other end gasped for breath, his strength already depleted. Emmanuel exerted a steady pull on the chain, certain now of his superior strength. Work at the Victory had not been a waste. A hand appeared on the edge of his peripheral vision and then a rounded stomach bumped against his shoulder blades. Fat and weak. Not the ideal build for a strangler. The chain gave way altogether and fell to the floor. A dog began to bark in the backyard.

Emmanuel swiveled a half circle, caught a skinny arm in his grasp and twisted hard. His assailant lost balance and tipped backward. The body slammed into Emmanuel's chest and momentum swung against him. He crashed onto the wooden floor and the weight of his attacker's body pinned him down and pushed the air out of his lungs.

A fine curtain of hair covered his face and blocked out the room. He twisted to the left so the body was in front of him, held close in a parody of a satisfied lover's pose. His hands touched rounded hips and the swell of a stomach, taut and curved as a globe. A tremor of movement and the distinct kick of life pulsed under his palm. Emmanuel sat up, stunned.

His attacker was heavily pregnant, with white-blond hair and curiously sloping eyes of Prussian blue. From her position on the floor she swung a fist, but Emmanuel caught her wrist and pinned it against her side.

She struggled against his hold and spit out words in Russian. Emmanuel didn't need a translator to understand: if curses worked, then he'd be blind and infertile by nightfall. He let her expend her energy till she was exhausted and gasping for breath.

"Stop," he said quietly. "Stop."

"*Da.*"

Emmanuel stood up and pulled the girl off the floor. She

pressed a hand to the small of her back and straightened up. The material of the black shirt tightened against her full breasts and stretched across the swell of her pregnant belly. The girl tugged at his sleeve and pointed to a darkened side room. Emmanuel shook his head. There was no chance he would walk into an unlit space with the person who'd just tried to strangle him.

"English?" he said. "Do you speak English?"

"*Nyet*." She jabbed a finger into his chest and demanded, "American? American?"

"No," he said. "South African."

"American? *Da?*"

"No. *Nyet.* Not American."

His answer didn't satisfy her and she cursed him to his face. Clearly his nationality was a bitter disappointment. It wasn't the first time. The women of France and Germany knew from experience that American servicemen's ration packs were fatter than those of their English or Canadian counterparts.

The dog continued to bark outside. Emmanuel went to the window. A slope-backed German shepherd ran the length of a low fence line that separated the patchy yard from the lush row of monkey apple trees and flowering creepers. He checked the perimeter and the feeling of being watched returned. The dog's restless patrol continued.

Emmanuel failed to find anything out of the ordinary and turned back to the woman, who had finally fallen silent. She pointed to the side room.

"You first," Emmanuel said, and wrapped the silver chain around his hand. Risk nothing, gain nothing. He fell into step behind the woman. The dog barked and snarled again.

The room was narrow and built along a bank of windows that faced the backyard. Heavy curtains kept out daylight. The pregnant woman stood in the middle of the floor.

Emmanuel tugged a curtain open and sunlight poured in, bright white after the darkness. He blinked hard and turned around. A great ox of a man with a bristly beard and watery green eyes sat in a deck chair. The tropical light glinted off the silver barrel of an automatic pistol in his hand. A Walther PPK.

"Fuck," Emmanuel said. He raised both hands in surrender. Europe was filled with the graves of soldiers who'd tried to outrun the firepower of this particular German-manufactured sidearm.

The woman squatted next to the deck chair and whispered harshly into the man's ear. The word "American" was repeated again and again amid the torrent of Russian, a little sharper with each use. The hand holding the pistol was white-knuckled and shaking.

Emmanuel kept still and observed. The bearded man was wide-shouldered and wide-necked, the deck chair barely able to hold his girth. Standing with the Walther in his hand, he would be in complete control of the situation. So why was he still sitting?

The woman continued whispering and the man drew in a sudden sharp breath. His jaw clenched and his fingers twitched around the metal grip of the Walther before it clattered to the floor.

Emmanuel and the woman lunged for the gun simultaneously. He blocked her advance with a shoulder and sent her flying back. There'd be time later to feel guilty about tackling a pregnant woman, but for now the Walther was his, and that felt good.

Emmanuel approached the man, who had hauled his bulk from the deck chair. Two attempts to put him out of action, both failed. The Russian couple weren't professionals.

"Sit," he said. "Now."

The man collapsed back into the canvas and drew a ragged breath. The pain had passed and color had returned to his face. He glared at his own hands, disgusted by their inability to hang on to the gun.

"English?" Emmanuel said.

"A little."

"Good. What's your name?"

"Nicolai Petrov."

"Who is she?" Emmanuel pointed to the woman, who was sulking in the wake of her failure to secure the gun.

"Natalya Petrova." The man breathed out the name, then said, with a hint of pride, "Wife."

"She's your wife?" There must be a thirty-year age gap between Nicolai Petrov and the petulant blonde.

"Yes. Mine."

Natalya chewed her fingernails, bored by the two older men talking in a language she didn't understand. Emmanuel suspected that unless the conversation, in any language, was about Natalya, she wasn't listening.

"This is your house?" he asked.

"It belongs to my cousin Kolya." Nicolai made the name sound like a disease. "He has gone to work at the whaling station. We are visiting here from Russia."

The Russians were a married couple on a family visit. The

attempted strangling and the ambush with the Walther still had to be explained, however.

"Why are you trying to kill me?" Emmanuel said. "First with the chain and then with this gun."

Nicolai shrugged. "Kill or be killed."

"I didn't come to harm you." Emmanuel crouched by the burly man's chair but kept the sidearm close to the ground. "I came here to find out about the boy who gave you the mermaid drawing. It was three nights ago. Do you remember him?"

Nicolai frowned and then shook his head after failing to translate the question from English to Russian.

"How long have you been in Durban?" Emmanuel went back to basics. One question and then one answer at a time, until the link with Jolly Marks was made.

"Here?" The Russian indicated the sunroom.

"Yes," Emmanuel said. "How long?"

"Three days."

That put the couple in Durban at the time of Jolly's murder. Emmanuel tucked the Walther into the waistband of his trousers and pulled Jolly's notebook free. The steel handcuffs tucked into a jacket pocket rattled and Nicolai sat up straight. The Russian man recognized the sound the way an orchestra conductor might recognize a note from a favorite instrument.

"Please." Nicolai fumbled with the buttons of his heavy wool coat and pulled a diamond and ruby ring from the lining. He held it out in the palm of his hand.

"Please," he said. "Take and go away."

Emmanuel ignored the bribe and removed the documents that stuck out from the breast pocket of the Russian man's winter garment. Two American passports in the names of

Nicholas Wren and Natalie Wren were unmarked by immigration stamps for South Africa or any other country. A healthy Nicolai, sturdy and handsome, smiled from the black-and-white photo glued to the identification page. Natalya had managed a pout.

"Real diamonds and real rubies," the Russian man said. "I give you for the passports."

"Don't worry." Emmanuel replaced the documents. "I'm not going to take them or the jewelry."

Natalya hovered next to the deck chair, her focus on the ruby-and-diamond-studded ring. She held her hands out for the jewelry the way a spoiled child might demand sweets.

"Not a chance," Emmanuel said, and tucked the goods back into Nicolai's winter coat. He flipped Jolly's notebook to the mermaid illustration and held it up for Nicolai to examine. Natalya poked him on the shoulder and Emmanuel shrugged her off.

"I'm not giving you the ring," he said.

She poked him again, harder. He turned and faced her so she got the full visual effect of his annoyed expression.

"*Nyet,*" he said. "Don't ask me again."

Natalya clutched his hand and dragged him over to the window, where she drummed her knuckles against the glass. She stopped and there was silence. Emmanuel pulled her away from the window. The quiet stretched out.

"Shh . . ." He motioned for her to keep still and checked the backyard through a crack in the heavy curtains. The German shepherd's body lay slack against the wire fence. Its pink tongue dangled from its mouth. Yellow leaves blew across the empty yard and lifted into the air.

Emmanuel shoved the notebook into a jacket pocket

and backed up two steps. Whoever had killed the dog was still out there somewhere. Exodus and the car were at the front. He moved to the deck chair and leaned in close to Nicolai.

"Can you move?" he said.

"No. I not leave here. They kill me."

"Someone's already killed the dog," Emmanuel said. "We have to leave this place. Now."

The emotion in Nicolai's pale green eyes was pure and animal. Emmanuel had seen it in the faces of soldiers in battle and knew that others had seen it in him, too. It was the fear of death.

"Go, Natalya." The Russian man pushed himself out of the deck chair. "I will follow."

The sound of a boot kicking at the back entrance echoed through the house. Natalya opened the front door and ran between the ridiculous ceramic statues with lumbering grace. Nicolai followed with a limping stride that rocked his wide shoulders from side to side.

"Move!" Emmanuel urged them on from the rear. They passed a statue of a yellow-eyed wolf cub by the gate. A few feet more and they made it to the parked DeSoto. Exodus spun around at the sound of the passenger door opening and watched the burly man dripping with sweat slide across the leather.

"Start the car," Emmanuel said. "Now."

The engine turned over. Natalya was no longer at the passenger door. She was running back to the house, blond hair flying in the breeze. Emmanuel went after her.

"What is going on?" Exodus called out from the car window.

"Keep the motor running," Emmanuel shouted, and sprinted back to the shabby building. Natalya was inside, dragging the polished leather suitcase across the floor. The wood panels of the back door splintered against the crate of empty bottles pushed against it.

"Jesus Christ." Emmanuel snatched the suitcase. He wasn't going to die for a handful of old photographs and Grandma's brooch. Inevitably people ran into danger for their memories.

"Run, Natalya."

She took off and Emmanuel followed. The case was heavy and halved his speed. The back door gave way and the crate of empty vodka bottles toppled over with a smash. Boots crunched the shards of broken glass littering the kitchen floor. There was a heavy thud, the impact of flesh meeting a hard surface and then a groan.

Emmanuel gained ground. Nobody followed. Exodus had turned the car to face the dirt road. The leather suitcase thumped into the back of the DeSoto next to Natalya and Nicolai.

"Go, go, go." Emmanuel clambered into the front seat and slammed the passenger door closed. The car accelerated and the tires kicked up dirt. Bushes scratched against the doors and the passenger-side mirror exploded. Chrome and glass flew into the air. Natalya screamed. A second bullet went wide and hit the feathery tops of a flowering reed bed.

Emmanuel peered through the dust cloud trailing them. There was a flash of white skin and a dark suit. It was impossible to make any kind of identification. Natalya was doubled over, with her hands jammed over her ears, but Nicolai held himself upright, cool under fire.

"Come on. Come on, girl." Exodus shifted the gears and stamped on the accelerator till the DeSoto's six-cylinder engine roared. The car fishtailed onto the main road doing fifty. A big black Dodge with a dent in the front grille was pulled over to the side with its bonnet open. There was no driver or annoyed passenger near the vehicle. No one had walked the dirt road to ask for help.

"That's his car," Emmanuel said. "He parked it up here and worked his way around to the back of the house."

"And who is he?" The gunshots had stripped Exodus of his charm and exposed the man himself: angry enough to chew iron nails.

"I don't know," Emmanuel said.

The fake mechanical breakdown, the silent disposal of the dog and the rear boundary attack were the marks of a professional killer. That word, *professional,* had come up at the scene of Jolly's murder. Neither Brother Jonah nor Joe Flowers seemed to fit that description. The pale-skinned tradesman, however, fitted it perfectly.

That suspicion didn't make the situation any clearer. There was no logical reason for the tradesman to tail him. One good thing had come from the ambush. He wasn't paranoid. He was being followed. That was a small consolation.

"Should have known . . ." Exodus muttered, and overtook a rambling family sedan on a blind corner. "You look like trouble. But I think, No, he is okay, this one. He has the nice clothes and he has the money. Big, big mistake."

The sedan blasted its horn but Exodus didn't ease up. He stayed bent over the wheel with the accelerator pedal jammed to the floor. Vegetation flew past the windows in a smudge of green.

"Try to get us to town alive," Emmanuel said.

"My side mirror is gone," Exodus said. "Now we are running like dogs. Why is this, Mr. Emmanuel?"

Emmanuel couldn't offer an explanation.

They turned into the settlement of Fynnlands and the speedometer dropped to sixty. There was no sign of the black Dodge. It was too early to be relieved. They had to get off the Bluff and disappear into the back streets of Durban.

The DeSoto rumbled over the bridge and cruised past the mangrove swamp, then plunged between the redbrick warehouses and factories along Edwin Swales Drive.

"We have to get off the main road," Emmanuel said. Taking the major link road back to the town center would be too easy a trail for the shooter to follow.

"You're going back to the passenger wharf." Exodus was adamant. "What you and your friends do after that is your own business. "

"Think," Emmanuel said. "How did the driver of the black Dodge find us? Did he just take a lucky guess or did he follow us from the passenger wharf?"

"*Masende!*" Exodus used the Zulu word for testicles and hit the steering wheel with a fist.

"Exactly," Emmanuel said.

The Basotho driver turned left and headed for the suburban streets of Congella. Three pretty white girls in flowered cotton shifts and scuffed shoes played hopscotch on the pavement. They watched the DeSoto's progress with curiosity. Later, if the driver of the Dodge stopped and asked the girls if they'd seen a nice car with silver trim, they'd say, *The one with the kaffir and the white man sitting next to each other? That one?*

"Sunday-driver slow," Emmanuel said. "We don't want to attract attention."

"Then you must get in the backseat like a proper baas. These white people, they don't like a black man to drive for himself. We must only walk or ride bicycles."

The DeSoto's speed dropped to thirty miles per hour and they cruised through the sleepy Sunday streets. Cloud shadows scudded across the red-tiled roofs and darkened the slender fronds of the royal palm trees on the roadside.

"Who gave you the mermaid picture that I showed you at the passenger quay?" Emmanuel said. It would be just his luck to have rescued a Russian couple with no connection to Jolly Marks.

"The big man. He and the girl, they came together with the picture and the address for the house in the bush."

"Thursday night?"

"Yes."

"What time?"

"Maybe just before midnight. I was outside the Seafarers Club. Three pounds to drive to the Bluff." Exodus laughed without humor. "The money was too, too good. Now I see why."

"They had a suitcase," Emmanuel said. "That should have told you something strange was going on."

"The girl is ripe and the man was in a big hurry." A long pause was followed by a rush into speech. "I thought maybe the man wanted to stay at the house so he could have fun before the baby came."

"I see."

A simple explanation for the trip had not even occurred to Exodus. That was what working outside of the confines of polite society did: it blunted the idea of normal and sometimes destroyed it. Emmanuel wondered if he too had pushed his ex-wife, Angela, too far and asked her for things that were common in the world of soldiers and police detectives but unacceptable in a "decent" marriage.

"Chasing the money. Always chasing the money." Exodus was rueful. "That is where I'm at fault, Emmanuel."

"Did you see Jolly Marks that night?" His failure as a husband was fodder for a late-night drinking session sometime in the future.

The DeSoto's speedometer needle dropped to fifteen and two coloured boys on bicycles flew by. Exodus's dark hands gripped the wheel hard and his knuckles turned white under the pressure.

"A bad thing has happened to that boy," he said, and sucked air into his mouth like a rugby player who'd just been tackled and had the wind knocked out of his lungs. "That is why you are asking these questions."

"Jolly was killed in the freight yards on Thursday night somewhere between eleven p.m. and one in the morning." Emmanuel guessed at the times. The details of the coroner's report would never be made available to him.

"Ayyyee . . ." Exodus made a sound that combined both helplessness and despair. It was a uniquely South African expression of grief. "Who would do this thing?"

Exodus was visibly shaken and Emmanuel's gut feeling about him solidified. Exodus was an ambitious black man who loved money, American cars and nice clothes, but he was no killer.

"Could one of your clients with unusual tastes be involved?" Emmanuel said.

Exodus shook his head. "I do not touch that kind of business. The backroom fights, yes. The card games, yes. The man who wishes to lie with a man or a woman of any color, this I also do. Blood and children together I do not do."

Emmanuel circled back to the first question. "Did you see Jolly that night?"

"No," Exodus answered without hesitation. "Business, it was slow until this man came with the piece of paper with the address. I took the money and drove to the house. No problems."

"And after?"

"I went home to my mother's sister's house in Cato Manor. On Friday morning I drove three girls to a party at a sugar mill outside Stanger."

"A two-day party?" Emmanuel said. This was a chance for Exodus to get the events of the last few days straight. Only a watertight chronology would satisfy the Detective Branch if they tracked down the Flying Dutchman.

"The men were having a party, but the girls, they were working. You understand?"

"Yeah, I understand."

This backed up what Khan had said about Exodus being out of town until Sunday. The Indian criminal knew what he was talking about. Emmanuel filed the fact away for future reference.

A hard metal click came from the rear seat and Emmanuel swiveled around to check on the Russian couple. Natalya had opened the lid of the suitcase and removed a hip flask and a small gold box. She picked four red tablets from the box and fed them into Nicolai's mouth.

"What are those?" Emmanuel said.

"Pain." Nicolai took a gulp from the flask that Natalya pressed to his lips and swallowed the pills.

Emmanuel leaned into the passenger compartment, determined to extract some information from the Russian man before the drugs took effect. "Who's trying to hurt you, Nicolai?"

"Many people."

"Why?"

"Because I am Nicolai Andrei Petrov."

"What does that mean?"

"I was not supposed to leave." The Russian leaned back in the seat and his eyes closed. "Now they will find me and make me go back."

"Who are they?" Emmanuel said, but got no response.

Natalya stroked her husband's wiry beard and laid her head on his broad shoulder. The couple rested in the way that soldiers rest after the fight. Emmanuel backed off. Many nights in the winter fields of Europe he had longed for the comfort of sleep himself. When they arrived at Château la Mer, he'd let Nicolai and Natalya have an hour of dreams. He couldn't afford to give them any more time than that.

"Where must I go to?" Exodus said.

"Willowvale Road in Glenwood," Emmanuel said.

15

HÉLÈNE GERARD SAT in the shade of the veranda and cradled a full glass of red wine. She wore a bright orange cocktail dress with a full skirt but no shoes. The DeSoto pulled into the drive and the Frenchwoman stood up and approached the stairs, smile at the ready.

"Detective Cooper, welcome back." She waved at the odd assortment of passengers in the fancy car. "I see you've brought some friends with you. Will they be staying?"

The tip of Hélène's nose was red and the skin around her eyes was puffed and swollen, the result of an afternoon of heavy drinking interspersed with tears. The brightly colored dress and the bare feet, resort wear for carefree days, had not chased the Sunday blues away.

"We'll be staying for a while," Emmanuel said, and opened the passenger door. He offered Natalya a hand but she ignored it and struggled out of the DeSoto. She massaged the small of her back and swore in Russian: a modern-day Eve, cursed with the nurturing of male seed and the bearing of children.

"This is Natalya," Emmanuel said. "She doesn't speak English but she might like a meal and a bath."

"Yes, of course." Hélène navigated the stairs from the porch to the car slowly, hands gripping the railing for balance. "I'll make sure she has everything she needs, Detective Cooper."

"Thanks."

Emmanuel watched the drunken Frenchwoman and the pregnant Russian climb the stairs to La Mer like invalid companions on an excursion. Hélène hesitated at the front door.

"You'll tell the major?" she said.

"Of course."

One day soon, Emmanuel figured, the mystery of the sad French Mauritian woman and her absent husband was going to be solved.

"Thank you, Detective."

Hélène mimed the actions for washing hair and eating while she led Natalya into the house. Emmanuel leaned into the passenger compartment of the DeSoto and discovered Nicolai slumped against the leather. The whites of his eyes showed between half-closed lids and a faint heartbeat pulsed at the base of his neck.

"Nicolai." Emmanuel slid into the car and tapped a bristled cheek. "Nicolai. Are you awake?"

"Tired," Nicolai mumbled. "I sleep, yes?"

"Not yet," Emmanuel said. "Soon."

The big man struggled to sit up but did not have the strength to shift his large frame off the seat. Blue smudges darkened the skin under his eyes.

"Lie back," Emmanuel said, and the Russian collapsed

into the folds of his winter coat. The painkillers might have had barbiturates in them. It hardly mattered. Pills or not, Nicolai was too weak to help the investigation for a few more hours. The run of bad luck continued. He dumped the leather suitcase on the bottom stair.

"Give me a hand," Emmanuel said to Exodus. "We have to get Nicolai into bed. I'll take his shoulders. You take his legs."

Exodus left the sanctuary of the DeSoto reluctantly. Mixing in white people's business was part of the job, but this situation was more complicated than dropping a man off at a hush-hush multiracial brothel or setting up a private poker game.

Emmanuel pushed Nicolai across the seat and together with Exodus maneuvered the Russian up the stairs and into La Mer. The interior of the house was dark and cool. A teakettle whistled in the kitchen. They carted Nicolai to Emmanuel's room and put him into the Provençal-style bed, where his solid body made a trench in the goose-down quilt.

"I must go," Exodus said, and backed out of the room quickly. He kept his gaze to the cypress pine floorboards so that it was clear to Emmanuel and to anyone else that while he had been in the house, he had not seen anything.

"Do you have any friends or relatives outside of Durban?" Emmanuel asked when the Basotho man had shuffled out onto the veranda.

"My father's brother is in Port Elizabeth."

"Stay with him for a few days." The police would stop searching for the Flying Dutchman the minute van Niekerk's forty-eight-hour deal expired.

"I will go straightaway." Exodus ran down the front stairs and unlocked the DeSoto's giant boot. He stowed the handsome fedora in a round hatbox and then pulled out the workman's overalls, which he slipped over the green suit and buttoned to the throat. The transformation from a worldly black man into a common servant had the quality of a magic trick. Then he lifted the carpet on the boot floor and removed a piece of folded paper, an exercise book and a pen.

"What's that for?" Emmanuel asked.

"A travel pass and a permission slip from the baas to say it is okay to drive his car to Port Elizabeth."

"What baas?"

"You." Exodus brought the pen and the notebook to Emmanuel and handed them over.

Port Elizabeth was seventy miles down the coast, but natives were not free to travel from one town to another without official consent from the government and their employer. A black man in a nice car was an invitation to the police to conduct a stop-and-search.

"What must I write?" Emmanuel said.

Exodus dictated. " 'This boy works for me. He is a good boy and a good driver. He is going to Port Elizabeth to do work for me. Please let him pass.' Sign your name at the bottom."

Emmanuel wrote the note word for word. He felt an embarrassment that had lain almost dormant since childhood. Nine years old, working part-time at the local garage, he was given the job of signing the weekend leave slips for the four Sotho petrol pump attendants: grown men with wives and children and gray hair sprinkled among the black, allowed to go home on the authority of a white child still in short pants.

"Much thanks." Exodus shoved the note into the work overalls and got into the car. He started the engine and reversed out of La Mer's driveway, an adult man armed with written permission to travel over land once owned by his own people.

The black Dutchman disappeared and Emmanuel leaned against the porch railing of La Mer. Twenty-five hours into the investigation, and he was no closer to knowing who had killed Jolly Marks or Mrs. Patterson and Mbali the maid. The list of suspects wasn't even a list, it was just a pair of names. Joe Flowers and Brother Jonah. Without the help of the Detective Branch and the foot police, identifying the driver of the black Dodge would be nearly impossible.

Emmanuel stretched the tension out of his neck and stared down at the sparkling white town below him. The pretty houses and colorful flower beds were ordered and peaceful. He knew from experience that perception and reality often had nothing in common.

—

A pain that could not be cured by morphine or any other drug pressed against Emmanuel's skull. The sergeant major's voice would come soon, spitting and swearing. Expect pain. Accept pain. Peace comes after the fight, not before. He decided to surrender.

"When you're ready," he said, "I'll listen."

The voice remained silent.

A light shone from the front window of Sister Anne's flat. Her father had been wheeled in for the night. The plan of attack was simple. He would enter the bedroom via the back window and catch Anne and Joe by surprise. If the window was locked, he'd kick down the front door and try his luck. Emmanuel threw the Walther PPK into the Buick's glove box.

Introduce a gun, and a simple plan split into a dozen new scenarios that mostly involved blood and a free ride in the back of a caged police van.

The wind had picked up and brought with it the smells of diesel and salt. Jolly's little sister emerged from the building and sat on the top step with her baby doll wrapped in a rag quilt. The night settled around her, and strands of hair lifted from her shoulders in the wind. Emmanuel locked the Buick, climbed the stairs and sat down next to the girl. The aroma of fried onions drifted from the hallway.

"It's late. What are you doing out here?" he said.

"Baby can't sleep. It's too quiet inside and she likes to watch the lighthouse blinking."

The intermittent flash of yellow from the Bluff lighthouse danced across the harbor but didn't reach the shore.

"Do you remember who I am?"

"You're a policeman." She rocked the baby doll back and forth in the cradle of her arms.

"That's right. I talked to you the other day," he said. "Do you know the girl Anne who lives above you?"

"*Ja.* Anne has kittens."

"Have you seen her tonight?"

"She took her pa inside. He was coughing."

"Is she at home, do you think?"

Susannah lifted the doll to a shoulder and stroked its spine with a tenderness that forced Emmanuel to look away. Old memories resurfaced. A fresh grave marked by a baby's rattle instead of a cross. Women crouched in the rubble with their children held close even though their own bodies were no protection against bombs or bullets. He'd seen prams ushered through decimated towns by hollow-eyed females dressed in tatters. In war, women protected life as though it were a tiny flame in the wind.

"She's fixing a stew for Joe," Susannah said. "He's got a big head, like Punch and Judy."

"Joe? Are you sure?"

She reached into the folds of the rag quilt and withdrew a coin. "Joe gave me a penny when he came through the back-yard. He said I must buy sweets with it."

"Was Anne waiting for him?"

"*Ja*. She let him into her window and then she asked my ma for some onions." Susannah pulled a second coin from the dirty bundle. "Anne gave me this one. If any of the police come, I must run and tell her quick."

"I'm a policeman. Why didn't you run and tell her?"

"Baby will wake up if I move. When baby's asleep, I'll go tell."

Running Joe down would not be easy. He was big and fast and he knew the neighborhood. Catching him by surprise was the trick.

"*A commander uses the weapons at hand, soldier,*" the Scottish sergeant major said. "*The girl is old enough to do the job. Send her into the field.*"

Susannah hummed a lullaby and Emmanuel rubbed the back of his neck where the neat razor cut of his hair met the skin. He was off his dial. He still took orders from a voice in his head eight years after being demobbed from the army. To-night, that seemed to make a kind of sense.

"How high can you count to, Susannah?"

"One hundred and forty-three. Jolly taught me."

That would give him enough time to make it into the backyard via the gate that led to the back lane. It might work.

"Will baby be asleep by the time you count to one hundred and forty-three, do you think?"

"Maybe," Susannah said. "She has bad dreams that come in through the windows. Maybe she'll drop off at one hundred and ten. That's her favorite number."

"When baby's asleep, will you knock on Anne's door and tell her the police are out the front?"

"*Ja.*"

"Good," Emmanuel said. "Remember, the police are at the front. Not the back or the side. At the front."

That should push Flowers through the fire escape window and into the yard. The yellow door he'd seen from Anne and her father's bedroom led to a disused back lane. Joe would likely exit through there.

"Shh . . ." Susannah whispered. "Her eyes are closing."

"Tell Anne and go back inside," he said. The port at night was no playground. "Okay?"

The girl nodded and Emmanuel sprinted to the corner. He checked over his shoulder. Susannah was on her feet, gently rocking the sleeping doll in her arms like a tiny Madonna. Shoulder-wide alleys that ran between the buildings offered the quickest way to the back. Emmanuel squeezed into the first one and worked around crumbling drainpipes and piles of rusty cans thrown out from kitchen windows on the upper floors. He prayed Susannah was slow up the stairs or he was going to miss Joe Flowers altogether.

The narrow back lane ran parallel to the road, with the rear of the blocks of flats on either side of it. A yellow square marked the gate that led into the yard of Jolly Marks's former home. Emmanuel moved in. Footsteps clanged on the fire escape. He and Joe were going to arrive at the gate at roughly the same time.

"Attack is the best form of defense, soldier," the sergeant major growled. *"Lay him flat."*

The yellow gate creaked open and Emmanuel crashed into it with his shoulder. The wood swung inward and met Joe coming out. The prison escapee fell back, winded. Emmanuel held him down on the dirty concrete slab under the washing lines. A window opened and a man in a grubby undershirt leaned out, a hand-rolled cigarette pinched into the corner of his mouth.

"What the hell is going on? I'll get the police on to the two of you. Now piss off."

"I am the police," Emmanuel said, and the man withdrew and shut the window behind him. The metal scrape of curtains closing sounded across the yard as the inhabitants of the slum dwelling shut the trouble out of their lives.

"Got any weapons on you?" Emmanuel patted Joe down. "A knife or maybe a gun?"

"Nothing," Joe gasped.

Emmanuel checked the suit pockets and dug out a packet of loose tobacco, rolling papers and a stub for admission to *A Woman's Face*, an MGM movie on continuous show at the Oxford Cinema from nine a.m. to ten p.m. The cinema tearooms were the perfect hiding place for criminals and recalcitrant schoolboys. And the ticket included a cup of hot tea and a biscuit at intermission.

"Tell me about Jolly Marks," Emmanuel said.

"Don't know him."

Emmanuel knocked Joe's box head against the concrete. It thumped like a watermelon tumbling off a fruit cart.

"Jolly was a member of the Zion Church. He lived across the hall from one of your special sisters. You knew him. Don't lie to me. "

"Oh . . . him."

"*Ja*. Him."

"Haven't seen him. Honest."

Emmanuel thumped Joe's head again. "When was the last time you saw him?"

"Back then." Joe groaned. "Before I went to Durban Central."

"You sure about that?"

"*Ja*. Why are you asking me about that kid? He wasn't right in the head, that one. Him and his sister both."

"Stay away from his sister." Emmanuel pressed Joe's muscular body into the hard concrete till air wheezed from his lungs. "Stay away from the girl or I will hunt you down. Do you understand?"

"Can't breathe . . ." Joe gasped, and Emmanuel eased off. With the sergeant major riding shotgun, inflicting harm would be easy, even enjoyable. That was what he had to guard against: the deliberate step into darkness.

"You get off my Joe." The fire escape stairs rattled and Anne leaned her bony elbows onto the railing. "He came out of Durban Central to take care of his ma. She's sick."

"You don't look like his mother," Emmanuel said.

"And you look like you enjoy having Joe under you like that. I knowed you was funny when I seen that fancy suit."

"Shut up and go back inside, Anne."

"He's my man," she said. "I stay with him."

Such bravado in defense of a thieving pimp. The gift of the perfume had done its job.

"Suit yourself," Emmanuel said. "If you come down here, you'll be interfering with police business and then you and Joe can cozy up in the back of a van—all the way to the cells."

Anne remained silent. For a moment, she was the tough heroine of an imaginary film but without the benefit of good lighting and makeup.

Emmanuel returned to Joe. "Where have you been since leaving Durban Central? Hanging around the docks at night?"

"No ways," Joe said. "There's police everywhere. I've been with my ma."

"Don't forget shopping. That's nice stuff you got for her. A gas stove, sugar, apples. Where did those things come from?"

"I found them."

"*Bullshit,*" the sergeant major spat. "*Put the pain on and this fucker will talk. Open him up.*"

"You found them?" Emmanuel worked his knee into the small of Joe's back. "Tell me where."

"Okay. Okay. I got a friend; he works on the port railway. He got them for me. Off the back of a freight car."

"For free? That's a good friend."

"I exchange things," Joe said.

"What things?"

"Things. Things my friend wants."

"Like what?"

Joe motioned in Anne's direction and Emmanuel lifted the pressure. The bony girl was too young to understand the difference between being used and being loved. Maybe her whole life would follow that pattern: poor, underfed and uneducated, always in search of a man to fill the empty spaces inside her.

The smell of burned onions and meat drifted out of an open window.

"You better take care of that stew," Emmanuel said. "Unless you want to burn the place down."

Anne jumped up and climbed back through the window. A woman should stand by her man, but life kept happening. Dirty dishes had to be washed, the laundry folded and the cats fed. The window closed.

Emmanuel lifted Joe, settled him against the fence and looked into his broad face. "Was Jolly Marks part of your exchange scheme?"

"No. No ways. Never."

"I told you not to lie."

"I ain't lying. That kid was strange. The whole family is strange. Not my cup of tea."

"Where were you on Thursday night? That was your first night out."

"With my ma. I went to see her, first thing." Joe's throat muscles constricted and a tear rolled from the corner of his eye. "The clinic hasn't got medicine and she's not doing so good—"

"Stop," Emmanuel said. "Stop."

There was no space in his head for a sentimental criminal who exchanged his girlfriend's body for apples and sugar and boxes of candles.

"It was your first night out," he said. "Shut in prison for months. You expect me to believe that you didn't come straight down to the harbor to look for some fun?"

"I would have," Joe admitted. "But I didn't have money."

"You don't need money. Your sisters earn it for you."

"*Ja*, but all the good earners are gone. All that's left is her upstairs, and she has to look after her pa most of the time."

Emmanuel said, "Did you see Jolly Marks that night?"

"Why do you keep asking me about him?"

"Jolly Marks was murdered the night you escaped from Durban Central. His body was dumped in the shunting yard. What do you know about that?"

Joe tried to scramble to the gate but Emmanuel pushed him down. The light leaking from the windows of the flats was sufficient to illuminate Joe's jug face. Unadulterated fear and disbelief glittered in his hazel eyes.

"You going to hang a murder on me?" Joe said. "Of a kid? No way."

"I asked you if you saw Jolly that night. You still haven't answered yes or no."

"No. No. No. I never saw him and I never spoke to him. Beat me if you want, but I ain't going to sign a paper that says I killed a kid. I've done plenty wrong, but murder? No way. "

"Have you ever been to the Dover apartments on Linze Road in Stamford Hill?"

"Why would I go there?"

"Answer the question."

"How the hell would I get there?"

"You drove," Emmanuel said. "In the big black Dodge with the silver trim."

"What?" Joe's forehead crumpled into deep furrows. "I don't know what you've got me lined up for, but I'm not signing. You and your friends can bounce me around the cells all night. All day, even. I'm not going to clear a murder off your books just because you can't find who really did it."

To load an unsolved crime onto a suspect already in custody, one with a list of previous convictions, was the oldest trick in the unofficial policing manual. The national government's rollout of regular "crime drives" demanded that the police make visible progress in the direction of a safer, cleaner, whiter world.

The sergeant major said, *"What friends? He said, 'You and your friends...' "*

Twin shadows elongated across the back fence: one was broad-shouldered, with a hand resting against the clip of his service revolver, the other slim and unobtrusive.

"Take it easy, Joe," a male voice said. "We won't let him pin those murders on you. We already know who did them, don't we, Cooper?"

"Christ above," the sergeant major said. *"These fuckers must have had an eye on the building and seen you come in. Don't let them give you any shit."*

"Detective Head Constable Robinson and Detective Constable Fletcher." Emmanuel got to his feet. "I thought you'd be in town arresting flashers and patriotic drunks. You could beef up your arrest numbers by rounding up a couple of natives who slipped into town without their passbooks."

"Joe Flowers's apprehension will cover us for a month or two," Detective Constable Fletcher said. "Your arrest is going to make us golden till the end of the year."

"My arrest?" The van Niekerk deal had twenty hours to run. He should be in the clear.

"When the time comes," Robinson said, "the major and his friend won't be able to protect you. They'll cut you loose and we'll be ready and waiting. You'll swing for those murders."

"Up you get, Joe." Fletcher unclipped a pair of steel handcuffs from his belt. "Time to go back to Central."

Joe sprang to his feet and made a run for the gate. Fletcher caught him by the shirt collar and jerked him back like a fish on the end of a line.

"My ma." Joe tried to twist free. "I got to take care of my ma. She's sickly."

"Should have thought about that before you stabbed those chaps in the pub." Fletcher twisted Joe's arms and snapped the cuffs on. "Your ma can come see you on visitors' day."

"The black Dodge," Emmanuel said to Joe. "Tell me where you got it from."

"What am I going to do with a car? I got no license. I—"

"Shut your mouth, Flowers." Fletcher shook Joe with bone-rattling force, then said, "This man is our prisoner, Cooper. You are not entitled to question him."

Robinson grabbed Joe Flowers by the shoulder and spun him to face the flats. "Stay here, Fletcher. You should have a talk with Mr. Cooper."

Emmanuel calculated the distance to the exit. Too far to sprint. Same for the fire escape stairs. He was squeezed between the heavyweight detective and the building. No help there.

"My ma . . ." Joe called out a last request. "You tell Miss Morgensen from the Zion to take care of my ma. You hear me?"

"I'll tell her," Emmanuel said. He knew what it was like to

lose a mother. Robinson pushed Joe through the back door of the flats and paused to give Fletcher the go-ahead nod.

"Shhh . . ." The sound came from a corner of the yard. Jolly's little sister, Susannah, and her china-faced baby doll huddled in the semi-gloom. Her dark outline rocked back and forth in an attempt to find a rhythm that would bring both her and the blue-eyed baby peace. Emmanuel turned to the girl and Fletcher's fist came in a blur. His head snapped back with the force of the blow and his body briefly experienced the sensation of flight. He gained altitude and flew back to meet the hard wood palings of the fence. The pressure in his head receded. This was real pain: hot and sharp and to the bone.

Emmanuel slumped to the ground and the rear door to the flats swung shut behind Joe Flowers and Robinson. Robinson condoned violence, but he didn't want to be a witness to it. By leaving Fletcher to inflict the pain, he thought he stood above the dirty work.

"Joe's ma wasn't always a sick old lady. She was a brothel keeper back in the old days." Fletcher strolled over to the row of overflowing garbage cans. "She made a fortune during the war with all the military boys sailing in and out of Durban. She gave discounts for first-timers and suddenly the whole British fleet were virgins." He pulled a lid free. "She lost it all to a con man who said he was an Irish baron. He promised her a castle and a title and a fountain of Guinness beer bubbling in the garden."

Fletcher's continued banter suggested they were two friends who'd bumped into each other accidentally in a darkened yard that smelled of rotten fish.

"Sad story," Emmanuel said. Every criminal had one. He struggled to a sitting position. Fletcher whipped the tin lid through the air and smashed it against the back fence. The wood shuddered and flexed. Emmanuel got to his feet. The next swing was coming at his head.

"Very sad . . ." Fletcher hit the lid against the steel post of the wash line and the metal screamed. "The noise is so Detective Head Constable Robinson thinks I beat the crap out of you. The only reason I used the pole instead of your face is because Major van Niekerk said to keep hands off. "

"*Hands off?*" the sergeant major said. "*That's a joke. He hit you like a sledgehammer.*"

"Very kind of you." Emmanuel wiped blood from his cheek. "I obviously misjudged you, Fletcher. Bet you like the ballet as well."

"No, that's the major you're thinking about. He's got season tickets to the playhouse. Shakespeare and all that. I like the horse races and the fights. You?"

"I like the fights, too," Emmanuel said. "Saw Joe Louis box an exhibition match in Europe during the war. Are we friends now, Fletcher?"

"We're friends till the major tells me different."

"You let an Afrikaner tell you who to be pals with?" Emmanuel said. It was a low shot, to be sure, but worth taking. The skin on his cheek was cut and beginning to swell.

Fletcher shrugged. "It's better to have powerful friends than powerful enemies. Doesn't matter if they're English or Afrikaner."

Despite appearances, Fletcher was not thick. He'd worked out that van Niekerk's coattails were worth hanging on to.

"And when the major says to take the gloves off?"

"I'm going to make sure you land arse-first onto the street."

"You can try," Emmanuel said.

Fletcher's grasp far outweighed his reach. The major had other police detectives who could drive and punch a bag on the payroll. Fletcher had no idea he was expendable.

"I'll give your regards to van Niekerk," the heavyweight detective said, and patted Emmanuel on the cheek with a callused palm.

"Tell him if he touches you again, you will break his fucking arm," the sergeant major breathed.

"What did you say?" Fletcher's hand dropped.

"Touch me again and I'll break your fucking arm."

"Huh." Fletcher laughed. "You couldn't break my little finger, but you'd still try, wouldn't you, Cooper? I got to admire that in a man."

"Pointless bravery?"

The dented angles of Fletcher's face showed that he believed broken ribs and cut lips were a badge of manhood.

"Bravery is never pointless," Fletcher said. "A man's got to stand up and be a man or else take up knitting."

Emmanuel knew plenty of men who'd joined the army with heroic visions and then found out the biblical truth of the battlefield: that all flesh is as grass to be cut down and wither away.

"Have you been following me all day, Fletcher?" A car and a handgun were tools of the police trade, easily picked up by two members of the Detective Branch. Either Fletcher or Robinson, both in the standard dark suits favored by plainclothes detectives, could have been the figure lurking on the street corner this afternoon.

"Nah. Got lucky," Fletcher said. "We passed around a hat at the station for Jolly's ma, to help out with funeral costs. Saw you and the old lady leave when we came to drop off the donation and decided to stake the place out."

"Stuck in the car all day," Emmanuel said. "Hell of a way to spend a Sunday."

"Got lucky a second time. Robinson had to take his little girl to a princess tea party, so we came back after sunset. Bingo. There you were, sitting on the steps like a fucking welfare worker."

Emmanuel checked Susannah. Her eyes were shut tight and the baby doll was clutched in her arms.

"Third lightning strike with Joe," Emmanuel said. This explained the run of dead ends that had come his way in the last two days. Fletcher and Robinson had stolen his luck.

"Thanks for Joe." Fletcher winked. "My name is going to look good in the newspaper."

"Don't forget the free drinks," Emmanuel said. "Dangerous prisoner apprehended. The public loves a hero."

The heavyweight detective's battered face lost its friendly expression. "Arse out on the street," he said. "With a mouthful of gravel."

"If the hangman doesn't get me first," Emmanuel said, and Fletcher grinned.

—

Emmanuel bent over to retrieve the scattered contents of Joe Flowers's pockets and the yard tilted. He sat cross-legged and waited for the fog to clear. Susannah tiptoed to his side and knelt on the cracked cement. The baby doll had evidently fallen asleep and she held it still. Emmanuel collected the rolling tobacco and the ripped bioscope ticket stamped with today's date. Joe had spent the afternoon in the dark, smoking hand-rolled cigarettes and watching Joan Crawford chew the scenery as a scarred Swedish beauty with revenge on her mind.

Emmanuel examined the tobacco. It was rough-cut and cheap, with not a hint of chocolate or honey. There never had been much sense to be found in the idea that Joe was the killer or the shooter on the Bluff, but the possibility had been something like a lucky rabbit's foot.

"Did you ever see Joe drive a car?" he asked Susannah.

"No, he doesn't have a car. Not even a bicycle. He runs good, though."

"That he does," Emmanuel said.

Joe's stable of sisters was down to one, so even a bicycle would be luxury transport. And there was the little matter of a lack of a driver's license, which was no bar to Joe actually driving but added another layer of improbability. Three days on the run and Joe's main concern had been his sick mother.

"Is Joe going to eat the stew Anne made for him?"

"Not tonight," Emmanuel said.

"Has Joe gone back to jail?"

"Yes, he has."

"That's where my pa is," Susannah said. "Do you have a ma and pa?"

"No."

"A sister?"

"Yes, but she's not here in Durban."

"Has she gone away like Jolly?"

"Something like that."

16

A SLEEPY NIGHT WATCHMAN in a knee-length wool coat and fingerless gloves waved Emmanuel through the gates and onto the gravel driveway of van Niekerk's house on the Berea Ridge. Fruit bats circled overhead and the coronation lights lit up the city center. He parked in front of the two-story Victorian building and considered his next move. Coming empty-handed to van Niekerk's door was not a pleasant feeling.

Joe Flowers, who possessed neither a knife nor a car nor indeed sufficient levels of cunning to commit three murders, was off the list of suspects. And a quick drive through the Point had failed to locate Brother Jonah, the sole person left to investigate. All Emmanuel had was a Russian couple who'd presented Jolly Marks's drawing to the Dutchman. He pulled the Walther from the glove box and rested it on his lap. The Cyrillic letters engraved in the metal might provide an explanation as to why the Russians were being hunted by a man driving a black Dodge. He pressed his fingers into the side of his skull. The spare morphine pill would be useful right now.

"*Are you going to sit there stroking your gun all night, Cooper, or are you going to go and tell the major that Flowers was a dead end? Maybe he has a fresh lead for you to chase up or maybe he can extend the deadline,*" the sergeant major said. "*You've got fuck-all to lose. Joe's in Central. Brother Jonah is AWOL. Exodus has fucked off to Port Elizabeth and the Russian is lights-out. As for the pregnant woman . . . well, take it from me . . . even if she could speak English, you do not want to disturb her sleep if you want children of your own down the track. Now get in there and ask for help.*"

"Don't breathe a word while I'm in there," Emmanuel said, and slid out of the Buick. He locked the car door and tucked the Walther into the waistband of his trousers. Being comfortably crazy was a fact he'd rather keep to himself.

"*Fine,*" the sergeant major said. "*I'll keep a lid on, but I'm not going to wait for permission to save your arse when the time comes. I'm a soldier, not a bloody nursemaid. Have we got a deal?*"

"Yes. We have."

Emmanuel took the veranda steps two at a time and pressed hard on the bell. A velvet Nat King Cole recording crooned into the night. Imagining the Dutch major sucking on a pipe while enjoying a mellow tune lifted Emmanuel's mood. The door opened and Lana Rose peered out through a curtain of cigarette smoke.

"Oh, it's you," she said.

"I've come to see the major," Emmanuel said. It was a shock to see her half dressed in van Niekerk's house after dark.

"The major's at a coronation party in Durban North. A proper coronation party with roast beef and trifle with claret for dessert. Larnies only. No house models or ex-barmaids allowed."

Larnies was South Africa's unique name for swells, the quality, the upper crust, the cream that rose to the top through good blood and money. Sugar barons, factory owners, judges and doctors, with a handful of London-based actors begged away from the Bulawayo Theatre season in Rhodesia to add dash to the mix.

"The major runs with that crowd?" Emmanuel was surprised. Few Afrikaners made it into the larnie bracket in Durban, the English epicenter of South Africa.

"In five years the major will run that crowd," Lana said. "Him and that toffee-nosed fiancée of his."

That was quick work. In less than six months the major had a fiancée, an on-the-side girlfriend and a clutch of policemen under his influence. Van Niekerk had a plan. He always did.

Lana drew deep on her cigarette and leaned forward, a movement that caused her to sway unsteadily. "You've got a cut on your cheek."

"Rough night," Emmanuel said. "I'll come back tomorrow."

"Don't be stupid. There's ice in the cooler and the major will be home soon."

Emmanuel hesitated, but Lana was already heading in the direction of the lounge room. She wore black satin-heeled shoes, and the hem of her white silk dressing gown swished against her bare legs. He closed the front door. Until Nicolai was rested and well enough to talk, there was nowhere else to go.

"I'll put ice in a serviette. Or I can try and find some"—
Lana searched for the right word—"iodine. That's it. Iodine."

"Ice will do," Emmanuel said, and entered a large room
with two leather couches and a hostess trolley laden with bottles of liquor. A full ashtray and a scatter of imported women's
magazines covered a low coffee table. Gilt-framed landscapes
of the Cape vineyards adorned the walls. Lana tipped a handful of ice into a cotton serviette.

"Sit," she said.

"I'll be fine." Emmanuel took the ice pack and pressed it to
the imprint of Fletcher's fist. Getting comfortable with Lana
Rose on van Niekerk's couch seemed dangerous.

Lana poured whiskey into a tumbler. "Are you in trouble,
Emmanuel?"

"A little," he said.

She offered him the glass and he drained half of it. It was
going to be a long night and, he feared, an unrewarding one.

"What else can you expect when you're one of Major van
Niekerk's boys?" she said. "Trouble comes with the job."

"I'm not one of van Niekerk's boys." He was an ex-soldier
and an ex–detective sergeant who'd fought through France
and brought murderers to justice. Being called a boy stung
more than the cut cheek.

"Of course you're not." Lana ground her cigarette out in
the ashtray and sank onto the couch opposite. "And I'm not
his girl."

This exquisite room was only a few miles from Lana's flat
in Umbilo but separated from it by an ocean of money. If Lana
won a string of trifectas at the July handicap horse races, then
she might end up in a house like this one. In reality, she had

bet herself on the major and won a temporary seat in the winner's circle.

"Okay," Emmanuel said. "I'm van Niekerk's boy and you're his girl."

"And that is why we are both here, waiting for him."

An awkward silence stretched out. The sound of a distant rocket, part of the coronation celebration, echoed across the harbor. Doing nothing while the clock ticked down to arrest and imprisonment on three murder counts was unacceptable. Emmanuel leaned toward Lana, who was massaging a thumb into the arch of her right foot. The satin shoes were for show, not for comfort.

"Are you from Durban?" he asked.

"I was born in Umbilo. The farthest I've been is Pieter-maritzburg." There was regret and impatience with the small-ness of her world.

"Do you know anyone who can read Russian script? I need a Russian sentence translated."

"Are you teasing me, Emmanuel?"

"Teasing you about what?"

Lana's eyes were almost black in the lamplight. "Do you know what it's like having a German mother and a Russian father in Durban? The last outpost of the British Empire? Do you know what it's like to be different here?"

Twelve years of running on the streets of Sophiatown and mixing with the blacks, coloureds and Indians: a "white kaf-fir" in the eyes of other whites. Four years at an Afrikaner boarding school pretending to be one of God's chosen people had done nothing to obliterate the memory of feeling like an outcast.

"Yeah," Emmanuel said. "I know what that's like."

Lana tilted her head and peered at him. She searched his face for proof that he understood. Difference in South Africa meant exclusion. Difference meant that a sense of belonging was always just out of reach. He looked back at her with the eyes of another outsider.

Lana lit a fresh cigarette from a pack that claimed to be the number one choice of doctors and nurses and took a long draw.

"*I* speak Russian," she said. "Just enough to get me out of trouble with drunken sailors and con men claiming to be the last surviving Romanov."

"Can you read the script?"

"A word or two."

So, the icon image in the medicine cabinet wasn't just for decoration. Lana was part Russian. Emmanuel pulled the Walther from the back of his waistband. The safety was on. He kept the gun in his hand but turned it so the text was visible. Lana raised an eyebrow in response.

"You need a gun translated?"

"Yes."

Lana reached for the Walther and Emmanuel held it back. The combination of too much whiskey, too many cigarettes and the major's engagement to a toffee-nosed larnie made her unpredictable.

"The safety is on," she said. "And the major will be back once he's tried to get into his fiancée's panties and failed. Again."

Emmanuel handed over the gun. The personal information about the major's virginal fiancée he could have done without.

Imagining van Niekerk fumbling with buttons and groping for a breast made him human, almost vulnerable, and Emmanuel knew that was a lie.

"Sit down and relax. Finish your drink." Lana threw herself back onto the couch and the silk gown parted to reveal the smooth line of a calf and the curve of a knee. She examined the engraving on the Walther's nickel plate with a frown.

Emmanuel sat on the opposite couch and downed the rest of the drink, eyes to the floor. Skin, silk and the dark cascade of hair over an exposed shoulder were all now out of bounds.

"Well?" he said.

"One of the words is *people,* but the rest is too complicated for me to translate," she confessed. "I do know it's a presentation weapon. A gift. Who does it belong to . . . someone important?"

"Not sure."

Nicolai Petrov was a sick old man with a heavily pregnant wife and two forged American passports. If he had been a hero of the Soviet Union, it wasn't helping him find safety in South Africa.

Emmanuel glanced at Lana, intrigued. "What do you know about presentation firearms?"

"My father collected guns. Mausers, Colts, Brownings and two Nagants engraved with the Russian imperial eagle given to him by Czar Nicholas himself. For meritorious service. That was the story after one bottle of vodka. After two bottles, the Nagant came with a country estate, a dacha and a lake. All lost in the revolution, of course." Lana ran a fingertip over the engraved text. "The owner is Russian?"

"Yes. That I do know."

"And you have his Walther."

"He gave it to me," Emmanuel said.

"A straight blowback-operated semiautomatic with double action, walnut grip and a chrome finish engraved with a personal message. This gun is for keeps."

"Jesus wept! Where does a woman learn such filthy talk?" the sergeant major whispered. *"You could build a skyscraper around the steel beam that's shot up under my kilt."*

Emmanuel brushed a hand over his face to dislodge the brusque Scottish voice. "Okay," he said. "I took the Walther from him."

"And he took it from a German." She pointed to a detail on the metal barrel. "Look."

Emmanuel got up and approached Lana reluctantly. The words *close enough to taste* sprang to mind when he took a seat next to her on the couch. Cigarettes, whiskey, expensive perfume and cordite: the thrilling scent of a bad girl who knew her firearms.

"A German imperial eagle." Lana pointed to the checkered walnut grip. "That's where the Walther stamp would normally be."

The thing about war was that guns changed hands on a regular basis, both voluntarily and involuntarily. They were another spoil traded and smuggled and propped up in display cabinets during peacetime, like postcards from the violent frontier.

"An officer's firearm," Emmanuel said. "Taken from a high-ranking German and given to a Russian after the war."

"But?"

"The man who owns it doesn't strike me as army, navy or air force. And his wife is not military barracks material, either."

"Ask them," Lana said.

"They're out of action for a few hours."

"Tumble their drawers and cupboards and see what you find. People leave all sorts of things lying around in plain view."

That was just the kind of illegal, no-holds-barred approach the Scottish sergeant major advocated.

"No drawers or cupboards to check. But there is one thing. An old suitcase." Natalya had risked her life to retrieve the leather bag from the house on the Bluff.

"Let's check it," Lana said. "Maybe there's something in it that I can make sense of."

"No." Emmanuel stood up quickly. "That's not a good idea."

"Why?"

"The major." That should be explanation enough.

"He's in Durban North sucking gin and tonics."

"You were expecting him."

Lana got to her feet and tucked the Walther into the pocket of her silk dressing gown. "Let him man his own pump for one night. It will do him good."

The manning of the major's pump is a thing for the two of you to sort out. In private and without my help, Emmanuel thought. He motioned for the Walther PPK. "Domestic arrangements aren't my strong point, so I'll be on my way."

"You asked for help, Emmanuel," Lana said, and headed for the door. "Have another drink. I'll be out in five minutes."

"I have eighteen hours to solve a triple murder," Emmanuel said. "Don't drag me into a personal situation with the major. Things are already too complicated."

"Eighteen hours." Lana considered him for a moment. "In that case, I'll be out in two minutes."

He stepped closer to her. This insanity was going to stop now. "This isn't a game. Three people are dead. Find another way to punish van Niekerk for being engaged to a larnie, one that doesn't involve getting in harm's way."

"Do you know what girlfriends and house models do, Emmanuel? They wait and they serve. That's it. Pet goldfish have more exciting lives."

"If you want excitement, take up hunting. This is a criminal case with guns, knives and very bad men."

"That sums up my life so far," she said. "You're twenty-four years too late to protect me from harm, Emmanuel, but it's nice that you tried."

She disappeared into the interior of the house and Emmanuel slumped down on the couch. Stopping Lana would be a snap. She was half drunk. Easy prey. But maybe there was something in the suitcase: a piece of information that could turn the case around.

"Ready?" Lana had changed into a blue cotton dress with a high neckline and a wide skirt that fell well below the knee. A woven straw bag dangled from her wrist, the Walther's new home. Flat walking shoes and a face wiped clean of makeup had transformed her from femme fatale into the hometown sweetheart whom soldiers of every stripe had fought to return to.

It was a sleight of hand.

"Eighteen hours," she said.

17

THE POLISHED LEATHER creaked and the silver locks snapped open at the first push. Clothing toppled out and scattered across the table on Château la Mer's redbrick porch where Hélène Gerard had set them up before disappearing inside. Emmanuel sifted through layers of lined coats, dresses, thick sweaters and cable-knit scarves. Nicolai and his wife had no plans to stay in subtropical Durban.

"German, English and French labels," Lana said. "All a couple of years old, by the look of things."

A small cardboard box with ripped edges was jammed against the bottom of the suitcase. Emmanuel removed the lid. A color image of Natalya in a crisp Red Army uniform glowered from the heavyweight paper. A Nagant rifle was slung over her shoulder and rays of sunshine broke the cloud cover and illuminated golden wheat fields. Woman, lover, soldier, farmer and pinup girl for the revolution. Cyrillic text ran along the bottom.

"It probably says something like 'A celebration of blood

and seed.' " Lana spoke with dry humor. "Russians dislike subtlety."

"The leaflets dropped onto battlefield soldiers were none too subtle, either," Emmanuel said.

By the close of the war the images employed by all sides were blatantly pornographic: German women assaulted by Russian men with ungodly phalluses, English girls pleasuring each other because their husbands were dead, sick or maimed, Frenchwomen prostituting themselves for a Yankee dollar. The leaflets were meant to fire up or disillusion the men. They'd either fight to protect their women or give up to go home to them.

"What's your guess for this one?" Emmanuel handed Lana another photo of Natalya, this time dressed in a color-ful peasant costume and holding a basket of unnaturally red apples.

" 'Spring harvest from the virgin lands'?" Lana threw back, then said, "That girl never picked a piece of fruit in her life."

"Only when the camera was rolling," Emmanuel said. Film was the perfect medium for Natalya. It allowed single and prolonged close-ups of her flawless face.

"You know her?"

"She's in the other room. Pregnant and sleeping."

"Oh."

"With her husband," Emmanuel added.

He retrieved the last photo. Iosif Vissarionovich Dzhugash-vili, better known as Joseph Stalin, sat on a brown velvet couch between two attractive women with glossy blond hair and slender legs encased in silk stockings. The women had straight white teeth unused to chewing boiled horsemeat or turnip dumplings. Natalya was one of them. A handwritten sentence was scrawled along the bottom of the photo in black ink.

Lana pointed to a word at the end. "I recognize that. It says *Iosif*. That was my father's name."

Emmanuel studied the signed photo again. A group of five uniformed military men was clustered behind the couch, but closer to the door of the palatial room, as if awaiting an audience with the great man. One of the officers had Nicolai's bulky frame but was clean-shaven and stood with squared shoulders.

"That could be her husband," Emmanuel said. "But he's too far away from the camera for me to be sure."

"One big star, maybe more, on the collar tabs of the jacket." Lana leaned closer. "The two-tone peaked cap and tunic could be NKVD. The state security service. If the photo was clearer, I could tell you more."

Emmanuel looked at her, in awe and in thrall of her casual knowledge of things military.

"My father wanted a son but he got me instead," she said. "I tried hard to make up for that mistake."

"What's your best guess on this man?" Emmanuel tapped the officer who most resembled Nicolai. He wasn't sure how important the answer was. He just wanted her to keep talking.

"A major or higher rank in the state security service," she said. "Does that fit the man in the house?"

"Not really," Emmanuel said. But then again, Nicolai had found the strength to haul himself from the deck chair in the house on the Bluff and he'd stayed calm when the bullets flew. It would also explain why the shooter on the Bluff had come after the couple. A senior NKVD officer would be a prime target for the English, the Americans and possibly even a Russian agency keen to reacquire a defector.

"Could be," he said.

"What's your connection to them?" Lana asked, and began refolding the heavy coats and scarves into the suitcase.

"Good question." Emmanuel jammed the box of photographs back into the corner, with the Stalin couch shot on the very top. There was something in Stalin's dark hair, dark eyes and cold smile that reminded him of Khan. "I followed a lead in the Jolly Marks murder that led to the Russians."

"Jolly, that's the boy killed in the freight yard?"

"Yes. The Russians were probably the last people to see him alive," Emmanuel said. "But beyond that I don't see a connection with his murder or the murders in Stamford Hill."

"One of the bar regulars is a railway policeman. He said an Indian gang that supplies children for the white slave trade killed the boy. Two scouts in fancy clothes panicked when the boy tried to run away."

That old fiction. No matter which way the English or the Dutch community turned, they were bedeviled by the insidious nature of darker people. Lawns left to die in the heat by insolent houseboys, beloved domestic pets deliberately overfed by careless housemaids and, lurking in the shadows of every European town, the terrifying and ever-present specter of dark-skinned men with an insatiable taste for white women.

"Indians didn't kill Jolly," Emmanuel said. The who-didn't-do-it list was the strongest aspect of the case so far. "It wasn't the Russians, either."

The only person who could be connected to all three murders was, in fact, Emmanuel himself. He was the strongest suspect, with good reason. Motive was immaterial because the Durban Detective Branch had evidence.

"*Excusez-moi.*" Hélène Gerard stepped onto the porch with a pot of hot coffee and a plate of homemade chocolate biscuits on a tray. She'd sobered up and smelled of lavender. Her hair was pinned back and her smile had been freshly painted onto her face. "I thought you might like something to eat."

"Thank you." Emmanuel said, and ignored Lana's stare. He had no idea why Hélène Gerard was so desperately helpful. Only the major knew the answer to that question.

"How do you take your coffee, Mr. Cooper?" Hélène poured dark liquid into a cup, and her knuckles appeared white against the pot's molded plastic handle. A fraction more pressure and the handle would snap into a dozen pieces.

"White. Two sugars."

The Frenchwoman's smile quivered like a live thing and every breath seemed to be a conscious decision to draw oxygen. Just holding the line. Against what, Emmanuel did not know.

"And you, mademoiselle?" Hélène asked Lana.

"White. One sugar. Thanks."

The metal spout of the coffeepot clanked against the edge of the cup. Hélène steadied and finished the task without spilling liquid onto the saucer. Her smile held.

"It's late," Emmanuel said. "Don't stay up for us. We can manage."

"You're sure?"

"Get some rest. I'll see you in the morning."

Hélène retreated to the door, then hesitated. "There's nothing else I can help you with? Please just ask."

"Everything is fine," Emmanuel said. "You've taken very good care of us. I appreciate it."

"It's been my pleasure."

Hélène slipped back into the house and closed the double doors behind her, ever the thoughtful hostess. Emmanuel stirred sugar and milk into the coffee cup. He waited and he listened. Hélène was spying from behind the door. He knew it as surely as he knew that she'd read over his identity cards while he slept.

"She really likes you," Lana said. "Or she's scared of you. I can't tell which."

Emmanuel moved across to the porch doors. Footsteps creaked on the pine floors of the interior corridor. Hélène Gerard was in retreat.

"She's scared, but not of me," Emmanuel said, and automatically checked the garden and the driveway for the source of Hélène's fears. A frog croaked near the marble-lady fountain but nothing moved. "Finish your coffee and I'll run you back to van Niekerk's."

"Did you find what you needed?"

"No." That was par for the course. Every new piece of evidence brought confusion, not clarity. "I still don't know who killed the Marks boy. Don't know why, either."

And that was what the deal stipulated. Find Jolly Marks's killer.

"So you're still in trouble?" Lana unclipped the straw bag, took out the Walther and slid it across the table.

"For now," he said. "Thanks for your help, anyway."

"What little it was worth." She looped the handbag over her wrist and frowned. "It's funny. I really thought I could read more Russian script than that."

Or maybe waiting for Major van Niekerk to stumble home drunk and horny held no appeal, Emmanuel thought. The information about the NKVD officer might prove useful once Nicolai resurfaced from sleep.

He secured the gun and made for the Buick. He had nothing to give van Niekerk. The major would have nothing to give the sinister man from the interrogation room. Emmanuel fished out the car keys but didn't insert them. The ornamental fountain splashed in the garden but there was another sound coming from the mouth of the driveway. He held his hand up to indicate silence. A clipped murraya hedge, shoulder-high and jungle-thick, shielded the house from traffic, and Emmanuel crouched low and moved quickly along its inner edge.

Lana closed the gap between them. He considered sending her back to the house, but if there was someone out in the dark, then double the hands meant half the work.

"The house is on a corner block," he whispered. "I'll check this part of the street. You check the other. Don't look over the hedge. Ever. Find a gap. If there's no gap, make one quietly. Understand?"

Lana nodded.

"Back on the porch in three minutes."

Lana crossed the garden, fleet as a bird's shadow. She crept along the hedge, her hands and eyes working in harmony to find an opening in the greenery. Her easy competence was disturbing. She had skulked and spied in absolute silence before. Enough times to make it appear natural.

Emmanuel avoided the driveway and moved parallel to the street, searching for chinks of light among the leaves and vines. He found none and carefully broke through the foliage one branch at a time to make a tunnel. The view did not improve.

Two black Chevrolets were parked on either side of the château's driveway in the ambush position. A slim male in a dark suit buttoned his fly and disappeared into the passenger seat of the closest vehicle. Pissing while on stakeout was a logistical nightmare. Twin points of red light glowed in the unlit interior of the second car. A quick smoke before a raid always calmed the nerves.

Down the street, half a block at most, a big black Dodge sat under a streetlight. There were plenty of Dodge motorcars in the city of Durban, but the chrome-rimmed headlights and the dent in the front grille made this one an exact match for the car at the side of the road on the Bluff. The dark silhouette of a man was leaned back in the driver's seat.

Adrenaline shot a message to every nerve ending in Emmanuel's body: *Run hard, run fast. Do not look back.* With speed he could make it through the darkened garden, over the fence and into the night. Then all he had to do was run and never stop, run and never sleep. Blood pumped through his veins and the cut on his cheek pulsed with fresh pain.

"*You will not retreat, soldier.*" The sergeant major was calm. "*You will not surrender. You will not raise a white flag. There're fifteen hours left on your deal with van Niekerk and letting these fuckers roll you was not part of that deal. They'll take what they want from the house and leave you holding the bag for the murders. That's God's honest truth and you know it.*"

Yes, he knew it.

"*Give them the slip,*" the sergeant major said. "*Give them nothing till you've had a chance to clear your name.*"

Emmanuel checked the time. One-thirty a.m. They'd come in an hour or so when they were sure everyone at La

Mer was sleeping. Timing was everything. The ability to drag suspects from their beds still numb and confused by sleep was power itself, a simple action that said, *We own the night. We own your dreams. We own you.*

Six months of fading into invisibility and tasting what it was to be nonwhite. Well, not tonight. Fifteen hours were left on the van Niekerk clock and he was going to use every one of them. The man in the Dodge and his friends would have to wait.

"How many cars?" he asked Lana, who stood on the veranda biting her thumbnail.

"One car at the end of the street," she said. "There's a man behind the wheel."

"All the exits from the house are blocked." Emmanuel looked down the unbroken lines of the hedge and the side fence. "They have us trapped."

"Do you know who they are?"

"I don't know names but I know who they are. I know what they are."

"Police?" Lana's tone was hopeful. Major van Niekerk's name would provide a quick way out of any trouble from them.

"No," Emmanuel said. "Security Branch."

Neither of them spoke for a moment.

"What are they doing here?" Lana said quietly.

"They're waiting. They're going to raid the house."

"Why would they do that?" Her skin paled in the mellow porch light. Major van Niekerk would never keep a girlfriend who'd been caught in the Security Branch net. There would be too much to lose.

"They're looking for something or someone," he said. "My guess is it's the Russians."

"So they'll arrest the Russians and leave?" Lana asked

"No way to know what will happen," Emmanuel said. "They might arrest one of us or all of us."

Lana stared across the garden. "When do you think they'll come?"

"Between two and four. Best time for night raids."

"That gives us . . ."

"Half an hour. An hour if we're lucky."

"What's the plan?" she asked.

"We find a way out and we take it," Emmanuel said. "You, me and the Russians."

Lana jerked a thumb at the house. "What about your Frenchwoman?"

"I doubt they're coming for her," Emmanuel said.

There was no way to stop the raid. All he could do was limit the damage done to Hélène and get out quickly.

He motioned to the hedge that separated Château la Mer from its back neighbors. "Our exit point will be across the yard and into the street behind. We'll break through the hedge if we have to."

Emmanuel split to the left and Lana to the right. They worked their way toward the middle of the hedge, looking for a break in the tropical vegetation. The servant's *kyaha*, like the one behind the Duttas' house, was built almost flush against the back boundary of the property. Servants needed to be close but not close enough to see through the bedroom curtains.

Emmanuel checked the lonely portal into the room. No

lights. No movement. The servant's room was empty. A place the size of La Mer should have at least one on-grounds maid. Hélène had invisible help and an invisible husband.

The space between the back wall of the *kyaha* and the hedge was pitch-black and narrow. Emmanuel squeezed in and fumbled toward the inky light that showed at the other end of the shack's boundary. His hands tangled in the foliage, then touched air and space.

"What is it?" Lana moved through the dark easily and rested a shoulder against the wall.

"A hole," Emmanuel said. "Feels wide enough to crawl into."

"The maid's secret passage," Lana guessed. "She probably used it to visit her boyfriend after lights-out."

Emmanuel crawled through the tunnel, which opened to a wide yard illuminated by a lantern that burned in the window of a mud-brick room a few feet to the right. White spider orchids in round-bellied pots lined a path to the back door of the main house. Lana emerged beside him and together they crouched low and breathed in the stillness of the night.

Emmanuel rose slowly. An empty driveway ran along the left side of the house. "That leads to the street. We'll find a car out there."

There was no need to say more. Lana knew what "find" meant.

"Let's get the Russians," she said, and they retreated to the tunnel.

The screech of rusted metal dragged against concrete shredded the silence. A nuggety black man flew from the doorway of the mud-brick room and ran straight for the back hedge. A wood knobkerrie, a native club, was raised high in the air.

"Stop," Emmanuel said in Zulu. "Stop where you are."

The man slowed but kept coming. Fear drove him. Fear and, Emmanuel guessed, the certain knowledge that if he failed to protect the delicate white orchids and the silver cutlery in the big house, then his work pass would evaporate. Without this job, he'd get sent back to a native location in the sticks and given an arid patch of dirt from which to scratch a living.

"Stop and listen," Emmanuel said quietly in Zulu. "We are not here to steal. We are not here to harm you or those whom you work for . . ."

The hard clicks and tongue-twisting consonants of the Zulu language had a rhythm and a melody that was unique, and to speak it, even here in the dark, unarmed, with a knobkerrie poised above his head, gave Emmanuel pleasure. The last conversation he'd had in Zulu was with Constable Samuel Shabalala, a man blessed with a simple eloquence that went to the heart of the matter and never danced around it.

"Does he understand?" Lana moved to Emmanuel's side, curious.

The wooden club dropped from the Zulu man's hand and he shuffled back. White women were more precious than the gold dug from the mines of Johannesburg. If a native raised even a finger to one of them, the white man's law came down like a fist.

"*Salani kahle*," the black man said, and retreated to the small mud building. "Stay well, *nkosi*."

"*Hamba kahle,*" Emmanuel said, returning the man's traditional farewell. "Go well."

The corrugated iron sheet, cut down to fit the doorway, scraped closed, and the lamplight inside the servant's room died. The orchid petals shone like distant stars in the darkened yard.

"What did you say to him?" Lana asked.

"I told him it is safer to dream than to be awake."

18

N O SAFE DREAMS for Hélène Gerard. Emmanuel's fingers curled around the silver handle of her bedroom door. Lana pushed herself up against the wall and tried to breathe quietly. Earlier, her calm had disturbed him, but now Emmanuel was glad of it. He needed an experienced woman who broke the rules and got away with it, not an innocent.

"Flick the light switch when I say, 'Now.' "

The light from the hall revealed a cavernous room. Curtains covered a bank of windows that opened to the veranda. The carpet muffled their footsteps and Emmanuel reached the side of the bed in silence. A dark mound under the blankets indicated a sleeping form. He reached forward, eyes adjusting to the dim light, and cupped a hand over a mouth.

"Now," he said, and the overhead bulb shone bright. The body in the bed surged forward and Emmanuel pressed down hard. Beard stubble pricked his palms. Hélène Gerard's frantic voice came from the opposite side of the mattress.

"Don't hurt him. Please."

A man in striped cotton pajamas jerked and spluttered under the covers, his green eyes alive with panic. Two silver framed photos tumbled from the side table and bounced on the carpet.

"Please." Hélène scrambled across the king-size bed on all fours, her flimsy nightgown bunched around her thighs. "Let him go."

Emmanuel lifted his hand and pulled back in shock, an involuntary movement that he immediately regretted. The man's face was scarred, and infected black lumps spread across the left cheekbone and over the bridge of his nose before disappearing into the hairline.

"Vincent Gerard?"

"Yes . . ." the man whispered. He was dark-skinned, dark-haired and had once been handsome. Beyond the man's facial disfigurement, he retained a faint glimmer of the fashionable French Mauritian partial to hand-tailored silk suits. Something terrible had transpired and now Vincent was a recluse, hidden away in his own house.

"It was the skin-lightening cream," Hélène said. "We wanted to make sure Vincent got European papers when he was examined by the Race Classification Board but the treatment backfired. The cream damaged his skin and then the rash broke out. We were married before the new laws came in, and now . . ."

Mauritians, once automatically considered "Europeans," had to be reclassified with the rest of the population and placed in a race group. Some retained their white status, but a great many others had been downgraded. A dark-skinned Mauritian and his blond wife had no future together.

"Major van Niekerk ate at our restaurant once a week . . . before the accident with the cream forced us to close," Hélène said. "He promised he'd sign a letter to say Vincent is white and that he suffers from a rare skin condition that can't be cured."

The solemn word of an Afrikaner policeman given to the Race Classification Board practically guaranteed Vincent his "white" papers. No wonder Hélène smiled till it hurt. Her marriage depended on it.

"What does the major get in return, Hélène?"

"I had to take care of you. Not tell anyone you were here. Call him with any news."

"Did you tell him about her?" He jerked a thumb in Lana's direction. She was halfway into the room, drawn by the mention of van Niekerk's name.

"No. I did try to call just after you came, but there was no answer."

Major van Niekerk was eating sherry-infused trifle at the coronation party in Durban North or he could be right outside Château la Mer. What was the real reason for signing the release papers?

"We have to move." Lana was anxious. "Now."

"What's going on?" Vincent Gerard said. "Is the major backing out of our deal?"

"No."

Emmanuel opened the top drawer of the armoire and rifled through the delicates till four pairs of silk stockings were found. There was no way to do what had to be done gently. He pulled Hélène from the bed.

"You're hurting me." She twisted away but Emmanuel kept hold of her arm. Hélène's fear had to be real or the raiding party would take their frustrations out on her and the beautifully ordered interior of her house. He pushed her down into a chair and pinned her arms behind her back. He did not look at her. If he did, he'd have to say, *I'm sorry. Forgive me.* A small hurt now to avoid real pain later. That was the trade-off.

Vincent Gerard growled and sprang forward with his fists clenched. Emmanuel pushed the Mauritian hard on the chest to stop him and Vincent flew back. His head cracked on the edge of a bedside table and he crumpled to the carpet.

"Vincent!" Hélène tried to get up from the chair, but Lana held her down by the shoulders. Blood leaked from a small cut just below Vincent's hairline.

Emmanuel remembered too clearly many long hours spent grilling suspects in stark interview rooms where proceedings ended with a confession that stated, "It was an accident. I didn't mean to hurt anyone." After a year in the Detective Branch, he felt that he could write the confessions himself. He might yet get that chance.

"Goddamn it . . ." He scrambled to Vincent's side. He'd come into the room to shield Hélène from the possibility of real damage, not be the cause of it.

"Vincent . . ." Hélène cried. "Is he alive?"

A heartbeat drummed against Emmanuel's fingertips. Thank God. A moan escaped Vincent's lips and relief unclenched the muscles in Emmanuel's face.

"He'll be all right."

Emmanuel lifted Vincent onto the wide bed. When he came to, the trouble would start all over again. The Mauritian wasn't going to sit quietly while his wife was tied to a chair and gagged.

Emmanuel retrieved a stocking from the floor. The French Mauritian couple smiled from the deck of a sailboat in one of the silver-framed photos lying on the carpet. No matter how he approached the situation, Hélène and Vincent would not emerge unharmed, and that left a bitter taste in his mouth.

"I'm going to tie you up," he said brusquely. "That's the only way to show the men who are going to raid the house that you had nothing to do with me. Do you understand?"

"What?" Hélène said. "I don't know what you mean."

"Six men, maybe more, are going to smash their way into the house soon." Emmanuel secured Hélène's legs to the chair. "We have to make sure they don't blame you for what's happened."

"I'll tell them." The Mauritian woman struggled when Lana pinned her wrists together and tied them. "I'll tell them."

"In a perfect world that would be enough," Emmanuel said. "But this isn't a perfect world."

He made sure the stocking didn't bite but double-knotted the material to ensure that it held fast.

"No—" Hélène said, and Emmanuel gagged her. He and Lana worked quickly and in silence, careful not to make eye contact.

"Should we tie him to the other chair?" Lana asked.

"We can't leave a dark-skinned Mauritian in a white woman's bedroom. The police will beat him. You know how these things go. The fact that they're married might make things worse."

"I know." Lana tucked an escaped strand of hair behind her ear. "What should we do?"

Emmanuel checked his watch. They'd lose precious minutes dealing with Vincent, but that was the way it would have to be. He'd done enough harm tonight.

"The empty *kyaha*," he said. A dark-skinned man hidden

away in the servant's quarters was a common feature of the
South African landscape. Vincent could be just another garden
boy for the baas and the missus.

"Of course." Lana understood the logic. "He'll be
invisible."

Emmanuel hoisted Vincent over a shoulder in a fireman's
hold. Hélène rocked her chair back and forth and strained
against the ties that bound her.

"He's safer out there than in here with you," Emmanuel
said. "Do you really want a group of white police to find Vincent in your bed?"

She shook her head.

"Get the doors," Emmanuel said to Lana.

They moved quickly through the house and out into the
lush garden. Lana ran ahead and opened the tiny servant's
room. The interior was dark and musty. A single camp bed
with a sisal mattress bumped up against a small table and a
chair. Emmanuel slid Vincent onto the narrow cot and lit the
paraffin lantern that was placed on the floor. He turned the
wick low. There were no sheets on the mattress and no curtains on the window. That didn't matter. The police team
would assume that Hélène Gerard was a stingy missus. Some
of the Security Branch officers might even applaud her for it.
A pair of blue work overalls was draped over a tool bucket
and the tip of a wool cap poked out from among the rusting
forks and trowels. Emmanuel grabbed the dirty overalls and
forced them over the fine cotton pajamas with white piping
along the collar.

"My fault . . ." Vincent mumbled. "It's my fault."

Emmanuel buttoned the overalls to the neck and ignored
the Mauritian, who wouldn't make much sense for a while.

He jammed the wool cap onto Vincent's head and pulled it down low.

"Here." Lana spread a thin blanket over Vincent's body. "That'll do the trick."

"I was selfish." Vincent clutched Emmanuel's sleeve. "I shouldn't have married her. Play with fire and you going to get burned. Even ten years back."

Emmanuel wanted to pull away but didn't.

"I loved her." The voice was slurred with emotion. "Down to the bone. All the way. Why's that bad?"

"It's not," Emmanuel said. "But the men who will come to this room don't want to hear that. You understand?"

"Shhh." Vincent put his finger to his mouth. "Big secret. Like when we first stepped out together. Don't tell no one."

"That's right," Emmanuel said. "Big secret."

"*Oui.*" Vincent curled into a fetal position and his scarred face relaxed. "She still loves me. Like this . . ."

Emmanuel waited till Vincent's eyes closed. Then he killed the lamp flame and exited the room. The garden was beautiful in the moonlight. If he had a match, he'd burn it to ash. Even in childhood there had been this contradictory impulse. Gazing out of the boarding school windows to the green summer veldt and a ridge of mountains glowing in the dusk, he had felt it: a rage at the careless beauty of South Africa and a desire to tear it to shreds with his bare hands.

—

The deadweight of Nicolai Petrov's drugged body strained the muscles of Emmanuel's back. The servant's room was only a few yards ahead, but every step was an effort. Maybe a trail of bombs raining down onto the garden would speed the process up. He'd never been able to regain the alacrity that he'd found under enemy fire. He'd never touched the same level of fear, either. At least while he was awake.

Emmanuel rounded the corner of the *kyaha* and placed Nicolai's body on the ground. A half-moon lit the path. The little red pills the Russian had gulped in the backseat of the DeSoto weren't just for pain. They must have contained powerful barbiturates, because he was still deep under. Lana manhandled the suitcase through the hole in the hedge while a sleepy Natalya crouched in the darkness.

"In. Fast." Lana pointed to the tunnel, and Natalya crawled through on her hands and knees, cursing all the way.

"You next," Emmanuel said to Lana. If the Security Branch men were on their tail, then he'd be the first one to face them.

"Hurry," she whispered, and crawled into the breach and out of sight.

Emmanuel lifted Nicolai by the shoulders and maneuvered his bulk to the mouth of the tunnel. The thick winter coat was ridiculous in the tropics but perfect for pulling a body across the ground. Branches ripped Vincent Gerard's expensive jacket and scraped Emmanuel's face and hands. The tunnel was built for one person only, and dragging a near-comatose male through it was a tight squeeze.

He stopped midway to rest his aching shoulders and catch his breath. Car doors closed on the street. The sound helped him find new strength. Three more tugs, and he and Nicolai emerged among the white orchids. There was no sign of Lana or Natalya. The pounding of rapid footsteps came from over the fence. A door smashed open under the force of a boot. Male voices shouted and he heard the men enter the house.

Emmanuel lifted Nicolai onto his shoulders and ran for the empty driveway. He stumbled but regained his balance. The Russian man groaned. Emmanuel pushed hard to the street. Lana and Natalya were still nowhere in sight. Where the hell were they?

He spun in a circle and saw brick walls, nodding rose heads and Lana at the open door of a green Plymouth. She'd hot-wired a car.

The engine idled.

"You drive," Lana said, and slipped into the passenger side while Emmanuel laid Nicolai onto the Plymouth's backseat. Natalya rested her husband's head on her lap and stroked his cheek. The lights of La Mer burned into the inky sky. Hélène would be face-to-face with the men now. Major van Niekerk owed her more than the "European" race papers after tonight.

Emmanuel took the wheel and eased the Plymouth onto the road. He gave the engine petrol. Houses flashed by and the car's waxed hood shone. His heartbeat roared in his ears. He shifted up to third gear. No roadblock. No sirens. Ten blocks from the raid now and cruising. The sleeping city hugged the wide harbor below and the engine of the hot-wired car hummed.

"You really are bad," Emmanuel said.

"You wouldn't have me any other way."

A dark pleasure glittered in Lana's eyes and Emmanuel was breathless. He wanted to touch her and taste her and lose himself in her just one more time.

Their gazes locked before Emmanuel broke away to check that the car was still on the tarmac. Natal mahogany trees lined the island in the middle of the road. Eyes to the front.

The cocktail of excitement and relief was more potent than booze or morphine. Lana made a sound, low and sweet, in her throat. Reality peeled away and flew to the wind.

Now. The word flashed like a neon beacon outside a desert oasis.

Now.

A few more streets and Emmanuel knew that he would pull over. A park, an unlit lane, a sleepy cul-de-sac, it didn't matter. Whatever came first.

The Plymouth bumped over a small branch blown loose from the tree planting on the island and curses came from the backseat. Emmanuel slowed the car, hands tight on the wheel. The Russians.

"Fuck," he muttered under his breath. The Russians were in the backseat.

"Not tonight," Lana said, and stared out of the window. A municipal park flashed by, pocketed with unlit corners and a stand of fever trees that grew thick enough to get lost in.

Not tonight. But maybe another one. Although, without danger and the exhilaration of a lucky escape, their lives played out on opposite sides of a great divide. The heat between them diminished, but a trace remained.

"I'll get us back to van Niekerk's," Emmanuel said. The major's house had tall walls, iron gates and a night watchman on guard.

"Okay," Lana said, and knotted her fingers together. An ex-barmaid from the moneyless end of Umbilo who had caught the eye of a clever Dutch major could not afford to throw that kind of luck away.

Natalya groaned and sighed in the backseat of the Plym-

outh and the sounds mocked Lana and Emmanuel all the way
to van Niekerk's house in the Berea.

———

Emmanuel leaned against the arm of the leather sofa, bruised
and aching. His back hurt from carting two barely conscious
men across the garden of La Mer, and the retreat of adrenaline
from his blood had left a hollow feeling of defeat. The available time to find out who had killed Jolly Marks, Mrs. Patterson and Mbali was now down to less than fourteen hours.

"Drink?" Lana stood by the liquor cabinet with two glass
tumblers at the ready. The Russians now occupied the guest
bedroom in the northwest corner of van Niekerk's Victorian
spread.

"Double whiskey and soda, please," Emmanuel said, and
eased into the middle seat of the chesterfield.

Lana mixed the drink and handed it to him before tipping
ice cubes into the second tumbler and pouring three fingers of
scotch. She gulped a mouthful and sank back into the leather
next to him. Ice chimed in their glasses.

"Did they hurt her, do you think?" Lana said.

"I hope not."

That was all Emmanuel could offer regarding Hélène and
Vincent Gerard's safety. In the absence of faith, hope was the
next best thing.

"When men like that get angry," she said softly, "they do
bad things, especially to women."

They weren't talking about Hélène Gerard anymore. Emmanuel put the whiskey and soda onto the low table and
turned to Lana. Strands of ink-black hair fell against the pale

skin of her cheeks and the ice cubes in her drink rattled against the glass. This was the postbattle stress. After the exhilaration came the fear and the reopening of old wounds.

"We did what we could with the time we had," Emmanuel said. It wasn't enough, he knew.

"We should never have left them. Those men will hurt them."

"That's not certain."

He removed the glass from Lana's hand before it cracked under pressure and placed it on the table next to the untouched whiskey and soda. No amount of alcohol would reverse the harm done to Hélène and Vincent. He cupped her hands in his; they were icy cold.

The front door lock opened with a hard click and Lana pulled free and jumped to her feet. She avoided Emmanuel's gaze and smoothed her hair into place before moving to the door.

"Kallie," she called into the corridor. "Down here. We have company."

Emmanuel retrieved the whiskey tumbler from the table. The liquor swirled golden in the glass but he left it untouched. He needed to keep his mind clear. It was time to get the truth about his release from custody and about the night raid on La Mer from the ambitious Dutch major.

He got up and placed both the half-full tumblers onto the silver trolley before pushing them out of view. No man, especially van Niekerk, would be pleased to find his woman enjoying expensive liquor in the company of an employee.

The major kissed Lana on the cheek and peered into the lounge room. "Cooper," he said.

"Major."

"You look like hell." Van Niekerk's lean face was touched with color after a night-long infusion of rich food and booze. Or maybe he had finally triumphed over his fiancée's brassiere. "Is there news?"

"You tell me," Emmanuel said.

"Meaning?"

"Hélène Gerard's house was raided less than an hour ago. We barely got out before they kicked the doors in."

"Did you get the Russians out?" van Niekerk said.

"How long have you known about them?" Emmanuel's stomach tightened. He had hoped, in the deepest part of himself, that the major did not have enough information to have planned the raid on La Mer.

"Hélène called me this afternoon. She said you'd brought a Russian couple to the house."

Anger replaced the fear and Emmanuel stepped toward the major. He didn't buy van Niekerk's apparent ignorance. Someone had given away Château la Mer's location to the man in the black Dodge.

"I left Hélène tied to a chair, scared for her life. Vincent was stuffed, bleeding, into the servant's room. You could have warned them about the raid but you threw them to the wolves."

"I had nothing to do with the raid. I'd never put that pressure onto Hélène and Vincent, not after what they've been through," van Niekerk said. "I was in Durban North all night, toasting the future queen."

"You were at a toffee coronation party till almost three in the morning?"

"The party just broke up twenty minutes ago." Van

Niekerk pulled his black tie loose and dumped it onto the sofa. "And watch your tone, Cooper."

"You didn't have to be there physically to be a part of the raid," Emmanuel said. "All you had to do was pick up a phone and call the Security Branch in."

"I'm drunk, Cooper." Van Niekerk rubbed a hand over his chin and cheeks. "But not drunk enough to call the Security Branch. For anything."

Van Niekerk was a one-man republic. Personal power and authority were all that mattered in his world. Sharing any spoil with Security Branch was out of the question, Emmanuel realized.

"Can you make the major a pot of coffee?" he said to Lana. "Black with a lot of sugar, please."

"Good idea, very good idea," van Niekerk agreed. "Bring it into my office with a packet of cigarettes. A couple of pieces of toast, too."

"*Ja,* one minute." Lana retreated toward the back of the house. Kitchen girl was on her list of jobs.

"There's a phone in the office." Van Niekerk followed Lana to the door. "Come with me, Cooper. I need to make a few calls."

They entered the darkened room and lit the lamps. The major fumbled in a back pocket and retrieved a silver chain with three different-sized keys attached. He tried to align the key with the lock but scratched a mark into the wood surface of the desk drawer.

"I'm stuffed," he said to Emmanuel, and threw the keys across the desk. "You do it."

Emmanuel unlocked the bottom drawer. Four leather-bound books lay inside. It wasn't a fiction. Some men really did have little black books filled with the secrets of others. The dock surveillance lists were also there. Dozens of policemen slept through the night in ignorance while the evidence for their undoing was right here at van Niekerk's fingertips. Were the sweat-making photographs uncovered during the Jacob's Rest investigation stashed in one of the other drawers?

"What do you need?" Emmanuel said.

"All of it." Van Niekerk sat behind the desk and unbuttoned his jacket. "We'll have to call in a few favors before the night is out."

Emmanuel removed the stack of books and placed them on the mahogany desk. His own name was in one of them, he was sure. Listed in which section: talented failure, hired hand or replaceable asset?

"Thank Christ." Van Niekerk greeted Lana's arrival with enthusiasm. "Over here, there's a good girl. I need two cups black and a cigarette before I pick up the phone."

Lana placed the tray on the desk and set out a plate with toast close to the major's hand. She poured a black coffee, added three sugars and stirred before setting the cup conveniently close to the plate. Next, she put a cigarette to her lips, lit it, drew on it and then handed it to the major. Emmanuel noted the red smudges of her lipstick on the filter. She had repainted her mouth. She began to pour a second cup of coffee.

"Cooper can take care of himself," the major said quietly, and Lana put the coffeepot down.

"Can I do anything else, Kallie?" Her smile was strained.

"Go to bed and get some rest. You look like you've had a long night, you and Cooper."

Even when drunk, the cunning Dutchman could grab

information from the air quicker than the most experienced detectives.

"Good night, then," Lana said, and left the office for the bedroom without glancing in Emmanuel's direction.

Major van Niekerk gulped his black coffee and arranged the books in a neat line. His fingers stroked the covers.

"What happened tonight, Cooper?"

"Lana was at La Mer when the raid happened. She helped get the Russians out."

"How did she get from here to there?"

"I asked her to help translate this." Emmanuel brought out the Walther PPK and showed it to van Niekerk. "There's a Russian inscription engraved along the side."

"Beautiful." Van Niekerk admired the gun before looking up at Emmanuel. "How did you know Lana spoke Russian?"

"I asked her if she knew anyone who did," Emmanuel said. "She volunteered."

"Just like that?"

If snakes smiled, Emmanuel imagined, they'd look just like van Niekerk did now.

"Yeah, just like that," he said, then, "Why did you sign my release papers, Major?"

"I told you."

"You told me a lie. Now tell me the truth."

"When did you figure that out?" the major said. Not many people got a step ahead of him. It made being caught out a rare pleasure.

"The afternoon you dropped me at La Mer. Your voice was calm but your hands were sweating. Why did you sign?"

The major lit a fresh cigarette and said, "I got a call in the middle of the party to say you were in police custody and about to be booked on three murder counts. Would I like to help?"

"How did this person know we were connected?" The major had kept all past history under wraps, even from Lana Rose.

"A very, very good question. One that I asked myself immediately. Johannesburg and Durban are a long way apart. Only someone with access to Detective Branch records could have known we had once worked together."

"You got me out because you wanted to find out who was digging into your records?"

"It was more than that, Cooper," the major said. "I wanted you set free and I wanted to know *why* the mystery caller was intervening. Prior to your arrest did you tell anyone your name and your old service rank?"

"Never," Emmanuel said, then recalled the freight yards. "No, that's not right. On the night of Jolly Marks's murder I told two suspects I was Detective Sergeant Emmanuel Cooper."

"The man who called me got your name and service rank from somewhere. Maybe the information came from the suspects."

"Unlikely," Emmanuel said. "One of them is a schoolboy and the other is Durban's dumbest gangster."

"The gangster . . . could he be a police informant?"

"I can't say for sure, but it would be a stretch." Parthiv and Giriraj had kidnapped him from the yards because they thought he was a detective. Not once had they used an "in" with the police to get out of trouble on the night of the murder.

"Did you tell anyone else you were a detective sergeant at Marshall Square?" Van Niekerk hit the question again.

"No," Emmanuel said.

"Are you sure?"

"Yes. Absolutely. Why?"

"Because if that's true, then your personal information had to be gathered at the scene of the Marks boy's murder," van Niekerk pointed out.

A shiver prickled across Emmanuel's back at the implication. "Someone else was in the yards that night, watching and listening," he said. "A policeman?"

"It was someone who could rush through an information request on you and have it turned around in a single day. My name would have come up."

"Do you have any idea who called you?" Emmanuel asked. During the course of the investigation he'd met only one person he suspected had access to high-level information: Afzal Khan.

"A *soutpiel*." Van Niekerk used the derogatory term meaning "salt dick," an Englishman who had one foot in South Africa, the other foot in England and his penis dangling in the sea. "The voice belonged to an officious little shit who thought a Dutch policeman and an ex-detective could be used and then dumped."

Not even a close match for Khan.

"Used to what end?" Emmanuel said. He'd been released to find Jolly Marks's killer.

"We got the answer to that question tonight, Cooper," van Niekerk said. "Jolly Marks's murder was the sideshow, the hook. Locating the Russians was the main game. You were set free to find them. How did you manage that, by the way?"

"The notebook," Emmanuel said, and experienced the sharp satisfaction that came from finding the corner piece to a puzzle. "The information that led to the Russians was in the notebook, but Jolly ditched it before the killer got to him. I think the notebook was the reason Jolly was killed."

The satisfaction ebbed away and left a sick feeling of dread in the pit of his stomach. That was what connected the three murders. The notebook.

"Mrs. Patterson and Mbali must have disturbed the killer when he came to the Dover to find the book," he said.

Good God above. If only he'd left the notebook in clear view instead of hiding it in the flour bin like a paranoid neurotic, two lives might have been saved. That decision couldn't be reversed. He had to face the dangers of the present situation.

"Now that I've located Nicolai and Natalya," Emmanuel said, "I'm expendable."

"Not as long as we have the Russians." Van Niekerk sprang to his feet and pulled a casement window open. Cool night air rushed into the room and he leaned out and yelled, "Barnaby, come here quick."

The black night watchman ran onto the wide veranda and crouched down. *"Yebo, Inkosi."*

"Lock the gates," van Niekerk said. "Don't let anyone in unless I give the okay. You understand? No one."

"I will do it." Barnaby took off across the lawn and the shudder of the huge gates scraping over gravel could be heard.

The major retrieved the silver chain and unlocked a dark wood sideboard with the largest of the keys. Handguns, single- and double-barreled shotguns and two wood and steel crossbows were stored on specially designed racks.

"Personal security concerns?" Emmanuel asked drily.

"I hunt." Van Niekerk selected a pearl-handled Colt and a leather hip holster from the munitions buffet. He holstered the weapon before locking the cabinet, which had originally been designed to hold heirloom china. "That *soutpiel* has no idea who he is dealing with."

"We have the Russians, we have guns and we have high walls," Emmanuel said. "But there's no point in us digging in. We need names and faces if we're going to get out of this. We need to know who we're up against."

"Let's start with the obvious suspects." The major opened a black book, found an entry and dialed. It took a while for the other end to pick up.

"*Howzit*, Tonk?" The conversation continued in Afrikaans, the language of Emmanuel's childhood and of his secrets and fears. He rarely spoke it now. Durban offered few opportunities to practice the Taal, and Emmanuel did not miss it despite the fact that certain words and phrases came first in Afrikaans and had to be translated back into English in his head. The Dutch language belonged to his father and that was enough to sour the use of it for all time.

Van Niekerk hung up the phone.

"It wasn't Security Branch," he said. "They have nothing till next Friday, and that's a raid on a union organizer's house in Cato Manor. Could the men at Hélène's have been regular police?"

"I don't think so. Detective Head Constable Robinson and Detective Constable Fletcher were staked out in front of Jolly Marks's home this afternoon. They stuck by the rules for my release. The men outside Hélène's house weren't playing that game."

"Someone with rank and information is pointing the way." Van Niekerk shuffled the books around and reordered them, mentally scanning the contents for information. "A policeman. I'm sure of it."

"A professional." Emmanuel told the major about the black Dodge from the shooting on the Bluff and the calculated nature of the attack. "The man in the Dodge must have known the location of Hélène Gerard's house before the incident on the Bluff because there's no way we were tailed back there."

"That's not possible . . . I was the only one with that information, Cooper."

"Maybe not." Emmanuel sat up straight. "The tradesman from the interrogation room. He bailed out a half block from the station. He could have followed us to Hélène's. It was a simple tag-and-release operation. Let a suspect walk free and see where he goes. Detectives use the same technique. Only this time it was used on us."

Van Niekerk ran a finger over the list of names in the Point surveillance notebook. The lamplight was bright enough to pick up the glimmer of pleasure in his eyes.

"I'm going to call some of my contacts and try and get the albino's real name," he said. "You talk to the Russians and find out who they are and what they're doing in Durban. We still need to figure out who killed Jolly Marks and the two women. Have you got anything?"

"One more suspect, an American street preacher with no surname or address. Haven't seen him since earlier this afternoon. He might have gone to ground."

"Find him. We need a head to slip in the noose for those murders," the major said coolly.

Three knocks rattled the office door.

"Come," van Niekerk said, and Lana dashed into the room dressed in the white silk dressing gown she'd worn earlier. The neckline billowed open and her slender hand plucked the lapels closed.

"It's the old man," she said. "He's soaked with sweat and his face is like ash. We need a doctor."

"Not good," van Niekerk muttered, and reached for the first of the leatherbound books on the desktop. "My medical contacts are all in Jo'burg. I've got one name on the Durban list but he'll be drunk till noon."

Emmanuel took that information in. Without Nicolai, the men behind the clandestine operation would melt away, but the three murder charges would stick. A hole had been torn into the breast pocket of Vincent Gerard's silk jacket and a paper edge poked out. Emmanuel pulled out the stained postcard and read the scrawled invitation again.

"I know a man," he said.

19

THE DAWN SKY was the color of a fresh bruise. Electric streetlights turned off in the city as the citizens of Durban rolled out of bed and into Monday morning. Emmanuel stood alone in the green blur of van Niekerk's garden. There was much to be thankful for. A phone call had confirmed that Vincent and Hélène Gerard were shaken but unharmed. Nicolai was still alive and the major was working through his stack of black books in an attempt to pin down the identity of the tradesman.

Still, Emmanuel was uneasy. Dragging Daniel Zweigman from his medical clinic in the Valley of a Thousand Hills was selfish. The old Jew had saved his life once and it had put him in danger. To ask for help a second time was greedy.

The heavy gates swung open and a dusty Bedford truck and a black Packard rumbled into the driveway. Emmanuel crossed the lawn and arrived at the front stairs moments after the truck's engine cut. A small man with white volcano hair in full eruption clambered out the driver's door clutching a battered doctor's kit. Wire-rimmed glasses perched at the end of an aquiline nose. It was Zweigman in all his glory.

"Dr. Zweigman," Emmanuel said.

"Detective Sergeant Emmanuel Cooper." The German's voice retained its characteristic dryness. "Perhaps it will also snow today."

They observed each other in silence. Emmanuel resisted the urge to brush the creases from the jacket and trousers of his battered silk suit. A cut cheek and discolored neck muscles told their own story. Zweigman pushed his smudged glasses up with an index finger and Emmanuel saw that his hands, fine instruments of healing, were now callused and rough. Lean times had found them both.

Zweigman smiled. "To be alive is the victory, Detective."

"Good to see you," Emmanuel said, and meant it. The disheveled German had put him back together after the Security Branch beating and made sure that only a few scars remained. "Sorry to drag you from the clinic on short notice."

"It is no matter," Zweigman said. "The clinic is only open three days a week until more funds can be found for a nurse and more medicine. Your timing could not be better. Now I have a surprise for you. Around here."

Emmanuel edged along the front of the Bedford's paint-flecked hood, still steaming with heat from the rough drive. A towering black man with broad shoulders rounded the bumper from the passenger side. He wore blue work pants and a long-sleeved cotton shirt under a khaki jacket.

"Shabalala . . ." Emmanuel said. "*Sawubona.*"

The Zulu constable from Jacob's Rest and his right-hand man on the controversial investigation into the murder of an

Afrikaner police captain was directly in front of him and larger than life.

"*Yebo. Sawubona,* Sergeant Cooper," Shabalala said, returning the greeting, and they shook hands.

"What are you doing here, man?" Emmanuel said. Hundreds of miles of dirt and tarred roads separated the tiny outpost of Jacob's Rest in the Transvaal and the port city of Durban.

"I have come from the clinic," Shabalala said. "My wife, Lizzie, and I are staying with the doctor."

It would have taken Shabalala and his wife two days of hard travel on ailing public buses, with corn bread and boiled eggs wrapped in cloth for sustenance on the journey. Emmanuel pushed away the feeling of shame. The Valley of a Thousand Hills was an easy two-hour drive from Stamford Hill. Only now, in a desperate hour, had he contacted the man who'd saved his life.

"Come." Emmanuel invited them both into van Niekerk's house. "We'll get a coffee and I'll fill you in."

"Good," Zweigman said. "Our official escort was not forthcoming with information."

"He was probably under orders not to say anything," Emmanuel explained, and climbed the stairs to the porch. The driver, one of van Niekerk's men from the coronation party, probably didn't know very much anyway. The major was a master at keeping his own counsel.

Emmanuel swung the door open. Zweigman entered the hallway, but Shabalala hesitated on the threshold. This was not the kind of house where natives normally entered via the front door.

"In," Emmanuel said to the Zulu constable. "The kitchen is out the back."

"Please," Shabalala insisted. Tradition demanded that European policemen enter before native ones, no matter what their rank. "You must go first, Sergeant Cooper."

They entered the house, where Zweigman examined a gilt-framed portrait of a sallow white man with thin, cruel lips. An early van Niekerk, no doubt, already calculating his share of South Africa's resources. A telephone rang in the office and Major van Niekerk's voice could be heard firing questions in Afrikaans. Lana had disappeared upstairs.

"I need your help," Emmanuel said to Zweigman over coffee in the light-filled kitchen. Shabalala stood at a back window and sipped tea while contemplating the profusion of colors in the garden.

"Medical?" Zweigman asked.

"Yes, but not for me. I've two people who need to be examined."

"Gunshot?" Zweigman asked. "Knife wounds?"

"What makes you think it's either of those?" Emmanuel was taken aback by the suggestion.

Zweigman laughed and indicated the opulent house. "Who knows what company you keep these days, Detective?"

"*Yebo,*" Shabalala said. "Very fine suit, too, Sergeant."

"The suit belongs to a French Mauritian. The house belongs to a police major."

"The clothes are irrelevant," Zweigman said. "It's your eyes that have changed. I think maybe your life, also."

"Well, you're exactly the same." Emmanuel was irritated by Zweigman's ability to ignore the surface scars and push a careless finger into the deeper ones. "You obviously have less money but you're still too clever for your own good."

"My curse and yours, also." Zweigman drained his coffee cup and soaped and scrubbed up over the porcelain sink. He dried his hands with a towel brought in earlier by one of van Niekerk's silent army of domestics. "Now please show me to my patients."

"This way." Emmanuel exited the kitchen and crossed the corridor to the guest bedroom. He knocked gently.

"*Da?*" Natalya appeared in the doorway, sleep-tossed and dressed in one of van Niekerk's Egyptian cotton dressing gowns. She ignored Emmanuel and sat down at a small table set with a breakfast of tea, boiled eggs and buttered toast soldiers. Nicolai was propped up in bed, pale and damp with sweat.

"Well," Zweigman said in surprise.

"This is Nicolai Petrov and his wife, Natalya," Emmanuel said. "Recently arrived from Russia."

"Ahhhh . . ." Zweigman digested that information. "Any English?"

"None for the girl, except the word *American*. Nicolai knows enough to hold a conversation."

"I will see what the problem is." The old Jew moved to the bed with the battered medical bag tucked under his arm. "I am Dr. Daniel Zweigman. You are Nicolai?"

"Yes."

"This beautiful woman is your wife?" Zweigman bowed low to Natalya and was rewarded with a dazzling smile.

The German doctor and the Russian shook hands and some kind of recognition passed between them. They were both men who had once been powerful and had a taste for beautiful young women. And both were far, far from home.

"I'll leave you to it," Emmanuel said. "Come through to the front porch when you're done."

"Fifteen minutes, maybe more." Zweigman snapped open the medical kit and removed a stethoscope and a glass thermometer.

Emmanuel backed into the corridor and closed the door. For a brief moment he'd caught a glimpse of the old Zweigman, the specialist surgeon with degrees lining the wall of a plush office in Berlin. He trusted Zweigman completely, would even trust him with his sister's life, but it occurred to Emmanuel that he didn't know the secretive German doctor at all.

—

Shabalala and Emmanuel sat down on the top step of van Niekerk's veranda and looked out across the harbor to the Indian Ocean. To Emmanuel's eyes, Shabalala had not changed. The murder of his closest friend, Captain Willem Pretorius, eight months ago, had not diminished his physical being in a way that could be seen. Maybe that was because Shabalala was a black man in South Africa. His pain had to be contained on the inside.

"Have you traveled well, Sergeant?" the Zulu constable asked.

"I have traveled far," Emmanuel said. "And things go well with you?"

"I am older," Shabalala said, and his statement lingered in the air. Neither of them had escaped the past.

"You have been many weeks at the clinic?" Emmanuel

asked. Something about the constable's earlier statement regarding his visit to Zweigman didn't sit right.

"My wife, Lizzie, and I stay with the doctor," Shabalala said, and Emmanuel understood. The Zulu policeman and his wife were not visiting the medical clinic; they now lived in the Valley of a Thousand Hills, far from Jacob's Rest and the bush farm where Shabalala had grown into a man.

"Why did you leave?"

"I became uneasy."

"I see," Emmanuel said.

The murder investigation had uncovered secrets that gave Shabalala the knowledge to destroy both lives and reputations in the small town of Jacob's Rest. Silence was one of the Zulu constable's strengths, but the very fact that a black man carried such information would have been the cause of tension, fear and even hatred.

"The Pretorius family," Emmanuel asked. "Did they come after you?"

The Afrikaner clan, rulers of the town of Jacob's Rest, had the most to lose if the real reason for their father's murder was ever revealed.

"No," Shabalala said. "The brothers keep to themselves and are quiet. Mrs. Pretorius, she has moved from the big house and out to the farm of her fourth son. She is not seen much in town."

A Zulu neighbor in Sophiatown had a saying: "Never plant a poisonous tree in your backyard. One day your children might be forced to eat the fruit." The Pretorius family and everyone involved in the investigation had, in some way, been poisoned.

"I'm sorry you had to leave your home," Emmanuel said.

If he'd walked away from the case and let the Security Branch do as they pleased, things would have been different. Shabalala's job and life would still be on track.

"The right thing was done." The Zulu constable was staunch. "There can be no shame in that."

The front door swung open and Zweigman shuffled out of the house. He perched between Emmanuel and Shabalala on the brick steps, the medical bag balanced on his knees.

"What's wrong with him?" Emmanuel said.

"Nicolai is being eaten away from inside. There is a growth in the stomach that will grow larger with time. I've seen it before."

"How long?"

"Impossible to predict," Zweigman said. "A few days, maybe a few weeks or months. All that can be done is to make him comfortable. I have given him a shot of painkiller."

"Can he be cured?"

"I do not believe so, Detective. There is no way to reverse the disease."

"And the woman?"

"She's close," Zweigman said. "When the child comes, I believe that Nicolai will take leave of us. The upcoming birth is perhaps what keeps him alive."

"To hold a child in your arms," Shabalala said. "That is the thing."

Zweigman rubbed the bridge of his nose where the glasses bit into the skin and said quietly, " 'Like arrows in the hands of a warrior, so are the children of one's youth. Happy is the man who has a quiver full of them; he shall not be ashamed, but shall speak with his enemies at the gate.' "

"*Yebo,*" Shabalala agreed. "This is the truth."

The biblical quote sounded like a lament to Emmanuel. Zweigman and his wife had once had children. Shabalala had once had a best friend. And Emmanuel himself had once had a job with the Detective Branch and a sister he could talk with openly. All destroyed by the fire of life. The magnetic force that drew the three men back together after eight months had a name; it was not fate or destiny or luck. It was loss.

—

Nicolai Petrov sat upright in the guest bed with the black-and-white photographs from the suitcase spread over the covers. The painkiller had softened the lines of pain around his mouth. Natalya gazed into a mirror and experimented with perfumes and lotions. Emmanuel pulled up a chair opposite Nicolai and sat down.

"Stills from Natalya's films?" he said.

"Some," Nicolai said. "She made many more. Dozens. These are the ones she wishes to remember."

"Where was this one taken?" Emmanuel indicated the photograph of Joseph Stalin on the soft brown velvet couch.

"Moscow," Nicolai said. "Comrade Stalin was moved to tears when *Triumph in Berlin* was shown. Natalya played the role of a field nurse."

"Stalin was a friend?"

"The great leader did not have friends. He had enemies and he had those wise enough to fear him."

"What camp did you and Natalya fall into?"

"Natalya was one of Iosif's favorite actresses," Nicolai said, and began to collect the photos. Emmanuel noticed the

Russian man's strong arms and shoulders for the first time. In his prime he would have towered above the crowd.

"What was your relationship with him?"

"I was an errand boy." Nicolai shrugged. "When Comrade Stalin died, everything that he loved was thrown out in the garbage. Natalya's work was part of the old regime... the corrupt regime. My work was no longer recognized. We left while we had the chance. It seemed the wise thing."

Errand boy. It was an interesting turn of phrase coming from a man who was built like a Borodino-class battle cruiser and whose hands looked like they could snap a spine.

"What kind of errands?" Emmanuel said.

"I did what I was ordered to do."

The Nuremberg defense worked just as well for members of the Russian security service as it did for the Nazis. An errand run on Stalin's order surely would have ended in blood.

"You worked for the NKVD?"

"Yes. I was a colonel."

Well, that explained the interest in the couple. The Americans, the British and even the Russians would consider the capture of a colonel in the NKVD a coup. South Africa's homegrown version of the NKVD, the Security Branch, would also be desperate for a taste of the action.

"Why Durban?" Emmanuel asked. The unmarked passports and the winter clothes suggested that South Africa was not the Russian couple's final destination.

"A last resort," Nicolai said. "We went first to England, but things did not work out for the best."

"Tell me."

Nicolai shifted against the tower of pillows and peered at Emmanuel with the sharp gaze of an experienced interrogator. "You are with state security?" he demanded.

"No, the Detective Branch. I'm just wondering why men with guns are after you and Natalya."

"Men that you have twice saved us from." The grizzled Russian leaned forward and Emmanuel caught a glimpse of the old Nicolai: brutal and strong. "Why did you do this?" Nicolai breathed.

Emmanuel didn't move back or blink. He recalled the statement Shabalala had made on the front porch and repeated the essence of it. "Helping you was the right thing."

"A dreamer . . ." Nicolai mumbled, and packed all the photographs away in the cardboard box. He jammed the lid into place and rested both massive hands on the top in an apparent effort to keep the past from spilling out.

"We defected to England," he said after a lengthy pause. "I took a file with me. The names of people the NKVD suspected of being British spies."

"To trade for your safety," Emmanuel said.

"Yes. The first two months were perfect. We were given a safe house and passports in exchange for the file. I was questioned many times by MI5 and the sessions were recorded. I told them everything I knew. Then a British agent was arrested in Stalingrad and my old masters offered to trade him back."

"For you?"

Nicolai's smile was tight. "Yes. The British had the file and many hours of recordings taken during questioning. They didn't need me anymore. I was only of value in a trade."

"You know this for a fact?"

Nicolai chuckled. "I brought other things out of Russia. I paid one diamond bracelet and two Black Sea pearls for details of the exchange. Natalya and I got out the night before they planned to come for us."

"You're still valuable to them," Emmanuel said. "That's why they've come after you. The trade is still on."

"Yes." Nicolai was matter-of-fact. "I have hunted men myself and I know that the hunt does not stop until the target is trapped or dead."

That meant the tradesman would keep up the pursuit, but Emmanuel's focus was elsewhere. Three civilians with small and ordinary lives were gone, their light extinguished forever. International intrigue was for the spooks who moved red dots across a map of the world and determined the fate of governments. The job of detective, on the other hand, was simple. A detective spoke for the dead. A detective sought justice for the boy lying in the blood and dirt, for the Zulu maid who'd never owned a new dress, for the sour Englishwoman with purple hair wound over plastic rollers. Their murders were Emmanuel's business. Solving their murders was also the only way he could avoid the gallows.

"You found your way from the docks all the way to that house in the woods." Emmanuel turned the conversation back to the last few days. "How did you do that?"

"That was nothing. Getting Natalya to love me . . . that was the challenge." Nicolai smiled at his self-absorbed wife, proud of her beauty and her youth. Stalin's henchman, hero of the people, captured not by a Panzer tank division but by a blonde with eyes the color of arctic water. It was clear that Zweigman's diagnosis of the situation was correct. Without

Natalya to focus his attention, Nicolai probably would have given up long ago. "I could not let them take us to a gulag. My darling wife would not have survived."

Oh, yes, she would have. Emmanuel had met a few Natalyas during the war. The beautiful and blessed females destined to sleep in feather beds and eat fresh bread no matter if the Communists, the Fascists or the Allies were in charge.

"Tell me what happened when you came ashore at the passenger quay," Emmanuel said.

"We had only an address, so we went to the yard with the wagons to see if there was a train to catch. Railway lines going all ways. Natalya and I, lost and in the dark. Scared, also. Natalya thought there was a man who followed us from the ship."

"How did you find your way to the house?"

"A boy helped us."

"Tell me about the boy."

"Ten years, maybe. Skinny, with dirty clothes."

"Was this boy alone or with someone?"

"Alone. He tried to run from us, and then he saw that Natalya was pregnant. I showed him the address for my cousin's house. That is when he made the picture, with the message *Please help,* which we gave to the black man with the car."

"There was no one with the boy . . . no one near him?"

"He was alone," Nicolai stated.

Emmanuel edged forward in his seat. "What did he do after he gave you the drawing?"

"He disappeared into the shadows."

Unbelievable. The Russian couple knew less than the English prostitute. Another dead end. Emmanuel worked his way backward through Nicolai's recollections, like an alchemist searching for gold in the dross.

"Can Natalya describe the man who followed you from the ship?"

Nicolai shrugged, his energy drained.

"Ask her," Emmanuel said. "Did she see him?"

The conversation between Nicolai and Natalya was brief. Natalya scooped cold cream from a jar and rubbed it into her face while talking.

"White . . ." Nicolai translated. "Black suit . . ."

This was where it would all end, Emmanuel was sure. A white man in a black suit.

"Dark hair," Nicolai continued. "To the shoulders. Like a wild Cossack."

Emmanuel swung to face Natalya. He touched his shoulders to indicate the length of hair, and the Russian beauty nodded. Fingers together, he drew an imagined widow's peak onto his forehead.

Natalya rolled her eyes at his pantomime and said, "*Da.*"

Yes.

Brother Jonah had been near Jolly when he died. He had attended a late-night meeting in a scrapyard where the term *Ivan*, a slang term for a Russian, was used. He talked like a soldier on a mission. And if Miss Morgensen was to be believed, he was also an associate of Afzal Khan.

Emmanuel left Nicolai to his memories and went in search of van Niekerk and a fresh set of clothes. He had less than nine hours to find the preacher and hopefully get a confession.

20

W HAT NEWS, COOPER?" Major van Niekerk sat at
the head of a long table in the shade of the porch. The
remains of an early-morning tea of raisin cake and scones with
jam lay on a china platter edged in gold leaf. Zweigman and
Shabalala sat side by side with a view of the pool and gardens.
They looked at Emmanuel with anxious smiles and he wondered what the major had said to them.

"Speak freely." Van Niekerk scratched the stubble on his
chin. "They know everything."

"Christ above . . ." Emmanuel leaned against the side of
the table. Why would the major pull Zweigman and Shabalala
deeper into this mess right at the point when they should be
on their way home?

"You're facing three counts of murder," Zweigman said.
"If the murderer is not found by this afternoon, you will be
arrested and placed in jail. Correct?"

"That's my problem, not yours." Zweigman and Shabalala
had saved him once already, a debt he still owed. He didn't
want them in danger again. "I'm grateful for your help, but

you have to go home now. I can't involve you in my troubles."
Not after Jacob's Rest.

Shabalala leaned forward. "You did not kill these people,
Sergeant. The man who did these things must be the one to
answer for the crimes. That is how it must be."

"And that is how it will be." Emmanuel pulled up a chair
and sat across from the doctor and the constable. He knew
from combat that the bond forged by men and women who
fought side by side was the hardest to break. What the three
of them had experienced in Jacob's Rest was the peacetime
equivalent. Almost like a family, they were tied together by
blood.

"You are my friends, not my men," he said, trying to ignore the struggle inside himself. He wanted Zweigman and
Shabalala gone *and* he wanted them by his side.

"*Yebo*, friends," Shabalala agreed. "And that is why you
will not do this alone."

The statement stopped Emmanuel cold. He had worked
five months at the Victory Shipyards breaking steel and hiding
from the past when two hours away were comrades. He wasn't
alone after all.

Shabalala poured him a cup of tea. Zweigman put a cake on
a plate and placed it in front of him.

"It's settled, Cooper," the major said. "Dr. Zweigman and
Constable Shabalala will be noncombatants. Strategic backup,
that's all. Did the Russians have any leads?"

"An American zealot preacher. Brother Jonah, he calls
himself. He works the Point and the harbor," Emmanuel said.
"He was in the freight yards on the night the kid was killed. I
think he might have something to do with Natalya and Nicolai, too."

"Why?" van Niekerk asked.

"Russians and Americans running around the docks in the middle of the night? Maybe it's a coincidence . . ."

"Do you know where he is?" van Niekerk asked. "A list of favorite places?"

Emmanuel shook his head. "Nothing yet."

"He has no woman and no friends?" Shabalala said. Such a thing was unthinkable for a Zulu. Social isolation was a form of living death.

"No woman." Emmanuel drank a mouthful of black tea and remembered his joyride in the back of the Silver Wraith. He also remembered Miss Morgensen's belief that Jonah had been in that car as well. Maybe Khan could help. He knew more than a little bit about what went on in the Point area and gave money to charities to keep up appearances.

"What about Afzal Khan?" Emmanuel thought aloud.

"Khan the Indian gangster?" the major said.

"The very one." A black-skinned man with a white body-guard and a silver Rolls would be well known to the police and to every citizen on the Point with eyesight.

"Do you know where this Mr. Khan is?" Zweigman chose a piece of raisin cake and broke it into bite-sized pieces over his plate.

"No idea," Emmanuel said.

The door connecting the porch with the interior of the house opened. Lana stepped out in black trousers and a man's white shirt, untucked. A cigarette dangled between her fingers. Smoking and in pants; no respectable venue in Durban would let her inside.

"Phone call from Jo'burg," she said to van Niekerk. "He said it's urgent."

The major got to his feet and moved to Lana's side. He stopped and said, "Cooper has to find your friend Khan the gangster. Can you get him in?"

"Of course." Lana's smile was brittle, the cigarette now pinched between her fingers. "I can try."

"Good girl." The major patted her on the cheek and disappeared into the house.

It was decided: the ex-barmaid who slipped through the dark like a fox and shrugged off threats from guns, knives and very bad men would lead Emmanuel back into the lion's den.

———

"I'll get out here," Emmanuel said, and Zweigman pulled the dusty Bedford truck into a parking space on Timeball Road. They were a block from the address Lana had given him. "I should be back in under an hour. If not, drive to the major's house and wait there."

"Go well, Detective Sergeant." Shabalala raised a hand in farewell.

Emmanuel stepped out on the pavement. It felt good to have backup and even better to know Zweigman and Shabalala were a block away from any potential trouble.

He started down Timeball Road, counting the building numbers along on the way. A boy ran past trailing a kite made from brown paper bags and butcher's string.

Up ahead Lana stood outside 125, a squat brown building that might once have been a printing plant or a garment factory. It was an unremarkable structure but for the fleshy Indian man who stood on the front stairs smoking a cigarette. A trio of rawboned adolescents exited the building and ran down the steps with boxing gloves slung over their shoulders.

Lana turned at Emmanuel's approach and his pace faltered. He'd seen her frightened, drunk and even softened by physical pleasure, but he'd never seen her angry.

"Hurry up, for God's sake," she said. "I don't want to be here all afternoon."

"I told you I was fine by myself. There's no reason for you to be here," Emmanuel said. Was that his voice? Defensive and bruised and hard done by?

"This isn't a candy store." Lana took a round compact out of her bag, flicked it open and checked her reflection in the mirror: red lips, black eyeliner, silky black hair and a tantalizing display of cleavage. "You need more than an address and money in your pocket."

"You could have left me to talk to him by myself."

"The major didn't think that was a good idea." The tension in Lana's body made it obvious that declining to help set up this meeting had not been an option.

"I'm sorry," Emmanuel said. "To drag you into this."

"It's my fault." She dropped the compact back into her bag and snapped the lock. "I was the one who asked you for a lift home, remember?"

That felt like a year ago and an hour ago. Memory seemed to bend time back on itself. One time frame could not be changed. There were now fewer than seven hours left till the Detective Branch served the arrest warrant.

"Come on," Lana said, and climbed the stairs. The hem of her skirt swished against her bare legs and the heels of her sandals clicked on the hard surface. Emmanuel fell in beside her and she nodded a greeting to the Indian guard. Closer up, Emmanuel saw that the guard was one of those men whose life was best summed up by a series of ex's. Ex-boxer, ex-wrestler, ex–barroom bouncer.

"Hello, Miss Rose," the fleshy man said, and pulled the door open. Emmanuel slipped in behind Lana, grateful for the easy entry but disturbed by the familiar use of her name.

A bare boxing gym with three practice rings, a row of punching bags and an old weights bench were set out in a long room with a concrete floor. A taut black man skipped rope in a corner, while an Indian and a coffee-colored man sparred in a practice ring. An older white trainer with a flattened face called out, "Move your legs, you lazy bastard!" It was unclear which boxer he was addressing. The air was thick with the smell of sweat and dirty socks. Emmanuel felt a burn in his chest: a combination of the odor and memories of bare-knuckled school fights.

Lana walked straight through the gym to the back wall. Despite the dress and perfume, she looked like a logical part of the scene. She opened a door and they stepped into a small room with bare walls and no windows. A line of wooden chairs was set up outside a second door, against which Khan's bodyguard, the British bulldog in a suit, lounged. Two Indian women and a mixed-race man sat in the stark space with cheerless faces.

"Hell's waiting room," Emmanuel whispered to Lana.

"How else do you get an audience with the beast?" she said, and walked over to the bulldog, who straightened up from his slouch. "Tell Mr. Khan that Lana wants to see him."

"He's busy." The guard gave a lopsided smile. "I'll let him know you're here when he's finished up."

A strangled grunt came from inside the office and Lana moved back into the middle of the room without answering. An old Indian woman with a face crosshatched by worry lines sat on one of the hard wooden chairs and twisted a lace hankie between henna-stained fingers. Emmanuel walked over to Lana, who peered into her handbag with a frown, searching for something.

"Got any cigarettes?" she asked, and sorted through an assortment of lipstick, perfume and powder compacts with shaky fingers.

"Afraid not," Emmanuel said, and watched the frantic search for another minute. Lana was on a first-name basis with these citizens of Durban's underworld, but it didn't make her any more comfortable. The sharp scrape of furniture moving across the floor came from the direction of the office and Lana snapped the bag shut.

"This man you're looking for"—her voice was tense—"is he the one who killed Jolly Marks?"

Emmanuel knew she was making conversation to keep from imagining what might be happening behind the closed door.

"Brother Jonah was in the yards on the night Jolly was killed," he said. "That makes him a person of interest."

The old lady in the corner gave up strangling her hankie and leaned forward. "The police say it was Indian boys who did the killing. Two of them. Maybe the Dutta brothers," she whispered.

Emmanuel was certain that he had not mentioned the Duttas' involvement to anyone. Not even to the major. Only he and Giriraj knew that the brothers had discovered Jolly's body. The prostitute had not named them. They were just

Charras: dark men in slick suits with the cheek to think a red-haired Englishwoman would have sex with anyone for money.

"Who mentioned the Dutta brothers?" Emmanuel asked the old woman.

"No one." She threw a nervous glance at Mr. Khan's door and then fell silent. Nobody talked about Mr. Khan except Mr. Khan. That was the rule. If you broke the rule, something of yours got broken in return.

"So, maybe it was the Indian men." Lana tucked a dark strand of hair behind an ear. "Like the railway policeman at the bar said."

"Someone has certainly been spreading the word."

Emmanuel wondered if the police had taken Parthiv and Amal in for questioning and, if so, how they'd gone from a description of "two Indians in sharp suits" to suspects with names. The old woman's stare suggested that Mr. Khan was involved. If so, had Khan obtained that piece of information directly from the freight yards or had one of the scores of Dutta aunties and cousins gossiped over a fence?

The office door swung open and a brown-skinned girl in a flowered dress staggered out. Emmanuel judged her to be around eighteen. She looked neither left nor right but straight ahead to the exit. The mixed-race man seated in the waiting room got to his feet and walked to her side. They shared the same looks: dark hair, brown skin and light green eyes. A father and daughter, Emmanuel thought. The man touched the girl's arm, but she shrugged him off in disgust and hurried out to the gym and the street. The man followed, his shoulders slumped.

Khan's offer to supply Emmanuel with a woman, "any color, any size," took on a sinister edge. Sprinkled across Durban, in suburban houses, harborside flats and shantytown shacks, were females with debts to the Indian gangster.

Just how had Lana made Khan's acquaintance?

"He'll see you and your friend now, Miss Rose." The Brit waved them into the inner sanctum and then closed the door behind them.

The contrast with the waiting room was stark and, Emmanuel suspected, deliberate. Khan's office had a hand-knotted Chinese carpet spread across the floor and was furnished with heavy wood cabinets that glowed with polish. A courtyard bright with blossoms and vines could be glimpsed through an open window. A sullen parrot peered out from a bamboo cage that dangled from a stand to the right of a wide oak desk.

Books, pens, loose paper, a black Bakelite phone and the heavy wooden box from the Rolls were pushed to the edges of the desk—on which, Emmanuel felt certain, the girl had paid off her father's debt. Khan looked up from securing the top button on his baby-blue shirt and smiled at Lana.

"It's been a long time," he said.

"*Namaste,* Afzal." She walked over to a cabinet and lifted the hatch to reveal a bar stocked with nonalcoholic drinks. She tipped ice cubes into a tumbler and filled it with guava juice, then placed the drink within Khan's reach. "This meeting is a favor for a friend," she said.

Emmanuel knew that the favor was for van Niekerk and not for him. He shrugged off the thought.

"Mr. Cooper." Khan's dark eyes narrowed. "I said we would see each other again soon."

"You were right." Emmanuel made an effort to relax. How did Lana know what drink to pour the biggest Indian gangster in Durban? The answer to that question began to dawn on him.

"So . . ." Khan leaned back while Lana Rose slid the pens and loose paper back into place on the desktop and straightened the wooden smoking box. "Why are you here, Mr. Cooper?"

"I'm looking for Brother Jonah, the street preacher."

"You need salvation?"

"Information. Brother Jonah can help."

"I only give information to friends," Khan said. "Fuck off."

Lana moved to Khan's side and leaned against the edge of the desk. She was close enough to straighten the collar of his shirt.

"Consider him a friend of a friend," she said.

"Really?" Khan's hand snaked out faster than a mamba's head and encircled Lana's wrist. The flesh of his thumb rubbed against the blue veins visible under her pale skin, an action that was both intimate and violent. "How good a friend is Mr. Cooper?"

Emmanuel moved forward but Lana kept him in place with a glance that said, *I will handle this.* He eased back, repulsed by the beautifully furnished room, the luxury car, the custom-made suits. Afzal Khan spent a fortune to disguise the fact that he was just a thug.

"Not too rough," Lana Rose said. "I bruise easily."

Khan seemed fascinated by her skin, but the expression on her face was one of parental boredom. His fingers tightened their hold but she did not react.

The desk phone rang and Khan released her to pick up the

receiver. "What?" he barked into the mouthpiece, annoyed that a pleasurable moment had been spoiled.

Emmanuel motioned to Lana. The meeting was over. He'd find Brother Jonah himself if it meant lifting every garbage lid on the Point. The price of Khan's help, to be paid by Lana, was too high.

"Let's go," Emmanuel said. His anger made him feel twelve years old again, barefoot and running along a dirt lane in Sophiatown with his sister's tiny hand clutched in his. The sound of their mother's cries for help made the night blacker and colder than any he'd ever known. With every step away from the three-room shack and its blood-splattered walls, he'd promised himself that when he was older and stronger, he'd stand up to men like his father and Afzal Khan.

"Yes, let's go." Lana grabbed her handbag from the desk and followed Emmanuel to the door. The Oriental rug muffled their footsteps but the click of the door handle was sharp.

"Wait." Khan sat forward with the telephone cradled between his ear and shoulder. "There is an address that might be useful."

Emmanuel kept his back to the room for a long moment. Five minutes ago the information was out of reach, and now it was being handed over for nothing. What was Khan up to?

"If the address is useful, I'll take it," Emmanuel said, and moved back into the office. A muffled voice could be heard on the other end of the telephone line but it was impossible to pick up words. Khan scrawled something onto a piece of paper, folded it in half and slid it across the desk.

"Here," he said. "Try this."

Emmanuel opened the page to check the information. A

Signal Road address was scribbled in bright red ink. The Indian man put the receiver down in the cradle and pulled the wooden smoke box across the desk. He lifted the box lid and extracted a pouch of tobacco and a stack of rolling papers. "Be careful. More than one person at the meeting might scare Jonah off, and it would take hours to find him again."

"I'll be alone," Emmanuel said, and tried to figure how Khan, with the weight of the Durban underworld on his shoulders, knew about Brother Jonah's state of mind.

"Good luck," Khan said, and smiled. A bright spark of emotion lit up the dead center of his pupils like the headlights of a ghost train in a tunnel.

Emmanuel left the office. Lana closed the door behind them. Funny how accents could bend words so they seemed to take on another meaning. Khan's "Good luck" sounded strangely like "Good-bye." The people in the waiting room stared at them with a mixture of anxiety and envy.

"Be quiet till we're outside," Lana said, and they exited the building to the sound of boxers' gloves smacking muscle. "Now keep moving in the direction of your car. Don't look back and, for God's sake, do not run."

"Okay."

Emmanuel kept a quick pace and fought the urge to check the street behind them for danger. They skirted a group of grubby-faced white boys playing marbles on the pavement and walked on. The Bedford truck came into view.

"That's us," Emmanuel said.

"Keep going," Lana said when they drew level with the driver's window. "We'll stop behind the truck and talk there."

Zweigman leaned out to say something, but Emmanuel spoke first. "Give me ten minutes. I'll tell you the news then."

Lana ducked behind the truck's covered bed and listened. The click of the boys' marbles hitting together made the only discernible sound.

"That was a nice move back in the office," she said after her breathing slowed to normal. "Pretending to walk out on Khan. He hates being ignored."

"I wasn't pretending," Emmanuel said. Tiny red bruises marked the surface of her pale skin. "I don't like the way he does business."

"You, me and the rest of Durban." Lana held out her hand. "Let's see the address."

He gave her the paper. Khan's "good luck/good-bye" was fresh in his mind. Was the Indian man involved with Jolly Marks's murder?

"I know this place." She flicked the edge of the page with her fingernail. "It's an old rope storehouse. Hasn't been used for years. Not to store rope, at any rate."

"How do you know that?" Emmanuel asked.

The disquiet born in Khan's office resurfaced. Lana had strong ties with both the police and the criminals in Durban. She was van Niekerk's girlfriend but her loyalties might lie elsewhere.

"My father was a stores supervisor." It was clear from Lana's smile that his confusion amused her. "He worked in this building for five years before he retired. Khan owns it. It's a strange place for a person to stay. There's not much there besides shelves, pulleys and an outdoor toilet."

"A dead end?"

"There's something at the storehouse." Lana handed back the folded paper. "Khan could have sent you away empty-handed but he didn't. Don't meet with this Brother Jonah alone. Take your men with you. It's important to have backup."

"They're not my men, they're friends."

"Friends with transportation are extremely useful, Emmanuel." Her tone was brisk. "And the Zulu will come in handy. You'd be surprised how many Europeans are still scared of them."

"You think it's a setup?"

"Or Khan has found God and the good fairies on the same day. Take your pick."

Emmanuel pocketed the address. "Okay. I'll go in on foot and see what the situation is."

Lana gave an impatient sigh. "Drive there in the truck and park a few doors away. If Brother Jonah is hiding, three people at the door will scare him away. You'll have to go in alone. Your friends will wait fifteen minutes, then come looking. Do you still have the Walther?"

"Yes." Emmanuel was taken aback by the speed of the suggestions.

"Good. You might need it." Lana dug into her white leather handbag and removed a tattered telephone book with faded gold letters on the front. "This will also be useful. It's Khan's."

"You stole it?"

"Yes."

"You stole it just right now?" Emmanuel said, feeling like Khan's parrot.

"He shouldn't have left that mess on top of his desk," Lana said, and gave Emmanuel a look that demanded, *Do you have a problem with that?*

"Why did you take it?" Emmanuel heard that stranger's voice again. This time suspicious and bemused.

"A favor for a friend," she said, and smiled.

Did she mean him or van Niekerk? With the clock winding down, it barely mattered. The phone book was his. Besides, if Lana and Khan had been intimate, it was now over. The theft of the book made it clear that she was firmly in van Niekerk's camp.

"Thanks." Emmanuel put the book into his pocket. There was a part of himself, not too deeply hidden, that delighted in her criminal ways.

"Should van Niekerk send in the troops?" Lana asked, and fished a set of jangling car keys out of her bag.

"Not yet," Emmanuel said. "We'll go straight to the storehouse and try to find Brother Jonah. An hour or two and we'll head back to the major's."

"Watch your back," Lana said, then hurried off in the direction of Point Road. She'd parked a few streets away and come to Khan's office on foot, like a thief.

Emmanuel put on his hat and a mental flash of his ex-wife appeared: shy and pretty, sitting on a London bus and wrapped up against the freezing winter. The war was over but life was still grim. The physical wounds on his body were healed. Angela, sheltered and innocent, seemed proof that softness could still exist in a hard world. She was his opposite and Emmanuel had married her because of it. Hoping for . . . what? A new man to emerge, happy and content with life?

Lana disappeared around a corner, hips swinging, heels clicking. It was no wonder his marriage to Angela had failed. He'd asked too much of her. His buried childhood, the war, police work and an attraction to women with experience of life's dark places . . . he couldn't change who he was. There was no cure for the past. Whether or not he got out of this, he resolved to write to Angela and wish her well.

Emmanuel moved back to the passenger side of the truck and leaned into the open window.

"A meeting has been arranged?" Zweigman pushed the keys back into the ignition and rested his hands on the wheel, ready to start the trip.

"I've been given an address," Emmanuel said. "It could turn out to be nothing."

"Or something?" Shabalala said. He'd tracked and hunted his whole life around Jacob's Rest. He knew about trails and ambushes.

"Brother Jonah might be at this address. I have to take the risk."

"I will drive," Zweigman said, and turned the key. The engine spluttered, then settled into a rhythmic chug. Shabalala opened the door and motioned for Emmanuel to get in.

"Okay." Emmanuel gave up the fight and squashed into the Bedford. He needed backup. He'd been alone too long. "Go down Timeball Road. Take the next left."

Emmanuel kept low but stole a glance at Khan's office a half block ahead. An Indian woman and two young men approached the front steps and talked to Khan's guard, who flicked a spent cigarette into the gutter and disappeared inside.

"What are they doing here?" Emmanuel wondered aloud. Maataa, Parthiv and Amal were dressed for a formal occasion. Both the boys wore ironed suits, and Maataa's purple sari glittered with gold and silver thread.

The door pushed open and Khan appeared on the top step.

He smiled and shook hands with Maataa, then reached over and slapped Parthiv's shoulder like a jovial uncle. Amal stuffed his hands into his pockets to avoid physical contact, and the unlikely quartet filed into the brick building. It was not an impromptu meeting. Khan had been expecting them. The Duttas' loyal strongman, Giriraj, was nowhere in sight.

"Is everything well, Sergeant?" Shabalala asked.

"Yes." Emmanuel concentrated on locating the next turn. He glimpsed port cranes and harbor tugs between wide brick warehouses and shipping agents. A tight bunch of Afrikaner rail workers took a smoke break on a corner.

The urban landscape became a blur. His mind was back in Khan's windowless waiting room and on the old woman with the henna-stained hands. Emmanuel suspected the Dutta boys' names had come from the murder scene directly to Khan. And now the Duttas had been invited to his office. To declare war or to initiate peace?

21

ZWEIGMAN TURNED ONTO Signal Road and slowed the Bedford down. The truck crawled past the offices of the harbormaster, a two-story Victorian building with a dash of Gothic, and continued on to the address Khan had provided.

"There it is." Shabalala pointed to a utilitarian wood and iron warehouse with double-fronted doors barred with a heavy piece of wood. "You will not be able to get in that way, Sergeant Cooper. Maybe there is an entrance by the side."

Zweigman parked the truck in front of a row of trim workers' cottages detailed with lace ironwork on the verandas. An old black man and woman, stooped with age, hauled buckets of wood into one of the small cottages for the evening fire.

Emmanuel got out of the truck and checked the time. Ten minutes past one. He had to be back by twenty-five past or Zweigman and Shabalala would pile out of the car and follow him into the storehouse.

"Fifteen minutes." Zweigman withdrew a fob watch from the medical kit. "Your time has begun, Detective."

Emmanuel took off without a good-bye, an old superstition from the war, when saying the words out loud was tempting the gods to grant your wish. He moved to the store-house. A wide driveway, built for truck access, led to a side door.

A tortoiseshell cat slept in a spot of sun that hit a steel ramp leading to a loading bay. Emmanuel tried the handle to the loading dock doors: no movement. He circled around to the backyard. A brick outhouse crumbled amid knee-high weeds, and the rusted remains of a woodburning stove leaned against the brick wall in defeat. A paint-flecked rear door was also locked.

Emmanuel returned to the side dock and knocked four times. The cat awoke and sprang with agile grace from the platform and into flowering weeds. He hammered again, louder.

"Hold on, there. Give me a minute."

Separate metal locks turned with rusty clicks. Emmanuel checked the Walther on the chance that Brother Jonah's easy manner was a ruse.

The door opened. Emmanuel stepped back and almost lost his balance. Brother Jonah was completely naked but for a small white towel wrapped around his waist. His Jesus hair was tied back in a ponytail and beads of sweat covered his wiry frame. If fat was a sign of sloth, the street preacher was clear of that sin. He was lean muscle wrapped in skin.

"Sister Bergis's friend." The street preacher made the con-nection. "The one who refused to share his name."

"It's Brother Emmanuel." Emmanuel held out a hand and tried to maintain a neutral expression. A knife, a gun, a sham-bok or a metal chain, those things were on the list of possible hazards. A near-naked man with a ponytail was not. "I've come seeking answers to some questions that are bothering me. Can you spare a few minutes of your time?"

"I offer guidance where and when I am able." Brother Jonah gave Emmanuel's hand a quick squeeze and retreated into the storehouse. "So long as you understand that man's time clock doesn't mean anything in here. Nature is in charge. She's the one who rides shotgun on all our earthly journeys and I am her servant."

Emmanuel nodded even though he had no idea what Brother Jonah was talking about. A row of grimy glass brick windows positioned just under the roofline admitted a minimum of light into the interior of the wood and iron building. Pigeons roosted on three wide beams that ran across the width of the ceiling. Steel shelves, mostly empty, took up uneven lengths of floor space. Wooden crates stamped with the stag and crown emblem of an imported whiskey brand were packed on a middle shelf. One of the trucks that rolled out of the Point freight yards with stolen goods had unloaded here in this warehouse.

Emmanuel checked the shadows for movement and detected nothing. An aurora of hard white shone like an industrial sun in the far corner of the storehouse.

"My workplace is down there." Brother Jonah closed the door and Emmanuel followed him toward the light source. The evidence did not back up Khan's comment about the preacher being scared off. Nakedness and vulnerability went hand in hand. When people sensed danger, they clothed themselves and they armed themselves. Failing that, they hid. Stand and fight or run and hide were the simple rules that governed human response to a threatening situation. Brother Jonah had answered the door naked but for a towel, a very small towel. He appeared to not have a worry in the world.

The light grew brighter and Emmanuel palmed the Walther. The unofficial motto of the special air services, "Bullshit baffles brains," came to mind. A naked preacher rambling about Mother Nature in the middle of an abandoned storehouse was the perfect distraction. The real danger was hidden in the unlit corners.

"Another day or so," Brother Jonah said, "and my work will finally be done."

Emmanuel let the evangelist get three steps ahead of him. "What work is it that you do?" he said. "I thought you were a preacher."

"Salvation is my major occupation." Brother Jonah wiped sweat from his neck and dried his fingers on the towel. "But I pick up odd jobs here and there to feed the body."

The major muscles of his back and arms moved beneath the skin. It was a body that didn't take much feeding.

"What's this job?" Emmanuel asked, stopping short of the circular white glow that hit the concrete floor. His eyes adjusted to the contrast between barely lit darkness and the manufactured light of a huge overhead lamp that was positioned a foot or so above head height. Smaller lamps with bare bulbs shone directly into a glass box resting on a laminated tabletop. A deep pile of ripped newspaper and grass was piled inside the glass container. Heat radiated from the lit circle.

"Helping nature," Brother Jonah said, and entered into the lamp glow. "Come take a look."

Emmanuel edged closer but held back till he was certain

there was no movement on the outer edges of the circle. He mentally fixed the position of the back doorway and slipped the Walther back into the hip holster.

"See?" Brother Jonah pointed into the pile of grass and ripped newspaper. Three pale blue eggs lay in a hollow scooped into the middle of the man-made nest. "Had them under heat for twenty hours already. They'll be ready to hatch soon."

"You're incubating eggs." Emmanuel removed his hat and fanned it to generate a breeze. The heat lamps raised the temperature, but not high enough to warrant removing every stitch of clothing. That decision was a personal one, made, he suspected, simply because the preacher liked being naked.

"Whom are you working for?" he asked. He had to make a spoonful of sense out of Brother Jonah's incubator before turning the interview back to Jolly Marks and the Russian couple.

"Mr. Khan. He's crazy about exotic parrots and birds. Likes to rear them by hand." Brother Jonah thumped the muscles of his chest and arms with tight fists and sucked in deep breaths. "You should get that jacket and shirt off, Brother Emmanuel. Get the heat into you. It opens up the lungs."

"I'm fine," Emmanuel said. "So, you work for Mr. Khan."

"Now and then." Brother Jonah began a series of deep knee squats. "A monkey could do this job, but Mr. Khan likes to have white men working for him and he pays for the privilege."

"I'm sure he does." White staff was the ultimate symbol of power for a nonwhite man. Proof that money could turn the world on its head and make it spin anticlockwise.

"Sister Bergis looks down on me. I know." Brother Jonah

moved on to knee lifts. "But I'm not on the teat of a rich missionary society. My work is funded out of my own pocket."

"Khan pays that much for egg incubation?" Emmanuel let a trace of disbelief color the question. Selling stolen whiskey was a good business with a regular customer base. That was probably how the preacher earned his keep.

Brother Jonah stopped the exercise routine and placed both hands on his hips. "You shouldn't listen to Sister Bergis," he said. "Lonely women have powerful imaginations. They fill their time with stories. That comes from an empty womb."

The preacher stared beyond the circle of light to something on the far wall. Emmanuel turned quickly, anticipating the swing of a club or a fist, and saw a full-length mirror propped against the wall. Brother Jonah admired his reflection in the looking glass: a man who believed he was formed in God's own image.

"Yeah, Sister Bergis has some crazy theories about you." Emmanuel faced the preacher with a smile. "She thinks you were a soldier. A fighter. I told her you were a man of peace. That you probably sat the war out in a conscientious objector cell."

"I fought in the Pacific." The veins on the preacher's forehead stood out from anger. "Hand-to-hand with the Japs. Europe was a cakewalk compared to what we did out on those islands. And that was just the half of it."

"The Pacific. That was hard fighting."

"And for what?" Brother Jonah stripped the towel loose and dried the sweat from his legs and chest. "The Russians have half of Europe under godless sway and we handed Japan back to the Japanese. The world's more dangerous than ever, Brother Emmanuel. I expect that's what's brought you to me. The pitiful state of things."

Emmanuel certainly hadn't come for the naked preacher show that was being lived out in three inglorious dimensions within arm's length.

"I'm here to talk about the murder of Jolly Marks. Why do you think he was killed?"

"The will of God." Brother Jonah resecured his towel. "We have to accept it, even when we don't understand it."

"You were in the freight yards that night," Emmanuel said. "I thought you could give me a more down-to-earth perspective on what happened. Maybe tell me what you were doing there."

Brother Jonah stilled. "That information is given out on a need-to-know basis, and I determine that you do not need to know a thing. Get my drift?"

"I can place you in the yards on the night Jolly Marks was killed," Emmanuel continued as if he hadn't been interrupted. "You followed a pretty blond girl from the passenger wharf. What more do I need to know? You're not a man of God; you're a night crawler. Did Jolly know that?"

"I'm a soldier in the Lord's army," Brother Jonah said quietly, and adjusted a heat lamp to shine a more direct light. "My guess is that you're an undercover policeman. Am I correct? Nothing wrong with that job, but you're not equipped or trained to handle this kind of situation, son."

"How hard can it be if you're involved?" Emmanuel said. The "son" tag riled him. There was a fifteen-year age difference between them at most. A couple of thousand miles separated the European and Pacific theaters of war. Brothers in arms, maybe, but even that was a stretch. Besides, one unstable father was enough to last two lifetimes.

"See, that's your ignorance talking," Brother Jonah said. "The personnel for every mission are handpicked to ensure victory. I was chosen and you were not."

"Chosen to murder children and old ladies?" Emmanuel laid on the contempt. "That's some mission you were handpicked for, brother. The angels must be pleased with the three new souls you sent up."

"Your wires are crossed. This mission was recon. Forward scout, locate and identify. No casualties reported."

"You were there but no one got hurt on your watch." Emmanuel translated the military-speak into plain English. "Jolly had his throat slit. That qualifies as serious hurt even by Pacific war standards."

"Same place, same time, different universe," Brother Jonah said. "Here's a heads-up from me: If you want to find that boy's killer, look for a sick individual with an eye for children. A devil in disguise."

A pigeon flew off a beam in the roof.

"I'm looking at him," Emmanuel said.

"Jesus Christ." Brother Jonah the preacher took a backseat to Jonah the battle-weary soldier. "I took an oath before God and man and the whole Pacific Ocean. No more blood. Not one drop to be spilled by my hand so long as I live. Amen. Hallelujah. I did go forth and I did sin no more."

That sounded mighty convincing, but Emmanuel needed facts, not biblical quotes. "You were in the rail yard that night?"

"Nothing illegal about walking from the passenger terminal to Point Road."

"Was Jolly Marks there?"

"Caught a glimpse of him, sure."

"You didn't speak?"

Brother Jonah shrugged. "No. He was working. I was working."

Emmanuel loosened his tie. The lamps magnified the tropical heat twofold and his mouth was fast becoming an arid hollow. The pressure in his head was beginning to build. He'd need to drink a gallon of water the moment he left the storehouse.

"Did you see anyone else that night?" he asked.

"Shadows," Brother Jonah said, then smiled at a sudden memory. "Oh, yeah, and a bald Indian man tuning a white whore's motor in an alleyway. Sounded like he found her starter button and pressed it real good."

Giriraj and the prostitute.

"No one else?"

"Nope." The preacher fiddled with his ponytail, twisting the lanky hair around bony fingers.

"So my witness was wrong," Emmanuel said. "There wasn't a blond girl and an older man in the yard that night."

"Not that I remember."

"You didn't follow them from the passenger quay?"

"I did not." Brother Jonah adjusted the lamps again, careful not to make eye contact. His face and arms were beaded with sweat despite the recent wipe-down.

Everything the preacher had said about Jolly Marks had the ring of truth, but he'd lied about shadowing Natalya and Nicolai from the passenger quay. Nicolai was the "Ivan" being talked about at Larsen's scrapyard.

"Who hired you to follow the Ivan?" Emmanuel said. "Was it Khan? The police?"

The preacher hesitated, thrown by the use of the slang word for a Russian, then said, by rote, "That's classified."

Emmanuel tried to establish a clearer picture of events. Brother Jonah believed he was God's soldier handpicked for a specific duty. He admitted being in the freight yards and even to seeing Jolly Marks but believed the "mission" was pure reconnaissance. Maybe Jonah was the one blindsided by all the spook bullshit.

"Here's something I think you really do need to know," Emmanuel said. "Jolly Marks talked to the Russians that night. He helped them get to a house on the Bluff. Someone killed him to try and get that information."

"Crap. A night crawler messed with that boy."

"No. He was killed to get to the Ivan."

"Forward scout, locate and identify." Brother Jonah jabbed a finger in Emmanuel's direction. "That's all."

"That was just the first part of the plan," Emmanuel said gently. He knew what it was like to be a soldier and to march through night and day, from one fight to another, on the orders of commanders who controlled the big picture and told you nothing. "The real aim was to capture the Russians and exchange them. Jolly was a civilian casualty."

Jonah's wiry body tensed and a flicker of doubt crossed his face.

"Tell me who's in command of this mission, and together we can sort this mess out," Emmanuel said.

A metal shelf rattled in the dark and the tortoiseshell cat from the steps streaked into the circle of light and crashed against a table leg. The glass egg container skated across the laminate but hit the raised metal edge of the tabletop and held steady. Pigeons flew up to the pitch of the ceiling.

"I must have left that door open." Brother Jonah grabbed the cat by the scruff of the neck and held it aloft. "How many times do I have to tell you to stay out, miss?"

Emmanuel stepped back from the cat's claws and the incubator lights cut out. The storehouse plunged into darkness. Two torch beams swung between the shelves and threw disks of light onto the walls. Fast, running footsteps clacked across the concrete floor. Emmanuel dropped to his knees and crawled in the direction of the back door. His head hit a steel shelf. He moved to the left and reoriented himself.

"What the hell is going on?" Brother Jonah shouted. "Who is that?"

A high-powered beam located the preacher's face and he threw a hand up to shield his eyes. The cat flexed its back and broke free. A spill of light from the torch beam gave a candle's worth of illumination. Emmanuel glimpsed the outline of the back exit and moved toward it. The second beam split the dark and shone on the door handle.

He was trapped.

"Still locked," a male voice called. "He's in here somewhere."

Emmanuel turned sixty degrees. Brother Jonah's reflection bounced off the full-length mirror resting against the wall. Emmanuel's impulse was to rush, but the rusted discipline of the battlefield held the reins steady. He crawled to the mirror and levered it forward so there was enough space to squeeze in behind. He pressed his body behind the glass and rested the weight back. Escape was impossible. Invisibility was the second best option.

"Mr. Khan is going to hear about this," Brother Jonah railed. "You are going to be in a shitstorm of trouble. Mark my words."

"Where is he?" a cool voice said. "Where's Cooper?"

"Who the hell is Cooper?" The preacher's voice crackled with ill humor. "And get that light out of my face. I can't see a damn thing."

Emmanuel stayed still and tried to figure out what was happening on the other side of the mirror. Two men with high-powered torches. Not Fletcher or Robinson of the local police. One well-modulated voice: educated South African. The other, local but far less polished.

"Cooper." Anger heated the cool voice. "The man you were talking to. Where is he?"

Emmanuel's heart thundered. He placed the voice. It belonged to the pale tradesman from the police station. He was sure of it.

"I can't think with that light in my eyes. Can't see a thing, brother. Dip that from my face and we can talk."

The beam of the flash angled downward and Emmanuel made sure to stay within the edges of the mirror. A shuffle of feet was followed by a grunt of recognition from the preacher.

"Oh," Brother Jonah said. "It's you. That's perfect timing. We need to talk about the Ivans."

"Did Cooper mention them?"

"Yeah . . . and a lot more." Brother Jonah's voice hardened. "Seems you lied to me, brother. You said no blood. You broke that promise."

Steel smacked flesh and the preacher's body crashed into the mirror. The glass cracked and the back of the mirror hit Emmanuel's face hard. Hot clusters of pain exploded along the ridge of his nose. He pressed his mouth shut to hold in a gasp. Brother Jonah's slack arm dropped into view at the side of the mirror.

"*Do not break cover,*" the Scottish sergeant major whispered. "*It's the tradesman. He's the one who's been following you for the last couple of days . . . He's after the Russians. He fucked up twice already, once at the house on the Bluff and then at Hélène's. If he finds you now, he and his friend will make you piss blood till you tell them where the Ivans are.*"

"Back to the side entrance," the tradesman said. "We'll work our way to this end of the building and check every crack and shelf on the way. We'll flush him out."

"And this one?" the second man said.

"Leave Brother Jonah. He'll be right in a little while. The boss will give me no end of uphill if I kill him. He's still annoyed about the others."

The others. Emmanuel pressed his body flat to the wall. Jolly Marks, Mrs. Patterson and her maid were collateral damage. They were not human beings to the tradesman but impediments to the success of the mission. The tradesman's certainty that the same man had killed all three victims came from the fact that he had killed them himself.

Emmanuel tried to catch his breath. The mission to capture the Russians was a fox hunt and he was the hound, released from police custody by the tradesman to run the prey to ground. The deal struck in the interrogation room, to find Jolly's killer or face the gallows, was a fantasy. The tradesman would kill him as soon as he had the Russians. Like the three murder victims, Emmanuel was expendable.

Even during war, the concept of collateral damage and "acceptable losses" was obscene. He clenched his hands into fists and anger pulsed through him.

"*Cool down, laddie,*" the sergeant major said. "*Use your head. It's dark out there. They have torches and guns. Get out and get away. Fuck them up later. It's called a tactical retreat.*"

Footsteps receded across the concrete surface and in the direction of the side entrance. The flashlights dimmed and left behind a molasses-colored void.

"*Now.*" The sergeant major breathed. "*Edge out and head for the back door quick-smart.*"

Emmanuel pushed the mirror forward and a broken shard fell from its cracked surface. Another piece shattered into a dozen refracting needles and a torch beam searched the perimeter of the floor.

"The mirror is falling to pieces," the tradesman said. "Move out."

Emmanuel eased sideways, careful to avoid the glass scattered across the floor. Images of Brother Jonah crumpled on the ground were captured and distorted multiple times in the broken mirror, as if in a circus fun house. He made for the wall and traced fingertips along the wooden slats. Beams of white swept right to left in a block pattern, searching the shadows. Emmanuel moved faster and found the raised metal handle of a deadbolt.

He sucked in a breath and his lungs cooled. The sequence of events was simple. Open the bolt, open the door and run. Three quick steps. The torch beams swept closer. Emmanuel twisted the deadbolt open. There was a hard click similar to the hammer of a gun hitting the chamber. He pushed at the door and sunshine flooded into the storehouse.

"There."

Emmanuel sprinted into the weeds and scrambled over to the abandoned woodstove. He prayed Zweigman and Shabalala were late. Two civilians against two armed men was no contest.

He approached the rusted metal stove at a run and found a foothold on the front burner. He hoisted his weight onto the top. The legs of the ancient cooker gave way with a metal sigh and the top listed like a ship plunging to the lower depths. Outstretched arms couldn't prevent him from falling into a bed of kaffirweeds.

He lifted his head and saw a narrow space behind the outhouse and a mound of red bricks tipped against the back fence. He crawled toward the narrow passage and edged into it with an inch to spare at either side. Amid the bruised greenery and the building debris, he crouched in the classic soldier's pose: waiting on the cusp of danger.

"Where the fuck is he?" the tradesman said. A flash of translucent white skin and the sleeve of a midnight-blue suit jacket sped across the narrow space behind the outhouse.

"Next yard?" the other voice said.

"Could be. Check over the top. I'll comb this area. He's here somewhere."

Emmanuel crouched lower. The tight hiding space was a perfect short-term solution. Long-term, it was the equivalent to being a tin duck in a shooting gallery. Five minutes into a grid search and they would find him. He held his breath, listened and heard nothing. He waited.

The throaty chug of an engine and the crunch of wheels on the side drive broke the tense silence in the unkept yard. A long blast of a horn was followed by the slam of a door.

"Hello, is anyone home?" Zweigman's voice called out. "Is this the Empire Storehouse? I have a pickup."

"Shit." The tradesman's voice was hard. "We have to move out. Circle back in five."

"One look at this gun and he'll clear off quick," the tradesman's partner said.

Emmanuel's heart tried to escape through his shirt. Zweigman had survived the war, but not in uniform. He was a healer, not a fighter.

"Keep it holstered," the tradesman said. The collapsed stove groaned under a new weight. "No more civilian casualties. We'll double back later and take this place apart."

The second man grunted and the adjoining fence creaked. Two heavy feet thumped to the ground from a height. The search team had gone into the adjoining yard.

"*Go, go,*" the sergeant major ordered. "*I'll fall back now that reinforcements have arrived.*"

Emmanuel scrambled to the mouth of the small space and looked out. Sky, weeds and rusted metal, but no men in suits. The tradesman and his sidekick were in the next yard behind the fence.

"Hello." Zweigman's voice came closer. "Hello. I have a pickup."

Emmanuel cleared the corner of the outhouse and cut across the choked ground. Zweigman saw him coming. Emmanuel signaled for quiet and the German doctor withdrew to the passenger side of the Bedford, pulled open the door and slid into the front. Shabalala was now behind the wheel. Emmanuel jumped through the door Zweigman had left open and the Bedford rolled down the drive.

Shabalala took a left onto Signal Road. An Indian vegetable seller with two baskets suspended from a bamboo pole balanced across her ropy shoulders labored along the sidewalk. "Brinjal. Potato. Onion." Her plaintive call filled the air. "Fresh brinjal."

The storehouse faded to a smudge of mud brown behind them, indiscriminate from the other industrial buildings that fronted the road.

"Your nose is bleeding." Zweigman pulled a cloth handkerchief from his pocket and gave it to Emmanuel. "It's clean," he said.

"Thanks."

"You found Brother Jonah?"

"Yes, but two other men found me before I had a chance to finish questioning him."

"The man who gave you the address, this Mr. Khan," Shabalala said. "He is the one who sent them."

"Has to have been," Emmanuel said, and glanced out of the window. "I was in the storehouse long enough to figure out that Brother Jonah isn't the killer."

"Bad news," Shabalala said. "You are still up to your neck in cowshit, Detective Sergeant."

"Just to my armpits," Emmanuel said. "I know who killed those people. I just don't know his name. Or where he lives."

"This is progress?" Zweigman said with a laugh.

Emmanuel took out the book Lana had liberated with her fingers and held it up. "Khan has the name of the man I'm looking for. The number is probably in this phone book."

"But how will you know which name is the correct one?"

"I won't. Khan is going to tell me."

22

A WHISTLE BLEW A long, sharp note and Shabalala eased the truck to a stop in front of a row of two-story terraces with deep verandas overlooking tended squares of green garden. A black man watering a fruiting kumquat tree retreated into the house and closed the door.

Shouts and the pounding of running feet came from the pavement. Emmanuel peered at the side mirror. Three black men in hard-worn clothes most likely picked at random from a mission charity basket flew across the street and disappeared into an alleyway. Another shrill whistle cut the air. Emmanuel scrambled out of the truck. He didn't want the others caught in a net intended for him. Zweigman and Shabalala joined him on the pavement.

A lanky black man in gum boots and blue overalls flew by, wild-eyed and sweating. The snarl of police dogs followed him.

"Black Maria," Shabalala said, and pointed to the street corner. A caged police van, painted gray and not black as the name suggested, lumbered into view. Native men and women of all shapes and sizes scattered before it, like marbles spilling from a schoolboy's pocket.

"A passbook raid." Shabalala spoke without emotion. This was the job of the police. To round up all the natives without proper passes and ship them back to the native locations. A black man without proper permission to be in the city was naked in the wind, a thing to be swept up and thrown out into the countryside.

"Hell of a raid." Emmanuel pointed to four policemen with German shepherds straining against leather leashes. A squad of foot policemen blotted out the wall of the building behind them in a solid box of olive drab uniforms.

"What is happening?" Zweigman pressed back against the truck door, pale and trembling. "Where are the police taking these people?"

Emmanuel sensed the depths of the doctor's fear. A roundup of members of a particular race to be transported out of the public eye must surely bring back memories of Germany during the war.

"Every month or so the police raid an area and scoop up all the natives who don't have proper passes," he said quietly. The scene was so typically South African that it was a surprise to have to explain it. Even children knew what this wild scattering of natives meant. "Those who are in the city illegally run and hide. Those who are caught are sent back to the native locations to fend for themselves."

"I have heard but never seen." Zweigman rubbed his forehead while he recovered from the old fear that had so clearly overtaken him.

A police whistle blew a piercing note. The uniforms broke rank and ran like a khaki tide into the main streets and the alleyways. The nonwhites who did not run stayed still. The dog squad moved toward the Bedford, and the dogs raked the sidewalk with their wet snouts, their mouths open, their canine teeth visible. An item of white cotton clothing hung from the pocket of the lead handler's trousers.

"You should get into the truck, Detective," Zweigman said. "It is better not to be seen."

"I'll be fine," Emmanuel said, and turned to Shabalala. "You stick close."

"*Yebo.*" The native constable understood that out of uniform and without official police papers, he was just another black man forced to account for himself in a white world.

A scrawny Indian man crouched in a doorway like a praying mantis. Even though Indians and mixed-race people didn't need passes to stay in urban areas, the laborer kept his head bowed and his hands held up in a gesture of supplication. A dog wheeled in the direction of the figure in the doorway and the handler loosened the lead. The animal leaped forward and snuffled at the Indian's clothes and hair, eager to establish a trace scent.

"Got something, boy?" the dog squad policeman urged his canine partner on. "Got something?"

The German shepherd fell back, disappointed. The laborer remained glued in place.

"Go into the truck, Sergeant," Shabalala said. "I will be fine here with the doctor."

"Not until I figure out what's going on." This action was more than a raid to net illegal black workers.

Emmanuel pulled the van Niekerk–issued Detective Branch ID from a pocket and moved to the line of police dogs. He zeroed in on a red-faced boy who was struggling to keep his dog under control. The fresh recruits responded better to rank and title. Cynicism was still a few years off.

"Constable." He flashed the Detective Branch ID. "What's going on? You've got the whole Point in an uproar."

"Where have you been, Detective Sergeant?" The uniform smiled and tussled with the dog lead. "We got him."

"Who?"

"The Indian who killed Jolly Marks." The constable was dragged away by canine force and his words were cut by the whimper of the excited dogs. "He ran, but we'll find him."

The dogs set off at a lope. Pedestrians scattered from the pavement, and the way lay clear for the police hounds. The laborer in the doorway had not moved. Emmanuel had not moved, either. The constable's cheerful promise was a heart-stopper. Zweigman and Shabalala came over to him.

"They are not looking for you, Detective Sergeant," Shabalala said. "They are looking, I think, for an Indian man."

Farther down the street, the dogs stopped to examine a dignified Indian in a pin-striped suit. The scent didn't hold and the dogs set off again, panting.

"They're after the Indian who killed Jolly Marks." Emmanuel repeated the constable's words even though there was no sense in them. Two Indian suspects had mysteriously shrunk to one. The sharp call of police whistles and the thundering of boots on the pavement meant that a fistful of money was being thrown at the apprehension of Jolly's killer. Someone had loosened the law enforcement purse strings. This effort was for the arrest of a child killer. It was interracial. It was a propaganda opportunity that could not be squandered.

"A witness gave the police a description of two dark-haired Indian men who were seen near the crime scene. Now it's down to one Indian and they're pretty sure he's guilty," Emmanuel explained. A slew of uniformed police cut across the end of Browns Road. He pointed to them. "Look at the number of cops. The Black Maria is to mop up any stray natives flushed out in the search. Dozens of pass violators and a child killer caught in a single afternoon. Whoever is in charge of this operation is going to get a promotion."

"You are no longer the prime suspect. The mistake has been rectified," Zweigman said. "You are free."

"Someone let me off the hook and now an innocent Indian man is on it instead." Emmanuel shoved his hands into his jacket pockets, bunched them into fists. "Neither one of us is guilty."

And there was still the outstanding matter of the double murder at the Dover apartments. Emmanuel felt certain that his name would still be on those arrest warrants.

"The man you talked to at the storehouse, he is the one the police are searching for?" Shabalala said when Emmanuel showed no joy at being released from the hangman's noose.

"No. Brother Jonah is white and American."

"Then who are the police after with their guns and dogs?" Zweigman puzzled aloud.

"I think I know," Emmanuel said, and moved off the pavement for two black men who were running full-pelt for the alley. Their rubber shoes, fashioned from discarded car tires, hit the pavement with hard slaps. Two light-haired boys, similar enough to be twins, stuck their heads out of a stationary Chrysler and giggled at the chaos of the natives and the police running around in all directions.

On the opposite side of Browns Road, Amal Dutta lurched from door to door in a frantic search for something.

"Amal." Emmanuel hurried across the asphalt and touched the boy's shoulder. The teenager's body vibrated with harried breath. "Slow down. Stop. What are you looking for?"

"Giriraj." Amal took great lungfuls of air. "I have to find Giriraj."

"Why?"

"I . . . I . . ." The words petered out and Amal slumped against the wall and his lungs wheezed from lack of oxygen.

"Sit." Zweigman appeared at Emmanuel's shoulder and talked directly to the stricken boy. "Sit down on the step and put your head between your knees. Good."

The doctor squatted in front of Amal and placed both hands on his shoulders. "There is enough air for every living thing. Take a deep breath. And another. Good. One breath at a time."

Shabalala wove through the crawl of traffic and joined Emmanuel on the footpath. A crowd of Afrikaner and English rail yard workers gathered on the corner of Point Road, all whispers and pointed index fingers. It was clear that, for once, the opposing "European" sides agreed on something. Emmanuel moved to block their view of Amal. Outraged citizens could so easily turn into a mob, and community-minded action into a full-scale riot.

Balmy Durban was no stranger to savage outbreaks of bloodshed. Beer hall riots and intertribal fighting claimed dozens of lives. Anti-rent-rise protests in the late forties had ended in the frenzied looting of Indian stores and the savaging of shop owners and innocent bystanders. The civil English façade was a hair's breadth away from chaos. And that was the essence of empire: the unspoken tension between civilized appearance and stark reality.

Emmanuel squatted next to Zweigman. Shabalala stood to protect their backs. The Zulu constable also felt the low tremor of suppressed violence that traveled in the air like an electric charge before a storm. Police guns were the thunder and lightning.

"Tell me," Emmanuel said to Amal.

"The police are looking for Giriraj."

"What for?"

"Because of the boy we found in the rail yard. Because of him." Amal licked his lips, miserable. "The policemen want him for that."

"For the murder?"

"Yes."

"Did you call and give them Giriraj's name?"

"No. Never."

"Parthiv?"

"Not him, either."

"Who, then?"

Amal glanced the length of the street, then leaned forward. "Mr. Khan." He whispered the name like a witch casting a spell. "It was Mr. Khan. He knew that Parthiv and I were in the rail yard near the boy's body. He said to Maataa, 'If the police know this, they will arrest your sons. They will go to jail and they will hang for that white boy's murder.' "

The meeting between the Duttas and Khan wasn't a peace initiative. It was a promise of disaster for the Dutta family.

"Khan blackmailed your mother," Emmanuel said.

"No." Amal's smile was cynical. "Mr. Khan said it was an exchange of information."

"Of course," Emmanuel said. "Tell me about this exchange of information."

"Mr. Khan said that the police did not have to know about me or Parthiv. He could fix this problem."

"But . . ." There was always a "but."

"The detectives knew that Indian men were in the rail yard. Mr. Khan said he had to give the police something to use. Just one name in exchange for our freedom."

"Giriraj."

"Maataa said no. Parthiv said no. I said no." Amal struggled to his feet. Emmanuel and Zweigman stood at either side of him while he fought back tears. "Mr. Khan told us that Giriraj was a bad man. A thief. A liar. That he stole from us and spent the money on prostitutes."

Khan's informers had been working overtime. He probably knew more about Jolly's murder and the plan to capture Nicolai and Natalya than the Detective Branch did.

"Then," Amal continued, "he picked up the telephone and dialed a number and asked to talk to a . . . a . . ."

"Detective Head Constable Robinson." Emmanuel supplied the name but Amal shook his head in response.

"No. It was a British Raj name."

"What do you mean?"

"Two surnames joined together," Amal said, then continued with the story. " 'Whose name shall I give the police?' " he finished imitating Khan, then fell into an uneasy silence. The end of the story was being played out on the streets around them.

High-pitched whistles screeched like metal birds and police wheeled as people ran past them. Giriraj came flying around the corner, crossed the tarred road and poured on the speed. The white port workers raised a shout and a group of them gathered and ran after the Indian man.

"Giriraj!" Amal shouted, but the Dutta family bodyguard was deaf to everything except the police whistles and the thunder of footsteps behind him.

Humans found it remarkably easy to turn against each other, Emmanuel thought. If someone was a different color, had a wandering eye or was left-handed, then turning against him became even easier. How elemental and comforting to believe that wrongdoing could be identified by a physical trait. The police and the others were after Giriraj, but all Indian men—fat, thin, tall and dwarfed—were, for the duration of the hunt, courting danger. Amal took off after Giriraj, and Emmanuel raced after him.

"Giriraj!" Amal's plea blew away on the wind.

Traffic crawled, then stopped when a squad of uniformed policemen swarmed across the road and veered in the direction Giriraj had fled. Emmanuel glanced over his shoulder. Shabalala and Zweigman were still with him, and behind them were more rail workers and police. If they stopped they'd be trampled under the momentum of the crowd.

Amal slowed. Emmanuel grabbed his arm and urged him on. "Keep running," he said, and dragged the boy along the pavement by force of will.

Ahead was a busy four-way intersection strung with electric tramlines and anchored on the corners by traffic robots. Trucks and cars idled at the red light. An ordinary Monday afternoon. Durban's image was still intact and bathed in mellow light. Giriraj, trailed by pursuers, got closer to the corner.

The traffic light turned to green. Cars surged into the intersection. Giriraj jumped the lip of the pavement and hit the crosswalk in full flight. A car braked hard and a horn blared. Giriraj skirted the front bumper of a maroon Mercedes and disappeared behind a delivery van. A second vehicle blasted its horn, a long, sustained note of alarm. The electric lines of the tram shook with the force of a sudden deceleration. Brakes screeched. A flock of seagulls shot skyward.

Emmanuel found extra speed and cut in front of Amal. Traffic in the intersection seemed cemented in place. A sweaty man, four back from the lights, craned out of his driver's window and tried to find the reason for the holdup. Across the line of ornamented car bonnets, Emmanuel glimpsed a gray-haired woman with a hand held against her mouth, the universal sign of distress that he'd seen countless times at crime scenes and in war zones: a scream held back.

Emmanuel edged past the delivery van. Heads were craned out the windows of a tram. Two women on the sidewalk clutched each other's arms. A uniformed driver with his hat askew and his face pinched red stood immobile in the doorway of the tram. He was shaking.

"He ran . . . He ran straight in front of me. I couldn't stop."

Emmanuel cleared a path through a small circle of onlookers. Giriraj lay on the asphalt, his limbs arranged at the impossible angles affected only by the dead. The oiled surface of his bald head was riddled with cuts, and a leather sandal had been thrown onto the opposite sidewalk. Emmanuel knelt to check for a pulse. Zweigman joined him on the road and Emmanuel pulled back and let the doctor take charge. He suspected that they both knew the result of the examination. A mortuary van, not an ambulance, would attend the scene.

"Giriraj . . ." Amal broke through the circle of onlookers. "Giriraj."

Emmanuel stood up and tried to block Amal's approach.

The boy scooted to the right and dropped to his knees beside the once-mighty body of Giriraj, now crumpled and vacant.

"Help him," Amal pleaded of the white-haired doctor. "Please."

"He is beyond help and beyond hurt," Zweigman said. "I am sorry. He is gone."

The tram driver turned away and the ticket conductor patted his back with a rough hand in the way of a man unused to displays of emotion.

"I didn't see him . . ." The driver's voice was a coarse whisper. "He ran out of nowhere. There wasn't enough time to stop."

"I know." The conductor sat his work companion on the footpath. "Plenty of witnesses who saw what happened. You won't get the blame."

The pursuit teams, the rail workers and the police arrived in separate waves of blue and olive drab. A bulky sergeant, sweat-stained and fragrant, began moving the crowd off while the rest of the squad set up a human cordon around Giriraj's body.

"Step back," the sergeant barked. "This is a crime scene. Everyone back four steps."

Emmanuel motioned Zweigman away from the body, then leaned down and spoke close to Amal's ear.

"Time to leave," he said. "Now."

"I'll wait." Amal was dry-eyed. "I'll wait for the ambulance to come."

Emmanuel checked the crowd. The stunned tram passengers and the disappointed dockworkers struggled for a better view. Constable Shabalala stood head and shoulders above the gathering. Any minute now elements of the crowd would shift focus from the dead man to Amal. They would want to know who he was, this young man kneeling by the side of a child killer.

One of the uniforms stuck on crowd control called out, "Did we get the right one, Sarge?"

"The witness is on her way," the sergeant bellowed. "She'll do a formal identification here on the spot."

A whistle blew and the throng split. The tram passengers craned their heads toward the new movement. Detective Head Constable Robinson and Detective Constable Fletcher pressed through the crowd, the witness tucked safely between them.

Emmanuel crouched and took hold of Amal's wrist. "If I have to break your wrist to save your life, I will. Now move. Quickly."

He tugged Amal to his feet. They stood almost face-to-face with Fletcher and Robinson.

"Her?" Amal gasped in recognition and Emmanuel wheeled them both sixty degrees so the witness saw their backs.

Zweigman glimpsed the fear in Amal's face and felt the urgency of the ex-detective's movements. "This boy is going to be sick," he shouted. "Make way. Please. Make way."

The crowd and the police gave them plenty of room. A path opened and then closed like a zipper as bodies hemmed in behind them. Soon all three were part of the great human tide. Emmanuel shouldered through the spectators and cut across to Shabalala. The Zulu constable was the perfect barrier to shelter behind. Zweigman joined Shabalala to form a line of cover. If the detectives looked in their direction, they would see an old man and a tall native brought into the city to help his master with the heavy chores.

The detectives led the witness over to Giriraj's body and Robinson held on to her slender arm. She was unsteady on her feet and swayed with the breeze.

"Is that really the same woman?" Amal whispered in disbelief.

"Yes," Emmanuel said. "She's cleaned up."

The prostitute from the rail yard had come dressed in a dark brown frock that buttoned to the throat and fell well below the knee. The loose garment covered the details of her body. Her face was free of makeup, her hair pulled back into a neat bun. A plain gold chain was her only adornment. Compared with the sparkling nighttime wear she favored, this was practically sackcloth and ashes. Still, there was something about her that didn't sit right. Despite all her efforts to appear respectable, an aura of sexual availability clung to her. Emmanuel couldn't figure out why. The prostitute held a hankie to her nose like a Victorian heroine in a penny dreadful novella, and he saw bright color glint from the white cotton. She'd forgotten to remove the flecks of devil-red polish from her long nails.

Detective Head Constable Robinson drew in a breath and let it out slowly while the witness completed her pantomime display of shock and grief. He appeared uneasy, despite being on the brink of solving the brutal murder of a white child.

"This him?" Robinson asked.

"*Ja,*" the woman said. "That's the Indian. He followed Jolly Marks."

The crowd murmured in response to the information. The prostitute continued to stare at Giriraj's body, mesmerized. A memory flickered across her face and she stepped back, lost in thought.

"And . . . ?" Robinson prompted after the silence had dragged out long enough.

"He . . . he had a knife in his hand," she said.

A few women tut-tutted, while their husbands rued the fact that the Indian was already dead and would not be dragged through the courts and then killed by the proper means: a rope and scaffold.

Amal grabbed hold of Emmanuel's jacket sleeve and whispered, "That's a lie. Giriraj never carried any weapons."

"I know," Emmanuel said. "But there's nothing to be done about it now. If she fingers you as one of the Indian men in the yard that night, the detectives will turn you inside out."

"But this is wrong," Amal hissed. "This is all a lie."

"Getting arrested won't make it right," Emmanuel said.

He studied Fletcher's and Robinson's tensed shoulders and blank expressions. They sensed something was rotten, too, but faced with a difficult case and a likely suspect who could no longer defend himself, they let the scene play out.

"You sure it's him?" Fletcher scratched his neck and peered down at the collapsed heap of flesh. "You told the crime scene guys that it was two of them: black-haired and in suits. This one is bald, with sandals."

The prostitute licked dry lips. "I was scared," she mumbled. "He'd seen me. He said he'd cut me if I told the truth."

"What kind of knife was it?" Robinson knelt on the tarred road and patted Giriraj's body down with brisk hands. He reached into a pocket and withdrew a small lump wrapped in white muslin. The prostitute leaned forward—a horse to a sugar cube.

"Hashish. No weapons." Robinson threw the white-wrapped nub to his partner and spoke to the star witness. "Did you get a good look at the knife?"

"What?" The woman fiddled with the gold chain around her neck, her hungry gaze on the lump in Fletcher's palm.

"The knife," Robinson repeated. "What did it look like?"

"Sharp," she said. "I was scared. He said he'd cut me."

Tricky situation, Emmanuel acknowledged. A spellbound crowd, a dead man and a distressed woman. No matter what Fletcher and Robinson thought of the witness's evidence, they were in no position to question it. A scared white woman trumped a dead Indian with a lump of African Black in his pocket any day. They had to play it safe and keep the witness and the crowd on their side.

Robinson smiled. "But you're not scared anymore. You found your courage and decided to tell us the truth. Is that right?"

"*Ja*, that's right." She spilled tears and the detective stood up and laid a hand on her shoulder. The crowd responded instinctively to the weeping woman. They projected the image of their own mothers, sisters or aunties onto her, no matter the reality.

Emmanuel wondered what the tears were for—the loss of Giriraj's tender alleyway ministrations or the cessation of the regular smoke delivery. Probably both. Giriraj provided the streetwalker with pleasure and comfort in a life that had little of either.

"Very brave of you," Robinson said. "To come forward and identify Jolly Marks's killer."

"I had to." The woman sobbed. "I had to . . ."

Stripped of makeup and washed with tears, the prostitute radiated a strange purity. Truth seemed to shine from her. Emmanuel figured that was because she was finally telling the truth. The decision to come forward and identify Giriraj was not hers. She had to. There was no choice involved.

The woman turned from Giriraj's body and stumbled blindly to the edge of the burgeoning crowd. Robinson snaked his heavy arm across her shoulder to weigh her down and stop her wandering. The spectators pressed against the ring of police cordoning off the scene.

"You've done well." Robinson injected sincerity into the textbook interview wrap-up. "We couldn't have solved this crime without you. Jolly's mother can sleep easy tonight."

The prostitute's sobs increased and Robinson signaled Fletcher to clear the way. An eager uniformed constable parted the wall of blue overalls, and the rail yard workers stepped back and assumed the stiff posture of an honor guard. Robinson guided the prostitute into the breach while the crowd looked on, mesmerized by the fragile white woman being led to safety.

"God bless you, miss," a passenger on the halted tram called out, and fluttered a hankie in farewell. The prostitute gave a royal wave and disappeared into the corridor of blue.

Emmanuel craned above the sea of hats and heads to catch the dying moments of the drama. Tucked into the crowd but still in plain view, a British thug in a suit, whom Emmanuel recognized as Khan's bodyguard, watched the prostitute. Robinson held the witness steady and the rail workers ushered them through to an empty strip of pavement.

"Shameless . . ." Amal hissed. "That woman is shameless."

"She can't afford shame," Emmanuel said. "Any more than you or I can afford risking a heart-to-heart talk with the police."

The rail workers broke apart and began to drift back to the freight yard. For a moment, real justice had been within their reach, the Indian a half block away from punishment. Now all that was left was work. Lines of sooty railway cars in need of decoupling and mile upon mile of hypnotic steel track.

Khan's bodyguard wove through the dispersing workers but kept two paces behind the detectives and their star witness. He had the grace of a rhino on an ice floe and knocked shoulders with a man attempting to roll a cigarette. The impact spilled cut tobacco over the bodyguard's suit and drew a curse from the smoker. The prostitute glanced over a shoulder and caught sight of Khan's man. Her face was drawn with lines of fatigue but her eyes sparkled. Life on the docks was patterned after the ocean: a cycle of rising and falling tides. Giriraj's death had brought the streetwalker to the center of attention, but the spotlight would last only a minute before shining somewhere else. Soon this drama would end and she would go back to a life filled with nameless men and dirty boxcars.

A payout, Emmanuel guessed. The sparkle in the prostitute's eyes when she saw Khan's man was anticipation. She had acted her role and now it was time to collect her reward: a few folded notes and a chunk of hashish to keep away bad dreams of the innocent man sprawled on the tarmac.

Afzal Khan was behind this perversion of justice, but Emmanuel couldn't figure what the gangster had gained from it.

"Move back," the sweat-stained sergeant in charge of crowd control yelled. "Make way for the mortuary van."

The spectators moved back slowly, reluctant to leave before the door to the van was locked and the blood washed from the road.

The conductor pulled the stunned driver upright and they inspected the damaged tram. "A quick trip to the workshop and she'll be good as new," the conductor said, and shuffled his feet to cover the sound of the driver's quiet tears. The driver touched the faint dent in the front of the vehicle made by the contact with Giriraj's body, trying to absorb the reality of what had just happened.

"I am responsible for what happened," Amal said. "More guilty than the driver."

"You are not to blame for this accident," Emmanuel said. "Mr. Khan gave your family an impossible choice."

"And how must I live with this feeling inside?" Amal said.

The mortuary van reversed at an angle and drew parallel with the stricken tram. The passengers filed down the stairs under the eager watch of a police constable and regrouped on the pavement. Two Indian girls in smart cardigan sweaters and A-line skirts split from the group and walked away. They had seen enough.

"Do more good than harm," Emmanuel said to Amal, and immediately regretted his words. He was perhaps the least qualified person to dispense wisdom on the subject of feelings. A taste for painkillers and the voice of the phantom sergeant major indicated that his own emotions were still a tangle. And this country . . . with its pettiness . . . He wondered what qualifications he had to tell anyone anything while he hung on to his white ID card and his detective's badge—no matter how temporary they might be.

He took another tack. "Do not become Mr. Khan," he said.

Amal said, "I can do that."

The mortuary attendants, a fat coloured man and a muscular Indian, both dressed in medical whites, swung open the van's double doors and pulled out a trolley. A policeman picked up Giriraj's stray sandal and threw it on the corpse's chest.

The sweaty sergeant lit up a cigarette and smiled at the morgue staff. "He's a big bastard. That's one hundred percent pure Punjabi muscle. I'll finish my smoke and give you boys a hand."

The attendants hung back. They would have to wait until the police sergeant was good and ready. Giriraj lay sprawled across the roadway, just another load to be picked up and stored for burial.

Zweigman said, "Perhaps we should go."

They turned and left Giriraj in the care of the nonwhite attendants who would drive him in their "nonwhites" vehicle to the "nonwhites" section of the morgue, where he would rest among other dark-skinned souls.

Ten doorways from the scene of the accident, Maataa and Parthiv sat on the second step of a stone staircase that led to the front door of a garment import-and-export business. Their shoulders touched. Clove cigarette smoke cocooned them from the bustle of the street. Maataa's glass bracelets jangled when she drew on the cigarette and handed it to Parthiv. They did not talk. They gazed at the pavement.

"Oh." Amal was taken aback by the harmonious family scene. "They were here all along."

"Probably waiting for you," Emmanuel said.

Amal hesitated, then approached the steps. His mother shuffled over to make room. He sat beside her and all three kept the silence.

Parthiv passed the cigarette back to his mother. She drew on it deeply and passed it to Amal. The baby of the Dutta family inhaled and coughed when the smoke hit his lungs. Tears ran down his face. Maataa did not laugh and Parthiv did not call him a weakling. They sat and finished the cigarette. The Duttas were going to survive the events of today.

"What now?" Zweigman asked when the Bedford truck came into view. The street bustled with human traffic pouring away from the accident scene.

"We're going to have a talk with Khan," Emmanuel said.

"This man will talk?" Shabalala sounded doubtful.

"We'll find a way," Emmanuel said. He caught sight of Robinson and Fletcher across the street. They were in conversation with the red-haired prostitute. She'd stopped crying and her body was rigid with tension. Khan's bodyguard leaned against the wall of a coffee shop two buildings farther up and looked on.

"I told you." The prostitute's voice was shrill and her fingers twisted the gold chain that hung around her neck. "He said he'd find me and cut me."

The expression on both detectives' faces was a mixture of boredom and contempt. Being a policeman meant talking to liars every day of the week. Good ones. The whore was terrible at it.

Emmanuel checked his watch. Less than three hours were left before van Niekerk's deal expired. Still, he was impressed

by Fletcher and Robinson's perseverance. They knew something was wrong and they weren't ready to walk away. The
truth mattered to them.

"Let's go to Khan's office." Emmanuel turned back to
Zweigman and Shabalala. "His bodyguard is across the street,
keeping an eye on the witness. That's one less obstacle to deal
with."

The German shepherds could be heard around a corner.
The Point was crawling with armed policemen as the mop-up
of natives continued. They moved closer to the row of two-
story terraces where the Bedford was parked. Driveways split
off the main road and led to warehouses. A Rolls-Royce Silver
Wraith was parked in the loading dock of a building with a
sign saying ABEL MELLON. DRY GOODS WHOLESALER.

Emmanuel walked past the car and stopped when they
were across the driveway and shielded by the walls of the next
building.

"That's Khan's car in the loading dock," he said to Zweigman and Shabalala. "I think he's in it."

"With all the police?" Shabalala said. "That man is without
fear."

Emmanuel thought about it for a moment. It was an odd
place for a well-known Indian gangster to park his Rolls. Even
Bergis Morgensen was able to identify Khan's car. A more
cautious man would have stayed away.

"Maybe Khan has nothing to be afraid of," Emmanuel
said, and took the stolen notebook from his pocket. He opened
it to the letter *A*. "What did Amal say about the policeman
Khan threatened to call?"

"He had a British Raj name," Zweigman said.

"With two surnames," Shabalala added.

Emmanuel scanned the entries, which were sparse and written in a sloping hand. *Anderson. Advani. Absolem.* He moved on through the *B*'s and *C*'s without finding a double-barrel surname. The last name in the *C* listings, scribbled hastily in pencil, caught his attention and he read it aloud. "Detective Sergeant Emmanuel Cooper."

Had Khan known who he was all along, or was the entry more recent? He kept flicking through the alphabet. Time was winding down. *Smith. Saunders. Sidhu . . .*

"Here." Shabalala pointed to an entry written along the vertical length of the page margin. Emmanuel turned the book sideways to read the name scribbled down in black ink.

"Edward Soames-Fitzpatrick." He smiled. "Now, that's a British Raj name."

"What is that?" Shabalala pointed to a squiggle of letters that had been added to the front of the name, almost as an afterthought. The writing was smudged and almost illegible. Emmanuel tried and failed to make sense of the scrawl.

"May I?" Zweigman said, and politely took the book. "I have long experience reading my own handwriting." The doctor pushed his glasses onto the bridge of his nose and peered at the letters like a Gypsy reading tea leaves.

"Col," he said. "C-O-L."

"Colonel Edward Soames-Fitzpatrick," Emmanuel said. Yes, that matched what van Niekerk had said about the voice on the phone. An officious little shit who thought a Dutch policeman and an ex-detective could be used and then dumped. A *soutpiel.* Emmanuel closed the phone book, thought again, thumbed to the *V*'s but did not find van Niekerk's name.

"Let's go get this bastard," he said.

"With what weapons?" Shabalala asked.

Coming to battle without guns had been the ruin of the mighty Zulu army.

"This book."

23

EMMANUEL, SHABALALA AND Zweigman approached the parked Rolls-Royce almost shoulder to shoulder. The rear window of the luxury car was open and smoke drifted out from the interior. Khan was home. Two black employees of Abel Mellon Dry Goods sat on the loading dock enjoying a cup of tea and a bag of fried fat cakes. They watched the odd trio of men for a moment and then retreated into the building. Emmanuel slammed the phone book against the passenger window of the Rolls.

"Is this yours, Khan?" he asked. "My friends wanted to take the book to the police station, but I convinced them to talk to you first."

A lock clicked. The silver door opened. Emmanuel stepped aside and waited for the cloud of smoke to clear. Chocolate wrappers littered the carpeted floor of the limousine and the scent of cannabis bud was strong. Khan's eyes were bloodshot and hooded.

"You're supposed to be gone and gone," he said.

"Not yet." Emmanuel peered into the Rolls. The Indian

gangster was alone. He must have started smoking the moment he knew Giriraj was dead.

"Move over," Emmanuel said.

Khan paused and then scooted across the leather seat. Emmanuel climbed in. He kept the door open to the fresh air and to Shabalala and Zweigman, who watched the main street for the arrival of the Detective Branch.

"You threw Giriraj to the dogs," Emmanuel said. "What was that worth to you?"

Khan's eyes darkened. "In this country," he said, "a man like me has to make his own luck. Where's the reward for being good if you are nonwhite? I will never be able to live in the Berea or sit on a bench on the Esplanade."

"The government made you into a criminal?" Emmanuel didn't believe that for a moment. Fascist dictatorship or ballot-box-stuffing democracy, men like Khan fed off human weakness for personal gain. "What exactly did you get for Giriraj?"

Khan lit up another hand-rolled cigarette and leaned back into the leather. "Giriraj was worth two trading licenses in Zululand and one here on Marine Parade."

Nonwhites were granted a limited number of licenses to set up businesses or to trade in areas of the country that were officially closed to them.

"A good deal," Emmanuel said drily. "Who did you give Giriraj up to, Soames-Fitzpatrick?"

Khan smiled and drew on his smoke. "If you live past this afternoon, Cooper, I'll hire you. Musclemen I can buy by the pound. Men with brains are another matter."

"Tell me about the colonel." Emmanuel checked his watch. Two and a half hours to go before the Detective Branch issued the warrants. If he didn't get answers soon, he'd be employed in the prison laundry or farmed out to a widget factory at ten pence an hour till the execution date . . . that's if the tradesman didn't get to him first.

"I never met this Fitzpatrick," Khan said. "But he called me to ask for help. It's like I said: good men are hard to find."

"You hired men for him . . . men like Brother Jonah?"

"Very good." Khan removed a piece of loose tobacco from the tip of his tongue and flicked it to the carpet. "Now I understand why Lana Rose is fucking you. She has a weakness for clever policemen." The Indian man's smile was filthy. "Tell me, do you and the Dutch major take turns? Or do you have her at the same time?"

Emmanuel grabbed Khan by the throat and exerted a steady pressure against the larynx. "Even stupid police are a step up from a gangster who makes a young girl pay off a family debt on his desktop and then trades a human life for money."

Shabalala's hand thumped on the roof of the Rolls, and Emmanuel let go of Khan, who drew in a ragged breath and slumped back in his seat. Emmanuel looked into the alley.

"They have come for you," Shabalala said.

Emmanuel got out of the Rolls. Detective Constable Fletcher and a young foot policeman he did not recognize were walking to the car with hands to their gun holsters. The loading bay door was locked and the wall behind the Rolls was over seven feet high. There was nowhere to go.

Emmanuel raised his hands and approached Fletcher. He wanted to put distance between himself and the two men who'd followed him into danger. This was his problem. The burden of the two murders at the Dover could not be shared.

"You're early," he said.

"Shut up, Cooper."

Fletcher grabbed Emmanuel's arms and pinned them to his back. Steel handcuffs bit into his wrists. The constable unclipped the Walther from its holster and stared at the shiny silverwork like a child who'd won the lucky dip. Fletcher pushed Emmanuel roughly toward the main road.

"You're in the shit," he said. "There's no getting out of it this time."

"Where are you taking him?" Zweigman asked, and was ignored by the detective constable and the young policeman.

A black Ford was parked at the curb with the engine chugging. Fletcher opened the door and pushed Emmanuel into the backseat. The door slammed shut.

"Thank Christ." Major van Niekerk was in the driver's seat and his face was tense and hard. He was in neat civilian clothing and freshly shaved.

The door opened again. Zweigman and Shabalala stood on the sidewalk with Fletcher, who now had the Walther held loosely in his hand. The young constable stood in the background and sulked over the loss of the pretty gun.

"In," the major said. "Now."

Zweigman and Shabalala clambered into the Ford without question and waited for an explanation. Emmanuel sat squashed against the window and regained his calm. The major looked over his shoulder.

"You need to get out of Durban, Cooper," he said. "The warrant for your arrest will be issued in a couple of hours and it will take me longer than that to find out who's actually running the mission to secure the Russians. I've got a name but I'm not a hundred percent sure it's the right one."

"Colonel Edward Soames-Fitzpatrick," Emmanuel said. "He hired Afzal Khan to help him."

"Fuck. I thought it was someone else. How's Khan involved?"

"He just helped frame a man named Giriraj for Jolly's murder and threw him to a mob on the Point. Poor bastard got hit by a tram before they could arrest him. The charge will stick. Khan also bought a witness. That's one of the murders cleared from the board."

"Leaving the other two for you." Van Niekerk checked the side mirror and the pavement for movement. "This is a mop-up operation, Cooper. With the three murders cleared, all that's left is to bring in the Russians. I'll handle Khan in person, but you have to disappear till things are set straight."

"Where to? Your house was my fallback position."

"A place called Labrant's Halt. It's a way station in the Valley of a Thousand Hills. Lana and the Russians are already on the way. They'll wait for you there."

Zweigman leaned forward. "I know this Labrant's Halt. It is only a few miles from the turnoff to my clinic. Our mail is delivered there."

"No." Emmanuel pinned van Niekerk with a hard stare. He knew what the major was planning and he could not ask Zweigman and Shabalala for more than they had already given. "We have to find another place."

"There's no time. Think about it. The Russians need a doctor and you need a place to keep low. You'll also have Constable Shabalala to watch your back."

"We'll go back and question Khan together, right now."

"And then what? When the deal time is up, you'll have no time to run and you'll have nowhere to hide. For just this once, let go, Cooper."

"Excuse me, Major," Zweigman interrupted politely. "What will become of Detective Cooper if he remains here in Durban?"

"Jail," van Niekerk said. "And then maybe a rope."

"In that case, it is settled." Zweigman turned to Emmanuel. "I extend to you a new invitation to visit my clinic."

"I can't ask that of you," Emmanuel said.

"You are not asking. I am offering."

Shabalala leaned forward but hesitated in the presence of an Afrikaner major.

"Go on," van Niekerk said, giving permission for the native constable to speak.

"The traffic will be slow because of the accident with the Indian man," Shabalala said. "We must leave now if we wish to get out of town in time."

"I will drive to Labrant's Halt," Zweigman volunteered. "If you are still uncomfortable with visiting my clinic, Detective Cooper, there will be ample time to make another plan. Agreed?"

"Agreed," Emmanuel said.

"Give me the keys to the Bedford and take this car," van Niekerk said. "The truck will be too slow."

The major and Zweigman exchanged keys. They were headed for the Valley of a Thousand Hills two hours out of the city on a rough macadam road.

"You okay, Cooper?"

"Fine, thank you, Major." He couldn't imagine the Afrikaner blue blood feeling as he himself did now . . . humbled by the sacrifice of others.

"Give me forty-eight hours to sort this out. I'll send word with Fletcher when it's safe to move. Can you keep still for that long?"

"Of course."

"Good, because you'll be useless to me and to the Russians in jail." Van Niekerk offered a hand. "Good luck."

"To both of us." Emmanuel shook on the wish.

The major climbed out of the Ford and waited for Zweigman to start the car and drive away. The getaway slowed to a crawl two minutes after leaving. Emmanuel checked out the back. Bumper-to-bumper traffic inched along Point Road. A policeman directed cars around the stranded tram. The mortuary van had departed the scene but a contingent of police brass mingled on the footpath. Giriraj was the department's catch of the day. A tall colonel with muttonchop whiskers stood with his legs apart and his hands on his hips. Emmanuel recognized him from Jolly's murder scene, where he lent moral support to the uniforms. He was also the dictionary definition of a *soutpiel*. Edward Soames-Fitzpatrick? The name seemed to fit.

The last straggle of onlookers parted and Major van Niekerk walked to the colonel's side. They talked for a few moments, both men genial and relaxed. Emmanuel's chest tightened. Van Niekerk knew the *soutpiel* colonel. The Dutch policeman was his mentor and his protector but Emmanuel was not blind to his faults. He knew that while Khan and van Niekerk were on opposite sides of the law, they shared one particular trait: self-interest.

Major van Niekerk would not protect the Russians unless there was something tangible in it for him.

Labrant's Halt was a long wooden shed built on the lip of an escarpment and surrounded by an ocean of dun-colored hills. An EMPTY sign hung from the lone petrol pump. A white Plymouth sedan was parked under a bare jacaranda.

Emmanuel leaned into the open driver's-side window. Lana, Nicolai and Natalya were in the car, sipping orange fizzy drinks through paper straws. Shabalala and Zweigman joined the conference.

"Where to?" Lana asked. Dust from the unsealed road dirtied her cheekbones, and her hair was whipped by the wind.

"That decision is for the detective sergeant to make," said Zweigman quietly.

Emmanuel knew the decision was his, but the consequences of his actions affected everyone. Going on the run with the Russian couple was unrealistic. On the backseat of the Plymouth were a heavily pregnant woman and a sick man in need of medical supervision. Outside stood a doctor, an experienced police constable and a fugitive looking for a place to disappear. Major van Niekerk was right. Zweigman's isolated medical clinic in the hills was the perfect solution.

"I would like to bring some small thing for your wives, to say thank you." Emmanuel addressed Zweigman and Shabalala. "What do you suggest?"

"Chocolate biscuits, the ones with the cream center. Lilliana has a weakness for those."

"Dried fruit," Shabalala said. "Or the licorice with the many layers."

"I'll see what they have."

Emmanuel moved to the screened-in porch that fronted

the building. A dozen Zulu men dressed in a mix of overalls and traditional clothing made from animal hides and printed cloth milled around the side entrance through which natives were served. They nodded a polite greeting, which Emmanuel returned before entering Labrant's Halt. Five months in English Durban, and he'd missed this . . . the feeling of being in black Africa.

The shelves inside Labrant's were half stocked, but he found the cream-filled chocolate biscuits and a small bag of licorice allsorts, both he hoped less than a year old. He added rice and sugar and a tin of roasted coffee beans.

Lana entered the store while he was paying the spindly white man who worked the shiny till.

"The ladies' room?" she asked, and a key was slid across the length of the wood counter. White ladies had access to the relative luxury of a long-drop toilet attached to the back of the building. Nonwhites learned to dig and squat.

"Out in a minute," Lana said, and disappeared among the dusty shelving. Emmanuel carried the sweets out to the Ford, feeling guilty at the insignificant price paid for his safety.

"How are the Russians doing?" he asked when Zweigman returned to the sedan with the medical bag tucked under an arm.

"They are holding up well, but Natalya has begun to have contractions. I think we will have a baby by morning." Zweigman smiled and dug a handful of coins from his jacket. "I will buy a small bottle to celebrate the occasion."

"I'll get it," Emmanuel said, and swung back to Labrant's before Zweigman could object. Through the mesh wire he glimpsed Lana sliding a pound note to the owner. The store telephone was on the counter and angled out toward her. She'd called someone.

Emmanuel hesitated in the doorway. He wanted her . . . that was understandable, given the night they'd spent together. Did he trust her? That was a different matter altogether.

24

Tiny birds darted like careless arrows across the rutted dirt track. Bleached grass grew tall beneath the marula trees. The Ford crested a hill and dropped down to a deep valley. The tenuous track came to a fork by the edge of a shallow river and Zweigman maneuvered the car left and along the stony bank. Constable Shabalala had taken the wheel of the Plymouth for the rough drive into the hills and now steered in behind the dusty Ford.

The narrow road wound steadily upward and ended at a circle of compacted dirt ringed with bright mountain aloes. A low stone house with a thatched roof sheltered under the limbs of an ancient fig tree. Weeds grew between cracks in the walls and lizards scurried across the heated surface.

Three dwellings, each smaller than the next, clung to a wide, flat plateau that faced onto a deep valley. A winter vegetable garden with cabbages, pumpkins and spinach ran parallel to the buildings, which were built in a semicircle. Chickens scratched in the dirt. The rusted arms of a windmill remained indifferent to the breeze.

Emmanuel was surprised by the dilapidated sprawl. This patch of hillside was hard country. Poor country. The old Jew appeared to have even less money than when he'd been a shopkeeper in Jacob's Rest.

"The clinic." Zweigman climbed out of the Ford. "Come, Detective, I will give you the grand tour."

The dry tone indicated that the doctor had read his thoughts and found them amusing. Emmanuel reached for the Walther, ready to unclip it and store it in the glove box. Lilliana Zweigman was fragile and Daniel Zweigman refused to own or hold a firearm, possibly a reaction to living through six years of war. Carrying a loaded weapon into their house would be wrong.

The hip holster was empty. The eager foot policeman had taken the Walther in the loading dock of Abel Mellon Dry Goods and Fletcher had not returned it. Emmanuel was unarmed.

"Come," Zweigman said.

Emmanuel grabbed the brown paper grocery bag and waited for the Plymouth to pull alongside before getting out. Shabalala helped the Russians from the backseat and kept an arm under Nicolai's elbow to help support his weight. A dirt path snaked across a grass verge in front of the houses. Zweigman paused at the edge of the garden and pointed to the first and largest of the stone houses.

"This is the clinic," he said. "When we have enough funds, it will be expanded out to the back. Two, maybe three rooms more."

They walked on. The winter vegetable patch grew up to the left. A small shed took the space between the clinic and the next stone house, which had a wide veranda and a view of the hills.

"That is our home," Zweigman said, and then pointed to the last building, not much larger than the shed but with flowered curtains at the two small windows. "That is the Shabalala house."

Emmanuel wondered how they would all fit. The parcel of land was large, with expansive views, but the buildings were small. A hen scratched through leaf litter under a tree and Natalya made a comment in Russian that sounded as if she'd swallowed a mouthful of vinegar. Emmanuel glanced at Lana for an explanation.

"The country atmosphere is not to her liking," Lana said drily, and they continued toward the doctor's snug stone home. Nicolai leaned heavily against Shabalala and each step he took was an effort. The rough ride into the hills had taken a toll on him.

Lilliana Zweigman and Lizzie, Shabalala's wife, stood on the veranda of the middle house and watched the procession of uninvited guests traipse toward them. Something in the way they stood, framed by the beams of the veranda, the last light reflected in their eyes, suggested they had both been beautiful in their youth.

"Ladies." Zweigman had pulled ahead five paces in order to give advance warning. "We have guests. Let me introduce you and we can all have some tea."

The doctor supplied a smile for each introduction but the charm had worn thin when he came at last to Emmanuel.

"You both know Detective Cooper, of course," he said.

His wife's fingers twisted the top button of her jacket till the thread almost snapped, and her breath could be heard rasping in the country quiet. Zweigman climbed the front stairs and touched her arm gently. Her panic subsided but did not disappear.

"How could we forget the detective sergeant?" Shabalala's wife, Lizzie, said, and an awkward silence followed her wry comment.

Emmanuel understood the women's fears. His murder investigation in Jacob's Rest had landed them all here on this lonely plateau far from home. If he'd left buried secrets buried and turned away from the truth, their lives would have continued on familiar paths. They had all paid a heavy price for his inability to walk away.

"Hello, Lilliana. *Unjani*, Lizzie." Emmanuel followed Zweigman up the stairs and presented the bag of groceries. He felt he was the Fourth Horseman of the Apocalypse who came bearing biscuits and licorice to divert attention from the danger and destruction that followed in his wake.

—

"Why here?" Emmanuel asked Shabalala when the fire in the rough stone circle was ablaze and the wood crackled and hissed. "He's a qualified surgeon. Why not Cape Town or even Durban?"

Shabalala rested on his haunches with his forearms balanced on his knees and threw a stick into the fire. A red sun hung over the crest of the hills. Emmanuel sank down next to the Zulu constable and waited. Good manners prevented Shabalala from offering a personal opinion without first giving the answer proper consideration.

"I think he is paying," Shabalala said. "For something he did, or did not do, in his home country, during the war."

A scatter of loose stones on the garden path preceded Zweigman's appearance at the fireside. He dragged a dried tree branch behind him and his face dripped sweat. His shirtsleeves were rolled to above his elbows and his pants legs up to his knees. "Fuel," he said, and propped the branch against the stack of logs and kindling already collected from the bush. "The temperature will drop soon and we will need the fire."

The women and Nicolai were in the middle house and it was by unspoken agreement that the able-bodied men settled down outside till bedtime. Sleeping arrangements were made: Shabalala and his wife in their house, Nicolai and Natalya in with the Zweigmans, while Lana was squeezed into the storage hut and Emmanuel was billeted on the clinic floor. He'd slept in colder and rougher places.

The sun dipped lower and the shadows lengthened across the ground. Night in the tropics came quickly. The light went out like a blown candle. The evening star was faint on the horizon.

"Mr. Shabalala," Lizzie's voice called into the gathering darkness. "I need a man to help me. Are you that man or shall I get another?"

The constable moved toward the middle house with a smile and a shake of his head. Zulu tradition called for women to be meek and obedient, but his wife was her own person.

Emmanuel glanced at the clinic buildings. They were strikingly similar to the stone and thatch house that Davida stood outside in his dreams. Even the hills etched against the sky echoed the landscape in his mind.

"Do you hear from Davida?" he asked when Zweigman sat down beside the fire. The doctor and his wife had been like surrogate parents to the coloured girl. "Is she safe?"

"She is well," the German man replied, and threw small twigs into the center of the flames where the fire was white-hot.

"And happy?" Emmanuel said.

A foolish question, he knew, but it didn't stop him from wanting proof of the impossible: a happy ending for at least one of the victims of the Security Branch's violent intervention.

"She is not unhappy," came the enigmatic reply.

The red disk of the sun disappeared and darkness swallowed the hillside. Not unhappy. There was a kernel of hope in that bare statement. To be injured but not destroyed was a small triumph.

"I'm sorry to involve you in this business with Nicolai and Natalya," Emmanuel said. "Especially after Jacob's Rest. We'll be gone in forty-eight hours and you'll be safe."

"The only safe place is the grave," Zweigman said. "That was one of my grandfather's favorite expressions. He was a peasant with dirty fingernails and stained teeth, so naturally I didn't believe anything he said. I was a medical student destined for great things. I knew everything."

The fire blazed in the stone circle and Emmanuel held his hands out to the heat. Zweigman rarely spoke of the past. Details of his life in Berlin before and during the war were still a mystery.

"After the Security Branch beating," Emmanuel said, "you promised that you'd tell me how you came to be serving behind the counter of a general store in South Africa."

Zweigman frowned. In Jacob's Rest, the detective had been beaten with professional thoroughness that resulted in broken bones and black bruises that mushroomed across his skin. Most patients with injuries so severe recalled only the pain.

"You remember?"

"Every word," Emmanuel said.

The doctor brought his hands up to the flames and examined the chipped fingernails and the rough skin encrusted with dirt. He smiled into the firelight.

"You should have seen me fifteen years ago, Detective. I was quite the specimen. A surgeon at Charité-Universitätsmedizin, with private consulting rooms furnished to the best of taste. Everything was always the best. The tailored suits, the wine in the cellar and the pretty girls I kept company with, even after I was married. That was Dr. Daniel Zweigman. Not the most clever Jew in Berlin, but one of them." The silence that followed was heavy with self-recrimination. "When rumors of war began, Lilliana came to me. She had a cousin in New York who was willing to take us in, find us an apartment and jobs. I said no. Members of the National Socialist Party came to me for treatment. I was Zweigman the healer, Zweigman the first choice for families of quality. I was safe. My wife and three children were immune from the madness. Then it was too late to escape."

The night settled on them, black and heavy. The Zweigmans were childless now and thousands of miles from Berlin.

"Lilliana and I survived the camps but our children did not. That's what broke Lilliana in the end: being alive when there was nothing left to live for." The doctor turned to Emmanuel. "Nicolai and Natalya can stay here as long as necessary. It is better to light a candle than to curse the darkness."

25

E MMANUEL SLID FROM under the spread of blankets. The mountain air had a bite and he dressed quickly. Both sleep and dreams eluded him. Outside of the clinic the night was a soft velvet curtain drawn over the land. A lonely moon hung in the sky amid an explosion of diamond-bright stars. The cold breeze carried the scent of dirt and river stones up from the depths of the valley. He could hear distant water running over rocks. He walked to the edge of the grass plateau and stared into the abyss.

Weak lights flickered on the crest of a hill. On the wind came the sound of an automobile engine laboring up a rise. Twin lights grew stronger. Headlights. Emmanuel checked the sky for signs of dawn but it was still too early. The lights descended into the valley and came to a stop at the junction. The car hesitated before turning left along the river. Emmanuel guessed it was the tradesman and his unseen accomplice from the rope storehouse. He felt their presence in his blood. They were headed for the clinic. Nicolai had been right when he'd said that this hunt would continue until the hunted was trapped or dead.

He cut across the grass flat to the building occupied by Shabalala and Lizzie and rapped on the window. The creak of bedsprings was followed by a sleepy groan.

"Shhh . . ." Shabalala made the universal sound of comfort and opened the door. He was puffy-eyed, a gray blanket wrapped around his broad shoulders.

"Visitors," Emmanuel said.

"I will dress."

Shabalala retreated into the hut and Emmanuel returned to the verge. The headlights flickered through the tall grass that pressed onto the dirt track. In half an hour the car would be at the circle of aloes. Shabalala ran to Emmanuel's side and gazed into the valley.

"What is it they seek?"

Emmanuel said, "They are here for the Russian."

"This man can hardly keep one foot in front of the other. What value does he have? Is he a chief of something?"

"He was once a chief. The men in the car want to exchange him for one of their own."

The interior lights in the Zweigman house turned on and Natalya's primal groans traveled out into the night. The thump of footsteps was followed by a murmur of voices.

"The baby is come," Shabalala said. "I will fetch my wife. She knows what to do."

"Get her," Emmanuel said, and studied the laborious movement of the car headlights on the narrow track. The tradesman and his partner were traveling into unknown territory. That would slow them but it would not stop them.

Shabalala emerged from the hut with Lizzie, who held a

lantern high into the darkness. She skirted the vegetable garden and headed for the main house. The door opened and Lilliana Zweigman hurried her inside.

"I will go out to them," Emmanuel said when Shabalala
returned to his side. "I don't know that there is a way to stop
them. But it is worth a try. At least I might be able to slow
them down."

"Until the young one comes into the world," Shabalala
said. "Maybe that is all the time that is needed."

"Yes, maybe." Emmanuel blew into his cupped hands. In
Durban, early winter had a residue of subtropical heat, but the
mountains were icy, especially at night. "I'll get a coat from
the old man's suitcase and a torch from the storeroom, then
I'll set off."

The storeroom door creaked open and Lana Rose
stood in dim candlelight. She was fully dressed, with a crocheted blanket wrapped around her. "What's going on?" she
asked.

"Natalya is about to have her baby and there's a car coming up from the valley." Emmanuel studied Lana's face. "Any
idea who's in the car and how they got directions to the
clinic?"

She looked into his eyes. "How would I know that?"

"Who did you call from Labrant's Halt?" he asked, and
shouldered into the storeroom. Two candles burned in the interior. "Maybe you passed on directions to the clinic then."

"I couldn't even find this place with a map," she said,
hands on her hips. "Shabalala drove out here, remember?"

That was true.

"Who did you call?" he said, and continued searching the
shelves for a torch. There had to be one here somewhere.

"The major," she said. "I had to let him know where the next stop was after Labrant's."

Emmanuel located a silver torch and pressed the switch. The beam was bright and narrow. Lana stepped into the light.

"You don't trust me," she said.

"I don't know anything about you."

"Did I imagine the night we spent together?"

"Okay. I don't know *very much* about you."

She shook her head. "You are the brightest and the thickest man I've ever met. We've done more than just fuck, Emmanuel. I don't hot-wire cars and steal from Indian gangsters every day of the week, you know."

"No. But you have done those things before," he said. "And now you're the girlfriend of a major in the police service. That's a big jump."

"You want to know why?" Lana stepped closer. "My father was a gambler and a thief and not much good at either." She spoke clearly and quickly. "He used the rope storehouse on Signal Road to hide stuff he lifted from the freight yard. I helped him pack and sell whatever he'd stolen. Sometimes I helped him steal the things myself. Mr. Khan bought a lot of it. Khan also hired me to serve drinks at private parties. He likes white girls to work the bar. I let him touch me but I never fucked him because Khan only respects what he can't have. You know what it takes to get out of that kind of life, don't you, Emmanuel?"

He nodded. Even now, decades later, he was still amazed that he'd escaped Sophiatown and a life interrupted by regular jail time.

"And the major?" he said.

"He pays my bills. When I've got enough money, I'm going to move to Cape Town, where nobody knows me, and I'm going to start over again. There. Do I have your trust now, Emmanuel?"

He was stopped cold by the onslaught of information but had no doubt that Lana would have it all . . . down to the very last wish.

"Yes," he said. "You do."

"Good. What do I need to know?"

"The men in the car are coming for the Russians. I'm going to try to stop them. Stay with Nicolai and keep an eye on Lilliana. She panics easily."

"Okay," Lana said, and they moved in tandem across the grass to the stoep of the main house. She disappeared inside.

Shabalala wrestled the Russians' suitcase onto the steps. The interval between Natalya's groans had shortened and the sound of them had deepened.

"Beautiful." Zweigman's voice was calm amid the vocal work of childbirth. "You are doing beautifully, my dear. We will move to the clinic and by morning there will be a baby."

Shabalala opened the case and threw Emmanuel a thick wool coat with a fur collar. A pair of leather gloves followed.

"We must move," Shabalala said, and selected a long scarf, which he double-looped around his neck and then tucked into the lapels of his police-issue winter jacket.

"Ready, Sergeant Cooper?" he said, and for a fleeting second the operation felt real to Emmanuel. The Detective Branch ID and Shabalala by his side. That was where the fantasy ended.

"There are things to be done here at the clinic. Important

work," Emmanuel said. Despite the very real props, this was not an official investigation in which a native constable was obliged to follow the orders of a ranking officer. "You don't have to come with me."

"It is woman's business and doctor's business." The Zulu constable removed a homemade slingshot from his pocket and stretched the rubber till it snapped back with a twang. "We must go. Our business is elsewhere."

"*Yebo,*" Emmanuel said, and they set off at a run to the circle of mountain aloes. Emmanuel's torch played over the stone walls of the clinic and the circle of dirt that led to the approach road. They would move downward to meet the car.

"Carry on," Shabalala said, and stopped to collect a handful of pebbles, which he dropped into his coat pocket—ammunition for the slingshot. Emmanuel waited. They set off again and ran hard to put the lights of the Zweigmans' house behind them. The thump of their feet on the dirt track was the only sound.

Small circles of light from the stone houses grew dim and were soon eaten by the darkness. The clinic disappeared into the bushland. Emmanuel slowed and swung the beam of the torch along the sides of the road, on the hunt for an obstacle to place in the tradesman's way. A fiery-necked nightjar swooped low over the ground and caught a white moth in its beak before ascending into an acacia tree.

The throttle of the car engine grew louder.

"There." Emmanuel steadied the beam on a broken tree branch with spreading limbs. "We'll block the road with that."

They heaved and pulled. The branch was unwieldy and clung to the underbrush. Headlights appeared through the dry grass.

"Together." Shabalala counted in Zulu. "*Kanye, kabili, kathathu . . .*"

Muscles strained and lungs burned with the effort required to break the tree limb free of its bush mooring. Wood creaked and the branch shot into the road. Emmanuel stumbled but Shabalala grabbed him by the coat sleeve. The lights rounded a bend.

"Quick," Emmanuel said. "Hide."

They cleared the road and crouched in the long grass. A car appeared on the straight. Twin shafts illuminated the tree branch, which lay to the left of center. Not so much of an obstacle as an annoyance. It would not stop the tradesman for long.

"We have to get them out of the car. Distract them." Emmanuel glanced around for ideas and came up empty.

Shabalala pulled the slingshot from his pocket and said calmly, "This I can do."

The black Dodge slowed to a stop and the tradesman from the police interrogation room stepped out of the passenger-side door. The breeze tugged at straw-colored hair and whipped it across his bloodless face.

"Cold out here," he said to the driver, then pointed to the tree branch. "This is the reason I hate the fucking country. Go slow. I'll guide you around."

He stepped forward and tried to push the branch out of the way. His hand shot into the air and he jumped back with a yelp.

"Shit." He examined the red indentation on his skin. "Something just hit me."

The windscreen of the Dodge crackled under a rain of stones, and the silver grille pinged like a giant xylophone. The tradesman skipped and twirled under Shabalala's barrage—

a drunk performing for loose change in a bush bar. Emmanuel smiled at the impromptu tap dance. The half albino was not calling the tune this time.

"Get down," the driver called from the safety of the Dodge. "Get down."

The tradesman threw himself to the ground and crawled behind the tree branch for cover.

"One stone left," Shabalala whispered.

"Wait till he stands up," Emmanuel said. After that, the plan ran out of steam.

"I'm coming after you, Cooper," the prone figure yelled. "You'd better be bulletproof."

"Wait," Emmanuel said. "Wait."

The tradesman stood up, Colt revolver in hand. Shabalala's last shot hit him square between the eyes. He reeled back and fell against the hood of the Dodge. The car engine died and the driver's door opened. The tradesman came upright by force of will. Lazarus with a six-gun.

"Now I've got something for you."

The Colt was aimed directly at the patch of grass where Emmanuel and Shabalala crouched. A bullet shredded leaves from the shrubs to their right. Far too close for comfort.

The tradesman walked forward and squeezed out a bullet for every step. He undid his coat buttons. Two gun handles poked out from his trouser waistband.

"Get out of the car." The order was given calmly. "Bring the torches."

"Run," Emmanuel said to Shabalala.

—

The land sloped down to the river. Emmanuel and Shabalala tore through the night and met tree branches and thornbushes along the way. It was too risky to use the torch. They ran and tumbled on the decline like children in a game of blindman's buff.

The sound of footsteps kept pace with them and a torch beam pierced the undergrowth. The tradesman was fast and determined. And he was armed. Bullets pinged into tree trunks.

"There is a river in front of us," Shabalala said. "We must cross it before the very white one comes."

"*Yebo. Yebo.*" Emmanuel pushed harder and tried to ignore the arrow of fire piercing his side. He had a stitch. Work at the Victory had built strength but no sustained endurance. They had to split up soon or he would drag Shabalala down.

Moonlight made a silver ribbon of the river and cast an eerie glow onto the far bank. The water was knee-deep and glacial. Emmanuel's muscles cramped, but he kept up with Shabalala, who did not flag. They broke onto the opposite shore and plunged into the marula trees.

Four minutes of hard upward slog, and Emmanuel stopped to suck in air. The pain in his side was sharp and burning.

"We have to split up," he told Shabalala. "Fork out on the hill. We'll have a better chance of losing them if we do that."

The moon was a pale disk in the sky. The tradesman and his partner were out of the car and probably disoriented. So was he. The plan had worked too well.

"We'll meet back at the clinic," he said.

Shabalala was a police constable, not a nursemaid for an out-of-shape detective. Somehow he'd find the way back to Zweigman's stone house.

"Hurry," he said when the Zulu man didn't move. "I'll be fine, soon as I catch my breath. Go now."

Shabalala hesitated, then slipped into the shadows of an acacia thicket. The crunch of footsteps receded. From the darkness the faint words, "Stay well, Detective."

"Go well, Constable," Emmanuel said, returning the farewell, and kept low among the native forest. A splash sounded from the river. Running headlong into the bush was one option. Ambush was another. He listened to the tradesman's fumbling approach, then moved slowly down the slope and closed the distance between him and his pursuer.

Hissed breath went past on the right. Emmanuel wheeled and found himself behind the dark outline of a man. A twig snapped underfoot. The tradesman swung around and Emmanuel surged forward with fists clenched. He landed two punches to the midriff and heard the satisfying crunch of a body going down to the ground.

He straddled the prone mass and flicked on the silver torch. A young white man with lumpy skin and a chipped front tooth gasped for breath amid the decaying leaves. He wore a loose black suit. A decoy. Emmanuel patted him down for weapons but found none. The tradesman had sent this boy out into the bush while he went on to the clinic to secure the Russian couple.

"Where's your gun?" Emmanuel asked, holding him down.

"Back there," he said. "In the river. I dropped it by accident."

"How many in the Dodge?" Emmanuel pulled the terrified boy upright.

"Three."

"Do they have guns?"

"Only the one with the fair hair. He has a few. Three, maybe."

The Colt was sure to be near empty but the other weapons would be loaded. That amounted to a bullet for every inhabitant of the clinic plus spares.

"Detective Sergeant . . ."

"Shabalala," Emmanuel called out. "Over here."

The Zulu constable crashed through the bush. "The car, it has gone to the clinic."

They both knew what that meant and broke into a run toward the river. This time there would be no stopping for breath. The acned decoy tried to match their speed but soon dropped off and collapsed on the dirt track. He'd be lucky to find his way out of the bush before morning.

"Three men are in the car." Emmanuel ignored the bonfire scorching his lungs. "Three guns."

"Two guns," Shabalala said. "The pale one fired six shots at us from the road."

26

CLUSTERS OF LIGHTS burned on the ridge. The black Dodge was parked in the circle of aloes next to the Ford and the Plymouth. Emmanuel and Shabalala slowed and stayed flush against the wall of the main building. Childbirthing cries and grunts came from within the clinic. At least Natalya was still alive.

"We have to get a visual of the buildings," Emmanuel said. "Behind the Dodge and then to the aloes."

On the count of three, Emmanuel and Shabalala scrambled to the car and then to the line of bright succulents. The grass verge in front of the buildings was empty. Trees swayed in the breeze and a metal clicking came from the clinic. A short man in a dark suit stood at the door and tried to turn the handle.

"Where is he?" The question was screamed into the night and a chair crashed through the window of Zweigman's stone house. Wood splintered into the air and the tradesman appeared on the porch.

"Spread out," he yelled. "Search every corner of this place. Now. We have to find Petrov!"

A white man tumbled out of the Zweigmans' front door, awkward in a dark suit normally reserved for court appearances when instant respectability helped sentence reduction.

"I already looked. Both houses are empty," he said. "Maybe there's someone in the other building."

"First building," the tradesman shouted across the vegetable patch. "Report."

"It's locked," the short man on the clinic porch yelled back. "There's someone inside. Sounds like they're sick."

"Check the houses again, and this time go around the back, too." The tradesman closed his jacket against the chill. "I'm going to get into that locked building."

The men split to either side of the vegetable garden and Emmanuel and Shabalala fell back into the thick brush that grew almost to the back boundary of the clinic. The old fig tree creaked in the wind.

"They can't find Nicolai," Emmanuel whispered. "He must have got out."

"I will go ahead and see if the man is hidden in the bush somewhere," Shabalala said. "You must keep still, Sergeant. Listen for the wood dove. When you hear it, come to the sound."

"Okay."

The part-Shangaan constable was an experienced tracker and hunter. If anyone could find a group of people in the dark, he could. He melted into the night.

Emmanuel rested for a moment and listened. He heard Natalya in labor and Zweigman's gentle voice crooning exhortations. Then another voice joined in.

"Close, my girl." It was Lizzie, Shabalala's wife. "Very close now."

She was in the clinic with Zweigman and directly in the tradesman's path.

A wood dove called and Emmanuel inched forward, every snapped twig and brush of thorns louder than a shotgun to his ears. Another distinct coo, and he made out the murky silhouette of a group huddled together behind the storeroom. He crawled close to Shabalala.

Nicolai rested against the trunk of a marula tree. He was barefoot and shivered with cold despite the crocheted blanket draped over his flannel pajamas. Squatting on either side of him, like avenging angels, were Lana and Lilliana. They'd armed themselves in the kitchen: Lana held a bread knife and Lilliana a rolling pin.

"My child," Nicolai whispered. "Has my child come?"

"Almost." Emmanuel gave the crocheted blanket to Lana, then unbuttoned the coat taken earlier from the Russians' suitcase and swung it across Nicolai's shoulders.

Shabalala unhooked the long wool scarf from around his own neck and gave it to Lilliana, who wore bed slippers and a quilted dressing gown fastened by a sash.

"Lizzie?" the constable asked the assembled group when it was clear that his wife was not hiding in the bush.

"She's in the clinic with the doctor. The pale man from the car is headed there," Emmanuel said.

Shabalala crept forward but stopped when the short man from the stoep appeared in the space between the storehouse and the clinic. He hesitated at the building's edge, too nervous to advance.

"Hello . . . anyone there?" The question was called out in a quavering schoolboy voice.

"Here," Lana called back softly. Emmanuel turned to stop

her, but she was already up and moving to the shed. "I'm hurt. Help me."

"Wait, Sergeant," Shabalala whispered. "She is bringing him to us."

"Please, help me," Lana called again, and the man moved in her direction, still wary but compelled by the primal need to help a wounded female. He stepped out of the light that spilled from the clinic window and into the darkness. Shabalala waited till he reached the edge of the brush, then grabbed him around the waist and pulled down hard. The man slammed into the ground and Emmanuel kept him there with a knee to the chest.

"Quiet." Emmanuel pressed a hand to the man's mouth. "Take off the sash for your gown, Lilliana. We need it."

The German woman set the rolling pin down and untied the fabric sash. It took almost a full minute—fast, given that her hands shook with the shell-shocked jitters of a war veteran. Which, Emmanuel realized, was exactly what she was. Despite never having worn a uniform, Lilliana Zweigman, like him, had seen too much of the war.

Emmanuel tore the fabric in half and gagged the man, then tied him to a tree trunk with the second half. He turned on the torch. Nicolai was sweating heavily in the frigid air.

"He needs medicine," Shabalala said.

"The . . . medicine . . ." Lilliana stuttered. "In our house. The medicine."

"The other man is still in there," Emmanuel said. "We have to clear him out of the way and then concentrate on getting the tradesman. The locked door will keep the others safe for a while."

"I'll handle the man at the house," Lana said with chilling

confidence, and set off along the back perimeter of the clinic buildings like a cat stalking her prey.

Shabalala whistled low. "Ah . . . a man must have the heart of a lion to stop that one."

A gunshot roused the birds roosting in the trees. There was a brief twitter of discontent before quiet was restored.

"Stay here with Nicolai," Emmanuel said to Lilliana. "Don't come out until I say it's safe. If anyone comes back here, hide. Understand?"

The German woman nodded and Emmanuel ran with Shabalala to the corner of the storeroom overlooking the grass verge. The tradesman stood on the clinic stoep. White splinters showed out of a new bullet hole in the wooden door.

"Come out," the tradesman said. "Or I'll keep shooting. It's a small building. I'll hit something eventually."

He shot the door again and the lock shuddered under the impact. Natalya's childbirthing cry turned into a yelp of fear.

"Double around to the drive," Emmanuel said to Shabalala, who was crouched next to him. "Set up on the other end of the porch. We'll press the tradesman from both sides."

Shabalala slipped into the bush and Emmanuel lifted his head higher to get a better view of the stone building. Lantern light spilled out from the front windows, bright enough to see by.

The clinic door opened and Zweigman stepped onto the stoep. The shattered wood door closed behind him. A lock turned. The German doctor raised his hands in the air. Emmanuel kept below the level of the porch and inched closer.

"Move," the tradesman said to Zweigman. "I want the Russian colonel."

"He is not here. Only his wife is inside."

"Hand her over." The tradesman's voice was hard. "I want her out here, now."

"You cannot have her," Zweigman said. "She is in labor and cannot be moved."

"I'll be the judge of that."

"No," Zweigman said. "I will be the judge of that. This is my clinic and she is my patient."

Emmanuel spied over the veranda edge. The tradesman had the gun barrel pressed to Zweigman's forehead, but the doctor stood still.

"Get out of the way or I will kill you."

"So be it," the doctor said. "But I will not move."

Yesterday afternoon, in the rope storehouse, the tradesman had said the "boss" didn't want any more civilian casualties. The stubborn old Jew was about to make himself the exception to the rule.

"Fucking kike . . ." The tradesman grabbed Zweigman by the lapels and lifted him into the air.

Emmanuel surged up the steps, taking them two at a time, and knocked the tradesman sideways. Their bodies slammed into the clinic and the gun clattered to the stoep. Emmanuel pinned the pale man against the stone wall. They grappled.

"Get the gun," Emmanuel shouted to Zweigman. "Get the gun."

Zweigman retrieved the gun and lifted it to hip height. Thank God. Emmanuel did not know how much longer he could keep the tradesman pinned. The German threw the revolver off the stoep and into the garden.

"Christ above," Emmanuel muttered. Fear of guns was fine in theory, but Zweigman's phobia had lost them the advantage. He tightened his hold on the tradesman's arms but felt no slackness in the muscle, no sign of weakening. The fight would last a while longer. Where the hell was Shabalala?

"Doctor." The lock to the clinic door clicked open and Lizzie peered out. "Doctor, hurry. It is time."

Zweigman hesitated, torn between two crises.

"The baby is almost here," Lizzie said, and the German disappeared into the stone building. The shattered door closed and the lock clicked.

"Back down," the tradesman said when he failed to break Emmanuel's hold. "I work for Major van Niekerk. He sent me here."

"I don't believe you."

"You're an idiot, Cooper." The tradesman's breath smelled of cool mints. "This clinic is in the boondocks. How do you think I found it at night? I was given detailed instructions by the major himself. He wanted the Russians extracted with no civilian casualties."

"He could have done that when the Russians were under his roof in Durban," Emmanuel said, but a poisonous seed had been planted. Van Niekerk was the only one who had known for sure where Emmanuel and the Russian couple were hidden. Lana had even called to confirm their final destination.

"The Berea house was too public. Van Niekerk wanted to keep his name out of this. He gave you and the Russians up to my boss in exchange for a promotion."

Emmanuel's grip slackened. He'd seen the major talking to the *soutpiel* colonel on Point Road. Had they been arranging the deal then? The tradesman sensed the doubt in Emmanuel. He threw his head forward and delivered a full-force head butt, a Liverpool kiss that knocked Emmanuel off balance. He staggered back, dazed.

"You just don't know when to stay down, Cooper."

The tradesman moved to deliver a king hit, but his fist was caught by Shabalala's giant hand and crushed. The Zulu constable forced the pale white man facedown onto the stoep. After a few moments of groaning and flailing, the tradesman collapsed, exhausted.

"You are hurt, Sergeant?" Shabalala asked.

"Just my pride," Emmanuel said, and patted the tradesman down for weapons. He was clean.

"Where's the other gun?" he asked.

The tradesman laughed and Emmanuel checked the main house. A gun could be trained on Lana right now. He quickly walked to the steps.

"Keep that one down," he said to Shabalala. "I'll check on Lana at the Zweigmans' house."

"You're in big trouble, kaffir," the tradesman said. "Hope you like prison food."

Shabalala settled his great weight onto the tradesman's back and smiled. "This one will not move," he said.

The rolling silhouettes of mountains were now visible in the breaking dawn. Night lifted and early birds began their chorus. The murmur of the river came from deep in the valley. Nicolai rounded the corner of the stoep, moving slowly. A tall man stood at his shoulder. A jab to the back pushed Nicolai forward. The third gun was accounted for.

"Colonel Edward Soames-Fitzpatrick," Emmanuel said, and enjoyed the surprised look on the tall man's face. "The commander in chief."

"Detective Sergeant Cooper." The colonel squared his shoulders. "Move aside."

"On whose authority?"

"The South African police."

Emmanuel said, "The police aren't interested in Nicolai. He's committed no crimes in South Africa."

"This is a national security matter."

Bullshit. With a silver spoon.

"Where's Security Branch?" Emmanuel kept an easy tone. "They're in charge of national security."

A baby's cry came from inside the clinic, weak at first and then much stronger.

"My baby," Nicolai said. "I want to see my child."

The colonel pushed the gun barrel hard into the Russian's back. "Let Dennis off the floor and we'll leave peacefully, Cooper. If you don't, someone will get hurt."

Dennis? Dennis was a guy who went to the pub on Friday nights, then staggered home to listen to a BBC radio serial with a cup of hot Bovril. The newborn wailed again and Emmanuel focused on Nicolai, who was still a valuable asset.

"Walk to me, Nicolai," Emmanuel said. "The colonel needs you alive. I promise he's not going to shoot."

Nicolai hesitated, torn between fear of death and the desire to hold his newborn child. He took a halting step in the direction of the clinic, and then another. Fitzpatrick moved to the side and aimed the gun at Emmanuel.

"You're right. I'm not going to kill the Russian. He's too valuable. You and the kaffir are another matter."

Sweat trickled between Emmanuel's shoulder blades. A gun barrel aimed midchest was a problem, but of more concern was Lilliana Zweigman, who crept across the grass with the wooden rolling pin held above her head. She had taken off her slippers to move more quietly, but her whole body shook. *Stop, slip away and stay safe,* Emmanuel begged silently. Lilliana had survived a long and miserable war. She could not die in the soft light of an African dawn.

"Look—" The tradesman tried to shout a warning, but Shabalala gagged him with a hand and kept his pale head pinned to the stone floor of the veranda. Nicolai walked slowly to the stairs and his stumbling feet covered Lilliana's advance.

"Let my man up," the colonel said. "Or I will shoot the kaffir."

Swing wide, swing hard and inflict maximum damage. Emmanuel's instructions were loud in his head but remained unspoken. Instead he stepped back and kept the colonel's focus on the veranda.

"There's no need to hurt anyone," he said. "Lower the gun. You'll get what you came for. Just put the gun down."

Lilliana whipped the pin through the air. The impact was bone-crunching. A shot thundered from the firearm and lodged in the wall of the storeroom as Soames-Fitzpatrick toppled into the dewy grass. Emmanuel jumped the steps and stamped on the colonel's hand till his grip on the gun weakened.

"Go," he said to Nicolai. "Go and see your child."

"*Da.* Yes." The Russian man climbed the stairs, drawn on by the newborn's insistent wail. He hit his palm against the door. "Natalya. Natalya?"

Zweigman opened the clinic door for Nicolai and checked for wounded on the stoep and in the garden. He saw his wife in the predawn light, an avenging domestic goddess with a rolling pin in her hand and an unconscious man at her feet.

"Lilliana." Zweigman closed the gap between them fast. "Are you all right?"

"Yes."

Emmanuel pocketed the colonel's gun, a Browning Hi-Power that easily could have put both Lilliana and Shabalala in the grave. He flipped the prone figure over and slapped him hard on the cheek.

"Please." Zweigman knelt beside the dazed man and completed a quick examination. "An egg-sized contusion and a hairline skull fracture. He will make a full recovery."

"Good," Emmanuel said. "I need him alive and talking."

"In a short while, when the disorientation clears up," Zweigman said, and got to his feet. He moved to Lilliana's side. "Oh, *liebchen*, did you do that?"

She nodded.

The doctor took his wife in his arms and held her. "I am so proud of you."

Lilliana's strange hiccupping laughter turned to sobs that shook her body. A woman's cries normally chilled Emmanuel. Yet now, only a few feet away from Lilliana's heartbreak, he felt no need to run. He would have given his life to bring his own mother back, but the past could not be bargained with or changed. He'd spent hours, weeks and years picking apart his memory of that night in Johannesburg to find the moment when the twelve-year-old Emmanuel could have stopped her death. No one's life should be held ransom to the past while the world kept spinning. Lilliana was in pain but alive and here to see another day.

The colonel swore and Emmanuel checked his condition. Sweaty and thin-lipped but with a spot of crimson on the cheeks.

"Shabalala," Emmanuel called. "Bring that one to the Zweigman house and we'll secure both of them."

"*Yebo.*" Shabalala hauled the tradesman to his feet and led him down the steps and across the plateau to the house. Lana appeared at the corner of the kitchen garden with the last remnant of the colonel's ragtag army in tow: a nervous youth with greased hair and heavy jowls who'd been left to search the Zweigmans' house.

"Are you hurt, Emmanuel?" Lana said. "I heard shots."

"I'm fine. Who's he?"

"This is Stewart." The young man mumbled hello. "He owes Mr. Khan twenty pounds, which he was told he could work off if he gave him a hand tonight. He says he didn't know about the guns or the Russians."

"Mr. Khan told us it was a parcel pickup," Stewart said. "It was supposed to be easy."

Emmanuel hit the colonel between the shoulder blades. "A national security matter, and you recruit boys with gambling debts."

"I didn't recruit anybody," the colonel said. "Dennis was in charge of that."

"Oh, I understand." Emmanuel pushed the colonel toward the main house. "You're not responsible for this fuckup. The men under your command are the problem."

"What about them?" Lana indicated the Zweigmans, still locked together.

"They'll be all right," Emmanuel said. In truth, he couldn't remember seeing the German Jewish couple so close.

The doctor turned to his wife. "Come," he said. "Let us go and meet the baby. He has white hair and big lungs."

So, Nicolai has a son, Emmanuel thought, and prodded the colonel into the big house. Jolly Marks and Mbali the Zulu maid had been a son and a daughter to their respective parents. Their deaths and that of the landlady had to be accounted for.

"Sit," Emmanuel said to the colonel when they entered the small kitchen, where Shabalala already had the tradesman handcuffed to a chair. The woodstove crackled. Lana filled a kettle and placed it on a burner, while Stewart, the hapless gambler, slouched in the adjoining room and pretended to read one of Zweigman's medical tomes. Emmanuel pushed Soames-Fitzpatrick into a chair and secured his hands with ties taken from the curtains. The colonel sat with a stiff back and a stiff upper lip.

"Check the Dodge, Shabalala," Emmanuel said. "See if there are any more weapons hidden."

"*Yebo.*" The constable ducked out the side door and cut back to the black car. A rooster crowed and a golden light brushed the treetops.

"I can't wait to see van Niekerk," the tradesman said. "I'm going to tell him how you fucked up tonight, and then I'm going to tell him you fucked his girlfriend. You'll be lucky to keep your teeth."

Lana tensed but set up a row of teacups on a sideboard. Her escape route to Cape Town, funded in part by van Niekerk's generous financial contribution to her everyday expenses, was now in doubt.

"Why would the major believe a word you say?" Emmanuel asked.

"Because I saw you with my own eyes. Van Niekerk won't be happy paying for something that's being handed out for free. If you uncuff me now, he'll never have to know."

"You followed me to Lana's flat and then to the Dover the next morning," Emmanuel said. The man leaning against the wall of the hardware store with the newspaper hadn't been a civilian waiting for a bus. "But first you had to tail me from the bar to Lana's apartment. Why follow me at all?"

"Van Niekerk's orders. He doesn't trust you."

"No, that's not it." Emmanuel was certain. For all his faults, the Dutch major had always shown absolute trust and faith in him. The tradesman had tailed him long before van Niekerk was involved in the investigation. "You were in the freight yard on the night of Jolly's murder. That's how you knew to follow me. You were there. And you probably had Brother Jonah on lookout as well."

The tradesman's eyes were cold. "You're a drowning man, Cooper."

Shabalala entered the kitchen with the same dented tool-box the tradesman had brought with him to the interrogation room. He rested it on the tabletop.

"No guns," the Zulu constable said. "Just this."

The metal box, for all its plainness, exerted a strange power over the occupants of the kitchen. No one moved. Then Lana stepped back, anticipating an unpleasant surprise.

Emmanuel unclipped the box and opened the lid. The scent of chocolate-and-vanilla-flavored tobacco wafted out of it. He removed three hand-rolled cigarettes.

"A gift from Mr. Khan," he said. "He helped you recruit your little army. An unstable preacher and a group of unlucky gamblers who don't know one end of a gun from the other."

Next, Emmanuel pulled out a rusty penknife. The white paint from the handle flaked off in his palm.

"Jolly Marks's knife, taken from the crime scene. You heard my name and my old police rank on the night of the first murder. You've been chasing me ever since. Waiting for me to find the Russians."

"Why would I remove a piece of incriminating evidence from the scene?" the tradesman said. "That makes even less sense than your other theories."

Emmanuel considered the child's weapon for a moment. Keeping it made sense if you discounted common sense and went deeper.

"There was a private in my platoon," he said. "A quiet lad from Liverpool, and ordinary. Or that's what I thought until another soldier found a necklace made from human teeth hidden in a rucksack. The private claimed it was a harmless souvenir, but he enjoyed looking at the necklace the same way a dog enjoys digging up old bones to chew on. You kept the penknife for the same reason."

"You're sick, Cooper," the tradesman said.

Emmanuel foraged under layers of newspaper stuffed into the box to keep the contents snug, and touched a handle. He withdrew a scalpel with dried blood splattered over the edges of the silver blade. Very much a grown-up's weapon.

"No theories or conjecture," he said. "I'll leave that to the judge and the jury."

The colonel sat bolt upright at the mention of a trial. "The mission was to find the Russians and secure them. He's the one who lost them in the freight yard and then killed the boy for his notebook. That went against my direct orders. I said no civilian casualties."

"Mrs. Patterson and her maid, Mbali?" Emmanuel pressed for more information.

"Same thing," the colonel said. "Get the notebook and get out. That was the plan. He turned the whole exercise into a bloodbath, in direct contravention of my orders."

"You are responsible for your men, Colonel."

"I'm not in charge," Soames-Fitzpatrick said. "MI5 wanted the Russians but they didn't want to ask the National Party for help . . . not with Malan in London talking about a republic run by Afrikaners. They decided to take an informal approach. They recommended Dennis and assigned me to get the job done."

Informal approach? The job? The British security agency had used the colonel to do their dirty work. If the mission succeeded, the glory was theirs; if it failed, they could deny any knowledge and leave Soames-Fitzpatrick to hang.

"Three people died," Emmanuel said.

"Against my direct orders."

If the colonel mentioned his "orders" one more time, Emmanuel would have to kill him. There was more to leadership than barking commands down a phone line.

"Stop talking, Fitzpatrick." The pale-skinned killer was unnaturally calm in the face of the colonel's attempt to dump full responsibility for the failed mission into his lap. "Make excuses up the chain of command, not down. The word of an ex-detective, a kaffir and a barmaid? Save your breath."

The tradesman was right, Emmanuel knew. Unless Major van Niekerk backed him, the allegations of three murders and an international conspiracy to capture a member of Stalin's inner circle would not stand. Jolly Marks's death was already neatly pinned on Giriraj and even with the scalpel there was no real evidence to link the double homicide at the Dover to the tradesman. The contents of the metal box would look like nothing more than a desperate attempt by a reclassified ex-detective to clear his name.

"You've got nothing, Cooper," the tradesman said. "The only way out of this mess is to free Soames-Fitzpatrick and me and step away. The colonel will do what he can to clear your name from the double murder charge. That's the only way you'll escape the rope."

"I'm tempted," Emmanuel said. "But I can't get past the fact that you killed three innocent people. That just doesn't feel right."

"You don't have the power or the connections to do a thing about it." The tradesman's eyes lit with pleasure. "Admit defeat and you might get a chance to live out your days amongst the kaffirs and the Jews."

"*Do it,*" the Scottish sergeant major roared out of the darkness, full of rage. "*Do it, soldier.*"

Emmanuel rounded the table and slammed the tradesman's forehead into the wood surface. The metal box slid over the lip and crashed to the floor.

"That was for Jolly Marks," Emmanuel said. "And this is for Mrs. Patterson and Mbali her maid."

He slammed the fair head down twice more and heard bones crunch. Good. Blood dotted the wood tabletop and trickled from the tradesman's nose. Even better. The tradesman moaned in pain.

"Sergeant." Shabalala laid a light hand on Emmanuel's shoulder. "Detective Sergeant . . ."

"Don't worry," Emmanuel said. "I'm done."

"No. Listen."

There was the slam of doors and footsteps on the circular drive and in the garden.

Lana ran to the window and peered out. "More cars. There are two men on the clinic porch. One of them looks like the major. There might be others."

"Stay here and keep an eye on the colonel and his friend." Emmanuel gave the Browning Hi-Power to Lana. He knew she could handle a gun. "Do not untie them. No matter what happens. Shabalala and I will go out."

They slipped through the side door and struck out for the winter vegetable patch. Muted voices could be heard from the direction of the clinic. A man approached with the collar of his lightweight coat turned up against the dawn chill.

"Fletcher?"

"The major wants you." The detective constable was ashen-faced and looked five inches shorter than he had yesterday afternoon. "He's waiting over at the other house with the doctor."

Emmanuel and Shabalala moved fast and found van Niekerk leaning against the veranda post of the clinic while Zweigman blocked the door. The newborn's cries had calmed.

"If you're the cavalry," Emmanuel said to the Dutch major, "you're late."

"The plan was to get here an hour ago, right on the tail of the colonel," van Niekerk said, and cast Constable Fletcher a sour look. "We took a wrong turn off the main road and ended up in a Zulu kraal. The chief of the kraal was none too happy. He thought we'd come to relocate him and his family to a native reserve."

"You gave the colonel directions to this place, didn't you, Major?"

"Yes." There was no shame or guilt in the admission. "It was the easiest way to flush out all the players and concentrate them in one place."

"A lot of things look easy from a desk," Emmanuel said.

"Okay," van Niekerk said. "I deserve that, but this is not how it was meant to turn out. The plan was to get here before any damage was done."

"He's lying," Zweigman said. "He wants Nicolai, just like the other men."

The major lit up a cigarette and puffed. "Let me explain the facts of life to you all. Nicolai and his wife have caught the attention of the British secret service, the Central Intelligence Agency and the Russian NKVD. There is no way for Colonel Nicolai Petrov to slip quietly into the night and disappear. Much as you'd like it to be so."

"We're just supposed to hand him over?" Emmanuel said. He caught movement out of the corner of his eye. A handful of men scattered across the grass verge and infiltrated the stone buildings. The door to the storeroom was kicked in and the interior searched. The gagged man was dragged out of the woods and pushed across the verge to a parked car. A startled bushbuck flew through the vegetable patch and out to the drive. Amateur hour was over and the professionals had arrived. This expeditionary force could do what they wished and yet they stayed well away from the clinic.

"I'd prefer that Nicolai come of his own free will," van Niekerk said. "His wife and child can stay. That's the deal. Nicolai only."

The door to the main house swung open and the colonel and the tradesman were bundled out and marched across the plateau by three armed men with blackened faces. Stewart, the hapless gambler, trailed behind. The last member of the colonel's army, the decoy ditched at the river by Emmanuel and Shabalala, was still out there somewhere.

"Will they be punished?" Zweigman asked.

"Not through the courts." The major smiled. "Nothing about this operation will ever appear in print or in official records."

Emmanuel checked the positions of the commando raiders. They were gathered along the perimeter of the clinic grounds, ready for a second surge. Their blackened faces showed no emotion. He didn't know what organization they belonged to. Not that it mattered. There was nothing to stop them from smashing into the clinic and securing Nicolai by force. With the operation officially blacked out, they were free to get the job done and damn the consequences. Emmanuel had seen what men were capable of when the leash of law and order was cut. A few graves hidden in the endless run of hills would never be found.

A heavy silence descended. Neither Zweigman, Shabalala nor Emmanuel could voluntarily place the sick Russian into the hands of an uncertain fate.

The clinic door pushed open and Nicolai appeared. He marked the men waiting on the perimeter and calmly buttoned his wool jacket.

"My son's name is Dimitri," he said to Emmanuel. "Please make sure that he and Natalya are safe. I cannot stay here and bring harm to you good gentlemen or to my wife. I have done things . . . This day was always going to come. *Spasiba*."

He walked across the porch and down the stairs. Major van Niekerk escorted him to a line of blue sedans parked in the drive. He opened the back door of one of them. Nicolai got in and the door closed with a thunk. Emmanuel moved forward, but Zweigman grabbed the sleeve of his jacket.

"Let him go. Nicolai's time is almost at an end. The safety of his wife and son is worth the sacrifice."

"*Yebo,*" Shabalala agreed.

The car containing Nicolai pulled away from the circle of aloes and disappeared into the wild grass. Van Niekerk strode back to the clinic with two commandos on either side of him.

"Cooper," he called. "Come over."

Emmanuel met van Niekerk halfway. Sunshine filtered through the tree branches, but no diffusion of light could soften the brute lines of the men's blackened faces. Lieutenant Piet Lapping and Sergeant Dickie Heyns of the Security Branch. The metallic taste of blood came to Emmanuel's mouth at the sight of pockmarked Piet Lapping, experienced interrogator and sadist for the state.

"Well?" the major prompted the Security Branch officer.

Lapping reached into his jacket pocket and took out an envelope, which he threw at Emmanuel like a hunter slinging a stone. "You've got more lives than a fucking cat, Cooper," he said before turning back to the parked cars. "One day you're going to run out."

The envelope hit Emmanuel's chest and he caught it before it dropped to the ground. It was a plain manila rectangle, unmarked and unstamped, yet he recognized the weight and feel of it. He double-checked the contents: a sympathy card to the mother of the young Communist found hanged in his jail cell. A single red rose embossed with the message *In your time of sorrow* was printed on the front. This was the card he had delivered to a shack in Pentecost Township six months ago and the reason he'd left the Detective Branch.

"Thanks for getting this back," Emmanuel said, and pocketed the envelope. "What did you get out of this, Major?"

"A promotion to colonel and the goodwill of the head of Security Branch." Van Niekerk smiled. "The reward for services rendered to the state."

"And the murder warrants for Mrs. Patterson and Mbali?"

"Withdrawn."

Lana appeared at the corner of the winter garden with a cup of hot tea in her hand. Cherry-red lipstick was perfectly applied to her mouth, but her disheveled hair seemed to suggest that she'd just gotten out of bed and was ready to be talked back between the sheets if the right man asked her.

"Ready to leave in ten minutes?" Van Niekerk said, and sipped the tea Lana gave him.

"Of course, Kallie." She kissed the major on the cheek and then disappeared into the garden. The Cape Town escape plan was back on track.

Emmanuel held out the Detective Branch ID and the race identification card. The fine for carrying false documents was the equivalent of six months' wages. Nonpayment meant prison time. It was back to swinging a sledgehammer at the Victory Shipyards.

"Keep them," van Niekerk said.

"What for?"

"Simone Betancourt. You can keep the papers because of her."

"I don't understand," Emmanuel said.

Simone Betancourt was the first murder he ever worked, tagging alongside Inspector Luc Moreau, a veteran detective on a mission to avenge the dead. A three-day plunge into the smoky nightclubs and gambling dens of postwar Paris led to a cheap street-corner hustler named Johnny "Big Boy" Belmondo. Johnny was handsome and big where it counted but light on brains. He'd killed and robbed the washerwoman on the million-to-one chance that the sparkling stones in her hairpin were real diamonds. An effort to pawn the jewelry revealed the diamonds to be worthless cut glass. A life lost to stupidity and greed. The files were placed in a cardboard box and stored in a dank room. Case closed.

Simone Betancourt. He was surprised van Niekerk remembered the case. Emmanuel had mentioned it once over drinks when the midnight-to-dawn squad were comparing notes on their "first."

"Five days of R & R in springtime Paris, and you could not let the dead lie. That's a burden for a soldier but perfect for a police detective." Van Niekerk sipped the hot tea. "Unlike you, I would have walked past. Unlike you, I would have stayed locked in the hotel room with my girl."

"I didn't mention a girl."

"With you there's always a girl," van Niekerk said.

Emmanuel left that time bomb ticking. If the major knew about his night with Lana, then a duel at sunrise was an option.

"The Detective Branch is recruiting native talent," van Niekerk said. "Shabalala would never rise above the rank of detective constable, but the pay is better than in the foot police, and he'd get to do more than shut down shebeens and arrest cow thieves."

"Detective Sergeant Emmanuel Cooper and Detective Constable Samuel Shabalala. Is that the payoff for letting Nicolai go without a fight?"

"Yes," van Niekerk said. "It is. Do you accept?"

EPILOGUE

THE BAR WAS a dim cavern favored by gamblers, taxi drivers and off-duty detectives at the end of the night shift. Emmanuel and Inspector Luc Moreau stood shoulder to shoulder at the counter, three drinks into the celebration of Johnny Belmondo's arrest.

Inspector Moreau said, "Long after the war has ended, this fight against injustice and cruelty will continue. This is how the world is rebuilt, Major Cooper, with one small victory at a time."

The barman, an amateur boxer with cauliflower ears and a surly mouth, poured shots. Luc Moreau lifted his glass.

"To Simone Betancourt. May she rest with the angels."

"To Simone Betancourt." Emmanuel downed the whiskey and motioned for another round.

The sun was rising and the neon lights of Montmartre flicked off one by one and a bright river of sunshine began to flow over the cobblestone streets. Two young prostitutes in high heels and low-cut silk dresses stopped to light candles at a roadside shrine to the Virgin Mary. They made the sign of the cross and tottered away.

Inspector Moreau lifted his glass again. They had an un-spoken agreement that this morning they would hammer the bottle. "To the other woman whose unjust death gave you a thirst for justice."

"What?" Emmanuel put his whiskey down.

"To the woman whose memory brought you onto this case," Moreau said. "The dead cannot be honored if they are not named. Even the unknown soldier has a marked grave, does he not?"

To honor the dead and have no fear of them . . . well, that was easier said than done. To bring them into the daylight and speak their names was dark magic. In a dim Parisian bar, half a world away from South Africa, Emmanuel conjured her into flesh: a silky-haired woman with green eyes and an easy laugh, absolutely careless with her beauty. Tired from working long hours but certain that her son would break free of Sophiatown and inhabit a world that she had only dreamed of.

"To my mother," Emmanuel said.

LET THE
DEAD LIE

Malla Nunn

Reading Group Discussion Guide

QUESTIONS AND TOPICS FOR DISCUSSION

1. Early in the novel, we learn that Emmanuel Cooper did not know his father, thus complicating the issue of his race. How does this affect Emmanuel throughout the story? Discuss what it would mean to be reclassified from a privileged group to a racial minority.

2. In the novel, lower classes are associated with violence and crime, and subsequently distinguished as "nonwhite." Is this indicative of the time and place? Does the depiction of race in the novel resonate with current issues?

3. In chapter 4, Emmanuel can tell by Parthiv's body language that he is lying to him. When else does Emmanuel realize he has been lied to and how does this affect his actions?

4. It could be argued that the Flying Dutchman is the least corrupt character Emmanuel comes across during his investigation. Would you agree with this? Who do you feel is the most corrupt?

5. What would happen if the United States issued a law where race or religious affiliation had to be placed on your identification card? Would it be allowed? What would you do?

6. In chapter 12, Miss Morgensen talks of feeling judged by Brother Jonah, even though he is physically not there. The author mentions the Christian belief of God seeing and judging all. Do other characters share this same be-

lief? Are other religious beliefs expressed? If so, do they sway the choices the characters make?

7. Dr. Zwiegman and Shabalala put themselves in danger when they agree to help Emmanuel. Why do they do so? What are some of the other underlying themes of loyalty and trust among the various characters in the story? Of betrayal?

8. Discuss the author's decision to frame the book with the story of Emmanuel in Paris. What do you learn about loss? About Emmanuel?

9. The Dutta brothers play a significant role in the plot. Why does Emmanuel feel an obligation to protect Amal?

10. Lana explains to Emmanuel that she is waiting, saving up money, until she can leave Major van Niekerk and start anew. How do you believe Lana justifies her relationship with the major? How does Emmanuel's opinion of Lana alter throughout the story and why?

11. Emmanuel shows few signs of weakness. The only glimpse into his psyche or hint of doubt is evinced through the phantom staff sergeant. How does the phantom staff sergeant motivate Emmanuel's choices and propel the story?

12. Have you also read *A Beautiful Place to Die,* the first book in the Detective Emmanuel Cooper series? If so, how does *Let the Dead Lie* compare? In what ways have Emmanuel and the other recurring characters changed over the course of the two novels?

ENHANCE YOUR BOOK CLUB

1. Research a film that is set in South Africa and watch it with your book club. Discuss your reactions to the various cultural images, including scenery, cultural motifs and music. Suggestions include *Invictus* (2009), *Catch a Fire* (2006), *Cry, the Beloved Country* (1995), *A Dry White Season* (1989) and *Goodbye Bafana* (2007).

2. Find a recipe for South African bobotie to your liking, such as the one here, www.cookstr.com/recipes/south-african-bobotie, or another traditional dish, to make and enjoy at your book club discussion.

3. Apartheid was the system of racial separation that existed in South Africa until 1993, when Nelson Mandela was elected president. Learn more for discussion at www.apartheidmuseum.org.

A CONVERSATION WITH MALLA NUNN

Where do you find inspiration for your stories?

Family stories about "the old days" are a great inspiration and an amazing historical source from which to draw characters and events. Add photography books, novels, news stories and a vivid imagination, and that about sums it up!

What gave you the idea to write this particular story?

Both my parents lived in Durban in their youth, and I heard a lot of stories about that time and place. That gave me the setting. The actual story spun off a very clear mental image of a young boy lying in the dirt of a freight yard. Like Emmanuel, I just followed my nose and found out what happened to the boy and why.

What is the writing process like for you? Do you generally know the plot of the novel before you write it or does it unfold as you go along?

I'd love to know the plot from beginning to end before I start! I generally write down fragments of the story as they come to me and then stitch it all together at various points. I do have a strong sense of specific events and conversations between characters before starting, and these mental scenes guide me into the world of the book. The word "organic" best describes my writing process.

Are any of your characters based on anyone in particular? Are there autobiographical elements to your work?

I draw bits and pieces from the people around me and from myself. I don't believe that anything is entirely made up . . . it's just rediscovered. For example, Emmanuel is an ex-soldier because many of my male ancestors were soldiers, and I remember meeting a few of the old men who'd lived through WWI and WWII. The novel is set near the harbor because my father was in the Merchant Marine and sailed out of Durban. I'm basically a story thief! I steal shamelessly from my parents, my relatives and my own childhood.

Lana mentions that she wants to move to another place when she has enough money, where no one knows her and she can start over. Is this a desire you have ever experienced

yourself? Do you think it is human nature to want to find anonymity and start anew?

The desire to start again is an essential part of human nature. It's important to be able to see a new future for yourself, your family and, in some cases, your country. My own personal history is very much driven by a desire to start fresh. My parents moved from Swaziland in southern Africa to Australia because they wanted to leave the past behind . . . to bury it forever. They didn't want us branded by our race and told where to live, whom to marry and what job to hold. My parents' choice changed our lives for the better. I'm a great believer in new beginnings. I live in Sydney but dream of living on a small farm with chickens and a vegetable patch and a huge, open sky . . . or maybe an apartment in New York? It's great to dream.

How were you able to write the character of Emmanuel from such a gritty, masculine point of view? Do you prefer writing male or female characters?

I had to work to refine Emmanuel's masculine voice, but getting to know Emmanuel has been a real pleasure. I love spending time with him. Emmanuel is much less of a "talker" than I am, so I have to really listen to him and try not to put words in his mouth. If that fails, my husband, Mark, is always on hand to alert me to "girly" moments in Emmanuel's dialogue and actions!

I don't have a preference for writing male or female characters, because I wrestle equally with the development of both. I like strong, believable characters, no matter their race, sex or age.

You paint a multicultural picture of South Africa, drawing on various cultures including Indian, Afrikaner, Zulu, Russian, Jewish and Greek, to name just a few. Was it im-

portant for you to involve many different cultures in your story? Can you talk about the different communities and how you decided to include them in the plot?

The community I was born into was pretty mixed. We were even labeled "mixed race." Because we were always the "in-between" people and because my family lived in the independent Kingdom of Swaziland, my relatives were drawn from different "tribes." There was nothing cool or hip about belonging to a mixed community back then because we were always overshadowed by the belief that race mixing was somewhat shameful and dirty. My multicultural South Africa is a simple attempt to reclaim history. South Africa wasn't just black or white: it was Indian and Italian and English and Zulu and Xhosa . . . to name a few.

Every one of the cultures included in my book was real and present in South Africa in the 1950s. Indians were (and still are) a huge part of life in Durban. They were brought out to work in the sugarcane fields of Natal by the British and many stayed on. Their influence on the culture has been immense. The British, the Zulus and the Afrikaners all shed blood in the fight for control of South Africa. These three "tribes" helped shape South Africa . . . for better and for worse.

Also, Durban is a port town. People come in and out on the tide. I used that fact to really mix things up a bit.

How were you able to understand the underbelly of the gangster and criminal world? Was this something you learned through experience, research or imagination?

I drew inspiration from old black-and-white photographs published in *Drum* magazine in the 1950s. The photos are gritty and urban and full of life. My father also told me stories about growing up in Durban that contradicted the sunny tourist postcard images. He knew Afrikaner boys who smoked weed and drank beer in darkened playgrounds . . . in the early 1940s. My mother talked about avoiding the botanic gardens at night because of the bad things that happened there. I just loved the contradiction between the rosy historical pictures and the underbelly of the city. Research and imagination did the rest.

You were born in South Africa. Did your own heritage factor into your desire to write a novel set in South Africa?

I was born in Swaziland in southern Africa, but the cultural and economic shadow of white South Africa loomed large in my childhood and shaped my parents' lives. We left southern Africa behind, but I still have the most vivid memories of my grandmother's farm after the rain and of white-robed baptism services held in outdoor pools, of funerals and weddings and the dusty playing fields of the boarding school. I grew up in a very tight-knit community, and the place and the people have never left me. I write about South Africa because it is literally "in my blood."

Emmanuel was given a "second chance" by the major. Have you ever been given such a second chance at something?

Absolutely. Three years ago I was a stay-at-home mom who worked part-time selling wine over the phone. I wanted to be a writer but felt I'd missed my chance. Today, I'm living a totally new life thanks to the fact that my husband, Mark, gave me the space and the time to write. My friends and family believed in me without seeing a word I'd written. Their support gave me the courage to take a second chance after years of stumbling.